DARK WITCH

HEARTSTONE ACADEMY

BECKY MOYNIHAN

Published by Broken Books
www.beckymoynihan.com

ISBN-13: 979-8-9883737-6-6

Cover design by Becky Moynihan
Cover images by www.depositphotos.com

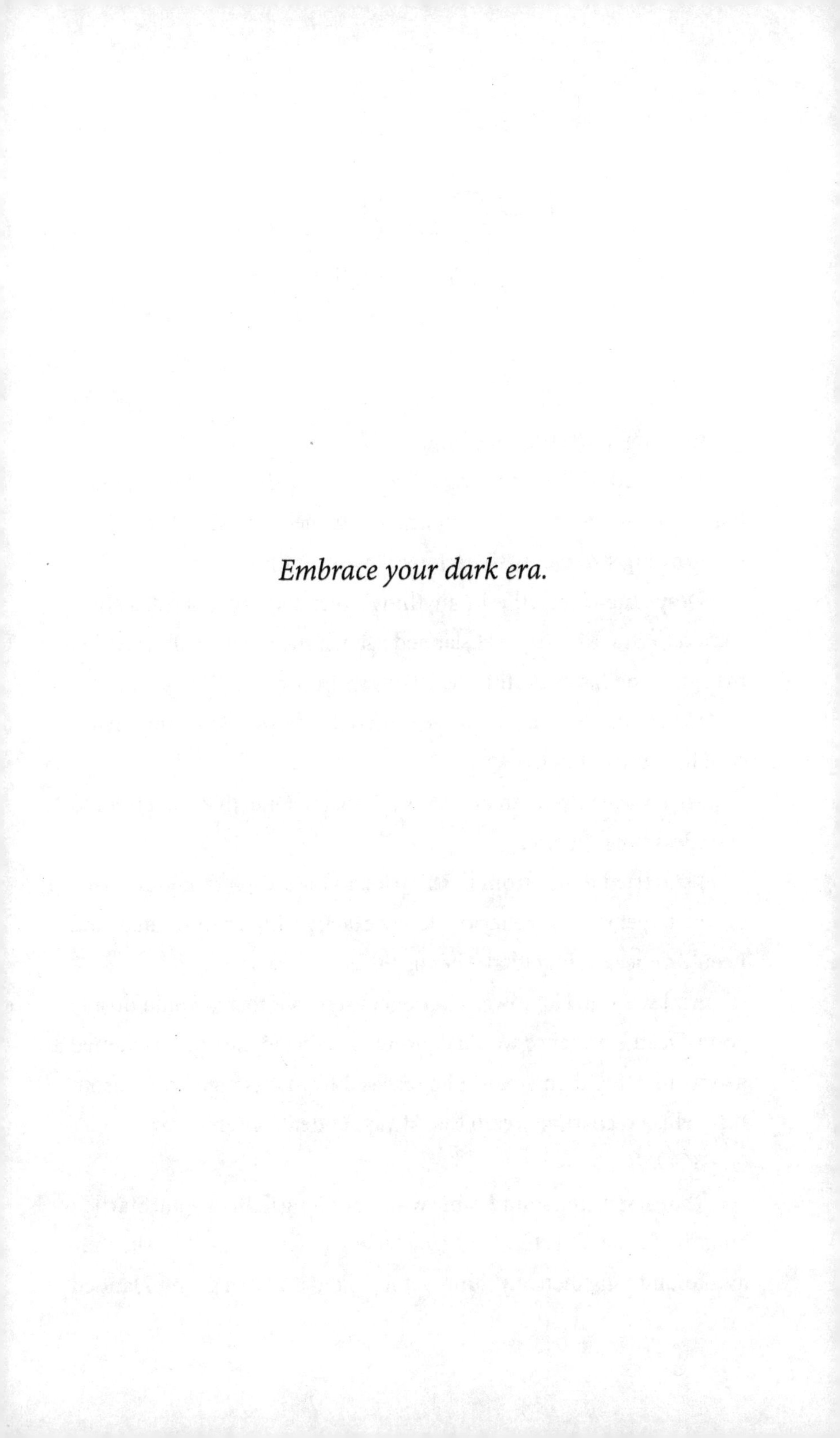

Embrace your dark era.

PROLOGUE

3 Weeks Earlier

Death clung to my skin like bitter smoke.

It smelled of dirt, decaying leaves, and despair, the odor so potent that I couldn't escape it. Everywhere I turned, the stench followed me, growing stronger with each passing second.

Desperate to breathe in anything other than that acrid scent, I started to run. My bare feet slapped against the wet asphalt, carrying me faster and faster until I was all out sprinting.

Hurry, hurry, hurry, I urged myself—despite knowing that I couldn't outrun it.

This was only a dream. A nightmare. One that I'd endured countless times before.

I still tried to flee from it, still tried to hide, even though I wasn't death's target in this scenario. I knew exactly who death wanted, and I couldn't bear seeing it take her again.

And so I ran. Not toward her but away—not that it would do any good. Death's presence would continue to cling to me until it claimed its victim. Only then would I be released from this nightmare. From this hellish recurring dream that always ended the same way.

BOOM!

The earsplitting sound came with a blinding flash of light. Startled and disorientated, I stumbled. The feeling of falling finally jerked me awake, and I instinctively flung out my hands. With a grunt, I landed on the road in an inglorious heap, my palms and knees taking the brunt of the impact.

As my scraped flesh lit up in pain, my senses sharpened, bringing me fully back to reality. It was nighttime, and I was outside in my pajamas during a raging thunderstorm. Blinking the rain from my eyes, I looked around to see where my nightmare had taken me. When I spotted Blackrose Manor's familiar Victorian-style turrets jutting into the night sky, relief filled me. I was still on Mayweather property, thank the ancestors.

Another fork of lightning lit up the stormy night, followed by a rumbling *boom*. My heart promptly leapt into my throat. Scrambling to my feet, I prepared to make a mad dash toward the house, but a whiff of something pungent froze me in place.

Dirt. Decaying leaves. Despair.

The scents of death still clung to me.

Fear shivered up my spine, and I spun around, certain I'd find *her* there.

When a slight figure in a white robe greeted me, her long hair plastered to her skull, I nearly jumped out of my skin. For a split second, I thought the impossible had happened. That an undead spirit had manifested into human form for the sole purpose of haunting me.

A name sprang to my tongue—*her* name—but before I could utter it, the robed figure spoke in a crisp British accent, "Oh, darling, another nightmare?"

As the concerned voice of my grandmother washed over me, I expelled the fear in a sharp exhale. "It's okay, Gran. You really didn't need to come out here."

Lightning forked through the raging sky again, making her irises almost appear white. In actuality, they were the palest of blues, a striking color she'd passed down to her son and granddaughter. I'd inherited her pale skin too but not her whitish-blonde hair. Mine was jet black like my mother's, except when light directly hit it. Then, the wavy tresses became a deep midnight purple.

"Nonsense," Gran said, stepping forward in her sopping wet robe to grasp one of my hands and turn it over. Another flash of lightning illuminated the bloody scrapes on my palm, and she clucked her tongue sympathetically. "It's been months since you last sleepwalked. I thought you were getting better."

I inwardly cringed when I heard the faint disappointment in her tone.

Studying my palm for another moment, she dropped it before saying, "Come. Let's get out of this dreadful storm and into dry clothing. I'll make you some honeyed Sano tea with a sleeping tincture to help soothe your restless spirit."

All too ready to leave this nightmare behind, I followed after her as she turned to head back inside. But I only made it a few steps before the smell of decaying leaves hit me again. My heart started to pound, and before I could think better of it, I was turning away from the house and following that godawful scent.

"Winter, what are you doing?" Gran called after me, but I was too busy sniffing to answer her.

A bone-deep intuition drove me onward, and I ignored the thunderstorm in my need to find the source of that smell. It grew stronger with each step, beckoning me forward despite my trepidation. Maybe what I was smelling was an actual body. Maybe someone had died and was rotting in the ditch beside our private drive. I hoped for it. *Prayed* for it. I didn't care how crass or morbid that made me sound. Discovering a body in the ditch was far better than the alternative.

But as the smell became suffocating, there was no dead body in sight. All I could find was . . .

With a frown, I stopped in front of our mailbox.

"Winter Snow, what on earth?" Gran questioned, arriving beside me just as I grasped the mailbox handle and pulled it down.

The second I spotted the black envelope inside addressed to me, her voice and the world around me muted. A cold foreboding crept up my spine, and that feeling of despair grew tenfold. Darkness edged my vision, and my hands began to shake.

Whatever was in that envelope would change my life—and I doubted it would be for the better. Everything in me recoiled from it, but before I could slam the mailbox shut, a muted voice said, "It's calling to you, darling. Open it."

Blinking rapidly, I pulled my gaze from the envelope to glance at my grandmother. Instead of trepidation, anticipation twinkled in her bright eyes. I flinched as another flash of lightning and crack of thunder reported through the sky, torn between curiosity and fleeing for my life.

Open me, the envelope seemed to whisper, muting the world around me once more. All on their own, my eyes went back to it, drawn to the foreboding mystery like a moth to a flame. When I hesitated, a sensation like cold fingers wrapped around my wrist, urging my hand upward and into the mailbox. I quickly yanked my hand back, but it was too late.

The envelope was tightly gripped in my trembling fingers.

Open. OPEN, the disembodied voice continued to prod me.

I glanced at Gran again, but her gaze was glued to the envelope with a fervor that sent another chill up my spine. Knowing I had no choice but to open it, I slid a nail beneath the silver wax seal and broke it. The second I exposed the letter within, the rain stopped pounding on my head. A purple light edged in shadows flared into existence before me, and a metallic scent bit at my nose, announcing the presence of magic.

My grandmother might be in her seventies, but her power hadn't dimmed in the slightest. With a quick flick of her wrist, she'd managed to conjure a shielding spell around us and a bright undulating orb that hovered eerily in the air.

Still shaking from the chilling sense of foreboding, I gingerly grasped the letter and pulled it out. As I unfolded it and began to read, I stopped breathing, knowing in just one sentence who the letter was from.

Dear Ms. Mayweather,

Congratulations on your admission to Heartstone Academy.

Before I could read more, Gran cackled with glee and sang, "Praise be to our illustrious ancestors!"

Numb with shock, I didn't react when she threw her bony arms around me and squeezed, clearly elated by the news of my acceptance.

"I'm so happy for you, Winter," she continued, pulling back to beam up at me. "After all that we've been through this past decade, our luck is finally changing."

I stared down at her, too dumbstruck to respond. She didn't seem to notice, grabbing the letter from my limp hands to reread it with a Cheshire Cat grin.

"Heartstone Academy, can you believe it?" she gushed, more animated than I'd seen her in a long time. "Why didn't you tell me you'd finally sent in your application?"

"I, um . . ." I stammered, still struggling to form words. "Surprise?"

"Oh, Winter, this is the best news I've had in *years*. I had my doubts, but I shouldn't have. You're a Mayweather, so of *course* the school would accept you. No other bloodline compares to ours, and fate is finally giving you the chance to prove it."

I opened my mouth again, needing to tell her the truth. But when one of her tears plopped onto the letter, I swallowed my confession. She was so proud of me, so proud of the granddaughter who could drag our family name out of obscurity. Against all odds, the most prestigious college in the world for witches and warlocks had accepted a Mayweather. This was a once-in-a-lifetime opportunity, and maybe Gran was right.

Maybe fate was finally shining her face on us.

This was my chance. My moment. I could change everything. *Everything.*

The scent of death chose that moment to invade my senses again, and I could have sworn I heard a voice on the wind. *Her* voice. Whispering a single word, an accusation that turned my insides to ice.

Murderer.

That one word immediately brought me back to reality, to the realization that I was the last witch on earth who should be attending Heartstone Academy.

I took in my grandmother's proud expression for another beat, then glanced down at the acceptance letter once more.

Whatever my decision, I knew one thing with absolute certainty . . .

I'd never sent in my application.

CHAPTER 1

Present Day

"Is this your idea of revenge?" I asked the twenty-year-old young woman in the mirror, noting that her skin looked extra pale today.

"Like the first snowfall of winter," Mom used to say.

Personally, I thought "ghostly" was a better description for my appearance. Much more fitting, especially considering I was talking to my reflection as if an undead spirit would possess it and answer back.

When nothing of the sort happened, I sighed and resumed applying my lipstick. The dark red color made my skin look even whiter, but it also gave my features the edge they desperately needed. Combined with the black smokey eyeliner framing my nearly colorless eyes, my face went from wide-eyed innocence to "Don't mess with me."

I finished applying the lipstick and paused again to scrutinize my reflection. She stared back at me unblinking, her expression cold and . . . haunted.

"*I* didn't do it, you know," I told her, dropping the lipstick on my vanity. "I don't know how Heartstone got my application, but I swear I never sent it. If it wasn't for my family, I wouldn't even be considering this."

Silence.

I sighed again, my nerves growing with each uttered word. This was a mistake. A terrible, terrible mistake. Probably the worst decision I'd ever made—one of the top five, anyway. But no amount of guilt-tripping myself was going to get me out of this.

I'd made a choice, and there was no backing out now. The Mayweather Coven—what was left of it—needed saving, and I was the only one who could do it.

If I didn't die first.

Ever since my acceptance letter had mysteriously arrived in our mailbox three weeks ago, I'd been plagued by an endless string of what-ifs. What if I'd unknowingly sent out my application during one of my sleepwalking incidents? What if my acceptance was a mistake and they kicked me out the second I arrived? Even worse, what if this was simply a sadistic joke meant to mock my family?

And, worst of all, what if I failed epically and came back home in a body bag?

That last what-if plagued me the most, especially since it was a real possibility. Heartstone wasn't like the other magical academies scattered throughout the world. The school had opened only two years ago, its sole purpose to birth the next generation of community leaders. Anyone who survived all four years earned a seat on the newly-formed council.

The Conclave of Magic was meant to replace the elders whose positions had remained empty for the past decade. Ever since they'd been excommunicated, our entire community had been without leaders. As a result, our powerful position in the supernatural world had diminished. What had once been a collective whole was now divided, the hundreds of covens around the world isolated from each other and directionless. Change was desperately needed, and so Heartstone Academy had been born.

The second I'd learned of the elite college, I'd started to draft my application letter. There were only three criteria for admission: You must come from a powerful bloodline. *Check.* Have mastered your magic. *Check.* And be prepared to face death. *Check.*

Deadly magical trials? Cutthroat students all bent on proving themselves worthy of being our next leaders?

No problem.

I was a Mayweather. Facing impossible odds was in my blood.

But I'd filled out that application as an eighteen-year-old naively determined to fix my broken world. Little did I know that it would only break more a few months later, that all of my resolve would vanish like smoke in the face of unthinkable tragedy.

And so I'd stuffed the application in a drawer and forgotten about it, resigned to live out my days in obscurity.

If only that acceptance letter hadn't come. If only that deep sense of family duty hadn't gripped me once more.

"Winter, are you ready? You're going to be late!"

As my grandmother's words filtered up the stairs, a million nervous butterflies burst alive in my stomach. Certain I was going to be sick, I jumped up from my vanity stool and rushed into the ensuite bathroom. Grabbing my hair, I pulled the black mass to the side right before dry-heaving over the toilet. Nothing came up. Probably because I hadn't eaten breakfast this morning—or dinner the night before.

"Winnie, Gran wants you downstairs!" a new voice yelled through my bedroom door, punctuated by a few pounding knocks.

"Coming," I called. Pausing another few seconds to make sure I didn't throw up, I straightened and turned toward the sink to study my ashen reflection in the mirror for the final time. "Please say you understand," I whispered to her, holding my breath as I waited, *prayed*, for a response.

I just needed a sign. One *tiny* little sign that I shouldn't do this, and I wouldn't.

Silence.

Swallowing my disappointment, I turned away and headed for the bedroom door. The second I opened it, a fluffy white furball scampered inside and leapt onto my bed.

"Really, Pearl?" I grumbled at my grandmother's cat familiar. "You could at least wait until *after* I'm gone."

The Persian blinked her yellow-green eyes at me, then slowly circled a few times before curling into a ball in the middle of my bed. I glared at her, and she stared back, her flat face devoid of expression.

Rolling my eyes, I left the devious feline to her devices, knowing this was a battle I wouldn't win. She went where she pleased and when she pleased, just like a regular cat. Even though she knew how much I hated finding her fur all over my stuff, none of my glares or threats fazed her.

When I hit the stairs, my ten-year-old brother raced from his room to join me, speaking a mile a minute. "Can I have your phone while you're gone? *Please*, Winnie? Just so I can text my friends."

"No," I immediately told him, frowning a little before adding, "And what friends? You don't have any."

"Yes, I do," Wyatt argued, annoyance edging his tone.

"Where? I've never seen them."

"Just because they're online doesn't mean they're not real," he said, his ire increasing. "I game with them every day, and we talk about all sorts of stuff."

I gave him a sharp look. "*Normal* stuff, I hope."

He returned my look with one that every little brother mastered. "I'm not stupid, Winnie. We only talk about human things."

"Good, but you're still not getting my phone. Those online friends could actually be fifty-year-old pedophiles."

His freckles shifted as he scrunched up his nose. "What's a pedophile?"

"Winter Snow, don't scare your brother," Gran chastised, her pale eyes disapproving as she watched us descend the stairs.

"Well, he needs to know that not everyone online is who they say they are."

"Yes, but he's only ten. Let him have his fun."

I arched a brow as we reached the bottom and joined her in the bright foyer, the morning sun beaming through the glass panes of the front door. "So I should give him my phone?"

She harumphed. "Hell, no. He already spends way too much time online."

A faint smile twitched my lips.

"Aw, Gran, come on," Wyatt pleaded, rounding his big puppy-brown eyes at her. "I'm gonna be all alone once Winter's gone. I need someone to talk to."

"You can talk to me."

Wyatt huffed and crossed his arms over his thin chest, looking so much like Dad with his stubbornly set jaw and white-blond hair that my throat tightened. Without warning, I turned and dragged him into a hug.

"Hey!" he protested, struggling to break free, but I only hugged him harder.

"I'm gonna miss you, Wy-Fi," I murmured, and he finally relented, wrapping his little chicken arms around me for a quick squeeze.

"I'll miss you too, Winnie," he mumbled back, then started to squirm until I reluctantly let him go. "But I still don't understand why you're going to school. I thought you liked your job at the diner."

One glance at Gran, and I cleared my throat to carefully say, "I did like my job at the diner, but it's in the human world."

"What's wrong with that?"

"Nothing. It's just . . . We're witches, Wyatt, not human. Going to this school could help restore our place in the community again. You know how important it is to have friends."

His blond brows pulled together in a troubled frown. "But they don't like us. What if they're mean to you or try to hurt you?"

I opened my mouth to reassure him, but my nerves suddenly returned with a vengeance, robbing me of speech.

"Then she'll remind them who they're dealing with." Gran spoke for me, a sharp glint entering her pale eyes. "Don't you worry, Wyatt. Your sister might have been denied the opportunity to hone her magic at one of our community academies in the past, but she's received the very best education possible from your parents and me over the years. Winter is more than capable of defending herself."

Worry still lined my brother's face despite Gran's confidence, and I couldn't blame him. He'd only been six months old when everything had fallen apart. The witch community meant nothing to him but turmoil and grief.

"Now finish saying goodbye, then go get ready for your lessons," Gran continued to tell him. "You have a potions test today, and don't forget our agreement. If you fail another test, you lose video game privileges for a week."

"Aw, Gran," Wyatt complained but knew better than to argue. Gran might *look* frail, but she was a queen lioness at heart who expected to be obeyed. I tousled my brother's hair, and he ducked away, waving at me with a quick "Bye, Winnie" before scampering out of sight.

Staring after him, I inhaled a deep breath before facing my grandmother again. The second our eyes locked, I knew her discerning gaze saw far more than I wanted it to. Instead of questioning me, she scanned my appearance with a cluck of approval.

"It does my heart good to see a Mayweather in academy uniform once more," she said, taking in my crisp white shirt, black blazer, and black-and-silver pleated skirt. A black ribbon tie, black knee-high socks, and shiny dress shoes completed the outfit. Raising a hand to reverently touch the silver-stitched H and A crest on my blazer, she whispered, "It suits you perfectly."

I swallowed hard, feeling the full weight of my decision with those words. But, despite my many reservations, I had to do this. I had to do it for *them*. For my family. We'd been outcasts for far too long, so long that my brother had never even met others of his own kind. So long that he was acting more and more human every day.

His curiosity of the outside world was getting harder to suppress, but it wasn't the *supernatural* world he was curious about. In his eyes, the supernatural world destroyed his family, so why would he want to be a part of it? Humans were what intrigued him, and although Gran had forbidden us both from attending human schools, Wyatt continued to emulate them—especially *American* humans, to Gran's chagrin.

He'd become so immersed in acting like one that he still hadn't manifested a single spark of magic. He was only ten, but I knew Gran was worried. The Mayweathers were known for manifesting early. If his magic didn't appear soon, it might be a sign. A sign that he was . . .

I didn't finish the thought, afraid I'd make it true if I did.

Something cold settled around my neck, snapping me from my thoughts. "What's this?" I asked, glancing down.

I lifted the silver chain Gran had clasped around my neck to better see the pendant attached. It was a pentacle—a five-pointed upright star within a circle—a symbol that all witches knew well. Nestled in its center was a black stone. At first, I thought it was obsidian, but upon closer inspection . . .

A sharp gasp left me, and I looked up at Gran in disbelief. "Is this what I think it is?"

"The rarest gemstone in the world, so rare that humans aren't even aware of it?" Her lips curved into an impish grin. "Yes, darling. It's a heartstone."

I blinked. "But . . . but *how?* Witches haven't been able to find more heartstone in decades."

She shrugged. "They haven't, but I've been secretly saving this little stone for a special occasion, and that time has finally come."

"Oh, Gran," I whispered, my throat tightening with emotion. "I . . . I'm truly honored, but I can't accept something so precious."

"*You* are precious, more precious than any stone," she adamantly replied, her expression sobering. "You were destined to carry it, especially considering where you're going. This amulet will protect you when I cannot, acting both as a shield and an amplifier to compensate for the absence of your coven. Never take it off."

"But first years aren't allowed to bring any personal items with them to school, including jewelry," I reminded her.

She waved my words away. "Nonsense. All the other families and covens will be protecting their scholars in a similar fashion. It's the witches' way." Reaching up to fist the amulet, she closed her eyes and chanted, "Shadows mine, aid my spell. Cloak this necklace, shield it well."

The necklace faded, then completely disappeared.

"There," Gran said, dropping the now invisible pendant. "The invisibility spell won't last forever, but if it wears off, repeat those words to keep it hidden."

I nodded, oddly comforted by the feel of the cool gemstone against my skin—even if I couldn't see it. "Guess we should go, then,"

I said, hating how thin my voice sounded.

Gran solemnly nodded. "Yes, it's time."

Taking a step back, she raised her hands and, with a confident sweep of her arms, conjured a human-sized portal between us. The edges shimmered dark violet, and inside the mysterious depths of its center was a void of pitch-black nothingness, swirling and grasping, threatening to swallow whole anyone who trespassed. "The Ether" was what we called the endless space between the earthly plane and the celestial. Only witches and their familiars could enter this realm, but not all who did came back out whole.

And some didn't come back out at all.

I wasn't afraid of entering it, though, especially with Gran as my guide. She'd been traveling by portal for decades and had never once lost her way.

Sweeping a final glance over Blackrose Manor—praying this wouldn't be the last time I saw my childhood home—I stepped around the portal and accepted my grandmother's outstretched hand. Together, we entered the black hole and were immediately transported to another dimension. Wind snatched at my hair, throwing it into my face as the world sped by impossibly fast. Gran firmed her grip on my hand, the only anchor keeping me from the Ether's clutches. Seconds later, we exited the screaming maelstrom, our feet landing on solid ground. *Sand*, more specifically.

Pushing my windswept hair back, I immediately noticed the time change. The sky was a dull gray, the sun still struggling to breach the horizon. I was used to seeing mountains, the rural town of Plymouth where I grew up sitting at the foot of one, but these mountains were far bigger. Instead of being covered in trees, they jutted up into the sky like giant rock behemoths, jagged and dusted in white. The air was also thinner and chillier than back home. We were *in* the mountains, not at their base.

"Where are we?" I asked, turning in a circle to take in the gorgeous panoramic view. We were standing on the sandy beach of a crystal clear lake, a glacier-fed river nearby steadily pouring into it. A thick border of pine trees surrounded the lake, not a single road or man-made building in sight. Birds chirped in the trees, but other than that and the gurgling water, I couldn't hear any signs of life.

"Sorry, darling, but I'm not allowed to tell you," Gran replied, letting go of my hand to tuck a few strands of white hair back into her otherwise pristine bun. "As your guardian, I was given permission to drop you off at this location, but all first years must face their initiation into Heartstone alone and without prior guidance. You'll pass through the magical wards as soon as you leave the beach, and that's all I can share. What happens after that is completely up to you."

The reminder sank like a rock in the pit of my stomach, but I nodded anyway, valiantly trying not to show how nervous I was.

This wasn't a typical college drop-off experience. Heartstone was an *elite* college for young and powerful witches and warlocks. Only the best were admitted, but I had to *prove* that I was the best. It made sense that I'd have to prove my worth from day one. Otherwise, the school wouldn't have a reputation for being cutthroat and dangerous.

Not to mention deadly. Every year, students died at Heartstone.

A foreboding chill suddenly crept over the peaceful landscape. The wind picked up, and I caught a whiff of something, a scent that didn't belong in the fresh mountain air.

Despair.

Cold fingers of dread raced up my spine, and I couldn't suppress a shiver.

No doubt seeing the fear bleeding into my eyes, Gran abruptly reached up and grabbed my face, pulling it down to hers before saying, "You're a *Mayweather*. Show them all what you're made of. Prove that you belong. Reinstate your place. Do it for yourself, but also do it for me and your brother. Do it for your parents and for your aunt Clarice, rest her soul."

"Yes, Gran," I replied, feeling my heart begin to race.

"Don't bow to anyone. You're *royalty*; they've just forgotten. Remind them that Mayweathers used to sit on the throne. It's your birthright to rule, and once you've conquered this challenge before you, Mayweathers will rise again."

"Yes, Gran."

Her sharp nails dug into my cheeks, her eyes boring holes into mine as if she could etch her next words into my brain. "Do whatever it takes to survive, but you *must* stay away from Thorne Hudson at all costs. Considering his family's position, I can only assume they had something to do with your acceptance to Heartstone. The Hudsons want nothing more than to make a mockery of you, to see you fail, to see you *dead*. This is your chance to prove just how resilient Mayweathers are. You *deserve* to be at that school, Winter. Don't let them destroy the last hope we have of reinstating our position."

At the mention of *his* name, my heart practically pounded out of my chest.

"Yes, Gran," I whispered, my voice reed thin. "I love you."

"Oh, my darling, I love you too," she murmured back, lifting up to kiss my cheek. "May the spirits of our ancestors guide and protect you on this journey. Now go. I've already lingered too long. The others will get a head start."

With that, she let go of me and turned to form another portal. As it sprang into existence and she stepped forward to enter it, I almost cried out for her to take me with. Instead, I viciously bit my tongue, forcing my feet to stay where they were.

Gran threw one last glance at me over her shoulder, her gaze brimming with love and pride. I smiled at her, though it was forced. She smiled back, then swept inside her portal and vanished from view.

The portal disappeared, leaving me utterly alone.

The moment she was gone, I immediately felt small and insignificant, completely inept to the task before me. I was just one witch, a *disgraced* one in a great big world that wanted to crush me like a bug. How had I convinced myself that I could do this? I had no clue what awaited me behind those invisible magical wards. I could fail in an instant, proving to the entire witch community that the Mayweather name truly was dead.

So many what-ifs. So many doubts and fears.

It was only by the power of my grandmother's parting words that I managed to push aside my fear and move. One step, then two, my shoes sank into the soft sand as I made my way across the beach. When only one step remained between the beach's end and the unknown, I lifted my chin and plowed ahead, bracing myself for whatever awaited me.

The second my shoes hit grass, the world around me changed. A deep gloom plunged the morning into night, and the temperature dropped by several degrees.

Before my eyes could adjust to the sudden darkness, a bloodcurdling scream lit up the night.

CHAPTER 2

Yup, it was official. I was going to die.

The scream wasn't mine, but it might as well have been.

A few sporadic flashes of light illuminated the eerie darkness, revealing what was hidden inside.

Chaos.

I stared in rising horror as a young woman around my age conjured a cerulean orb of magic, only to be knocked off her feet a second later by a . . .

I blinked. Blinked again.

The forest of pine trees was *alive.* Every time a ball of magic lit up the night, the trees reacted, viciously attacking the magic wielder.

Another terrified scream punctuated the air, followed by a terrible snapping noise as roots shot from the ground and wrapped around the girl. She screamed again, only for a root to wind around her head and muffle the sound.

"Run!" a male voice shouted from nearby, and I glanced over to see him blast a tree with fire. As the orange ball exploded against its side and started licking up the bark, an inhuman noise came from its depths, sounding way too much like an agonized wail. Within seconds, the entire tree was up in flames, burning so hot that heat gusted across my face.

The stench of burning wood hit me, along with a scent combination that immediately turned my blood to ice.

Dirt. Decaying leaves. Despair.

The tree was dying.

"RUN!" the Fire Elemental bellowed again, nearly colliding with me as he charged past.

The foreboding presence of death kept me locked in place, all while my survival instincts fired off on all cylinders. *Run, hide, fight. Run, hide, fight.* A part of me wanted to return to the beach, to the safe haven a mere step behind me. It would be easy, *so* easy to hide, to resume my pitiful life of obscurity. Another part wanted to save the dying tree and make sure the girl trapped by roots was okay.

I did neither of those things, knowing that this was a test. A *trial.* This was my initiation, and if I made the wrong choices, I would fail.

As I hesitated, my grandmother's words came back to me. *"Do whatever it takes to survive, Winter."*

Whatever it takes. Whatever it takes.

I reached up to grasp the invisible amulet around my neck, knowing what she'd want me to do.

Run.

Listening, I burst into action, using the flames from the dying tree to follow after the Fire Elemental. Every few yards, he would lob a fiery orb at the trees nearby, and they'd screech in fury. The more he did it, the angrier they became, until—

Crack. Groan. Snap.

One of the trees suddenly fell, narrowly missing me as it careened like an arrow toward the fleeing warlock. With a thunderous *boom*, it hit the ground, and I lost sight of the warlock. The impact shook the forest floor, so violently that I pitched forward, sprawling on my hands and knees. Roots and rocks dug into my flesh, but I barely felt the pain, the world around me abruptly muting as I sensed death nearby.

I stopped breathing, my spine going rigid when I felt its phantom touch seconds later, coating my skin in goosebumps. But it wasn't here for me. I started to tremble anyway, knowing that I was helpless, *powerless* against it. Whenever death came, it never left empty-handed.

Frozen with fear, I stayed where I was for several long moments. Only when the fires burned out and plunged the forest into darkness once more, only when the stench of death finally faded away, did I try to move again. My hearing returned, but the world was still hushed, as if Mother Nature herself had paused to observe what had just happened.

Please only be the tree, please only be the tree, I silently chanted to myself, unwilling to accept the worst case scenario.

Picking myself up, I followed the fallen tree's length, moving slowly so I wouldn't trip over a root.

Please, please, please.

I could barely see a few steps ahead of me but didn't dare conjure an orb, my intuition warning me that the trees would attack me if I did. They'd probably been enchanted to react to magic, so I forced myself to endure the suffocating darkness—darkness that had once felt like a friend to me but not for a very long time. Now it felt like a malevolent stalker lying in wait.

When I reached the spot where I'd last seen the warlock, I swallowed hard and inched closer to the fallen tree.

Please.

One step. Two. The toe of my shoe struck something. Not a root or even the tree, but something that felt a lot like a limb. Like a body. Like—

"Dear ancestors." I whirled around, clamping a hand over my mouth as bile surged up my throat.

It was the Fire Elemental. The tree had *crushed* him.

Even without visual confirmation, I knew he was dead. This wasn't the first time I'd dealt with the aftermath of death's claim. The hopeless despair sank deep into my bones, sucking the very life out of me. Weakness stole through my body, and I waited for the feeling to ease its grip on me, torn by what to do next. I should keep running, but . . . but someone was *dead*. Even though I knew students died at Heartstone Academy every year, seeing it firsthand was a shock to my system.

He didn't even get the chance to prove himself. Didn't even get to step inside the hallowed halls of the prestigious school he'd wanted so badly to attend.

Just like that, his life had been snuffed out. All those years of training, of preparing, of *hoping*. For what? For *this*?

Doubt assailed me again, even greater than before. I couldn't do this. The stakes were too high. Gran would understand if I backed out, if I returned home where it was safe. Right?

Before I'd even finished the thought, I knew the answer. I was a Mayweather. A *Mayweather*. Mayweathers never backed down, and they most certainly never hid from a challenge. We might have been forced out of our community ten years ago, but Gran and even my parents had never stopped fighting to prove their worth. The Mayweather bloodline was legendary in the witch community, going back decades, *centuries*. That reputation was sacred, even more so now that it was hanging on by a thread.

I could restore that reputation. I *had* to restore it. It was my solemn duty as a Mayweather to protect the family name. Nothing else was more important.

Including my life.

With that reminder burning in my gut once more, I shoved aside my doubts and forced myself to move again. Not toward the fallen warlock, but away, knowing that the longer it took me to reach the school, the more I would have to prove. Portaling wasn't an option since I had no clue where the campus actually was. I could levitate to at least acquire a bird's eye view of the terrain, but doing so would expend a lot of energy—not to mention the trees might not approve.

Walking it was.

As I left the warlock behind, I focused on covering as much ground as I could without attracting attention. I'd spent the majority of the past decade in obscurity, so that shouldn't be a problem. I was used to blending in with humans, to living in the shadows. I *was* a shadow, slipping through the trees without detection. I might not be buddy-buddy with my magical affinity anymore, but it cloaked me all the same, allowing me to access its dark world.

With each passing step, the night's foreboding chill grew, the wind moaning through the trees like a melancholy ghost. Intuition tugged me northeast—not a heightened sense of direction but something deeper. A knowing. An *awakening*. One that often felt sinister in nature.

This way, it breathed, urging me onward with cold prodding fingers. *This way to your destiny*.

Lured by the telltale rush of flowing water, I decided to follow the river upstream, walking along its rocky edge and picking up speed despite the sharp incline.

This wasn't so bad. As long as I didn't use magic, I could—

I was suddenly yanked into the freezing river, gasping in shock only for my mouth to fill with water. As my head went under, I instinctively pushed toward the surface, but something shoved me down deeper. I slammed into the riverbed, unable to see up from down through the dark current.

Sharp rocks dug into my flesh, ripping my new uniform and skin to shreds. My lungs screamed for air, and I flailed my limbs, desperate to reach the surface. When I couldn't find it, something dark—darker than the churning waters trying to drown me—stirred within my veins.

Use me, it said, the words a soft hiss of command. When I ignored it, still grasping and clawing to reach the surface, the darkness hissed more urgently, *Use me!*

I stubbornly clenched my jaw, refusing to give in, refusing to *drown*. I was stronger than this. I was a *Mayweather*.

USE ME.

No! I internally shouted at the darkness, deciding then and there that drowning wasn't such a bad way to die after all. All I had to do was swallow, and it would be over. No more responsibility. No more guilt. No more pain. I would be free of it all.

At peace.

A word I didn't have the right to utter. To *feel*.

What was I thinking? I couldn't die this way. I didn't *deserve* a peaceful watery grave.

Use meeeee.

It was the sense of despair, the chill creeping into my very soul that finally weakened my resolve. Death was near, seeking out a new target.

Only this time, his target was *me*.

With the threat of my impending doom so close, my survival instincts kicked into overdrive. Before I could stop it, the darkness in my veins surged up, ready to strike out at anything and everything. Fear gripped me, not because death was breathing down my neck, but because I was about to expose the part of me I'd carefully locked away. The part of me that had a mind of its own, that was *dangerous*.

A scream built in my head, one of terror, of helplessness.

I couldn't stop it. Couldn't *control* it.

Nooooo! I wailed at the darkness, struggling to push it back down. But it was relentless, a leviathan fighting to break free of its cage. It had been so long, *too* long since I'd let it out. There was too much pent-up energy, and I was too rusty. Too *scared*. My magic was about to explode, and there was nothing, *nothing* I could do to stop it.

Just as the pain from keeping it contained grew unbearable, just as my body started to convulse from the lack of oxygen, the pressure keeping me under the water vanished. I raised my head and immediately breached the surface, sucking in a frantic gasp. A mixture of air and water speared down my throat, and I succumbed to a violent fit of coughing.

The fresh pain in my chest was the perfect distraction, though, and I nearly cried out in relief when I felt my magic pause. I quickly locked it up, shoving it down, down, down so it couldn't escape again.

That was close. *Too* close.

As I continued to drag in life-giving air, my body shook uncontrollably, hyped up on fear and adrenaline from the near disastrous event. Although I could no longer sense death, my fear remained. It had never left empty-handed before. I'd robbed it. Cheated it out of its victim. Did death ever seek revenge? I didn't know and didn't want to stick around long enough to find out.

Shivering and no-doubt looking like a half-drowned muskrat, I struggled against the current toward the riverbank. As I did, I spotted movement on shore. A girl, a *witch*, was following the river upstream like I'd been doing. Her back was to me, so I only caught a glimpse of her long swinging braid. Right before she faded into the gloom, she glanced over her shoulder at me still struggling in the river. Her skin was darker than mine by a few shades, but the bronze hue was light enough for me to see her lips curve into a wicked grin.

Why, that conniving little devil.

Her smile confirmed what I'd already begun to suspect. *She* had done this to me. Based on how the water had held me under, she must be a Water Elemental. It had been stupid of me to think that a *spell* was the only thing I'd be up against in this trial. Heartstone Academy was cutthroat, but so were the students. We were each other's competition, after all. The more students that failed earlier on, the less competition we'd have to face later.

This girl obviously wasn't afraid to eliminate her competition, and if I was going to survive this world, I'd need to adopt that same bloodthirsty attitude. For a moment, I'd almost forgotten, almost convinced myself that the other students and I were fighting the same battle and not each other. That delusional moment had nearly been my undoing, and I couldn't make that mistake again.

These students would sooner kill me than help me, especially when they found out who I was. I had to protect myself, to be smart, or I was going to wind up as Heartstone's next casualty.

By the time I made it onto solid ground again, the Water Elemental was long gone. So much for thinking I'd be the first student to complete the trial. At this rate, I'd end up last. Well, *almost* last. I couldn't forget the girl trapped in tree roots and the crushed warlock.

More aware of my deadly surroundings than ever, I ignored my fresh injuries and took off along the riverbank again, determined to make up the time I'd just lost. My socks squelched in my waterlogged shoes with each step, my hair and clothing stiffening with the growing chill. I could easily utter a spell that would have me dry in seconds, but one glance at the trees nearby, and I clamped my shivering lips shut.

The Water Elemental had risked using her magic, but something inside me, some instinct warned me not to reveal mine. I'd rather arrive at the school last than not at all.

At least an hour went by without spotting a single soul. My intuition sharpened the farther I went, letting me know that I was getting closer to my destination, but the weather had taken a turn for the worse. The higher I climbed into the mountains, the colder the temperature became, the harsh winds tearing at my hair, clothing, and exposed skin. Each step became harder to take, my ragged breaths gusting from me in white plumes as I struggled to keep climbing. It was only when the snow began to fall at an alarming rate that I truly started to worry.

"You've got to be kidding me," I mumbled unintelligibly, my jaw practically frozen shut. If it wasn't for my little dip in the river, I could handle the snowstorm. I was used to them, to the freezing temperatures and harsh winds from my winters spent in New Hampshire.

But this? This was unbearable. I couldn't survive this. Not with my damp clothing and hair sucking up all my body heat.

I had to risk using my magic.

That or portal back home with my dignity in shreds. The latter wasn't an option, so magic it was.

The spell I chose was considered simple magic, the energy use minimal. Any witch or warlock could do it, no matter their affinity, most learning how to at an early age. My dad had taught me when I was only twelve, and I thought of the memory now as I raised my stiff hands and, with a little flourish, muttered, "*Arida*."

The barest of energy illuminated my fingers a deep purple as my magic responded to the spell with focused precision. Within seconds, my hair and clothing were bone dry, including my socks and shoes. I immediately felt better, but before I could breathe out a relieved sigh, the world around me blurred white.

Snow and wind swirled around me like a tornado, screaming their fury. They tore at my clothes and whipped my hair into my face, beyond pissed that I'd dared use my magic. Little shards of ice joined the maelstrom, mercilessly pelting my exposed skin. I covered my face, but the storm was everywhere, pounding into me so hard that I was forced to crouch in the snow.

The storm roared and roared, stealing my sight and the breath from my lungs. I opened my mouth to drag in air, but snow and sleet filled it instead. Panic fluttered in my chest, and in an instant, the darkness within me surged up again.

Use meeeeee.

As more and more snow dumped on me, so fast that I was waist-deep in it within seconds, the fear of being buried alive nearly made me give in. But that fear wasn't as great as my fear of letting the darkness out after nearly two years of suppressing it. There had to be another way out of this, a way that didn't involve losing myself to the malevolent magic simmering in my blood.

Angry that I wouldn't let it out, the darkness shoved at the cage I kept it in, making it nearly impossible to think. Remembering another storm I'd recently been caught in, I quickly threw up my hands to conjure a shield. The snow and wind immediately stopped pelting me, thwarted by the invisible barrier.

But the storm didn't let up, screaming and pounding against the shield in search of weakness. Already exhausted from my near-drowning in the river and freezing hour-long trek, I knew I couldn't hold it back indefinitely. I needed to get out of here and fast.

Struggling to my feet again, I waded through the snow, my hands stretched out before me to better support the shield. I walked blind, my only guide the river to my right. No longer able to hear it over the raging snowstorm, I stuck closely to the edge, the slick, snow-covered rocks slowing my progress significantly.

Minutes felt like hours, but I kept going, one laborious step after another. If it wasn't for the instinct letting me know that I was still headed in the right direction, I might have lost hope. The storm was relentless, growing in volume with no signs of stopping. I slipped and stumbled over the rocks, nearly ending up in the river several times.

Everything ached, including my teeth, which were clenched tightly so they wouldn't clack together from the cold. My job at Rudy's Diner had kept me on my feet for nine hours a day as I'd bustled around waiting on tables, but it hadn't prepared me for this trial. I felt woefully out of shape, my legs like jello beneath me. My body screamed at me to sit down, to take a break, but if I did, I'd probably never get up again.

The air was growing thinner, and each breath was an effort as I doggedly plowed up the mountain. It might as well be Mount Everest at this rate, an impossible task that I had no hope of completing. I wasn't ready for this. Wasn't *prepared.* Not just physically, but mentally and emotionally as well.

Why the hell hadn't I told Gran the truth? That I hadn't even sent in my application to Heartstone, that this was all a huge *mistake?*

Minutes turned into hours turned into *days.* My body weakened, my *shield* weakened, on the verge of collapsing. I felt it thin, felt it crack beneath the storm's rage. Any second now, and it would be over. I'd given all I could give, and I had nothing left. Water sloshed onto my shoes, and I finally noticed how rough the river's current had become. A few steps later, and I understood why.

A waterfall. There was a freaking *waterfall.*

Which meant that I had to climb to the top somehow, and I didn't . . . I didn't have the *energy.* Just as defeat welled in my chest, just as my shield began to crumble to dust, my shoe landed on something flat. I glanced down and saw stone. *Stone.* Not rock. It was hewn into a man-made shape, a shape that instantly made me want to cry out in joy.

A stair!

I changed course and found another, then another and another, carved into the rocky mountainside to create a staircase beside the waterfall. Halfway up, my magic completely gave out. The snowstorm rushed back in and surrounded me, nearly knocking me backward. I blindly lurched forward and felt for the next step with my hands, crawling, *clawing* my way up.

I was close. I could feel it in my bones.

Just one more step. One more. I couldn't give up when I was this close. It felt like an eternity, but I reached the top. Unable to see a thing through the screaming storm, I continued to crawl, not caring how pathetic I looked.

One step. Just one step more.

I didn't know how long I crawled, blindly using my hands to follow the paved stone path beside the river, but I was suddenly there. As if someone had flipped a switch, the raging storm ceased and the air cleared, allowing me to see the world around me for the first time in what felt like forever. I was at the foot of a steep set of polished stone stairs, and when I lifted my gritty eyes, I beheld the towering might that was Heartstone Academy.

The building was huge, jutting up so high that the pointed pinnacles got swallowed up by the night sky. The design was like that of a gothic cathedral, imposing and sinister, built out of stone nearly as dark as the heartstone it was named after. Most of the tall and narrow stained-glass windows were devoid of light, making the structure appear that much more unwelcoming. The few lights I saw flickered weakly, going in and out of focus.

Or maybe that was my vision.

As I tried to stand, the ground dangerously tilted, and I knew that it was me. I was out of steam and fading fast. If I didn't make it up those stairs, if I passed out right before reaching the entrance, would they fail me?

Unwilling for that to happen, I dragged myself forward and started to climb one last time. One more step. Just one more. I was close, *so* close. I had to complete the trial. *Had* to. There was no other choice.

Every step was agony, my heart trilling dangerously fast as I pushed myself past my limits. Darkness edged my vision, my exhausted body on the brink of collapse.

One more step. Just. One. More. Step.

I barely remembered reaching the top. Barely remembered stumbling toward the menacing building's front doors. Barely remembered grasping one of the thick metal handles and pulling, *yanking* to pry it open.

But I remembered stepping foot inside. One step, and I was sprawled on the hard floor, unable to carry my weight a second longer. I managed to roll onto my back before everything dimmed, before the faces peering down at me blurred and started to fade. But as I succumbed to the darkness, one face sharpened long enough for me to recognize it.

A face I'd hoped to never see again.

A face that immediately flooded my mind with memory after painful memory.

A face that made me think of *her*. Of my best friend.

The friend that I'd murdered almost two years ago.

CHAPTER 3

Cold liquid speared down my throat. Not water, but something pungent, something that tasted like vomit.

My gag reflex kicked in, and I choked on the liquid, managing to spit it out.

"Come now," an annoyed voice snipped. "We don't have time for delicate sensibilities. Drink the Sano, Miss Mayweather."

Something hard jabbed into my bottom lip and pried it open. Before I could jerk my head away, more liquid filled my mouth. Knowing what it was this time, I begrudgingly swallowed it, cringing at the godawful taste. The fast-healing potion raced down my throat like liquid ice, immediately spreading through my body in search of injuries. As my aches and pains started to fade seconds later, I cracked my eyes open and was immediately greeted by an unfamiliar face.

A *sour* one.

The middle-aged woman's mouth was so pursed that I could barely see it. When she saw my eyes open, her scowl deepened even more. "Welcome back, Miss Mayweather," she said, not an ounce of warmth in her tone. "The student convocation is about to start without you, so you'd best hurry."

Rising from her chair with the now empty cup of Sano Elixir she'd practically forced down my throat, the woman sharply turned on her heel and marched off without another word. Based on the knee-length white coat she wore, I assumed she was a doctor.

Wait.

I shot up on the bed, taking in my surroundings with wide eyes. I was in the infirmary. Of *Heartstone Academy*. I'd made it. I'd survived the trial!

Giddy with relief, I scrambled off the bed and stood, already feeling ten times better. A quick glance down my front revealed that I was still in my uniform. My woefully soiled and tattered one. Dirt and crusted blood smudged my hands and the exposed parts of my legs, but the potion had at least healed my cuts and bruises. I reached up, grimacing when I felt how tangled my hair was.

"Chop-chop, Miss Mayweather," the sour doctor's voice snapped from somewhere beyond my partitioned-off cubicle. "Tardiness is a punishable offense at this school."

Her words had the desired effect, and I hurried from the cubicle, my shoes echoing against the stone floor. As I speedwalked down the infirmary's main aisle, I took in the vaulted ceilings and stone arches, noting that light dimly shined through the elaborate narrow windows on the room's right side. It hadn't felt like I'd been unconscious for that long, so I could only assume they'd dispersed the weather spell used for the trial.

Shadows still lingered in the corners, though, the light from the iron sconces on the stone walls casting the interior in gloomy shades. I passed by a couple dozen partitioned-off cubicles, all of them empty. When it finally dawned on me that I was the only student here, urgency filled me, and I walked even faster. Nearing the exit, I spotted the sour doctor along with two others. All three of them watched me leave, their expressions far from friendly.

Dear ancestors, did they treat *all* of the students this way, or was it just me?

Feeling all sorts of uncomfortable, I hurried even faster and yanked open one of the heavy oak doors, wanting to put this awkward situation behind me. But when I stepped into the hallway, I immediately stopped dead in my tracks, realizing I had no idea where to go. It was even more dimly lit out here, and there weren't any windows.

I was about to suck up my pride and return to the infirmary to ask for directions when a sudden shiver raced up my spine. Goosebumps erupted over my arms and legs, and I stiffened as a disembodied voice seemed to beckon me from down the dark hall, *This waaaay.*

I swallowed hard as I felt my intuition tug me in that direction.

This way to your destiny, it whispered through my bones. *This way to your fate.*

More like *doom*, I thought to myself, heeding the voice despite the foreboding chill in the air.

Without my intuition to guide me, I would have certainly become lost. The building was a maze of dark hallways and winding stairwells, and there wasn't a single soul in sight. The eerie silence was deafening, and I caught myself peering over my shoulder every few steps, half-expecting the building to come alive and attack me. Maybe my trial wasn't over after all. Maybe I was about to face a new challenge, one that would scare the living crap out of me.

I was halfway there already, my body tensing every time a shadow shifted in my peripheral. I didn't know what I expected my time at Heartstone Academy to be like, but I hadn't thought the very *walls* of the school would pose a threat. I really was on my own here. Truly and utterly alone. And if I stopped to think about that fact for even a second, I wouldn't be able to keep going, so I focused on the task at hand, on making it to the convocation in one piece.

It was the distant sound of clapping that alerted me to how close

I was minutes later. Relief filled me, and I hurried faster. As I rounded the corner, the hallway widened. Columns dotted its length, and I saw light illuminating the stone floor up ahead. Halfway down the hall, the space opened up. To the right was a wide staircase, and I glanced down the length toward what must be the entrance hall.

The vaulted ceiling soared high above, sloping upwards to form a central peak. A huge oval stained-glass window was positioned above the double entryway doors, Heartstone's silver and black crest proudly etched into the glass. The biggest wrought-iron chandelier I'd ever seen hung suspended in the middle of the foyer, at least three stories high with dozens of flickering candles lighting up its length. Not seeing an attached chain, I briefly paused to ogle the marvel.

It was enchanted. *Magic* kept it floating in the air.

Another round of clapping snapped me from my awe, and I looked left to see another set of double doors. They were closed, the clapping definitely coming from inside. My stomach swooped with nerves, but I didn't let myself think let alone hesitate. Like ripping off a bandaid, I marched to the heavy doors and yanked them open. They groaned loudly, and I cringed, hoping no one would hear. No such luck. The clapping abruptly stopped, and as I stood in the doorway, every single eye in the massive great hall turned to stare at me.

My mouth dried. Dear ancestors, this was the stuff of nightmares, the getting-caught-butt-naked-in-a-crowd kind. At how exposed I suddenly felt, I might as well be naked. All the hair on my body rose, my senses going on high alert. Before me was a room full of powerful magic wielders, of *predators*, and every single one of them was picking me apart with their eyes, searching for weakness.

I swallowed, the sound audible in the deafening silence.

Don't run. Don't you dare *run*, I inwardly hissed at myself, willing my hands not to shake, to reveal how utterly terrified I was. I'd already left a weak first impression by promptly passing out on my arrival. Falling apart right now would be the final nail in my coffin.

One gaze in particular pierced me like an ice pick, the cold fury behind it so palpable that my attention went straight to him before I could stop myself. Time slowed to a crawl as my eyes clashed with the warlock's. He was in an aisle seat toward the back of the room, which meant that he was closer to the doors. To *me*. Making it impossible not to see the anger brewing in his ocean blue eyes—eyes the same color as hers.

His were darker than usual today, stormy and cast in shadow from his thick lowered brows. *Her* eyes had never been that dark, that angry, especially not at me. But his had. The last time I'd seen him, he'd shown me just how angry, how terrifying he could become.

That horrible day came rushing back to me now, and I tried to swallow again. Tried and failed. His gaze dipped below my chin as if he'd just tracked the failed swallow, then dipped even lower, taking in my body with a cursory, *scathing* sweep.

He was suddenly on his feet, and my heart promptly lodged in my throat. Terrifying images of our last encounter pounded through me, my body breaking into a cold sweat as Thorne Hudson straightened—all six-foot-five of him—and squared off with me in the main aisle. A high-pitched shriek came from the red-tailed hawk perched on his broad shoulders, the added height making the warlock look giant-sized. The bird familiar thrust his massive wings out, filling the aisle with their five foot length.

At barely five feet myself, I couldn't help but be intimidated by their large presence. The duo were similar in coloring, all deep browns and russet reds, the warm shades the exact opposite of my cool ones. I'd always thought Thorne looked like a pirate with his tousled rich brown hair, deeply tanned skin, square stubbled jaw, and the small gold hoop glinting in his left earlobe. Hints of dark ink jutted from his white shirt collar and streaked down his large hands, the tattoos further accentuating his roguish appearance.

He might look like someone who spent all his time outdoors under a hot blazing sun, but nothing about Thorne Hudson's personality was warm. The twenty-four-year-old Cosmic warlock was as cold as they came, especially toward me. He might be good-looking—okay, fine, stupidly *hot*—but every single line of his handsome chiseled face was set in unforgiving stone.

For a second that felt like an eternity, we stared at each other, a million unspoken words simmering between us. The weight of them practically crushed me, and I almost looked away. Almost.

"*Do whatever it takes to survive*," Gran's words reminded me. "*But you* must *stay away from Thorne Hudson at all costs*."

I should have known better than to think I could do both of those things. Thorne didn't just hate me. He wanted me *dead*. And now here I was, standing before him alone and terrified, far from my coven and any form of protection.

This was his chance to finish what he started. To exact his revenge.

I could see it in his storm-filled eyes. The hatred. The desire for vengeance. He loathed my guts, and yet . . .

I couldn't blame him.

Not after what I'd done to his sister.

Knowing he could end me with a flick of his wrist, my hands began to shake. But instead of willing magic to them, instead of preparing to defend myself, I curled them into fists at my sides.

Do it, I silently threw at him, even as fear made me tremble harder, as the darkness within me rose up in response to his threatening presence. *Put an end to this*.

His eyes narrowed to slits as if he'd heard my message loud and clear.

Time all but stopped, the tension between us fit to explode. I waited for the inevitable, my whole body trembling like a decaying leaf about to be severed from its life source. I'd hoped to last longer than one day at Heartstone Academy, and although I was disappointed with myself, no one could cheat death.

Not even a witch who could sense it coming.

The tension became unbearable, but I didn't move a muscle, frozen in place by guilt, by the painful memories of my past. It was like my survival instincts had switched off, a deep sense of resignation filling me instead. I waited. Waited and waited for Thorne to lift a hand, to strike me down where I stood.

What are you waiting for? I wanted to scream in the awful stillness. *Do it!*

His right hand twitched, and I squeezed my eyes shut, too much of a coward to face my own death. I waited. Waited and waited for the agonizing blow.

Nothing happened.

The sudden sound of angry footfalls had my eyes snapping back open. I nearly swallowed my tongue at the sight of Thorne and his familiar only feet away from me and closing in fast. He kept coming and coming, his presence looming larger and larger, reminding me of just how *huge* he was.

At the last second, right when a collision seemed inevitable, I shifted to the side. He swept by me, his arm brushing against mine. The graze was featherlight, but I felt a sharp *zap* anyway. The electrical current shot through me like a mini lightning bolt, shocking my insides more than hurting them. The sensation wrenched a startled gasp from me anyway, one that he completely ignored as he stormed from the great hall.

Flustered, my heart trilling like a hummingbird's wings, I turned to watch him stalk down the stairs, across the foyer, and out the building. The front doors slammed shut behind him, echoing loudly in the dead silence that followed.

Not knowing what to do, I continued to stand in the doorway like a gaping fish. It was only when a male voice finally broke the silence that I turned back to the great hall, to the sea of faces still staring at me.

"Well, it would seem not everyone is pleased to see a Mayweather grace these hallowed halls."

The words had an immediate effect on the audience. The verbal response was visceral, ranging from shock to blatant fury. Several students shot up from their seats and started to shout, the flurry of words making their feelings about my presence more than clear.

"What is a *Mayweather* doing here?"

"She's exiled! She doesn't belong at this school!"

"She's *trash*. Kick her out."

"We don't want her here!"

I'd expected to receive some animosity, even though I'd only been ten years old when the elders and their families had been excommunicated. I still vividly remembered the trial, the anger and resentment when the community had cast us out. It didn't matter that I'd been an innocent child. All they saw was another Mayweather, and that made me guilty.

But it was clear that ten years of exile wasn't enough to cool the lingering grudge over what had happened. Witches weren't exactly the most forgiving bunch, that was for sure. My family's actions had disgraced the whole community, ruining not only their own reputations but the entire witch race.

A sin like that couldn't go unpunished, and it was my duty to pay the price.

But it was also my duty to *fix* it, to regain what had been taken from us. Which was why I didn't allow the hateful words being spewed to break me. The only way forward was to face their judgment, even if it hurt.

Even if it killed me.

Overwhelmed by the sheer force of the hostility, I focused on the far side of the room, on the male standing on the great hall's stage who'd outed me. He was tall and lean, his dark three-piece suit contrasting sharply with his fair skintone. Heavy stubble darkened the lower half of his face, his black hair cut short. Probably in his late forties or early fifties, he looked like a Keanu Reeves doppelganger. Nothing about him seemed overtly menacing, but the wry twist of his lips immediately put me on edge.

I know all about you, Winter Snow Mayweather, the smile seemed to say. *You can't hide anything from me.*

A bead of sweat slid down my spine, my instincts screaming at me in warning. A trap. This felt like a *trap*. Like a perverted game designed to oust me, to expose my deepest darkest secrets.

Maybe Gran had been right. Maybe the Hudsons *were* behind my admission to Heartstone, encouraging the school board to accept me for the sole purpose of publicly exposing my crimes. If that happened, this would all be over before it could even start. Just the thought of what they would do to me sent another shiver of fear through my body.

As the students' voices rose in volume, my trepidation grew. At this rate, I'd be dead before they could schedule a trial. Images flashed through my mind of my body up in flames as they burnt me at the stake. Humans had started the practice centuries ago, but the only ones burning witches these days were other witches.

The intense need to flee nearly choked me, but I stayed where I was, knowing this was the only way to prove myself. The man standing on the stage allowed the students to rage, watching me with his mouth still fixed in that wry twist. After a moment, it became painfully clear that this was another test. Another *trial.* Not the kind that ended with me burnt to a crisp, but I was being tried and judged all the same. One wrong move would seal my fate.

Sudden anger at how unfair this was washed over me, and I dug my broken nails into my palms. Thorne Hudson might have a valid reason to hate me, but no one in here actually knew me. They knew *of* me, of the name I bore like a scarlet letter. But they didn't know me or what I'd been through to get here. They didn't know about the constant guilt and pain I carried or the crushing responsibility I felt every day.

They didn't know, and they didn't care. I was nothing but an ugly stain to them. Something to be ashamed of, to hide, to erase, to throw away.

I was a mistake, and they wanted nothing more than to be rid of me.

Digging my nails into my skin hard enough to break it, I straightened my spine and bore the abuse, focusing on Gran's final words to me instead of the irate crowd's.

"Don't bow to anyone. You're royalty; *they've just forgotten."*

They'd forgotten, all right. They saw me as nothing more than a stray, flea-infested mutt.

Insults and threats continued to hurl through the air, striking me like stones. My lips quivered, but I clenched my jaw, raising my chin a notch for good measure. Something about the action caused the man on the stage to smile. It was creepy, not to mention downright sadistic. Was he *enjoying* my suffering?

He abruptly raised his hands and barked, *"Rigescunt indutae!"*

Just like that, dead silence fell over the student body. But I knew it was more than the commanding words that had shut them up. He'd cast a spell over the entire congregation. Hundreds of students were frozen where they stood or sat, many of them with their mouths still wide open.

"Really, Cyrus?" a new voice said, this one female. "Don't you think that was a little dramatic?"

With that same creepy grin still plastered on his face, the warlock glanced at the black woman sitting in a chair to his left. "Not in the least, Venetia. The students should know who's in charge at this academy, and that I don't appreciate uncivilized outbursts. The spell will only last a few minutes anyway."

The middle-aged woman pursed her full lips in disapproval, but instead of arguing, she swung her gaze to me and said, "Come, child. There's a seat for you up front."

I blinked, then blinked again, surprised to discover that I could move. But even more surprising was the kind smile the woman directed my way. Her umber-colored skin crinkled at the corners of her warm brown eyes as she beckoned me forward encouragingly. Unlike the warlock who'd frozen all the students—except for me, apparently—her black hair was poofed out in a large afro. One of the coils caught the light and seemed to move independently from the rest, but it was probably just a draft.

Not seeing a single trace of anger or judgement on her face, I immediately wanted to like her, to trust her. Maybe not everyone here hated me after all.

Careful, my intuition whispered, more like *hissed* to me. A reminder that letting my guard down at this school could have deadly consequences. Even the seemingly harmless ones could be the death of me if it served their agenda.

Still, I couldn't stand in this doorway forever, so I finally allowed myself to move. It was eerie walking down the aisle past row after row of frozen students. Their eyes didn't follow me, but I knew they could still see, still hear me moving past them. Now that I was inside the great hall, I could fully appreciate just how massive it was.

Columns with arches jutted up the sides, while curved buttresses braced the rounded ceiling several stories above. Stained-glass windows let in weak light behind the thick columns, and another huge round window bearing the academy's crest was positioned above the stage. Iron sconces high above further lit the space, but shadows still clung to its many corners, and I couldn't help but wonder if anything—or anyone—was hiding in them.

Each step I took echoed loudly against the stone floor, making the trek feel a mile long. When I finally reached the front, it immediately hit me how exposed I was. Hundreds of angry students were now at my *back*, and all it would take was one vengeful action to end me.

Despite how vulnerable I felt, I slid onto the empty aisle seat in the very first row, more than a little uncomfortable that the girl in the seat beside me was twisted around with an ugly scowl on her face. A scowl meant for me. My hand was halfway to my neck before I caught myself and quickly lowered it to my lap, silently cursing my slip. After the rough day I had, I'd worried my necklace had fallen off, but even though I couldn't see it, I suddenly felt its reassuring weight.

I clung to that invisible presence now, praying it would protect me from the mob at my back. I could already hear movement coming from the crowd as the freezing spell started to lose its grip. Another minute and hundreds of eyes would be boring holes into the back of my skull.

If only I had a familiar to keep an eye on them for me. Oh, what a *boon* that would be. But my prayers and even my summoning spells over the years had gone unanswered. Wherever the celestial spirit who'd gifted me a piece of their essence that fueled my magic was, they clearly didn't want to be associated with a screwed-up witch like me.

Couldn't blame them.

With my close-up view of the great hall's stage, I could fully see what I assumed were the academy's professors. None of them looked all that thrilled to see me, except for one. I spotted a few familiars among them, perched on laps or shoulders, and couldn't help but feel a bit envious.

Gran had always said it was only a matter of time before I got mine, that our pure and powerful bloodline had a way of drawing familiars in, but that was before we'd fallen from grace. What spiritual entity in their right mind would want to be tied to a pariah like me?

"Now that the final first year has arrived," the warlock standing center stage suddenly said, "we can commence with the convocation. Everyone, take your seats, please."

More movement. More shuffling. A few whispered grumbles reached my ears, but no one resumed their shouting. The eyes on me felt even worse than I imagined, though, their intensity so great that I missed the next few spoken words. But the second my *name* was uttered, I snapped to attention, my gaze locking on the warlock.

"—Miss Mayweather's presence isn't a mistake. The school board voted to admit her just like everyone else here today. She's a student and is to be treated as such, and that's all I'll say on the subject. Moving on, I'd like to introduce myself again to our late arrivals."

Meaning *me*.

"I'm Chancellor Cyrus Grimshaw, the chief executive officer of Heartstone Academy. It has been my honor to serve here for the past two years and to witness history in the making. I'd like to start off by congratulating our new first years on completing their Initiation Trial. This test wasn't easy, and not everyone passed. Some quit, and others let fear get the best of them. It takes great courage to face the unknown, especially without the aid of a coven, and only the bravest and strongest succeeded."

He stretched open one of his hands, and a large animal suddenly appeared from the shadows behind him. It was a greyhound—his familiar, I assumed—his brindle gray coat short and sleek. The tall, lanky dog soundlessly glided forward, carrying what appeared to be a note in his mouth.

When he placed the note in the warlock's hand, Chancellor Grimshaw accepted it with a murmured, "Thank you, Phantom."

The animal turned and retreated back into the shadows, vanishing from sight like his namesake.

Opening the note, the chancellor continued, "These are the names of the students who failed to complete the Initiation Trial and were therefore dismissed from the school . . ." He rattled off five names, his voice's inflection no greater than if he was reading a grocery list. "Among them was Matteo Danbury who's just been confirmed deceased. Let's take a moment to pray that his soul safely reaches the spirit plane."

I bowed my head with the rest of the congregation, but the second I closed my eyes, an image of the tree falling and crushing the Fire Elemental invaded my mind. I wrenched my eyes back open, tightly clasping my trembling hands in my lap.

After a brief moment, the chancellor started speaking again, smoothly switching topics as if the loss of a student wasn't worth dwelling on. "As you all know, our community has been at a terrible crossroads this past decade. Ever since the elders' botched attempt to stop the vampires from breaking their century-long curse . . ."

Me. He looked at *me*.

". . . we've been leaderless and divided. This tragedy has cost us dearly, not only because our power has been diminished, but because other supernaturals have *risen* in power and done so at our expense. Rumors abound that the royal vampire family has used witch blood to birth their next generation of heirs. There are even whispers that the queen herself is a witch."

Shocked murmurs rippled through the crowd, and my own eyes widened. A witch was on the vampire throne? How the hell had *that* happened?

"If that isn't blasphemous enough," Chancellor Grimshaw continued, "learning that hybrid werewolves exist has threatened everything we believe in. A werewolf in possession of magic is an abomination, and they've been using that stolen power to strengthen their packs. Magic is sacred, a sacrificial gift from the celestial spirits meant only for us. *We* are its keepers, not vampires or werewolves or hybrids that defile the natural order. That connection to the spirit world was what made our community more powerful than any other, and we *must* fight to restore that strength."

The students reacted to his impassioned speech with enthusiasm, clapping and shouting in agreement. He might have a creepy smile, but he sure knew how to light a fire under his captive audience.

"With the creation of Heartstone Academy, these tumultuous times can blessedly come to an end," he said, that passion brightening his slate gray eyes. "In this room are the sharpest, bravest, most cunning and powerful young witches and warlocks of our generation. The strongest of you will rise up to become our next leaders, claiming your earned spots on the Conclave of Magic to serve and protect our community. You will unite us. You will lead us to greatness once more, to the power and respect we rightfully deserve!"

The screams were deafening, triggering a deep-seated fear inside me that made my entire body stiffen. At least the screams weren't directed at me.

As the chancellor paused to soak up the crowd's enthusiasm, he dropped his gaze and looked directly at me. That smile crept over his face again, and I squeezed my hands together until they hurt. Something flashed in his eyes, something that looked a lot like excitement.

I hope you're ready, Miss Mayweather, his eyes seemed to say, to challenge. *This is where your life begins . . . or where it ends.*

My throat sealed shut.

Ancestors save me, I was so doomed.

CHAPTER 4

Never in my life had I felt so unwelcome.

After listening to Chancellor Grimshaw pump up the students for another hour, the first years had been dismissed to tour the extensive grounds. A pretty red-haired professor named Felicity Birch led our group, a little gray-and-red bird familiar flitting about her shoulders. But her cheerful-sounding name didn't match her current mood. Minutes into the tour, it became uncomfortably clear that *I* was the cause of the professor's sour attitude. Every time she mentioned a fact about the school, she alluded back to its purpose for existing in the first place.

"We never needed an elite academy like this in the past. If the elders hadn't failed us so disgracefully, we wouldn't be forming a new council at all."

"This school represents a fresh start. After what happened ten years ago, the community is done with elders. A council body made up of individuals who earned *their positions is the change we desperately need."*

"Heartstone wasn't designed for the weak. If you don't have what it takes to survive all four years, then you should leave now. The longer you waste our time, the more disgrace your failure will heap on your family and coven. Only the greatest witches and warlocks are meant to lead our community."

"Just because you were admitted to this school doesn't mean you're

worthy of a spot on the Conclave. You must prove yourself, a concept that should have been instilled decades—centuries—*ago. We wouldn't be having this discussion today if that had been the case.*"

On and on, she not-so-subtly jabbed at my family name, making it obvious she didn't think I belonged here. The entire tour, the other first years either eyed me disdainfully or ignored me completely. None of their faces were familiar, my years of magic training spent at home and not at an academy. It was clear most of them already knew each other, though, whispering amongst themselves congenially.

One of them cast more glances at me than the rest, her sepia-colored eyes watching me intently. If it wasn't for the long golden brown braid swinging from high on her head, I might not have realized who she was.

The Water Elemental who'd almost drowned me during the Initiation Trial.

When I met one of her glances with a "I know what you did" look, a wicked little smile curved her full lips. Flipping her braid back, she slid through the crowd until she was even with me before murmuring in a lilting Spanish accent, "If I'd known who you were, *sombra*, I would have held you under a little bit longer."

Before I could respond—not that I even had a response—she slipped away and rejoined a small huddle of other first years. A hulking guy with dirty blond curls draped a muscled arm over her shoulders and, before I could look away, glanced back at me with a sneer.

Yeah, yeah, everyone here despised me. Message received loud and clear.

The tour lasted all afternoon, and the only downtime given was a quick two-minute bathroom break. Professor Birch kept up a steady stream of monologue as she showed us every possible nook and cranny of the campus, inside and out. It was bigger than I could have possibly imagined, a compound of several buildings strategically placed near each other with a large open courtyard in the center.

Despite the fact that we were deep into what I now knew were the Canadian Rockies, the mountainous terrain surrounding the campus was devoid of snow, probably with the help of another weather-controlling spell. It was cold, though, the wind, gloomy sky, and light drizzle making it colder still.

By the time we made it back inside, I was chilled to the bone and starving. Lunch hadn't been provided, and I was starting to think that we were in the midst of another trial where the last one standing was declared the winner. Unfortunately, I hadn't eaten in over twenty-four hours, so that wouldn't be me. Just when I worried that I was about to pass out for the second time in one day, Professor Birch announced that it was time for dinner.

"Make your way to the dining hall in an orderly fashion. It's first come, first serve, so—"

The sudden rush of bodies drowned out the rest of her words, dozens of famished students scrambling to be the first in line. I thought about slipping inside the bathroom to wash my hands, then thought better of it, too hungry to waste even a few seconds. The throng shoved and jostled each other down the stairs and halls, all decorum vanishing as the need for sustenance overroad everything else.

I tried to jockey for position, but a sharp elbow to my shoulder sent me stumbling back. As my bruised bone began to throb, I glanced up to see the hulking warlock with dirty blond hair leer back at me before plowing forward like a linebacker. Realizing that fighting through this ravenous crowd would probably just earn me several more vindictive blows, I slowed, allowing the mass to thunder past.

By the time I reached the dining hall, hundreds of students were clambering for food at a huge buffet. It was pure chaos, but no one tried to sort the teeming bodies into an orderly line. Knowing that the only way I'd get anything to eat was by diving in, I straightened my spine and did just that. After several attempts, I finally managed to secure a tray, but snagging even a single scrap of food proved to be impossible. Minutes later, I had several more bruises and nothing to show for them but one small baked potato.

When no one came to refill the empty platters, I gave up with a quiet sigh and turned to find a seat at the packed tables. I chose the first corner seat I saw, keeping my head down so I didn't have to see any glares directed at me. My hands noticeably shook as I cut open the potato, my blood sugar so low that I almost shoved the whole thing into my mouth. Spotting a butter dish on the table, I forced myself to reach over, scrape off a piece, and carefully butter my potato. I might be hungry, but I wasn't an animal.

My fork was loaded and halfway to my mouth when I felt a presence at my back. I didn't know *how* I could feel it with all the commotion around me, but the air suddenly felt thicker. Heavier. Like a humid summer night before a storm erupts.

"You're in my seat," a deep voice rumbled like distant thunder directly behind me.

I stiffened, knowing without looking that it was Thorne. In an instant, a hush fell over the entire dining hall, everyone pausing what they were doing to take in the tense scene. Try as I might, I couldn't stop my heart from frantically pounding. I lowered my fork to the tray, not wanting anyone to see that my hand no longer shook from hunger but from fear.

It had been stupid of me to choose this seat without scoping out the room first. A single glance down the long table made it embarrassingly clear that I'd sat somewhere not meant for me. For one, there was a crisp white cloth covering the table, unlike the other ones. For another, there were flowers, lit candles, and several condiments laid out in fancy silver dishes like the butter I'd just pilfered. There were also stacked plates, silverware rolled into cloth napkins, and pitchers of ice water.

But, worst of all, there was a female server in a black and white uniform standing behind a nearby student. She glared at me with heavy disapproval, a heaping platter of chicken in her hands.

Realizing I'd made a huge mistake, every inch of me went cold. Worried that I was going to pass out again, I forced myself to keep breathing. My heart continued to race, faster and faster until I thought it would fly right out of my chest.

"First years don't sit here," a male voice said, but it wasn't Thorne's. It came from in front of me, not behind. I swung my gaze to the guy just as he pulled out the seat directly across from me and plopped down.

Based on the confidence oozing from him, I assumed he was a third year, one that had spent the past two years asserting his place on campus. The upturned tilt of his dark eyes gave away his East Asian heritage, along with the warm tone of his light olive skin. He wore his straight black hair longer on top and parted in the middle, his build like that of an Olympic swimmer.

The black-and-silver striped tie around his neck was loose, the first few buttons on his white shirt intentionally undone. One of his hands was on the table, an ornate ring with a topaz gemstone adorning each finger. So much for the "no personal items" rule applying to *all* students. He was handsome and definitely knew it, but the irreverent smile fixed on his full lips was what made me peg him as an entitled rich boy.

His smile abruptly morphed into a full-blown grin, and he drawled, "You've got a little drool, Mayweather. Right here." He lazily reached up to tap his chin, and I completely fell for it, lifting a hand before I could stop myself. When he belted out a laugh, I froze again, beyond mortified.

I'd thought nothing could top the insults hurled at me in the great hall, but this teasing—no, *mocking*—was so much worse.

Knowing that how I handled this hazing could further mark me as a weakling, I chose not to comment. I barely even blinked, my face expressionless as I watched the warlock get his rocks off at my expense. All the while, I was hyperaware of the fact that Thorne Hudson still stood directly behind me.

Waiting for me to vacate his seat.

When I was about to do just that with what little dignity I had left—okay, fine, my dignity was in shambles—Thorne spoke again.

"Riku."

One word, but the quiet way he said it dripped with authority.

The male across from me immediately stopped laughing, but his black eyes continued to twinkle with merriment as he replied, "Sorry, man, but you never told me she had Bambi eyes. You know how twitterpated I get for the innocent look."

Heat swamped my face, no doubt giving away how mortified I was by his words. Not because he'd compared me to a deer but because Thorne had *told* him about me. Then again, I knew far more about Thorne and his close friends than he would approve of, thanks to his sister. I even knew that the mocking male before me was Riku Tanaka, an exceptionally gifted Air Elemental. Terrified by what Thorne might have revealed to him, I felt the darkness within me stir.

Use meeee.

For a split second, I almost gave in. Almost allowed it to slip free for my own self preservation. Memories quickly crowded in, ones filled with pain and terror, and I instantly felt ashamed for my weakness.

Hurriedly tamping down the darkness once more, I rose to my feet on trembling legs. Whether or not I was about to be condemned in front of the entire student body, I was done being publicly ridiculed. But as I collected my tray and turned to leave, I nearly collided with a tall blond male blocking my path. Instinctively, I took a step back. And immediately realized my grave error when my spine bumped into something hard. Something *huge.*

ZAP.

The contact sent a swift electrical charge through me, just like in the great hall earlier. I went poker straight, not from the sharp shock, but from the sound that rumbled above my head, equal parts growl and irritated hiss. Dear ancestors, I was doomed. Thorne was for sure going to kill me this time. It was one thing to invade his school and sit in his seat, but violating his *personal* space?

Unforgivable.

"I'll kill you!"

The words he'd roared at me the last time we'd seen each other rushed back to me now, and I flinched before I could stop myself. The movement was small, almost imperceptible, but this close to me, there was no way he could have missed it.

Feeling raw, like my insides were exposed for all to see, I wanted nothing more in that moment than to fall apart. To prove to the entire student body that they were right about me, that I didn't belong here. The demons of my past were too big, and if I stayed here any longer, they were going to eat me alive.

But I didn't move a muscle. I stood my ground despite how pointless, how *foolish* it was. Thorne's shadow completely engulfed me, and with my unprotected back to him, he could end my life in an instant.

I waited for him to do just that, *certain* he would. It had been stupid of me to think that I could stay out of his way. The second I'd stepped foot inside Heartstone, I'd practically handed my life to him on a silver platter. And no one would fault him for killing me, not even the professors.

They might not know my secret, but Thorne did. And once he told them, it was game over for me anyway. I might as well let him do the honors since he more than anyone had a right to.

For the second time today, I closed my eyes and prepared for the inevitable. My hands still shook with fear, my heart frantically pounding, but I wouldn't cower or beg for my life. My dignity might be in shambles, but I was still a Mayweather. I would stand tall as I faced death. I would—

"What do you see, Oz?"

I wrenched my eyes back open as the blond warlock still blocking my path answered Thorne, "Shadows. Her aura is shrouded in them."

"She's a Darken," Riku lightly scoffed. "They're all shrouded in shadow."

"Not like this," Oz replied, reaching up to adjust his dark-framed glasses. Combined with the perfect curl on his forehead, he looked like a blond Clark Kent. I recognized him as Osmond "Oz" Parrish III, a talented Oracle and Thorne's other best friend. "The shadows emanating around her are darker. It's like they're *blocking* her aura, and they feel malevolent. You were right about her, Thorne. She's dangerous."

At that, the dining hall erupted into chaos once more. All the blood drained from my face when I caught words like "unhinged" and "crazy." Witches deemed unstable didn't just get locked in a padded room. No, their punishments were much, much worse.

I trembled like a leaf as the shouting continued, my fear so great that thoughts of portaling back home consumed me. The odds against me were too great. I couldn't survive, not with Thorne here. Not when an Oracle could *see* my darkness. The little hope I had of hiding, of keeping my secret, was fading before my very eyes.

The last thing I wanted to do was disgrace my family name even more by quitting, but I didn't see any other option.

It was either that or surrender to a fate worse than death.

Why, oh, *why* had I come here?

I was just about to cave under the insurmountable pressure when a female voice rose above the rest, snapping, "Silence!"

As the buzz died down, I glanced over to see that a professor had entered the dining hall. She was standing in front of the buffet area, her nostrils flared as she took in the student body with a heavy frown. At the sight of her, my knees immediately weakened with relief.

Wearing a black skirt suit that was tailor-made to fit her curvy figure, the woman waited for the commotion to completely subside before saying, "Everyone, take your seats. Winter, there's a spot for you at the first year table over there."

She pointed to the other side of the room, but her brown eyes stayed fixed on me. When they crinkled warmly, some of my trembling faded. As everyone moved to sit down, I finally unglued my feet, slipping out from between the two warlocks to claim my new seat. I landed at the far end of the table, not failing to notice that the spot beside me remained empty. Hostile eyes followed my every move, but now that a kind face had arrived, I latched on to her like a lifeline, ignoring everyone but her.

The professor waited for the room to settle before continuing in a much more even tone, "For those who don't know, I'm Professor

Venetia Holt, the vice-chancellor of Heartstone Academy. Although I don't believe in *freezing* the entire student body in order to get their attention, I will not tolerate riots at this school and will punish those who instigate them. From now on, there will be order in this dining hall. You are all adults, but if you refuse to act as such, you will be treated like children and sent to your rooms hungry."

Pausing for a moment to let that sink in, she went on, "If you haven't noticed yet, there's a hierarchy on this campus. The more trials you complete, the more privileges you earn, with those who finish last receiving the least. Since Heartstone has only been open for two years, our third years receive the most privileges. Their dining accommodations and living quarters far surpass that of a new first year, because they've *earned* those rights. We reward diligence and dedication here, two qualities that the future leaders of our community need to possess. With that said, here is the list of students who completed the Initiation Trial from first to last . . ."

As she pulled a slip of paper from her jacket, my stomach dropped.

Please don't be last, please don't be last, I silently pleaded, already dreading what my "reward" would be if I was in last place.

"In the number one spot is Alma Ramirez. Congratulations, Alma," Professor Holt said, focusing on a girl several spots away at my table. When I saw who it was, my stomach dropped even more. It was the Water Elemental who'd nearly drowned me. *Of course* she'd arrived first.

Professor Holt started to clap. A few of the other students politely joined in, but the majority didn't react—including every third year at the fancy table I'd been kicked off of.

My gaze briefly landed on Thorne who was now sitting in the seat I'd vacated. His hawk familiar was nowhere in sight, probably out catching his own dinner. Even so, his broad shoulders rose above the rest, allowing me to clearly see his face. A face that was currently fixed on—

I nearly swallowed my tongue as our eyes collided.

For a terrifying second, I couldn't look away, caught in the storm seething in his blue irises. But Professor Holt started to speak again, and I managed to wrench my gaze free, focusing on her like my life depended on it—which it did.

"For earning the first place position, Miss Ramirez will receive her pick of available living quarters. She'll also be able to choose her roommates if she desires them, which I strongly suggest. You all might be competing against each other, but it's essential you don't isolate yourself. We all know that a witch cannot survive without a coven, after all. The more allies you have, the higher your chances of surviving to graduation."

Great. Just great. She was looking at *me* while saying the words, as if warning me specifically that I wouldn't survive on my own. I needed trusted allies, ones that would watch my back. Problem was, everyone here would rather stab it.

The professor went on to name and congratulate the other first years, their rewards lessening the further down the list they were. I barely breathed the entire time, waiting for her to call my name. I waited and waited, my heart sinking with each name she uttered that wasn't mine.

"And finally," she said, carefully folding the list and tucking it back into her jacket pocket, "the last place position goes to Winter Mayweather."

No one clapped. Not even Professor Holt.

I'd already been humiliated several times today, but this? *This* was by far the worst. An unwelcome outcast at the very bottom of the school's pecking order. Couldn't get any worse than that.

Oh, but it could.

"For earning the last place position," Professor Holt went on, "Miss Mayweather will receive the least appealing living quarters available—the Jade Wing Tower."

At that, soft gasps and whispers rippled over the student body. When I caught the words "suicide", "cursed", and "haunted," my blood ran cold.

"She will not be allowed roommates," Professor Holt continued, raising her voice a notch above the hushed chatter, "and the only way she can improve her accommodations is by doing better in future trials. The same goes for the rest of you. Do well and earn favors. Do poorly and reap the consequences. *Audentia et Fortitudo*—Courage and Strength is Heartstone's motto. You'll need both to succeed here. That's all I have for you this evening, but as a reminder to our new students, wandering the halls past midnight is strictly forbidden and so is contacting the outside world. For your protection, there are wards in place that prohibit portaling inside the campus walls. Morning assembly in the great hall starts promptly at seven, so I suggest you retire early and get a good night's sleep. You're going to need it."

As suddenly as she arrived, she departed, but not before giving me one final look. It wasn't filled with warmth this time but was quietly apologetic. I managed a small smile for her, knowing it wasn't her fault I'd come in last place.

The moment she left the dining hall, the students resumed their eating and conversation. Right away, several first years tried to get Alma's attention, clearly hoping she'd choose *them* to be her new roommates. No one approached me, of course. I was the lowest of the low, more of an outcast now than when I'd arrived. And whatever was in Jade Wing Tower had them spooked. I couldn't expect visitors any time soon, that was for sure.

With no one to talk to, I dug into my baked potato. I wasn't even halfway finished when I caught Thorne rising to his feet. Riku and Oz also stood, both shorter than him but not by much. All three warlocks were an intimidating size on their own, but together, they were formidable. It was a wonder I'd been able to function earlier while surrounded by them. I wasn't even half their weight, and the top of my head barely reached their chests.

The room noticeably quieted as the trio left, all eyes following their departure. When Thorne vanished from view, something in my chest loosened, and I breathed a little easier.

As the chatter resumed, I heard a first year witch a few spots down wistfully sigh, "They're so delicious. What I wouldn't give to be sandwiched between those three."

I nearly choked on the bite of potato in my mouth.

"Riku is my favorite," the girl across from her remarked. "He's funny, charming, and I hear he'll sleep with pretty much anyone, including first years. No strings attached."

I cleared my throat rather loudly, but they continued their conversation as if I wasn't there.

"I like 'em ruthless and emotionally unavailable like Thorne. The more red flags, the sexier," the first girl said. "Plus, he's arguably the most powerful magic-wielder on this campus, maybe in the world. I'm not surprised he was named Head Prefect this year. What with his family having founded this school, he's basically Heartstone Academy's prince. We can't forget Oz, though. He might be quiet, but he has that sexy nerd vibe going for him. He's also wicked smart, can astral project, and his family is disgustingly rich."

"They're *all* rich, Nadine. Now that Thorne, Riku, and Oz have the best chance of earning spots on the Conclave, everyone wants to back their families. They've been dubbed the Arcane Three for a reason. Very few can wield magic like they can. They're royalty at this point, and everyone wants to get into bed with them."

"Literally."

"You can say that again. Do you think there's a chance they'll ever let us join their group?"

"No way. Those three have been thick as thieves even before being admitted to Heartstone, and they haven't allowed anyone else in their inner circle since coming here. There's a chance they'll *sleep* with us, though."

"Good enough for me."

The witches snickered, and despite how hungry I was, their conversation killed my appetite. Still, I forced myself to finish the potato, including the skin. Who knew when I'd be able to eat next. After the day I'd just had, I wouldn't take anything for granted here.

When some of the other students started to leave, I decided to get up as well. No sense sticking around to socialize when it was obvious no one wanted anything to do with me. Leaving my tray where it was, I stood, already knowing how to find Jade Wing after the extensive tour Professor Birch had given us. She hadn't taken us up into the tower, but there was no missing it.

I only made it a few feet before someone else stood from the table. Seeing the long golden brown braid down her back, my first instinct was to skirt around the Water Elemental without comment. But Professor Holt's words came to mind, and I begrudgingly slowed to murmur a quick, "Congratulations on your win."

Alma turned to me, her sepia brown eyes flickering in surprise. The look was quickly replaced by a jaunt lip curl as she replied, "Thanks, *sombra.* Too bad you received last place. Not that I would have considered you for a roommate before, but I definitely won't now."

Several of the students nearby chuckled, including the hulking blond guy who'd elbowed my shoulder earlier.

The urge to defend myself pressed at my windpipe, but what could I say? The next time you try to drown me, I'll fight back? I should have fought back the *first* time. Knowing that anything I said would only ostracize me further, I kept my mouth firmly shut and started to leave.

As I passed by her, Alma called after me in her lilting-accented voice, "Sleep well, *sombra.* I heard the last first year who lived in Jade Wing Tower jumped out the window to his death. That, or he was pushed. Either way, I'm sure his disgraced spirit will keep you company. Rather fitting, if you ask me."

Her audience laughed even more, and it took all of my willpower not to sprint from the dining hall in abject humiliation. When I was finally alone in the halls, the relief I was hoping to feel didn't come. I remained tense, dreading what awaited me in the tower. I could practically *feel* death breathing down my neck, his cold presence making all the hair on my body stand on end.

Each step I took toward my destination grew heavier, the weight almost more than I could bear. *This way,* my intuition beckoned me down the shadowy halls, morbidly drawn to what awaited us despite my trepidation.

Every time I passed by fellow students, they were in pairs or groups. No one walked alone but me, and I'd never been more aware of how vulnerable that made me until now. Still, I could barely focus on them, my senses sharply in tune with death's presence. I could feel, taste, and smell it, a sure sign that he'd claimed victims here before—or was planning to in the near future.

He kept me company all the way to Jade Wing, a constant foreboding shadow dogging my every step. When I found the narrow winding staircase leading up to the tower, fear gripped me so hard that I almost couldn't do it. Almost convinced myself that death was awaiting *me* at the top of those stairs.

Maybe that would be better. Then this torment could finally come to an end. All I had to do was jump, and this nightmare would be over.

The second I had the thought, I shoved it aside. I might be at my lowest, but I wasn't ready to give up just yet. I had fight left in me. I *knew* I did. So I pushed past my fear and stepped onto the first stair, then the next and the next, encouraging myself to take one more step. Just one more.

Five stories later, I was at the top, the lighting so weak that I could hardly make out the lone wooden door a few feet away. Darkness closed in around me, threatening to steal my sanity and consume me whole. Unable to stand it any longer, I raised my hand and willed a magical orb into existence.

Glowing strands of deep violet hovered just above my palm, allowing me to see the door better. I stared at the black handle for a few minutes, working up the nerve to touch it. Finally, I reached out with trembling fingers and grasped the metal. It was ice cold, as if no one had touched it in ages. That, or the tower really was cursed by the spirit of the boy who'd taken his life.

Not that I believed in such things, but I was completely freaked out anyway, certain a ghostly apparition awaited me on the other side—one with a broken neck and limbs.

I gripped the door handle for dear life, trembling so hard that I thought I would faint. How ironic would it be if I passed out, fell down the stairs, and broke my neck?

Stop it! I scolded myself, frustrated with my morbid imagination.

Shaking the image from my mind, I braced for whatever awaited me on the other side and pushed open the door.

CHAPTER 5

When the first thing I saw was a ghostly pale figure standing across the room, I almost screamed bloody murder.

A second later, I quietly cursed my stupidity, realizing the figure was my reflection. Even so, I struggled to slow my racing heart, half-expecting the figure to leap from the floor-length mirror and attack me. When a full minute passed and nothing happened, I stepped inside the room. A spider web promptly smacked me in the face, and I jerked my free hand up to swipe it away.

Fumbling along the wall for a light switch, I flicked it on, but nothing happened.

Great. No electricity. I'd expected my living quarters to be bad but not *this* bad. There was also a chill in the air, one that had nothing to do with death's continued presence.

Holding my magical orb higher, I began to explore the space.

Right away, I noticed the dark stone walls were curved, framing the room in a circular shape. A small, weather-beaten desk was the first piece of furniture I stumbled across. On its surface were a handful of candles, most of them tipped over. I righted them and willed more heat to infuse my orb, using it to ignite the wicks. As more light filled the room, some of my fear faded.

Until the flames eerily flickered, and a cold breeze stirred my hair.

I whirled around and immediately spotted the broken window. Shards of jagged glass were still stuck to the frame, a frame just large enough for a person to fit through. At the sight, my intuition went haywire, practically shouting at me that this was it. This was where someone had jumped—or been pushed—to their death.

Before I knew it, I was across the room and standing in front of the window. Glass crunched beneath my shoes, both the wind from outside and a phantom one only I could feel teasing my exposed flesh. My orb had fizzled out, and before I could stop myself, I reached up and touched one of the intact glass shards.

My vision immediately tunneled, and the world around me disappeared. Images flashed before my eyes, as if a projector screen had been placed before me. I watched, unable to look away as a redheaded boy about my age whirled around in terror. His mouth opened in a scream, but before he could utter a sound, something blasted him in the chest. He flew back, violently striking the window. Glass shards exploded into the air as he fell through and disappeared over the edge. Still unable to look away, I watched him plummet from the tower and strike the unforgiving ground below.

The second his neck snapped, the world around me returned with a jolt. I stumbled back, loudly gasping for air as if I'd been holding my breath. Bile surged up my throat, but I forced it back down, drawing in several deep breaths until my heart no longer felt like it would explode from my chest.

Trembling, *terrified* from being forced to watch the replay of someone's death, I felt myself start to unravel. After all I'd endured today, knowing that the student who'd previously lived in this tower had been murdered was the last straw.

I crumpled into a heap on the floor, unable to hold back a sob. The sound wrenched from me, echoing my loneliness and despair off the unfeeling walls. Pressure welled behind my eyes, and I thought for sure it would happen this time. The pressure built and built and built, but . . .

Nothing. Not a single tear.

Frantic to release the well of pain inside me somehow, I lifted my gaze to the floor-length mirror and screamed, "You were supposed to *be* here. We were supposed to do this *together!* To keep each other *safe!*"

The girl in the mirror glared back at me, dry mascara smudged under her pale eyes, her black hair a hopelessly tangled mess. Her uniform was dirty and ripped in several places, her ribbon bow tie missing. At the sight, her angry expression fell.

Everyone had seen me like this. *Everyone.* The chancellor, the professors, the students . . .

Thorne.

Even he had never seen me look this terrible before, not even after . . .

Instead of finishing the thought, I whispered to the miserable girl in the mirror, "I'm sorry. I'm so sorry I yelled at you. None of this is your fault. I just miss you so terribly."

No response.

Needing to talk to someone, *anyone*, I fumbled in my pockets for my phone but came up empty. My heart shriveled up even more when I realized that for the first time in my life, I had absolutely no one to talk to. Not my parents. Not Gran or my brother. They might as well be in another realm.

I was covenless. Friendless. Alone in a way that made it nearly impossible to breathe.

Remembering the necklace Gran had given me, I reached up and gripped it tight, hoping it would offer me a shred of comfort. When the amulet wouldn't even warm beneath my palm, I let go with a mournful sigh and curled up on the cold floor, too exhausted to make it to the rickety bed a few feet away.

Even with death clinging to the walls and images of murder replaying in my mind, sleep beckoned to me. I should at least lock the door in case someone decided to murder me next, but at that moment, I couldn't summon the energy to care.

As I allowed sleep to pull me under, something fluttered against my cheek. It was featherlight, barely a wisp of air. *I'm here*, it seemed to sigh, but I wasn't alarmed by the sound or even afraid. If anything, it made me feel less alone.

Before I could wonder about it, oblivion swept me away.

The showers in Jade Wing were ice cold.

And co-ed.

I'd meant to sneak down earlier before anyone else arrived, but I'd slept like the dead last night. Not even a killer in the room could have woken me. At least I hadn't been visited by nightmares or sleepwalked.

The sound of the clock tower bell chiming the hour had finally dragged me awake, stiff and sore from sleeping on the floor all night with barely enough time to take a quick shower before breakfast. Besides not wanting to face any hateful looks or comments this early in the morning, I wasn't exactly used to the whole sharing-a-bathroom thing.

I wasn't a prude, per se, but the only male I'd seen naked was my brother—and that was years ago back when I was changing his diapers. As for males seeing *me* naked, I'd never dated, let alone slept with anyone. My experience with guys was practically nonexistent, mostly because my parents and Gran had forbidden me from socializing with humans outside of work. And being an outcast cut off from the witch community, I'd had no other prospects.

Well, except for Thorne. But he'd only tolerated me for his sister's sake, and now that she was gone . . .

Yeah. He was the very *last* male who'd be interested in seeing me naked.

A towel and basic toiletries had been allotted to each first year, along with underwear and a few uniforms. None of us had been allowed to bring personal items, and I'd overheard more than one girl complain about the pitiful amount of grooming supplies in their toiletry kits.

"I got to pick mine," I heard a familiar lilting voice say from somewhere near the sinks. "Another perk of earning first place."

I peeked through the crack in the flimsy shower curtain, shivering under the cold water as Alma Ramirez showed a few girls her large toiletry bag. They oohed and aahed at the contents but were clearly jealous of what Alma had received.

"All name brand items. They spared no expense," Alma shamelessly bragged, pulling a lip gloss from the bag.

A huge male body blocked my view of her, wearing nothing but a towel around his waist that hung low enough to expose a little crack. "Can I borrow your hair gel, Almie?"

"Of course, Blaze," she told the hulking giant, who I recognized as the guy that had left a bruise on my shoulder. "You're my roommate. What's mine is yours."

"Thanks, babe," he drawled, accepting the bottle she handed him. As he turned to leave, I caught more naked flesh, this time in front. He was built like a heavyweight boxing champion, free of hair except for a dark blond trail under his navel. When I realized I could see the outline of his *dick* through the thin towel, I quickly jerked my eyes up.

And found him staring at me through the crack in the shower curtain, his lips twisted in a leering grin.

My heart jumped into my throat, and I quickly stepped out of view. But it was too late.

"You peeping at me, *stray?*" he barked. A second later, the shower curtain sharply whined as he wrenched it open, exposing me butt naked for all to see.

A yelp escaped me before I could swallow it. On instinct, I covered my breasts with an arm and reached for my towel that hung from a peg on the divider wall. Before I could grab it, Blaze's meaty hand got to it first. I watched in horror as the material disappeared from view, leaving me with nothing to cover myself.

For a moment, panic got the better of me. I didn't have to look in a mirror to know that it was written all over my face, giving away how utterly mortified I was. My eyes met Blaze's again, and the leering look in them was accompanied by something else this time, something that I could only define as lust.

As he raked his gaze down my front, I shivered uncontrollably, feeling violated in a way I'd never felt before.

"Wow, *sombra*," Alma crooned, sauntering up beside Blaze to openly gawk at me. "A little sun on that virgin snow skin would do you good."

Others joined them, taking in my naked body as if I were a sideshow attraction at a circus. Realizing that not a single soul was going to help me, I shoved my panic down, deep enough to fix an indifferent mask on my face and force my arms to lower.

One of the guys ogling me wolf-whistled as I exposed my breasts, but I didn't look his way, turning to switch off the showerhead. As calmly as I could, I gathered my things and stepped from the stall, relieved when the students shifted aside to let me through.

"Lookin' good, Mayweather," another guy taunted when I passed by him.

I kept my gaze straight ahead, glued to the exit too far away. Outwardly, my expression was wiped clean of all emotion, but inwardly, it felt like I was dying. The door leading up to Jade Wing Tower was all the way at the end of the hall. To reach it, I'd have to parade naked down the entire hallway where any number of students could see me. Last night, the hall had been empty, but this morning, it was *teeming* with bodies.

My hands itched to form a portal, but I wouldn't be able to conjure one even if I wanted to. I kept them firmly at my sides, not even allowing them to shield my breasts. As my humiliation burned hotter and hotter with each step I took, the darkness within me stirred, offering up its protection.

Use meeee.

I ignored it as usual, knowing that unleashing shadows simply to cover myself would be seen as weakness. No, I had to strut down that hallway as if being nude in front of dozens of peers didn't bother me.

Even if doing so would inwardly tear me apart.

The moment I passed from the bathroom and into the hallway, I died a little more. The passage was even busier than before, and every time a student spotted me, they stopped dead in their tracks to blatantly stare.

"Disgusting," a girl muttered as I swept past, instantly making me feel insecure about my body.

Several more wolf-whistles followed in my wake, along with a few catcalls, but I refused to acknowledge them. No one touched me, yet each judgmental look felt like nails gouging into my skin. All I had to do was make it to the end of the hallway. I could survive that long. There was no other option.

It felt like I walked down that hallway for an eternity, but I eventually reached the door leading up to the tower. With the hallway in a buzz from my walk of shame, I opened the door and stepped through, slowly shutting it behind me.

The second the latch clicked into place, my legs gave out, and I collapsed to the floor. Feeling sick to my stomach, I gulped down air, determined not to throw up. After a minute, I forced myself to stand and make it up the stairs.

Dirty. I felt *dirty*.

My shame was so great that I considered skipping breakfast, but the hunger pains in my stomach vetoed that idea. I quickly dressed in a fresh uniform and decided to use a little energy to spell-dry my hair, determined to face the vultures looking put-together with my head held high.

They could take away my dignity, but I wouldn't break that easily. I was a Mayweather, and they'd remember soon enough why my ancestors had been leaders of our community for generations. We didn't bow to adversity. It might knock us down for a while, but in the end, we always clawed our way back up, stronger than before.

Time for me to prove just how resilient Mayweathers were.

CHAPTER 6

Not surprisingly, breakfast was shaping up to be a disaster.

Based on the whispers filtering through the dining hall, the entire student body had been made aware of my walk of shame. I received more than one leering look from the guys, but Blaze's was by far the worst. Only able to scrounge up a bagel from the once again picked-clean buffet, I was just about to pass by Blaze and Alma on my way to the far corner seat when the curly-haired brute loudly said, "Hey, sweet cheeks."

A couple of the warlocks nearby snickered, all too aware that Blaze hadn't meant the cheeks on my face. I chose to ignore him, glad that at least Thorne and his friends weren't in the dining hall yet to hear all this. Servers bustled around the fancy third year table, but none of the professors were here, thank the ancestors.

Clearly peeved that I'd ignored him, Blaze swiftly turned in his seat and stuck a leg out directly in my path. I stopped with my tray in hand, staring straight ahead like an expressionless robot when what I really wanted to do was glare daggers at him.

"I was talking to you, stray," he said.

No comment. I didn't even blink.

His words had a ripple effect, though, and the roar of chatter faded as the other students paused to listen in.

Fantastic.

Pleased to have an audience, Blaze propped his elbows on the table behind him and brazenly drawled, "That uniform does nothing for your figure, sweet cheeks. I like you much better naked."

As dozens of students reacted with amused twitters and laughter, my face burst into flames.

I didn't think the embarrassment could get any worse, but at that exact moment, I saw three tall figures enter the dining hall out of the corner of my eye. Of course, they were none other than the Arcane Three. Fate wouldn't have it any other way. They paused in the doorway, realizing something was amiss, and it was then that I knew.

Not reacting would be a mistake.

Why, oh, why did *this* have to be the moment that I was forced to prove myself?

But there was no avoiding it. It was do or doom myself time. So I calmly swung my gaze to the gloating behemoth and replied, "And I'd like you much better with a different face, yet here you are."

Dead. Silence.

I immediately wanted to disappear as I felt the eyes of the entire room on me. Maybe reacting had been a mistake after all. Maybe—

The room suddenly erupted. Not with insults but *laughter*.

Realizing that it wasn't at my expense this time but at Blaze's, I blinked in shock. Alma's mouth slightly fell open, but Blaze was even more shocked, his ruddy cheeks noticeably darkening as his moment in the spotlight was epically ruined. By the way his forest green eyes were slightly bugging out, I could tell he was angry. No, *furious*.

Before he could retaliate, I stepped over his leg and went to my corner seat, knowing that I'd just made an enemy.

Well, a greater one.

Something told me that a guy like Blaze wouldn't let anyone get away with insulting him, especially me.

Despite their reactions to my comeback, the other students

swiftly returned to their food and conversations, leaving me to sit in my corner alone once more. The seats beside and in front of me were empty, and no one tried to fill them. They might have appreciated my comment, but none of them were lining up to make an alliance with me, that was for sure.

My eyes betrayed me and flicked toward Thorne and his friends. They were still standing near the doorway, but none of their gazes were on me, thank the ancestors. They were staring at someone, though, intensely enough that I couldn't help but follow their line of vision.

When it landed on Blaze, the bite of bagel I was about to swallow got stuck in my throat. The hulking brute was staring right at me, and as our eyes met, I saw something dark in his expression. A threat. A *promise.*

You're mine, the look practically hissed.

I forced myself to hold his gaze a moment longer, adopting a bored expression even though my heart had started to race. Yeah, I was poking the bear, but I couldn't back down now. Not when I'd already made a stand.

Ten years of hardcore training with my parents and grandmother had taught me that. By showing my hand, I'd proven that I wasn't a pushover. But I'd also proven that I was a *threat*, that I wouldn't back down without a fight. And I'd most definitely picked a fight with the blond-haired hulk, one that he wouldn't be backing down from either.

Stupid. I'd been *so stupid* to open my mouth.

This was going to end badly. I could feel it in my bones like a malignant tumor. He was no doubt powerful, hence why he was here, but I had no idea what subsect of warlock he was. The sooner I found out, the better I could prepare for what was to come.

Problem was, I doubted I'd be able to keep my darkness caged if he chose to attack. My emotions were too strong when it came to this idiot. What he'd done to me in that bathroom . . .

I couldn't help but want revenge, and that was bad. Really, really bad.

Regret tightened my throat, and I forced the bite of bagel down before I could choke on it. The *last* thing I needed was to make another scene by requiring the Heimlich Maneuver. Not that anyone would give it to me. They'd probably like nothing more than to see me writhing on the dining hall floor in the throes of death.

I finally broke eye contact with Blaze as if dismissing him, then stupidly snuck another glance at Thorne in time to see him whisper in the ear of another male student. The warlock scribbled something on a small pad of paper with a serious nod.

Frowning, I continued to watch them. They were standing at the fancy third year table now, talking low enough that I had no hope of overhearing them. As a server bustled toward their corner, Riku slid a hand palm down across the table. The male student deftly plucked up whatever had been under Riku's hand, read it, then smoothly tucked it in his pocket. Suspicion rattled in my gut, my frown deepening as I watched him do the same thing with Oz.

It was only when the male student moved down the table, repeating the process several more times with other third years, that I knew, just *knew* what he was up to.

Taking bets.

There was only one thing I could imagine the third years betting on, and that was whether or not Blaze would kill me.

Heat engulfed my face once more, but this time, it wasn't from embarrassment. I was *furious*. How dare they so callously bet on my life like that. Did they do this with all the new first years trying to prove themselves or did that special honor only apply to me?

Too angry to see straight let alone think straight, I got up and left the dining hall before I could do something suicidal, like confront the bastards. I'd already dug a large enough grave for myself this morning. No need to speed along my demise even more.

Unlike yesterday, I was the very first student to arrive at the great hall for morning assembly. I hadn't received my class schedule yet, but I assumed we would get them during the assembly. This wasn't like a normal university where students' chosen majors shaped the direction of their classes. We were all gunning for the same thing, so we all had the exact same classes. But since there were over one hundred students in the first year, they'd probably split us into groups.

Was it too much to hope that Blaze wouldn't be in any of my classes?

Probably. With my luck, he'd be in all of them. And so would Alma.

Not wanting to make the same mistakes as yesterday, I decided to sit in the front row again despite how uncomfortable it made me. Chancellor Grimshaw, Professor Holt, and the others were already on the stage busily talking amongst themselves. Their mouths silently moved, so I assumed they'd cast a sound-blocking spell to discourage students from listening in.

Noticing me, a few of the professors gestured my way. Not being able to hear what they said made me even more uncomfortable, especially when their expressions soured. I didn't need to hear them to know that my presence had an instant dampening effect on their moods. Chancellor Grimshaw glanced my way, his creepy smile making a swift appearance before he answered the disgruntled professors.

How mortifying would it be if they'd heard the gossip about my walk of shame? And what if they thought I'd done it on *purpose?* I was pretty sure that indecent exposure was a punishable offense.

Professor Holt caught my eye and briefly paused to give me a reassuring smile. I was too nervous to smile back but was grateful for her attention all the same. Within minutes, students started pouring in, filling the great hall with noise.

I pretended not to see or hear them, keeping my focus on the stage. But it took all of my willpower, especially when I heard a warlock say loud enough for me to hear, "You really saw her naked?"

"Front and back. Her tits are smoking hot, and she has a blue butterfly tattooed between her shoulder blades. You really missed out, man."

Pain lanced through my palms, and I glanced down to see that I'd gouged my nails through the skin. Blood welled in the cuts, and I quickly pressed my trembling hands together to stem the flow.

Breathe. Just breathe, I ordered myself, squeezing my eyes shut as fresh fury writhed through my insides. It was getting harder and harder to ignore the vicious gossip, to pretend the words weren't wreaking havoc on my psyche. But I couldn't afford to paint an even bigger target on my back. Any reaction now would reveal just how upset this morning's bathroom fiasco had made me, and an emotion like that would be like cannon fodder to these people.

So I kept breathing. In and out, in and out. Focusing on the air entering and leaving my lungs until the cold fury no longer felt like icicles inside my chest. The quote about sticks and stones came to mind, but I'd always hated how untrue that saying felt. I was pretty sure a good old-fashioned stoning would hurt less than the verbal beating I'd endured since arriving at this school.

Even so, my emotions were firmly under control once more as the last of the students filed in and the professors on stage took their seats. Like yesterday, Chancellor Grimshaw was the only one left standing, and as he raised his hands, the crowd ceased its chatter.

"Good morning, students," he said, the sound-blocking spell clearly no longer in effect. "I hope you were all able to get a good night's rest, because we have a full itinerary for you today. One thing we pride ourselves on at Heartstone Academy is an educational experience unlike any other. Most of you have already received several years of education at one of our community academies located around the world, but the training you'll experience here isn't anything like that. To better prepare our new students for what's to come, we've decided to incorporate a mentorship program this year."

Excited whispers swept through the crowd, and the chancellor held up his hands again to silence them.

"This program not only prepares our first years for the rigorous training and trials ahead but gives our upperclassmen a chance to experience the leadership role responsibilities they'll face after graduation. We used to rely on the elders to protect our entire community and also looked to them for wisdom and guidance. The Conclave of Magic will encompass the same roles, its members acting both as our shields and mentors. So before our second and third years think that this mentorship program gives the first years an unfair advantage, know that it is *crucial* to your own training."

He paused to let his words sink in, sweeping his gaze over the back half of the great hall before continuing on.

"The professors and I have voted on a lottery to determine which first year student will be paired with which second or third year mentor. It's completely random, and the pairing is final. This partnership will continue for the rest of the year, and before any upperclassmen think they can get away with throwing their first years to the wolves, their failure will be yours. Refuse to mentor them, and we'll assume you're not capable of leading our community someday. Venetia, if you please."

The chancellor stepped back as Professor Holt rose from her chair and claimed the center stage position. When she raised her hands, green magic encased them, giving away her affinity.

Earth Elemental.

"*Manifesto*," she intoned. With a sweep of her glowing green hands, she unveiled two black cauldrons on pedestals positioned on either side of her. "These cauldrons are enchanted to yield names randomly and without bias for the Mentor Ceremony. When I call out your pairing, you will both come up and swear a binding pactum to each other, that neither of you will intentionally cause the other fatal harm whilst the pairing is in effect. This will ensure the pairing remains fair and mutually beneficial."

Shocked exclamations rippled over the student body, and I felt my own face slowly drain of blood.

A *pactum?*

"It doesn't, however, force you to ally with each other," Professor Holt loudly said, cutting off the chatter. "Who you make alliances with at this school is your choice alone. But if you break your pactum, no matter the reason, what befalls one befalls both. I hope you have all been taught how dangerous pactums can be. Your very life depends on how seriously you uphold your promise."

Barely pausing to let us digest her warning, she raised her hands again and chanted, "Dutiful cauldrons, entrust me with the first pair. Thine servant entreat that it be fair."

Green smoke burst from the bowels of both cauldrons, along with two scraps of paper. They fluttered in the air above the professor before floating down to rest on her open palms. Glancing down at them, she spoke in a firm tone, "Our first pairing is Blaze McGrath and Sydney Wright."

No one made a sound as the two students stood and made their way to the stage. Realizing that the first year was none other than Blaze the Bully, I immediately felt sorry for the upperclassman chosen to mentor him. She wasn't much taller than me, pretty with blonde hair fashioned into a cute pixie cut. As she and Blaze moved to center stage and faced each other, neither of them looked happy about the pairing.

Chancellor Grimshaw stepped forward, drawing what looked like a small dagger from his coat sleeve. Offering it to Blaze, he said, "A shallow cut on the palm is needed to make the pactum binding. Both of you must willingly cut yourselves, then clasp your hands together to let the blood intermingle. Once you've both done so, you will recite your oath together."

Blaze accepted the knife, quickly slicing his palm before giving it to Sydney. She did the same, her mouth set in a grim line as she handed the dagger back to the chancellor and stuck out her hand for Blaze to clasp. He did so rather brutishly, his beefy hand completely swallowing up her dainty one. She locked eyes with him, scowling as he no doubt squeezed her delicate bones. Blaze's mouth twisted into his signature leer.

Poor girl.

"Blaze McGrath and Sydney Wright, repeat after me," Chancellor Grimshaw said. "I bind thee to me, vowing not to intentionally harm thine mortal body. Henceforth, may we remain bound for one year, provided our immortal souls still reside on this plane."

It felt like the entire great hall held its breath as the pair recited the oath. When they were finished, the two pieces of paper on Professor Holt's palms lifted into the air and caught fire, magical green flames swiftly burning them to ash.

"Their oaths ring true," she said, flashing them both an approving smile. "Well done. You may take your seats."

Despite knowing that Blaze couldn't harm her without harming himself, Sydney looked rather green as she wrenched her hand free of his and descended the stage steps. Blaze, on the other hand, looked smug as he watched her leave, sauntering down the steps as if he'd won something.

Several more pairings were called, each ending with a confirmation that their oaths to each other were genuine. Alma's name was eventually called, and a few first years gasped when she was paired with Riku Tanaka.

"So lucky," one girl whispered enviously.

"He's going to bone her, for sure," another wistfully sighed.

When the pair clasped hands and started to recite their vows, each word spoken dripped with sensual promise. Based on the seductive smirks they kept giving each other, I doubted training and mentoring would be the only activities those two did this year. An image of them passionately making out invaded my mind, and I threw up a little in my mouth.

As she descended the stage, Alma tossed her braid back and gave me a pretentious little wink, one that clearly meant, *I won first place again. Too bad for you.*

Yeah, well, Riku wasn't the only powerful third year. I could be paired favorably, too.

But with my luck, probably not.

"Winter Mayweather," Professor Holt suddenly said, and I snapped my gaze back to the stage, realizing that my pairing was about to be called.

Please be someone who doesn't hate me, please, please, please, I silently begged as she opened her mouth to read the other name on her palm.

"And Thorne Hudson."

My heart plummeted to the floor.

CHAPTER 7

The world was crumbling, and I was falling, falling, falling.

Fate couldn't be *this* cruel.

I'd made mistakes. Terrible ones. But this? Binding myself to the person who hated me most in the world? How could I possibly follow through with something so wretchedly *wrong*?

I couldn't. I *couldn't*.

Anything would be more tolerable than this. Literally *anything*.

My ears were ringing, but the crowd's reaction to the pairing was strong enough to penetrate my shocked state.

"*Blasphemy*."

"She doesn't deserve that pairing!"

"It's sacrilegious."

"You can't bind the Head Prefect to the *stray!*"

Oh, that one was definitely Blaze.

"Silence!" Professor Holt snapped, her brown eyes devoid of warmth as she glared at the student body and some of the other professors. "The cauldrons have chosen, and it's not our place to question that decision. Now sit down and remain quiet. This ceremony is sacred, and we will all conduct ourselves respectably. Winter and Thorne, if you please."

I didn't know how I managed, but I left my seat and climbed the stage to stand in front of Professor Holt. She didn't smile at me encouragingly this time, but her gaze softened as our eyes met. I was still too numb to do anything other than keep myself upright.

This wasn't the first time I'd felt this way and probably wouldn't be the last, but I was definitely having an out-of-body experience. Everything was crystal clear around me, but it felt like this was happening to someone else. It *should* be happening to someone else.

Despite feeling like I was hovering above my body like a ghostly specter, I felt Thorne's large presence behind me and turned to face him. Unable to stop myself, I glanced up at his face and immediately wished I hadn't. It was stone cold. *He* was stone cold. Every line of his body was fraught with tension, and when our eyes connected, he practically turned into a pillar of ice.

His hawk familiar wasn't with him again, but all six-foot-five of him was plenty intimidating. He squared off with me a foot away, his closeness forcing me to crane my neck back in order to maintain eye contact. I would have liked nothing better than to look at my shoes instead, but instinct told me that would be a huge mistake.

No matter how uncomfortable it made me to stare into the face of pure hatred, lowering my gaze would prove to everyone here just how unworthy I was of this pairing.

But the longer I held his gaze, the darker Thorne's eyes became. It was like peering up at an angry sky about to unleash hell on Earth. If I wasn't still numb with shock, I'd be violently trembling right now.

The last time we'd stood toe-to-toe like this had been almost two years ago, and he'd been equally angry then. His furious shout in my face—"*I'll kill you!*"—rang through my mind now, cutting through some of my fog. Facing him again like this was suicide, but I couldn't make myself look away. Couldn't *move.*

I was trapped in his furious storm, and there was no way out but through.

Problem was, there was no way in hell I'd survive.

Still, I accepted the small dagger the chancellor handed me, barely feeling the pain as I sliced open my palm. When I held out the knife to Thorne, he clenched his jaw so hard that I heard his teeth grind together. Seconds ticked by and nothing happened. He stared at me and I at him, both of us stuck in a tense stalemate.

After a solid minute went by, he opened his mouth and spoke in a low tone, so low that I almost missed the words. "Pick again. Choose anyone but her."

Those words shocked me to my very core, completely erasing any feeling I had left in my body. If the students had heard what he said, they didn't react. The entire great hall was deathly silent as they waited to see what would happen next.

Thorne Hudson, the golden prince of Heartstone Academy, had openly rejected me in front of the entire school. With the power he wielded from his family name alone, he might as well have just expelled me. His words held the same weight as if he'd cast me from the witch community all over again. For good this time.

I should feel so many things right now. Hurt, embarrassment, *anger*. But I couldn't feel anything other than a faint sense of relief. At least this way, I would be spared the humiliation of trying to bind myself to someone who could never vow not to hurt me.

He *wanted* me dead. I knew that much. And not being able to finish what he started two years ago would probably drive him mad.

Chancellor Grimshaw cleared his throat, and I prepared to hear the inevitable as he replied, "Choosing another would break the enchantment and put all the students who've sworn pactums in jeopardy. One of your very own allies could reap the consequences of your decision, causing them to fail or worse. This in turn will reflect poorly on you, Mr. Hudson, something I'm sure you don't want after all you've accomplished here. You're Head Prefect. Is this the example you want to set for the other students?"

Oh, crap.

Thorne's nostrils flared, evidence that he was *not* happy with the chancellor's words. It wasn't blackmail, per se, but awfully close. If Thorne refused to bind himself to me, he could kiss his pristine academic record goodbye.

One second, the dagger was in my hand, and the next, yanked away as Thorne used it to savagely slice open his palm. Then, with no warning whatsoever, he grabbed my hand. I immediately felt a sharp *zap* at the contact, powerful enough to drive the numbness away and force me back into my body. As the electrical current streaked up my arm, fear pumped through me. All he had to do was crank up the voltage, and I was toast. *Literally*. Electrocuting me would definitely save him from having to pair with me. In fact, I should have expected him to do this.

Stupid. I'd been stupid to even come *up* here.

"*You* must *stay away from Thorne Hudson at all costs*."

Stay away. Stay away. This was dangerous. *Dangerous*.

With my heart hammering inside my chest, I tried to pull away. Thorne's grip ruthlessly tightened, and he jerked me closer, so forcefully that I stumbled forward a little. We were inches apart now, close enough that I could no longer maintain eye contact. Close enough that I could *smell* him. Fresh, wild, and sharp, his scent was like burnt matches mixed with ozone.

My gaze dropped to his chest mere inches from my face, putting me at a clear disadvantage, but it allowed me to see just how upset he was. Each ragged breath pushed his chest out, stretching the fabric of his white shirt taut. I glanced down at our locked hands next, noticing how white his knuckles were from how tightly he held on.

He might have a stone cold personality with a face to match, but his large hand was shockingly warm. It felt like holding a live wire, one that could burn me at any second. His skin practically buzzed with energy. It *was* buzzing. No, it was shaking, forcing mine to shake as well. Or maybe mine was shaking his. Either way, hot blood escaped our sealed palms, dripping onto the stage below. I assumed it was his since I'd only made a small, shallow cut. Realizing he'd cut himself too deeply, I felt a little twinge in my chest, something that felt a lot like guilt.

Dear ancestors, I was hopeless.

Here I was, about to make a binding oath with my greatest nemesis, and I was feeling sorry for him. Not only that, I felt *responsible* for his injury. He wouldn't be in this turmoil right now if any other name but mine had been picked. I'd been the cause of his anger and pain two years ago, and I was the cause of it now.

But it was too late to back out. Chancellor Grimshaw was speaking again, reciting the pactum oath that we were to repeat. So far, every pairing had been successful. The students hadn't just spoken the words; they'd *meant* them. When it came to magic, intention was everything. Words were empty without the will for them to succeed. Which was why I was certain, *certain* that our pactum would fail.

Thorne would never willingly bind himself to me.

We recited the oath in unison anyway, and I couldn't help but doubt my own intentions as I uttered the words. The last thing I needed was to be stuck with Thorne for the next year. I could practically hear Gran shout that he would doublecross me somehow. He wanted to kill me. *Kill* me. Then again, what better way for me to keep my enemies close? At least he wouldn't pose as much of a threat to me with a pactum looming over his head.

Maybe. Possibly.

Oh, who was I kidding? Thorne would never, *ever* bind himself to—

"The oaths ring true!" Professor Holt announced rather proudly, snapping me from my thoughts. I glanced over just in time to see our slips of paper disintegrate in a poof of green smoke.

Before I could fully realize what that meant, Thorne ripped his hand free and stormed off the stage. I watched him go, descending the stairs at a much slower pace in case my legs decided to give out. Blood still dripped from his injured hand, and he noticeably flexed it, whether from the pain or to rid himself of my touch, I didn't know. Instead of returning to his seat, he stalked on past and yanked open the great hall doors to disappear from sight.

Perched on the back of his seat, his hawk familiar lifted into the air and took off after him with a powerful flap of his wings. Whispers filled the great hall as the students took in the highly-charged scene. Riku started to leave his seat, but Oz grabbed his arm and gave him a subtle warning shake of his head.

Dear ancestors, this was bad. Really, really bad.

If I didn't have a big enough target on my back before, I sure did now. I'd made the Head Prefect storm from the room not once, but *twice* in under twenty-four hours. Anyone who wanted him as an ally—which was everyone in this room—would be thinking of ways to earn his approval.

What better way to prove themselves worthy of an alliance than to free him of a pactum he so clearly didn't want?

And the only way they could do that . . .

Was by killing me.

CHAPTER 8

By the time the Mentor Ceremony was over, it was lunch period.

Thorne didn't return to the assembly, but I had enough to worry about without fretting over where my mentor was.

Mentor.

How had *Thorne* become my mentor?

It was all anyone talked about the entire lunch period. Not about their new class schedules or even their own pairings. Mine was the most advantageous pairing of them all, and everyone felt it was unfair. Alma cast more than one perturbed look at me, but Blaze looked downright murderous as he stabbed the food on his tray, seeming for all the world like he wanted to stab *me* with that fork.

Since I'd needed to wash the dried blood off my hand before eating—most of it being Thorne's—I'd once again had to settle for the last few scraps of food. What I managed to snag didn't even come close to filling the gnawing hole in my stomach, but it was better than nothing.

When the Arcane Three didn't show for lunch, I knew without a doubt that it was because of me. Were they already concocting a plan to get rid of me? Thorne might not be able to kill me, but nothing about our pactum said that his *friends* couldn't.

Then again, all Thorne had to do was spill my secret, and our pactum would be null and void in an instant. Because I'd be dead. *Executed.*

But lunch period came and went, and there was still no sign of him.

Choosing to believe that no news was good news, I left the dining hall as soon as I was done eating, relieved that no one had tried to confront me this time. My first class was across campus in a building that sported a massive indoor arena for demonstrations. To say I was nervous about this class was an understatement. I'd have to publicly reveal my magic eventually, but I'd somehow deluded myself into thinking I could get away with only using simple magic.

Wielding simple magic in an *elite* Conjuring class?

That had failure written all over it.

If I didn't put on a show of some sort, *proving* that I belonged here, then I was screwed.

When I arrived at the arena, a professor was directing the first years into groups. "Name?" he asked a black-haired warlock with deep olive skin, and I remembered he'd been paired with Oz Parrish.

"Damien Lombardi."

The professor consulted his clipboard before pointing to a spot behind him. "Fire Elementals are over there."

Following the direction of his finger, I saw an orange banner on the wall with a ball of flame etched onto it. When I realized we were being grouped by magical affinity, some of my nervousness turned into tentative hope. Besides my own family, I'd never socialized with other Darkens before. Maybe our common ground would spark a truce of some kind, or at *least* a semblance of understanding.

Darkens were often looked upon with fear and suspicion, even inside our own community. Not because our magic was inherently evil, but because it was the most unpredictable—and dangerous if not properly harnessed. If anyone here could understand the magic coiled within me like a deadly snake, it would be my fellow Darkens.

When it was my turn to be grouped, the professor's stoic expression pinched, making his sharp features appear even sharper. Around thirty years old, the sandy-haired warlock wasn't overly tall or broad, but his dark brown eyes promised a world of hurt if I dared step out of line.

"Darkens over there," he said in a clipped tone, jerking his pointy chin to my left—and effectively dismissing me. "Next."

Not surprised by his reaction to me, I moved past him without comment, heading toward the dark purple banner with twisting black shadows on it. The students seemed to be avoiding the arena's open center, so I did the same, navigating the stone path around its circumference. Tiered amphitheatre-style seats circled the perimeter, giving the observers an unobstructed view of the flat circular center.

A large five-pointed pentacle was engraved in the stone floor, reminding me of my necklace safely tucked beneath my crisp white shirt, the tiny heartstone pressed against my sternum. It had kept me safe so far, albeit a little worse for wear. At least I'd survived the first day.

Columns lined the stone walls, punctuated by iron sconces that held actual fire. The flickering flames weren't the only source of light in the vast space, though. A giant dome rose above the arena, curved metalwork holding it aloft. But instead of glass panes keeping the outside elements from intruding, there was nothing. Looking up, I could tell right away that it was raining outside, the sky dull and covered in dark clouds. But not even a single drop of rain fell into the arena, making me aware that an invisible magic shield covered the dome.

Clever, especially for demonstrations.

As I approached the few Darkens already in the room, I tried my best to appear friendly, even managing a small smile despite my nerves. One of them noticed me and immediately gave me a cold look.

"It's her," she muttered to the other Darkens, who turned and also gave me cold stares.

The smile on my face faded.

All but the first one looked away again, dismissing me without a second glance. I tried to shrug off their reaction. After all, I didn't even know them. But I couldn't help feeling a little hurt that they'd cast aside one of their own so readily.

I was about to move around the group and take a seat when a sudden bout of stubbornness gripped me. Tossing aside my pride, I stopped in front of the girl and thrust out my hand. "Hi, I'm Winter."

Her eyes rounded in horror, and she glanced down at my hand as if it was about to bite her. She wasn't the only one caught off guard by the unexpected move. The other Darkens whirled around again to gawk at me, equally horrified by what I'd just done. Although my back was to the rest of the room, I was more than aware of how quiet it had suddenly become. Even the professor had stopped talking.

Great. I'd really put my foot in it this time. Or hand.

Despite how uncomfortable the moment had become, I kept my hand outstretched. Whether the girl accepted it or not, I wouldn't be the first to look away.

A lengthy moment passed before the Darken witch managed to school her expression and evenly reply, "I know who you are, Mayweather. We all do. But that doesn't mean you're one of us. Your family gave witches a bad name, *especially* Darkens. Look around. How many Darkens do you see here compared to the other subsects? We were persecuted too after what your family did, judged for crimes we didn't commit. Allowing you to poison our ranks would be the end of us. We would fade into oblivion like the Syphons, becoming myth rather than legend. I, for one, won't let that happen."

"Me neither," another Darken said.

"Nor I," said the third.

As one, they turned their backs on me, leaving me with my hand still hovering midair. When I felt it start to shake, I quickly lowered it to my side and did what I *should* have done, moving past the group to take a seat by myself.

Wow. That interaction had been much more painful than I'd anticipated. And humbling.

I knew the community blamed my family for a lot of things. Our name alone had taken on the role of bad luck. Hard year at work? Blame the Mayweathers. Going through a divorce? Blame the Mayweathers. Death in the family? Blame the Mayweathers.

But this was the first time I *actually* felt responsible for a complete stranger's misfortune. If I pestered the other Darkens into allying with me, it would only hurt their chances of making it to graduation. I might not know them personally, but they'd obviously been through a lot to get here. It would seem that I wasn't the only underdog at this school.

Busy ruminating on that surprising revelation, I almost missed the two familiar figures entering the arena. Oh, great. Mayweathers really *were* bad luck. None other than Alma and Blaze strode into my Conjuring class, greeting several of the other students as they did. Alma, of course, went to stand with the other Water Elementals under the dark blue banner sporting a cresting wave. But Blaze veered away to join the Fire Elementals, something I should have guessed from the start. Not all Fire Elementals were hotheads, but out of all the witch subsects, that one suited his personality most.

Plus, his name was *Blaze*.

Soon, around fifty students had entered the arena, seven or eight in each group—except for the Darkens, which only had four. Each banner clearly represented a magical affinity. The green one with a fully-bloomed tree was for Earth Elementals, of course, and the white one with swirling lines that represented wind was for Air Elementals. The Oracle banner was a sparkly cerulean blue, a third eye staring out from its center, while a star and crescent moon on an electric blue banner was for the Cosmics.

The final banner was red with a symbol in the shape of an hourglass. It represented the Syphons, even though not a single witch or warlock stood beneath it. They'd all been wiped out a century ago, tied to a curse from one Syphon witch's failings. Although the curse had been broken a decade ago, the only living Syphon at that time wasn't a part of our community. Just like with my family, she'd been labeled an outcast, a disgrace to our entire kind.

I could only imagine that they'd chosen to display the Syphon banner more as a cautionary tale than anything else. Actions had consequences, ones that could affect generations to come. And if I didn't heed that warning, I could very well cause Darkens to be wiped out next.

As the weight of that responsibility bore down on me, the professor left the entrance to stand in the arena's center. "Students, my name is Professor Larkin Seacrest, and I will be teaching your Conjuring class this year." The dome amplified his voice, making it echo loudly for all to hear. "Everyone here should already be able to conjure magic, but during the course of this year, you will learn to connect more deeply with your affinity. The deeper you connect, the greater your potential."

The lines of his face grew even more stern—if that were possible—as he continued on, "Only those who master their abilities will succeed in this class. You'll face trials of increasing difficulty that test those abilities, so prepare to prove yourself. Effort won't be enough. Even your best could fail you. Be willing to push yourself beyond your limits, and you might survive to the end of this year."

Pausing a beat, long enough for me to hear just how loud my heart was thundering, he then said, "You will complete challenges individually but sometimes as a team. As you all take turns demonstrating your abilities today—"

Wait, *today?!*

"—I suggest you pay close attention to your peers' skills. Study their strengths and weaknesses before forming alliances, because who you ally with could make or break you in the trials. Starting with the Earth Elementals and ending with the Darkens, you will each have one minute to demonstrate your magic. Show us why you were chosen as a potential leader for our community. Prove that you deserve a spot on the Conclave. First up is . . ." He consulted his clipboard before calling, "Levi Pierce."

As a warlock with dark auburn hair rose from his seat beneath the Earth Elemental banner, Professor Seacrest beckoned him to take the floor, then stepped aside, leaving the student alone in the arena's center.

When Levi hesitated, the professor said in a firm tone, "Impress us, Mr. Pierce. This is your chance to show the others why they should consider you as an ally. Your minute starts . . . now."

Levi immediately raised both hands and willed magic to them. Twin green orbs sprang into existence, and for a second—one blissfully naive second—I let myself hope that everything would be okay.

Until Professor Seacrest's voice snapped like a whip through the air, "You call that magic, Pierce? I said *impress* us."

Looking flustered, Levi let the green orbs fizzle out as he scrambled to think of a way to appease the unhappy professor. Abruptly falling to one knee, he slapped both palms on the stone beneath him and squeezed his eyes shut. One of the students snorted, and I glanced at the Fire Elementals to see that it was Blaze. He was staring at Levi's hunched form with disdain, clearly not impressed with the Earth Elemental's performance so far.

I bit my lip, suddenly nervous for the poor warlock. I knew all too well the pressure of being under a judgmental microscope. Hopefully he did something with his magic other than—

A faint tremor beneath my shoes had my eyes shooting downward, just in time to witness dark vines and roots erupt from the stone cracks. Startled exclamations and shrieks echoed throughout the arena as the plants snaked around the students' legs. A thorny vine attached to my left leg, and I watched with morbid fascination as the thorns punctured my thin sock, embedding deeply into my skin.

A furious bellow distracted me from the sharp pinpricks of pain, and I glanced at the Fire Elementals again to see Blaze completely tangled in thorny vines. As he struggled to pull them off, flowers popped open all around him, covering him in bright fuchsia. Several of the students snickered, including Levi, who now had his eyes open. Unlike the rest of the arena, the patch of ground beneath the Earth Elemental was blanketed in soft green grass and tiny white flowers.

Blaze glared at him, and I couldn't help but admire the warlock for standing up to the bully. I allowed a little smile to tease my lips, but it quickly faded when Levi abruptly swayed, nearly toppling over. The vine around my leg loosened, as if he'd suddenly lost control of it. I reached down and dislodged the thorns from my skin, not surprised when spots of blood saturated my sock. At least the material was black.

"Okay, Mr. Pierce, your time is up," Professor Seacrest said with a note of satisfaction. "An impressive display of concentration and control. Although, I should have mentioned that maiming your peers during demonstration is highly discouraged, especially if you don't want enemies right off the bat."

A few of the students chuckled, but most didn't look all that happy to be plucking thorns out of their skin. Blaze wrestled the vines off him, but not before they'd left several bloody scratches on his face and hands. He was *livid*, and it was nice not to have that attention directed at me for once.

As Levi slowly labored to his feet, clearly exhausted from expending so much energy, the professor stretched out his free hand toward the mess of greenery and uttered a quick obliterating spell.

"*Eradico*."

Just like that, the vines, roots, grass, and flowers withered and died, disintegrating to dust and seeping back through the stone cracks. The scent of their decaying rot reached me, and a shiver of awareness sliced up my spine. Death might not be breathing down my neck at the moment, but it was still here, still showing itself in unexpected ways.

Nothing was safe here. Not even a harmless blade of grass.

By the time the spell was finished, not even a stray thorn remained. Everything the Earth Elemental had conjured had completely been erased.

"Next up is—" Professor Seacrest began, but I was suddenly distracted, hyperaware of a presence. Not death's, I noted with a frown. No, this presence was far too *alive*. Too charged. Too *angry*.

Dread tightened my gut, instinctively knowing who it was even before I glanced toward the entrance and found Thorne there. He was leaning against the wall with his arms crossed over his chest, staring directly at *me*. A swallow lodged in my throat, and I hurriedly looked away, then silently cursed myself for looking away too soon.

What the hell was *he* doing here? Didn't he have his own classes?

Struggling to concentrate on the student about to give her demonstration, I pressed my palms together in my lap, feeling a slight sting from my healing cut. Even though my eyes were glued to the witch standing in the arena's center, my senses were wholly focused on the warlock in the entryway. I could no longer see his eyes on me, but I could *feel* them, their scrutiny so intense that heat flushed my skin. Refusing to squirm, refusing to show any sign that his presence flustered me, I studiously watched the demonstration.

And didn't see a single thing.

It wasn't long before the other students noticed his presence, pointing and excitedly whispering amongst themselves. A sharp throat clear from Professor Seacrest shut them right up. In no time, it was Blaze's turn to demonstrate. He strutted to the arena's center, arrogance oozing from his pores. One of the thorn cuts on his face slashed diagonally across, making him look even more menacing.

Not surprisingly, he put on a big dramatic show. With a jerk of his hands, he yanked the fire from the iron sconces toward him, then used them in a dangerous juggling act. "Playing with fire" took on a whole new meaning as he leapt and twirled with the fire, even managing to stick a flaming orb into his mouth without getting burned.

With his one minute almost up, he threw the flaming balls into the air above him and swirled his arms, willing the fire to do the same. Around and around the fire went, forming one giant ball of fiery energy. When it resembled a mini sun, he violently slashed his arms down.

I thought the fire would dispel then, maybe break apart and shoot back to the iron sconces. Only half of my attention had been on the performance, the greater half still stuck on Thorne. Which was why I didn't see the huge flaming ball streak toward *me*.

But I saw Thorne's expression change as it did. He was suddenly alert, pushing off the wall to stand at attention. It was enough to warn me of the danger.

I whipped my gaze to the fireball, intense heat blasting over me as it hurtled my way at breakneck speed. The other Darkens scrambled away, but I had nowhere to go.

Well, crap. It looked like my destiny was to go out in a blaze of glory after all.

CHAPTER 9

The darkness within me rose up at the threat, prepared to protect me from the blast.

No! I inwardly shouted at it, frantically trying to shove it down and raise my hands at the same time.

The second I covered my face, the flaming ball exploded like a detonating bomb. The sound was deafening, but I didn't cover my ears, too busy protecting my eyes from being burned in their sockets. I waited for searing pain to rack my body, for my clothing and hair to catch on fire. For my skin to melt off my frame.

Nothing happened.

The intense heat faded, and the fiery glow winked out.

A sudden voice cut through the smoky air. An *angry* one. I dared to crack open my eyes and peek through my fingers.

"I will not tolerate such undisciplined recklessness in my class, Mr. McGrath," Professor Seacrest shouted in Blaze's face. "This is a demonstration, not a trial, and any grievances you have with other students will not be aired in this arena. That stunt will cost you greatly, now get out of my sight. You're done here for the day."

"But, Professor Seacrest, I—"

"Out!"

Blaze's face turned beet red. He looked ready to argue some more, but instead, he whirled and stormed off. I watched him go, lowering my hands once more to my lap. My *shaking* hands.

That had been close. *Too* close. I'd almost become charred filet mignon.

Angry at him but equally angry at myself for not anticipating the attack, I worked on slowing my frantic pulse. Blaze cast me a scathing look, but in doing so, completely missed the look that Thorne was directing at *him*.

I blinked. Blinked again. Maybe my brain was fried from all the smoke inhalation, but Thorne didn't seem pleased that Blaze had almost finished me off. He actually looked . . . pissed. Like *really* pissed.

Hmm. Probably because *he* wanted that honor. Well, he couldn't try to kill me for at least a year, so he'd better get used to the idea of others trying to.

When Blaze was gone, Professor Seacrest resumed the demonstrations as if nothing had happened. Despite his ire, he hadn't even checked if I was okay. At least he'd stopped the fiery blast from pulverizing me. He might despise my family name like everyone else, but he didn't want me dead—in his classroom, anyway.

From my peripheral, I saw Thorne resume his spot against the wall, but his posture seemed stiffer than before. I snuck a glance at him, and sure enough, he was stiff as a board. A muscle jumped in his rock hard jaw, and I knew he was grinding his teeth together. His eyes were narrowed to slits, but they were no longer focused on me. He was watching the other students, even Professor Seacrest, so intensely that I couldn't help but frown a little.

Good grief, he didn't have to broadcast to the whole class that I was *his* to kill. That heated gaze of his practically shouted, *She's mine to destroy. Back off.*

Whatever.

The narrow brush with death had soured my mood, and when

Thorne swung that gaze my way, my scowl deepened. Making sure he saw how pissed off *I* was, I haughtily raised my chin and looked away, blatantly dismissing him. When I felt his eyes continue to bore holes in the side of my head, my bravado wavered. Had I seriously just snubbed the most powerful warlock in the third year? What was *wrong* with me?

Everything, apparently. Might as well own it. At least while my anger held.

Student after student performed their demonstrations, some more impressive than others. Most of them seemed to be showing off for Thorne rather than their peers or the professor. Couldn't really blame them. He was the school's Head Prefect. If anyone was going to advance them up the hierarchy ladder, it would be him. One word of affirmation, and they would shoot from the bottom to the top overnight.

He didn't appear all that impressed with the demonstrations, though. Even when it was the Cosmics' turn to perform their magic, his expression didn't change.

Despite my ornery mood, I grew more and more nervous the closer it came to my own demonstration. What could I possibly show them that wouldn't make me the laughing stock of the entire class? If I stuck to simple magic, word would spread like wildfire that I was without a doubt an empty name, one that needed to be erased once and for all.

So busy worrying about my own performance, I almost didn't notice when Alma Ramirez took the floor. I forced myself to pay attention to her, certain she'd try to target me somehow. She turned to murmur something to Professor Seacrest, and with a nod, he walked over to a table on the far side of the arena and returned with what looked like an empty glass vial.

Alma took it and faced the students again, a sly little smirk crossing her lips as she raised her free hand. In an instant, deep blue magic engulfed her palm and fingers. Focusing on the Earth Elementals across the room, she curled her fingers in a "come hither" gesture.

I couldn't see what happened right away, but one of the Earth Elementals suddenly gasped. Soon, they were all reacting, and I leaned forward in my seat to better see. When I finally realized what Alma was doing, I tensed all over.

Tears. She was stealing their *tears.*

The targeted witches and warlocks continued to gasp and exclaim as she coaxed the tears from their eyes and beckoned them forward. Instead of dripping to the floor, the tears floated in the air, following Alma's command by traveling across the open arena and slipping inside the vial.

She targeted group after group, forcing every student she focused on to give up their tears. Even her fellow Water Elementals cried like babies, whether they wanted to or not. When the vial was almost full, she turned to the last group, the Darkens.

While she coaxed the tears from them as well, it became abundantly clear that she wanted to save me for last. As I waited, I sat so straight in my seat that it probably looked like a poker was stuck up my butt. The waiting seemed to go on forever, but not even a minute had passed.

Please run out of time, please run out of time, I silently pleaded.

No such luck.

Finished with the other Darkens, she turned to me, that sly smirk of hers widening. I braced for whatever she had in store for me, instinctively knowing this wouldn't end well. She might not have plans to outright hurt me like Blaze had, but what she wanted to take from me didn't exist. I hadn't cried in *years*. No matter how hard I'd tried to force the tears out, they wouldn't come.

She was going to fail. She was going to fail in front of *everyone*. And it would be all my fault.

I should be glad to see her fail. She'd nearly drowned me, after all, almost causing me to fail the Initiation Trial. An eye for an eye, right? Gran would approve.

But as she curled her fingers at me, beckoning my tears to come forth, I felt no satisfaction when they refused to cooperate. She might fail to procure tears from my body, but that failure would only further mark me as a pariah. As an *oddity*. Just one more reason to shun me.

When no moisture leaked from my eyes, Alma's smirk slipped. Curling her fingers again, she tried a second time, but nothing happened.

"Wrap it up, Miss Ramirez," Professor Seacrest warned. "You're running out of time."

Alma's lips formed a tight line, and she curled all five of her fingers into claws. I felt the pull of her magic, the *command* to release my tears. She pulled and yanked, looking more desperate with each passing second. My eyes burned under the strain but remained bone dry. Her hand began to shake, her energy rapidly depleting as my body refused to bend to her will.

"Time, Miss Ramirez."

With a frustrated cry, Alma clamped her hand into a tight fist and *yanked*. I coughed. Coughed again as fluid rapidly filled my lungs. Pain stabbed my chest, worsening every time I tried to suck in air. My survival instincts kicked in, and I started to cough in earnest, desperate to clear my lungs, to *breathe*.

"*Enough!*" a deep voice barked.

Surprise trickled through me. Was that *Thorne*?

"Miss Ramirez!" another voice snapped, this one Professor Seacrest.

Alma dropped her hand with a gasp, and I immediately felt my lungs drain. Coughing a few more times to clear my windpipe, I raised my head to look at her. She was trembling all over, bewilderment and devastation written on her face. A lone tear slid down her cheek as she whispered, "*Dios mio*, that wasn't supposed to happen."

"I should say not," the professor said, striding forward to take the vial of tears from Alma before she dropped it. "I'm going to mark that down as a loss of control rather than a blatant attack on a fellow student, but the high bar you set in the Initiation Trial has just fallen, Miss Ramirez. You may take your seat."

More tears slipped down her face as she left the arena's center, her shoulders slightly hunched and golden braid falling limply down her back. One glance at the other students confirmed what I'd feared would happen. Their expressions ranged from disappointment to pity, the reverence Alma had garnered from her early win now tarnished.

But they weren't just looking at her. They were looking at me too, openly gawking as if I was an alien creature from outer space—just like I'd predicted. Too afraid to find out what expression Thorne now wore, I avoided glancing his way. He might have ordered Alma to stop, but I didn't for one second think he did so out of concern for me. Whatever his motives, he certainly didn't care if I lived or died.

The mood in the arena grew more somber after that. The students still needing to demonstrate actively steered clear of including me in their performances, casting glances at Thorne so often that I finally caved and peeked at him. Okay, he'd gone from pissed to downright angry. No wonder they were all looking at him. His dark mood was definitely affecting their performances. More than one student lost control of their magic, earning a frown and stern word from

Professor Seacrest.

At this rate, I could almost get away with doing simple magic. Almost.

I still needed to show off my Darken affinity somehow, but what could I do that wouldn't end in disaster?

Before I knew it, the Darkens were being called to demonstrate. Prudence Calloway, the brunette witch who'd spoken to me earlier, used her magic to engrave her name deeply into the arena's stone floor. She waltzed back to her seat with a rather wicked smile, leaving Professor Seacrest to deal with the fact that "Prudence was here" had just desecrated his sacred pentacle.

When my name was finally called, I thought for sure my legs wouldn't be able to support me. Unfortunately, they did, carrying me to the center of the arena before I could order them to run in the opposite direction.

"Your one minute, Miss Mayweather," Professor Seacrest began, "starts now."

I froze. Head to toe, I couldn't move a muscle. My heart stopped. My mind blanked. For several long seconds, I did nothing but sightlessly stare at my expectant audience. This was hell. This was *worse* than hell. I'd rather be *in* hell than stuck in the middle of this arena right now.

"Time is halfway up, Miss Mayweather," the professor said, his voice distant and echoey as if he'd called down a very long tunnel.

Great. I was epically failing this demonstration. What I wouldn't give to disappear right now. Every cell in my *body* wanted to disappear, so badly that I shut my eyes and wished for it to happen. *Willed* it to happen.

Disappear, disappear, disappear!

The magic in my veins stirred, eagerly responding to my cry. I was suddenly plunged into darkness, the world around me muting. I ripped open my eyes to a sea of billowing black smoke. No. *Shadow.* Panicking, I tried to wave it away, but . . . but where were my hands? Where was *I?*

No, no, no, no.

I'd disappeared, all right. I'd turned myself into a *shade.*

CHAPTER 10

I wasn't *actually* a ghost.

If someone kicked me right now, I'd feel it, and so would they. Magic had its limitations, at least on the mortal plane. Since my body was made of flesh, I couldn't just dissolve it into nothing. But I could hide it without uttering a spell, using the power of darkness to fool the naked eye into *thinking* I'd disappeared—similar to how human magicians used pyrotechnics and mirrors.

Gran had taught me how to do it a few years ago, making me practice the technique over and over until I could practically do it in my sleep. Which was probably why I'd done it even without meaning to.

Knowing that the illusion was strongest away from open spaces, I silently carried my shadow self toward a particularly dark spot along the arena's perimeter where the fire from the lit sconces barely touched. I didn't float above the ground like a wraith, but with my senses dulled to the world around me, I could fully concentrate on moving with stealth. Within seconds, I reached my destination. My conjured shadows perfectly melted into the naturally dark spot, allowing me to breathe easier now that I was out of the limelight.

From my position, I could clearly see the reactions to my sudden disappearance. Faces were slack-jawed, gaping at the arena's empty center. Even Professor Seacrest looked baffled, his brow pinched as he searched for his missing student. Certain my little trick had mystified Thorne as well, I looked his way, only to find him already staring at my dark hiding spot.

My mouth slowly fell open. How the hell did he know I was here?

Despite my rather impressive yet unintentional demonstration, his expression hadn't changed. If anything, his mood seemed to have darkened more. Sheesh. Did *nothing* impress this guy? Not that I was *trying* to impress him, but still.

"Time, Miss Mayweather," the professor said, still searching for me.

Knowing I couldn't hide forever, I reluctantly loosened my grip on the shadows. As they fell away, my senses fully switched back on. The abrupt change was overwhelming, and I swayed, catching myself with a hand on the wall to orientate myself. Dragging in a deep breath to chase the spots from my vision, I straightened and stepped from the shadows.

Some of the students' eyes widened when they spotted me, and Professor Seacrest whirled around to find me approaching from behind. I hid my trembling hands in the pleats of my skirt, not wanting everyone to see just how much that little stunt had drained me. It had been years since I'd done anything like that, years since I'd lost my grip on the darkness in a way that allowed others to see it.

I hadn't meant to let it out, but I'd wanted to disappear so badly, so I'd just . . . I'd slipped. At least no one had been hurt, thank the ancestors. Even so, that stunt had been stupidly reckless. I couldn't slip like that again.

Clearing his throat, the professor carefully schooled his expression before saying, "Not bad, Miss Mayweather. Shadewalking is an advanced skill for a Darken. You may take your seat."

Wow, was that an actual compliment? Maybe so, but it was a begrudging one. He might have been impressed, but he didn't want to be.

As I finished crossing the arena and sat down, I felt *way* too seen. Absolutely everyone was staring at me, their expressions ranging from jealousy to wary curiosity. Dare I hope that my unplanned demonstration had sparked some begrudging admiration in the students as well?

"Many of you show promise," Professor Seacrest began, thankfully drawing the students' attention back to him, "but most of you lack stamina and control. To become truly one with your affinity, you'll have to dig deeper. *Far* deeper. Mr. Hudson has graciously agreed to demonstrate what that looks like. For those who don't know, our Head Prefect is a Cosmic with a rare ability to manipulate storm matter using the energy of the universe. When it comes to mastering magic, none can compete with him, not even me. Mr. Hudson, the floor is yours."

When Thorne finally peeled himself off the wall and stepped forward, most of the students started to clap. Not only were they excited to see the Head Prefect in action, they most definitely wanted to earn some brownie points by showing their support. I didn't join in, my nerves returning with a vengeance now that he was about to unleash his magic. I'd only seen it once before, but I'd hoped to never see it again. The horror, the *terror* I'd felt as he'd gathered that raw power, that vast might, and directed it all toward me.

"I'll kill you!"

His promise from that fateful day sliced through my mind as he stalked toward the arena's center, removing his blazer and tie as he did. When he didn't stop there, when he started to remove his white *shirt* as well, the clapping dissolved into hoots and hollers. The girls went crazy, jumping up from their seats to cheer him on. Without my permission, my eyes followed his fingers while they deftly unbuttoned the shirt and tugged it from his pants. The shirt opened, and I tried to look away, to stop my gaze from roving over the broad expanse of tanned skin on display.

But I couldn't.

There were so many muscles, so many *tattoos*. He shrugged the shirt off, giving me an unobstructed view of his entire upper half, and I drank it all in like a parched desert nomad. Tattooed wings resembling a hawk spanned his whole chest, making the impressive width seem even broader. There wasn't any ink on his stomach, but the defined six pack stamped there was plenty intriguing to look at.

And then there were his arms. Thoroughly muscled, veined, and completely covered in ink. The dark tattoos looked like a violent network of lightning bolts, starting at the top of his neck and streaking all the way down to the tips of his fingers.

I didn't know how long I stared at him, but when I finally managed to drag my eyes to his face, I found him watching me.

Ancestors save me, what did I just *do?* Intense heat blasted my cheeks, embarrassment making me want to shadewalk into a dark corner again. Better yet, out of this room.

I didn't move a muscle, didn't even breathe, too busy pretending like I wasn't mortified that he'd just caught me ogling his chest. And stomach. And arms. Good grief, why did he have to be so breathtaking? It would be so much easier to despise him and his cold personality if he didn't look like Zeus.

Without taking his eyes off me, Thorne levitated his clothing toward the theatre seats and neatly set them down. A muscle feathered in his jaw as our gazes held, and I couldn't help but wonder if he was thinking about killing me right now.

He'd promised to, and I'd believed him. Almost two years later, I still did. A pactum wouldn't stop him. He'd find a way to finish me off somehow.

His chest expanded, then he abruptly looked away and swept those intense blue eyes over his audience before saying, "When I start, don't move. And whatever you do, don't try to interact with my magic."

Or you'll die, he might as well have added.

Everyone sank back to their seats, their attention riveted on him like insects to a bug zapper. If only they knew how deadly his magic was. They wouldn't be leaning forward in their seats, that was for sure.

Silence descended, everyone anticipating what Thorne would do. Everyone but me. I dreaded it, wishing I could be anywhere but here. What if he slipped? What if he "accidentally" lost control, and I just *happened* to be in the way? Would the pactum consider my death unintentional and dissipate our oath?

Thinking of the amulet around my neck, praying it would protect me, I watched Thorne widen his stance and close his eyes, his body loose yet balanced in preparation for what was to come. Nothing happened right away. Not even his hands lit up with magic. The silence became weighted as he stood perfectly still, looking for all the world like a frozen statue.

It was the slight shift in the air that warned me. The sharp scent of an impending weather change, a *violent* one. Something flashed in the sky above the dome, followed closely by a loud *boom*. As the sound vibrated our bones, we all looked up to see a powerful storm brewing outside. Rain pounded on the dome, but the invisible shield kept the storm at bay.

The storm that Thorne had *called*.

I glanced at him again to see that his hands were now halfway raised, electric blue magic dancing over his fingers. The lines of his body were taut, making his muscles stand out in sharp relief. I nervously clamped my hands together as he strained. No, *pulled*. Not visibly, but I could sense he was willing something toward himself. *Calling* it.

The storm outside was only the beginning.

I stiffened, suddenly knowing what he was about to do. Before I could prepare myself, a blinding flash of light lit up the dome, followed by a deafening *crack*.

The arena suddenly exploded into chaos. Wind and rain poured in, snuffing out the fire in the iron sconces. Yells and screams echoed through the air. Another flash lit up the dome, but it didn't stop there this time. It streaked down, down, down, so intensely bright that it momentarily blinded me.

A monstrous *boom* shook my bones, the force throwing me back in my seat. Freezing rain pelted my face, and angry winds snatched at my clothes. When a buzzing sensation charged over my skin, making all of the hair on my body lift, fear sliced through me.

It took all of my strength not to curl into a cowering ball. Instead, I managed to blink the rain and spots from my vision, desperate to see what was happening. When my vision cleared, the image before me stole my breath away.

A figure stood in the arena's center, completely enveloped in white hot light. Crackling blue edged the electric streaks of energy. The *lightning*. It raced up and down the figure, traveling so fast that I could barely track the movement.

It was Thorne. He'd called down lightning and was now *controlling* it.

A few tails whipped out, threatening to zap anyone or anything that got too close, but the majority stayed close to his body. The deadly light illuminated his face, revealing perfectly poised features and eyes still sealed shut. Wind stirred his hair, lashing it across his cheeks, but he didn't twitch even a single muscle. He was in a zen state, in absolute control over the dangerous element.

Just when I started to wonder what he planned to do with that lightning, his arms began to glow. No, his *tattoos* did. They lit up a bright blue, and the lightning whipping around him suddenly began to fade, to disappear. *Inside* the tattoos.

Dear elders, ancestors, and spirits. I'd known Thorne was powerful. I'd seen it firsthand. But no way in hell was I prepared to see a Cosmic harness and *absorb* lightning.

Seconds later, the lightning was gone. So was the wind and rain. The arena plunged into darkness, the only light the glowing tattoos on Thorne's arms.

Silence fell once more, the only sounds coming from beyond the dome as the storm receded. My skin continued to buzz from close contact with the powerful energy, intensified by the adrenaline sparking through me. Fear still raced through my blood, but now, something else did too. Something that could only be described as awe.

Never in my life had I witnessed such a spellbinding feat. For a heartstopping moment, Thorne had transformed himself into a deadly tapestry of art in the shape of a storm. He'd commanded that storm. He'd *become* that storm. It was in his veins now, corralled into submission by the magical tattoos adorning his arms.

As the tattoos' glow cooled and dimmed, Thorne lowered his arms and reopened his eyes. They immediately locked with mine, and I shivered, whether from dread or begrudging respect, I didn't know. Maybe both.

He was terrifying, no doubt about it. But he was magnificent, too. No wonder everyone fawned over him. He was literally a god made flesh.

Not that I would ever tell him that. His ego was probably already the size of Mount Everest.

Still, his demonstration made mine look like child's play, along with everyone else's. We definitely couldn't compete with his prowess, and I now understood why he hadn't been impressed with our performances.

He was a master, and we were but lowly apprentices. Our magic was laughable compared to his.

And now, he was my mentor.

Lucky me.

As my imagination swiftly conjured up the many ways I could fail in the upcoming days, Professor Seacrest uttered a quick spell to relight the iron sconces. The darkness lifted, revealing Thorne already halfway dressed.

"Let's give Mr. Hudson a hand for his unmatched display of *audentia et fortitudo*, everyone. Remarkable. Truly remarkable," the professor said, his usually stern voice brimming with praise. He started to clap, and the others joined in, many rising from their seats now that the danger was over.

Thorne didn't acknowledge the praise, grabbing his tie and blazer before stalking across the arena toward the exit. He was almost there when he abruptly stopped. His grip on his jacket tightened, then he turned back to face the room. I thought for sure he was going to sketch a bow or something, but instead, he looked directly at me again and said, "Let's go."

The clapping faded, all eyes swiveling toward me.

At the *command* in Thorne's voice, the blood in my face promptly drained.

Terrific.

My master was summoning me . . .

And I had no choice but to obey.

CHAPTER 11

The center of Thorne Hudson's attention was a very bad place to be.

Professor Seacrest hadn't even batted an eye when he'd ordered me to leave the arena with him. It was like the warlock had jurisdiction at this school beyond that of even a professor. I knew he was Head Prefect and all, but this kind of power far surpassed that.

The minute we were alone in the hallway, he threw over his shoulder, "Why didn't you shadewalk when that fireball was coming at you?"

Caught off guard by the abrupt question, I slowed, only to pick up the pace again when he didn't stop, his long strides nearly impossible to keep up with.

When I didn't respond quickly enough, he bit out, "Answer the question."

Despite how nervous I was to be alone with him, my eyes narrowed on his broad back. He might intimidate me, especially after that astounding demonstration, but I'd already been pushed around enough for one day. So instead of giving him a satisfactory answer, I simply replied, "I didn't think of it."

His shoulders noticeably tensed at that, a sure sign of his disapproval. We were certainly getting off to a great start. At this rate, we'd be best buds in no time.

Not.

Whatever his title at this school was, whatever notoriety I could gain by having him as my mentor, I had no intention of sucking up to him like everyone else. There was a volatile history between us, and despite the guilt that continued to haunt me, I wouldn't allow a Hudson to treat me like a doormat.

We walked in silence for a charged beat, then he said, "Not doing anything made you look weak."

"I'll keep that in mind for next time," slipped out before I could catch it.

His entire body went rigid, and I slowed again, certain I'd gone too far. It was one thing to give him evasive answers, but ones dripping with sarcasm? Bad idea. *Very* bad idea.

This was Thorne freaking Hudson. What was I *thinking?*

For the next several minutes, neither of us said a word. Every time it was on the tip of my tongue to ask him where we were going, I forced the words back down. He was piping mad, his body fully charged with electricity like a loaded battery. One misstep, and he could turn that deadly energy on me, pactum by damned. Not wanting to push my luck, I silently followed him down hallway after hallway like an obedient little shadow, a shadow that he seemed to have completely forgotten about.

A few minutes later, we entered the dormitory building, and my nerves started to fray. Where the hell was he taking me? To his *room?*

Sure enough, he headed straight for the wing reserved for third years. Right before stepping over the threshold, I came to a dead halt.

Thorne finally slowed, casting me an impatient look over his shoulder. "What are you doing?"

"First years aren't allowed in Sapphire Wing," I said in a way that silently communicated he should already know this. I just couldn't seem to help myself.

"They are if I say they are," he replied in an annoyingly perfunctory way, not at all snotty like the words would suggest. "I'm your mentor now, so where I go, you go."

Clearly done with the discussion, he faced forward and took off again, leaving me scrambling to catch up. I'd been here once before during the campus tour with Professor Birch, but she'd explicitly told us that first years couldn't enter upperclassmen wings under any circumstances. Guess that rule didn't apply when I was with the almighty Thorne Hudson.

Still, I felt more than a little uncomfortable being in a *restricted* area. I'd always been a rule follower. Well, *almost* always. But the one time I'd dared to break the rules had ended in disaster, so I didn't plan on breaking any more anytime soon. Being in the third year wing felt too much like crossing a line, and that feeling worsened with the knowledge that I was doing it with Thorne.

He was my mentor, but we were alone and heading toward his room. Everything about this situation spelled disaster.

I should leave before something awful happened, before he found a way around that pactum and killed me without any witnesses. The dorms were empty this time of day. We were utterly alone. *Alone.* Would he kill me swiftly or draw out his revenge with a little torture? He could torture me for *hours,* and no one would hear my screams.

Thoroughly convinced now that I was walking to my death, I nearly jumped out of my skin when Thorne abruptly stopped. He started to turn, and I went poker straight, the darkness within me stirring at my anxious state.

Use meee.

Yeah, right. Even if I finally allowed the darkness to defend me, speed wasn't on my side. A single lightning bolt from Thorne could have me down faster than I could think, let alone act. No, in a stand-off fight, magic that could travel at the speed of light would always win.

Knowing that, I pushed the darkness back down and braced for whatever Thorne had in store for me. But as he turned, he only did so halfway. Without even looking at me, he lifted a hand and muttered something under his breath, so low that I couldn't hear it. The sound of a lock scraping pricked my ears, followed by the slight creak of a door opening. One step, and he disappeared inside . . .

His dorm room.

Oh.

I blinked a few times, trying to convince myself that this wasn't a trick to lure me inside. He hadn't killed me yet, so maybe . . .

Maybe his room was protected by a sound-blocking spell, which would ensure no one heard my screams.

Frustrated with my paranoia, I huffed and took a step forward. As I did, Thorne emerged from his room again, this time with a huge bird on his shoulder. At the sight of me, the hawk screeched and flapped its massive wings. I stiffened again, suddenly aware that I'd made a grave mistake. Thorne had sworn a pactum with me, but his *familiar* hadn't. The bird of prey might not be able to kill me faster than I could blink, but he could do some irreparable damage, like peck and scratch out my eyes.

Imagining how painful that would be, I warily stared at the agitated hawk, certain Thorne was about to unleash him on me. The bird stared right back, its deep yellow eyes fixed on me like I was his next meal.

"Settle, Comet," Thorne told his familiar before securing the door with another muttered spell and wave of his hand. The bird protested with another shriek, yet he immediately pulled his wings in, his eyes all but daring me to try anything.

I stopped breathing when Thorne turned to walk back down the hall toward me, the addition of that blasted bird making him look like a Viking pirate god—if such a being existed. *Well, he does now.* I was gawking right at him like a tiny schoolgirl about to pee herself. He stalked down the center of the hallway like royalty, looking for all the world like he didn't see me. Certain he was going to plow me right over, I stepped sideways.

But not enough.

His arm brushed mine, and—*zap!*—a startling amount of energy shot from him and into me. A sharp *pop* announced the exchange, the electrical transference making all the hair on my body stand on end. As a startled gasp escaped me, I could have sworn he made a noise as well, something that sounded a lot like a scoff.

Upset by the unwanted burst of energy, I snapped before I could check myself, "Stop doing that."

"Doing what?" he tossed back without even slowing.

The hawk swiveled on his perch to face backwards, those penetrating eyes watching me like a—well, a *hawk*, as I turned to storm after them. "You know what. Stop *zapping* me."

"Stay out of my way, and you won't get zapped."

Why, that infuriating, egotistical—

"The pactum might consider that *intentional* harm, you know."

Comet shifted his feet as the line of Thorne's shoulders went rigid. Guess he didn't like being reminded of our pactum. Too bad. After a tense beat, Thorne rumbled back, "If I try to harm you, there won't be any 'mights' about it."

My throat closed. Okay, that sounded way too much like a threat. Or a promise. Time to shut my mouth before I angered him further.

Deciding not to ask him if there was a point to this little fieldtrip, I lapsed into silence once more. We exited the building but from the back this time, then climbed a steep stone pathway that led us away from the school and toward a grassy glen. Once again, no one was around but us.

It was no longer raining, but the sky was still glum, a layer of thick gray clouds snuffing out the sun. Wisps of fog clung to the wide open field, growing thicker near the edges where the trees met. The woods were dark, and as I stared at them, a foreboding chill crept up my spine, reminding me of what had happened during my Initiation Trial.

Only one student had died so far, but my intuition warned me that he wouldn't be the last. Whether by the hand of future trials or fellow students, the occupants of this school would be visited by death again. I could only pray he wouldn't be visiting *me* any time soon.

Distracted by my morbid thoughts, the sound of flapping wings startled me. I jerked my eyes to Thorne again just as Comet launched off his forearm and into the sky. The hawk climbed higher and higher, shooting above us until he was a tiny speck.

Thorne watched him go before saying, "I didn't want him caught in the storm earlier."

Realizing he was giving me an explanation for why we were out here, I simply nodded.

As we watched the bird circle over the field in search of prey, the silence became weighted. So many unspoken things. So much hurt, pain, and anger simmered between us. If there was ever going to be an opportunity to clear the air, it would be now. I'd tried to do just that two years ago but had epically failed. Now that he wasn't actively trying to kill me, now that no one was around to overhear, I could try again.

For her sake, I *needed* to.

My heart started to pound, the swirling nerves in my stomach making me feel sick. I opened my mouth anyway, determined to spit out what needed to be said.

"What happened this morning in the bathroom?"

Caught off guard by his question, I swallowed too fast and choked. He dropped his chin to watch me, and I felt heat rush to my face. Great. How much did he already know?

"Nothing," I quickly replied, hoping my embarrassment wasn't visible.

He studied me for a painfully long moment before looking out over the field and saying, "You won't survive this place without allies."

"So I've heard."

"You also won't survive if you're not willing to defend yourself."

That one gave me pause. I opened my mouth but nothing came out.

"Your demonstration was all flight and no fight. You hid and made yourself look small."

Ouch.

"You're not eating enough. You're not taking up enough space. Continue as you are, and you'll fail within the week."

I snapped my gaze to the side of his face. "And what do *you* care?"

"I don't. But your failure will reflect poorly on my leadership skills."

Double ouch but not surprising to hear. Facing forward again, I muttered, "At least you'll win your bet."

It was his turn to give me a sharp look.

"Didn't think I noticed that?" I dryly said. "Everyone here might hate me, but I still pay attention. So what did you bet? That Blaze would kill me before the day was over? Well, he had his chance and failed. Too bad for you that Professor Seacrest intervened."

He stared at me for another beat, then looked away with a slight head shake. "Not so observant after all." Before I could wonder about that statement, he continued, "Forget the bets. You need to be focused on the only thing that matters: staying alive. The odds are already stacked against you considering all the enemies you've made in less than two days, so if you don't have what it takes to survive here, then leave."

I blinked. "Leave? Right now?"

"Yes."

I didn't say anything for a long moment, trying to digest what he'd said. On one hand, everything he'd said about me was true. If I didn't adopt a cutthroat attitude, I wasn't going to last much longer. But on the other hand, this conversation felt way too much like reverse psychology, like he was trying to convince me that leaving was *my* idea.

Nope. I was *not* falling for that bull. If he wanted me gone so my impending failure couldn't tarnish his perfect reputation, then he'd completely forgotten who I was. Who my *family* was. We'd already been forced out of the community, already done our time in obscurity. No way was I leaving here for Thorne's sake. *Especially* not for him.

He didn't want me here? Didn't want me making him look bad? Tough. I was done feeling guilty for invading his personal space. I deserved to be here, and I wouldn't let a Hudson bully me into thinking otherwise.

Which was why I raised my chin and firmly replied, "Not a chance in hell."

Anger practically pulsed from him. Even with my gaze straight ahead, I could see the muscle furiously ticking in his jaw. Oh, well. This wasn't the first or last time I'd make him angry.

"Fine. It's your funeral," he quietly seethed through clenched teeth, making goosebumps erupt over my flesh. "Don't say I didn't warn you."

Okay, I was a bit freaked out now. Or a lot.

When he raised two fingers to his mouth and let an ear-piercing whistle rip through the air, I couldn't help but flinch. Immediately, his hawk familiar dropped from the sky and dove like a missile toward us. He looked like a feathered bullet aimed for my heart, and as he came in hot, it took all of my willpower not to duck behind Thorne for protection.

A split second away from reaching us, the bird thrust out his wings, taloned feet extended. A gust of wind from the flapping wings slapped my face, but I forced my hands to remain at my sides, even when those wicked talons flexed wide, more than capable of gouging my vulnerable eyes out.

Just when I thought a collision was inevitable, Thorne thrust his arm out, and the bird wrapped those deadly taloned feet around it. A tip of one wing struck my cheek before he neatly tucked them both in and climbed up to Thorne's shoulder.

A bit dazed, I didn't move a muscle as Thorne whirled and headed back down the stone pathway, not bothering to check if I followed. With our chat officially over, I stayed where I was even after he was long gone. I kept my eyes on the distant treeline, his final words ringing in my ears like a death knell.

"It's your funeral."

Your funeral.

Funeral.

Funeral.

Funeral.

Conjuring and Spellwork were my only two classes for the day, but by the time dinner rolled around, I barely had enough energy to snag some food before it was all gone.

At least I'd managed to score some meat this time. The conversation I'd had with Thorne might have unnerved me, but it had also lit a fire under my butt. I couldn't allow myself to waste away from lack of food. Now that I'd been given a taste of what this school would demand from me on a daily basis, I understood just how important it was to keep my energy up.

These classes weren't all listening and taking notes. They were advanced, requiring magical demonstrations more than anything. It felt like I'd been thrown into the deep end and expected to already know how to swim. Even though I'd been thoroughly taught all the magical subjects by my parents and Gran over the past decade, this place made me feel like a novice.

What's worse, none of the other students looked like they were about to fall asleep in their seats from the strenuous day. Annoyed at how low my stamina was, I ate every last scrap of food on my plate, washed it down with a large glass of water, then stood up, ready to call it an early night.

As usual, I'd sat alone in my corner of the dining hall. Thorne and his friends were across the room at their special table, but if they'd noticed me, I didn't know. I was too busy studiously ignoring them. After what Thorne had said to me, I hoped they kept their distance for as long as possible. I'd rather not have a mentor at all than deal with constant threats and insults. I doubted he'd teach me anything useful anyway, not when he so clearly wanted me to leave.

But as I prepared to exit the dining hall, I didn't fail to notice the heads that turned my way. Word had spread of my shadewalking demonstration, and reactions were mixed about me not being a complete dud. Still, not a single soul had approached me all evening.

If I wanted allies, it looked like I'd have to do all the legwork.

Problem was, I still didn't know who I could trust. If I picked the wrong person, my chances of survival would plummet even more.

For now, I decided that fending for myself was better than letting my guard down around someone who could later stab me in the back. Allies were important, but so was using common sense.

When I approached where Blaze and Alma sat, I felt my muscles tense. Although I hadn't meant to, I'd deeply embarrassed them both during our Conjuring demonstrations. Fewer students had been clamoring for their attention at dinner, especially Alma. It didn't help that neither of their mentors had approached them yet, just one more thing the student body had been gossiping about this evening.

Apparently, the only pairing that had met today was me and Thorne.

The other first years were obviously salty about that fact, still grumbling that our pairing was unfair, not to mention obscene. I'd felt both Alma and Blaze's eyes on me while I was eating, their ire felt from several feet away. So as I came even with them, I wasn't the least bit surprised when I heard Blaze say, "I'm not done with you yet, stray."

I could have kept walking. I *should* have kept walking.

But as I recalled Thorne's harsh, albeit true words about defending myself, I paused long enough to reply back, "I'm not done with you yet either."

At the promise, the *threat* in my tone, a few of the students within hearing range guffawed. I kept going, half-expecting Blaze to jump up in fury and lob a fireball at my back. Despite how exposed I felt in that moment, I forced myself to remain calm—at least on the outside. Without my consent, my gaze flicked to where Thorne sat and caught him watching me. I couldn't read his expression, but when our eyes met, I made a point to look away again in a clear snub.

Whispers followed in my wake, but I kept my head high and my gait even, determined to leave this room with dignity. Today had been utterly exhausting, but I wasn't going to show it. By the time I reached Jade Wing, I couldn't wait to collapse on the rickety bed in my drafty tower. Even with the constant chill and moaning wind coming from the broken window, I already knew I'd sleep like the dead again.

But when I finally dragged myself up the five flights of stairs and opened the door, something triggered my instincts. I immediately went on high alert, certain someone was waiting inside the room, ready to attack me. I thought about running the other way but only for a second. This was *my* room, as pathetic as it might be. Whoever was in it needed to leave, and it was my job to make them, even if that meant defending myself. Even if that meant . . .

Even if that meant *hurting* them.

Nausea swirled in my gut, but I forced myself to shove open the door and storm inside anyway. In a flash, I conjured a swirling ball of dark violet magic to my fingertips and shouted, "Who's in here?"

My eyes darted from shadow to shadow, searching for the intruder. I held the orb higher, my heart pounding out of control. Nothing happened. The air was cold but still. Not even a wisp of breeze from the window stirred it. Slowly turning in a circle, I carefully catalogued everything in the room, and that's when I finally saw it.

I froze, my insides turning to ice when I read the message on the floor-length mirror.

Leave or die.

The letters were a deep red and still wet, grotesquely bleeding down the reflective glass like . . . like blood. Except that it wasn't *like* blood, I realized with rising horror.

It *was* blood.

CHAPTER 12

"Who here has seen a heartstone?"

No one in my Amplifying class raised their hand, including me.

Liar, the little stone resting on my sternum silently accused, but I ignored it. No way was I going to risk exposing my one and only boon. After an entire week at this school, I was completely convinced that the invisible amulet around my neck was the only thing keeping me alive.

Survived my first week at Heartstone? *Check.* Grown increasingly paranoid that someone here—or many someones—was out for my blood? *Check.* Failed to make any friends or alliances? *Check.* Resorted to taking showers at night to avoid further humiliation? *Check.* Struggled to perform classroom demonstrations while also keeping my darkness contained? *Check.* Spelled and shielded my dorm room so no one could kill me in my sleep? *Check.* Pissed off my mentor multiple times a day simply by existing? *CHECK.*

Yes, I was still alive despite all the odds, but I was starting to crack under the constant pressure and loneliness. The threat written in blood on my mirror had shaken me to my core, and although I'd immediately placed protection spells around my room, the scare had triggered my proclivity for nightmares. More than once, I'd woken up in a cold sweat from dreaming about a faceless foe shoving me out that broken window to my death.

Although my sleep had been unsettling this past week, at least my body had stayed in bed every night. The *last* thing I needed was to wake up and find myself in a completely different location. Walking the halls past midnight was forbidden, and I doubted a sleepwalking excuse would spare me from being disciplined.

"As you all know," Professor Holt continued, drawing my attention back to her, "heartstones are the rarest, most powerful gemstone of known existence on Earth. One small stone can amplify a magic wielder's abilities to devastating proportions. That capacity for unmatched power is what inspired the founders to name this school Heartstone Academy. Every student admitted to Heartstone is a rare and powerful gem, but whether or not you have the capacity for unmatched power, only time will tell."

Her brown eyes rested on me for a second before moving on.

"Today, we will test out an assortment of amplifiers to determine which one enhances your magic best. Since amplifying can have dire consequences depending on the wielder's intentions, first years are not allowed to carry an amplifier on their person outside of class, the only exception being future trials."

A few groans rose up from the class. I inwardly winced, feeling guilty for already breaking the rule. Not that I would give up my amulet. Guilt I could live with, but surviving this place without my protection necklace? Probably not.

Ignoring the reactions, Professor Holt pulled aside a black cloth covering her desk to reveal a wide array of stones and gems in every color imaginable.

"Once you've made a connection with the best amplifier for your magic, it will become your signature relic. Although it's important not to grow dependent on a relic's aid, the most influential witches and warlocks throughout history used amplifiers when the need arose, be it to assert authority or to protect themselves and the community.

As an Earth Elemental, I'm naturally drawn to the emerald. Watch what happens when I wield my magic with and without the relic's assistance."

With a confident flourish, she lifted a hand and conjured a glowing green orb into existence. It was about the circumference of an adult fist, but when she picked up one of the emeralds on her desk, the orb flared brighter, instantly tripling in size.

"Amplifying is an advanced skill and requires a higher level of control, so if you've never done it before, practice extreme caution," Professor Holt warned before returning the emerald to her desk. The green orb noticeably dimmed, then vanished as she dropped her hand. "One of the trials you'll face this year requires the use of amplifiers, so I suggest you choose your relic wisely. A poor connection could endanger your life and even doom you to failure."

That got my full attention. I knew that every witch responded to amplifiers differently, but what if my hidden heartstone interfered with my connection to another amplifier? Drawing on the combined power of two completely different relics could harm more than help me. My magic was unstable enough as it was, and I could only imagine how dangerous it would become if I threw more unknowns at it.

With that troubling thought etched into my mind, my stomach lurched when Professor Holt called me up to test the amplifiers. I'd practiced with various stones before under Gran's watchful eye, so I already knew that my magic connected best with the darker ones. Black onyx and obsidian were great ability boosters, but my magic also paired well with amethyst and tanzanite.

The problem was, besides the heartstone, I hadn't touched an amplifier in nearly two years. I was out of practice with them. Even with the heartstone pressed against my skin for the past week, I hadn't drawn from it—not intentionally, anyway. I didn't know what to expect, and with Professor Holt plus an entire class of students watching me, my nerves could cause me to lose focus and put everyone here in danger.

A slight tremor shook my hand as I raised it to hover just above the stones without touching them. I immediately felt a pull to pick them up, their promise of power calling to my magic. I continued to avoid direct contact, my trembling increasing when I felt the darkness within me stir, drawn to so much potential power at my fingertips.

The heartstone isn't enough for you? I inwardly grumbled at it.

You do not use it. Or me, I could practically hear it hiss back.

Fair point.

I passed my hand over every gemstone. Once. Twice. Hesitating. Afraid to choose. On the third pass, someone behind me muttered, "Just pick one already."

Blaze.

"The connection process shouldn't be rushed," Professor Holt sternly chastised him before looking at me again, her expression softening. "Take your time, Winter. You're doing just fine."

Right. She had no idea just how *not* fine I was at the moment. One misstep, and I could put us all in grave jeopardy.

Just when I thought I wouldn't be able to choose, making it clear to the entire class that something truly was wrong with me, my hand passed over a deep purple stone and stopped.

The amethyst.

This one, my intuition firmly said. *Choose this one*.

Swallowing hard, I decided to listen to the prodding voice in my head and scooped up the stone. It settled against my palm, cold and lifeless. But when I lifted my other hand to conjure an orb, at the same time coaxing the stone to respond to my magic, it burst awake, instantly warming my skin. My orb tripled in size and flared brightly, the scent of a crisp winter's evening after a heavy snowfall permeating the air.

"Good," Professor Holt said, nodding in satisfaction. "Your connection is strong."

A relieved sigh silently fled me, and I allowed myself to relax a little. It was okay. I was okay. One relic was awake while the other lay dormant. As long as they weren't both activated at the same time, I should be perfectly—

Before I could finish the thought, my chest started to warm. No, not my chest, I realized with horror. My necklace. My *heartstone.*

It was awakening, responding to the command I'd given the amethyst. Panicking, I dropped the stone in my hand. It hit the edge of the desk and clattered to the floor, just as a powerful wave of energy rushed through my veins and ignited my magical orb. In an instant, I lost all control. With a loud *whoosh*, the orb transformed into a massive ball of destruction.

"Winter!" Professor Holt shouted, raising her hands to contain the angry magic.

Too late.

The twisting ball violently erupted in a spray of lethal shadows. The dark strands became razor-edged like obsidian blades, transforming into deadly shrapnel and hitting anything in their path—including me. Pain sliced through my cheek before I could protect myself, several students crying out as the magic found other victims as well.

As fast as the magic erupted, it vanished, but the destruction in its wake was catastrophic. Something warm trickled down my cheek, and when I lifted a hand to touch it, my fingers came away red with blood.

"What the hell?" an irate voice barked. Still reeling from what had happened, I didn't see Blaze jump up from his seat until it was too late. "You did that on purpose, you little freak, and I'm gonna make you pay!"

The furious Fire Elemental stormed toward me, blood from a deep cut right above his left eye dripping down his face. Flames engulfed both his hands as he prepared to retaliate, and the heartstone's heat intensified, a fierce need to defend myself rushing through my veins.

It all happened so fast that I thought for sure an altercation was unavoidable. The tension between me and the hotheaded warlock had reached a boiling point, and if I didn't meet him head on, he was going to kill me.

Already awakened and raring to go, the darkness inside me pushed to the surface. So close to getting what it wanted, I felt how eager it was, how excited. Excited to be unleashed, to be used. But that wasn't all, I realized with shock.

I could feel how much it wanted to hurt. To maim. To *kill*.

Horrified. *Terrified*. I burst into action, doing the only thing I could.

I fled.

Willing my body to disappear into the shadows, I slipped away before Blaze could use his bright flames to discover my position.

"You can't hide forever, you coward!" he roared after me. "You're mine, do you hear me? *Mine*."

Professor Holt shouted something at him, but the words were lost to me. I was already gone, slipping from the classroom and out into the hall, escaping the havoc I'd just wreaked like a guilty thief. The second I was out of sight, I released the shadows and ran. I didn't know where I was going, only that I needed to get far, far away. From the chaos. From Blaze. From *myself*.

But no matter how hard I tried, I couldn't escape who I was. I'd kept it bottled up. I'd ignored it. I'd done everything I could think of to deny its existence. But it was still there. Still waiting in the darkness. Still anticipating the moment when I'd slip up, when I accidentally set it free.

And I had. I'd *really* screwed up this time. How could I face anyone after that epic disaster? It was two years ago all over again, and I couldn't breathe. Couldn't cope as the awful memories started to crowd back in, painfully reminding me of why I'd chosen not to send in my application to Heartstone in the first place.

Somehow, I managed to stumble into one of the bathrooms without anyone seeing me. My chest was on fire, the memories plunging me into a downward spiral of panic and despair. I fell against the sink counter, gripping it for dear life as I shook like a leaf. Drowning, unable to find relief with even a single shed tear, I lifted my heavy head and stared into the mirror. The pale girl in it stared back, her equally pale eyes wide with desperation and guilt, so much *guilt*.

"Oh, Jewel," I choked out, watching my face crumple in abject misery. "I never should have come here. I'm sorry. I'm so sorry for f-failing you, for *everything*."

Strangled gasps left me as I struggled for air, the pain in my chest less than I deserved. I didn't know how much time passed, but the pain eventually faded enough for me to breathe again. The guilt remained, though. It never went away, forever haunting me lest I forget the grave sins I'd committed.

I'd just dampened a paper towel to clean the cut on my cheek when the bathroom door burst open, smacking the wall with a *bang*. I whirled, my spine snapping straight when Thorne stormed inside, heading straight for me. In an instant, he had me pinned against the counter, a sharp *zap* lighting up my insides as his arms brushed against mine. He trapped me between them, his hands coming down to grip the counter on either side of me.

The rest of his body didn't touch mine, but his *face*. Ancestors save me, his face was inches away, so close to mine that all I could see—all I could *smell*—was him.

"Do you have a death wish?" he bit out, his hot breath hitting my face and stirring my hair.

I struggled to swallow, leaning back on the counter as much as possible. The bare inch of space between our faces felt charged, *electric*. I could practically hear it crackling.

"Answer me!" he snapped, making me flinch.

Yes.

"No," I replied, my voice too quiet. Too subdued.

His eyes noticeably darkened, *hardened*. He didn't believe me. Still, he said, "Then why the hell did you *run* from that fight?"

I blinked. Seriously? He was angry that I'd run, not that my magic had *injured* people? Too drained to dredge up my own anger and disgust, I reached up to push him back. His chest was rock hard, the muscles firm and unrelenting. Not in the mood to marvel at his strength—or the fact that I was touching him—I pushed harder, *shoved*. He might as well be made of stone for all the good it did.

"Let me go," I demanded, my voice a little stronger than before.

But not enough. Not *nearly* enough.

One of his hands let go of the counter. Before I could take advantage of the escape route, he flashed that hand up and caught my chin. I jerked back in shock and broke his hold, then scrambled to make my escape. He stopped me in an instant, wrapping that hand around my neck instead, my *throat*. As his fingers squeezed, hard enough to cut off my air, I froze, my eyes flying wide.

Was this it, then? Had I finally made him snap?

Fear pumped through me as I stared into the depths of those fierce blue eyes, knowing that he could end my life in a split second. But there was a feeling of relief too, one I couldn't seem to quell every time this man held my life in his hands. It would be easy, so easy for him to take it. I couldn't deny that a part of me still wanted him to.

"Do it," I whispered aloud, even though I hadn't meant to.

His gaze dropped to my traitorous lips, darkening even more. "Don't tempt me," he rumbled back, the words warming my mouth.

His fingers spasmed on my throat, further digging into the vulnerable flesh before sliding up to my jaw. Firming his grip again, he forcibly turned my head to the side and picked up the discarded paper towel from the counter. As he raised it to my face, I stopped breathing, preparing for the pain. But unlike the unyielding hold he still had on my jaw, the swipe across my injured cheek was soft. Gentle.

"The cut is too deep," he said after a moment. "It'll scar if you don't take Sano."

My skin hummed, warming beneath his touch. It was suddenly all I could feel, making the pain disappear. Flustered, I tried to pull away again. This time, he let me, finally dropping his arms and straightening. I looked everywhere but at him, more confused than ever when I noticeably felt colder at the absence of his touch.

He could have *strangled* me. Hell, he'd been tempted to. So why did I suddenly feel . . . disappointed?

Great. I really *did* have a death wish.

Before I could sort out my messy feelings, he tossed the bloodied paper towel in the trash and headed for the door, muttering, "Let's go."

I stiffened all over. "What? No. I'm not going out there yet. I just . . . I need a few more minutes to clean up."

He stopped dead in his tracks, then slowly turned around again. I met his gaze and immediately regretted it, realizing that I'd once again pissed him off. Ever so slowly, he came toward me, each movement controlled, *coiled*—like a prowling predator who'd trapped his prey. He came and came, filling my world with only him once more.

Only when he was inches away, when his closeness forced me to tip my head way back in order to maintain eye contact, did he finally stop and quietly grit out, "Do you think you're special, Snowflake? Do you think I *care* that you're embarrassed to be seen with an injury your own magic inflicted? Well, guess again. You're not the damsel in distress here, and I'm most definitely not your knight in shining armour. I only care about *winning*, something I can't do if you run and hide every time you're afraid. So I'll say it one more time before I *drag* you out of here. Let's. Go."

As his threat washed over me, any lingering warmth I might have felt from his touch vanished. A cold, albeit quiet fury took its place, so potent that it took everything in me not to spit in his face. Instead, I wiped my expression clean of all emotion, not giving him the satisfaction of seeing how upset his words made me.

He stared at me for another beat, then turned for the door again. Curling my trembling hands into fists, I followed after him, my fury growing with each step.

I hate you, I threw at his back as he exited the bathroom, the only words in my head for the next several minutes. Every time we went down another hallway. *I hate you.* Every time we climbed another set of stairs. *I hate you.* Every time we passed by an ogling student. *I hate you, I hate you, I hate you.*

By the time we reached our destination, my mood was so dark that I could have strangled *him*. Realizing that he'd taken me to the infirmary didn't make me feel any better. He only wanted to erase the cut on my face before it scarred, because a scar represented failure, and failure was not an option for his little *student*.

But when we entered the wing, I noticed with a sinking heart that I wasn't the only injured one who needed Sano. Several first years were milling about, all of them from my Amplifying class. Fresh guilt battered me when I saw how many had been cut by my magic.

"There she is!"

The sound of someone charging toward us had my gaze flicking down the aisle. At the sight of Blaze, my heart dropped into my stomach. He was coming right at me like a bull, murder burning in his eyes. Before I could do anything, before I could so much as blink, a wall of pure muscle slid in front of me, blocking my view of him.

"Out of my way, Prefect," Blaze growled, too incensed to taper his sharp tone. I peeked around my unexpected shield as Blaze ground to a halt less than a foot away, the veins protruding from his neck. Thorne was a few inches taller, but Blaze was built like the Hulk. Not that size really mattered in our world when it came to strength. Some of the most powerful witches in history were my size or smaller. Still, Blaze looked ready to punch Thorne if he didn't move soon.

"Back off, McGrath," Thorne ordered, his quiet tone laced with authority. "You're not touching her while I'm here."

"Then leave," Blaze snarled back. "She attacked me. Her blood is mine."

"And you attacked her first. I'd call that evening the score," Thorne replied with bite.

Blaze's eyes narrowed, his mouth twisting into a leer. "Oh, I see. You're protecting the stray now. What changed? Did she start sucking your dick or something?"

Thorne moved. Lightning quick, he grabbed Blaze's shirt collar and yanked him close before saying in a deadly rumble, "Your foul mouth is going to be the end of you, first year. Spout off like that again, and I'll become your worst enemy. Now get out of my face before I teach you a lesson you won't soon forget."

He dropped his hands back to his sides, but his body remained rigid, prepared to fight. Blaze was equally tense, his chest furiously heaving from being publicly dressed down by the Head Prefect. He glared at Thorne for a solid beat, then must have finally realized how precarious his situation was.

His eyes flicked over the room, noticing that a crowd had formed, drawn to the possibility of an altercation. They looked eager, *excited* to witness a brawl between the Head Prefect and a first year. There was no doubt in my mind who they thought would win.

When I glanced back at Blaze, I found his attention now fixed on me. Instead of cowering at his hateful look, I returned it with equal intensity, channeling all the gall I felt at his lewd "sucking dick" comment.

He curled his lip at me, defeated for the moment but not done with me by a long shot. Without another word, he brushed past us and stormed from the infirmary. When the doors closed behind him, our audience continued to linger, staring at us with open curiosity. I could practically *hear* their swirling, invasive thoughts.

Was Thorne protecting me?

Was I sucking his dick?

The silent speculation made heat crawl up my neck. Thorne ignored them, resuming his course as if nothing had happened.

"I need a bottle of Sano, Dr. Haywood," he said upon spotting the doctor who'd practically shoved the pungent elixir down my throat a week ago. The middle-aged woman with graying brown hair brightened at the sight of him, but her smile slipped when she saw me.

“For her?” she asked, her lips puckering in disapproval.

“Does it matter?” Thorne rebutted, and the woman blinked at him in surprise.

“No, of course not, Mr. Hudson. I’ll get that bottle for you right away.”

She hurried to do his bidding, and I stared after her, more than a little disturbed by how quickly she’d deferred to him. They truly did treat him like royalty around here, a fact that annoyed me but would make Gran absolutely livid.

The Hudsons aren’t royalty, she would say. *They stole our crown from us, those backstabbing traitors.*

Even so, I couldn’t reinstate our position in the community by demanding special treatment. I might have hated how Thorne had spoken to me earlier, but he hadn’t been wrong. I wasn’t special here. If I wanted to be treated with the respect given to the Mayweather family for centuries, the respect they’d since lost, then I’d have to fight for it.

But earning anyone’s respect around here was proving to be harder than I could have imagined. After the chaos I’d just unleashed, I doubted even Professor Holt would look at me with kindness anymore.

Dr. Haywood quickly returned and handed Thorne a dark blue bottle. “Do you need help with the dosage?”

“No, I’ve got it, Dr. Haywood. Thank you,” he replied, earning himself another smile. A smile that soured again when she looked at me before moving to tend another student. “You sure have a lot of enemies,” he said the moment she left us, turning to head down the aisle.

You know why, I wanted to snap at him. Instead, I muttered, “Guess that makes me a special snowflake.”

A sound left him, a scoff that couldn't hide his amusement. Look at me making my mentor laugh. Miracles did happen.

When he stopped by an empty cubicle, waiting for me to join him, I suddenly realized what was about to happen. Um, nope. We weren't doing this again.

"You don't have to help me," I told him, reaching for the bottle he held. "I'm very familiar with Sano and know how to administer the right dosage."

"Tough," he replied, holding the bottle up just out of reach. "First years aren't allowed to take potions without supervision, including Sano."

I dropped my arm, frustration pricking my chest. "Seriously? I'm in the infirmary surrounded by doctors."

He didn't respond, his resolute expression saying it all. *Get your butt in here or you'll be dragged.*

I dug my nails into my palms, narrowing my eyes to slits. He didn't even blink, his self assurance *maddening.* Not wanting to make yet another embarrassing scene, I stalked into the cubicle and rigidly sat on the bed's edge. He sauntered in after me rather slowly, undoubtedly at my expense. He was enjoying this. Enjoying how *uncomfortable* it made me.

As he grabbed a cup from a cart nearby and pulled up a chair *way* too close to me, I struggled to hold still. All it took was a featherlight touch. A glancing brush as he stretched his long leg out beside mine and *ZAP!*

"Would you quit it?" I hissed, squeezing my thighs together to make myself smaller. Why? Why did he have to zap me every single time? It wasn't overly painful, but it threw me off balance, *demanding* my attention.

One corner of his mouth lifted. Not a lot, but enough that I suddenly knew, just *knew* he was doing it on purpose. He *wanted* me rattled. Wanted my attention. *All* of it.

Narcissistic sadist.

"I'm not the only one with enemies, you know," I chose to say out loud, watching his sadistic little smirk only grow at my not-so-veiled threat.

"I know. But you by far have the most, and anyone dumb enough to ally with you will have to take them on as well."

"Thanks for the reminder," I muttered. "Will you get on with it already? I need to take a long shower after this."

To wash off the feel of your hands on me, I said to myself but wished I had the nerve to say to his face.

He received the message clear enough anyway, and that stupid smirk disappeared.

Good. It was creepy seeing him smile. Distracting.

While he uncorked the bottle and began to carefully pour the dark elixir into a cup, a thought came to me, and I blurted, "How did you know where to find me anyway?"

"You left quite the mess in your Amplifying class, including a few drops of your blood," he replied without looking up at me. "I had Oz use it to track you."

Everything in me went cold. Blood rituals, no matter how small, were sacred. *Sacred.* I knew he hated me, but how could he *do* such a thing?

I was shocked, *furious*, but more than anything, I was terrified. Terrified of what else Thorne's friend had discovered about me with that blood. Oracles could read you, see *inside* you, and he could learn more from one drop of my blood than anything Thorne could ever tell him.

"That's sacrilegious. A complete invasion of privacy," I said, my voice trembling from all the emotions brewing inside me. "I didn't give him permission to use my blood."

Thorne stopped pouring to finally look at me. I tried to keep the emotions from my face, but judging by how still he'd suddenly become, I hadn't quite managed it. Studying me for a beat, he quietly said, "Relax. He only used the blood to draw a map of your location on the floor. None of your blood was ingested, and he properly disposed of it afterward."

I stared at him. Hard. Searching for a lie. When his gaze remained steady on mine, relief shuddered through me. I didn't respond, too busy shoving down all my emotions again. He handed me the cup of Sano, and I took it without comment, downing it in one go. The foul-tasting potion speared down my throat like an ice cold vomit cocktail, immediately searching for injury. Within seconds, it found the cut on my cheek and began to knit it shut.

As I reached up to touch it, Thorne grabbed my hand and murmured, "Wait."

My eyes flew back to his, but his focus was on my cheek. While he watched the cut heal, he continued to hold my hand as if he didn't realize it. Well, *I* sure did. Every inch of me was aware of his fingers wrapped around mine, not tightly in a demanding way, but firmly. *Securely*. My hand started to warm under his, my skin humming in a pleasant way.

Unsettled by my reaction to his touch, I twisted my hand free of his hold. He let it go, slowly straightening when I abruptly stood from the bed and scooted away.

"Are we done here?" I asked, looking everywhere but at him as he corked the bottle and rose from his chair.

"Yes."

"Good." I whirled to get away as fast as I could, but I wasn't fast enough.

"Training begins tomorrow," he called after me, freezing me in my tracks. "What happened today can't happen again, so you'll be working with me to control your magic. Every day during your free period, we'll meet at the glen. You know the spot."

I nodded that I'd heard, then quickly fled the infirmary. Training? With *him?* I shuddered from head to toe, knowing without a shadow of doubt that Thorne Hudson was about to make my life a living nightmare.

CHAPTER 13

The clouds overhead were thin enough that I could see hints of the sun for the first time in over a week. Thorne's hawk was circling high above on the hunt for prey, and the woods almost looked inviting for once instead of menacing. But I couldn't stay focused on my serene surroundings.

Not when Thorne was stripping again.

That and the arrival of his two friends made the nerves in my stomach do somersaults.

He'd just placed his tie and blazer on a nearby rock and started to roll up his white shirtsleeves when he caught me staring. Our eyes locked, and I immediately wanted to look away in embarrassment. Knowing he'd only see that as *weakness*, I kept my eyes on him, praying my cheeks weren't bright red.

At least he'd kept his shirt on this time. Those forearms, though. Why did it immediately become harder to concentrate now that they were exposed?

Annoyed at myself, I blurted the first thing I could think of. "What are they doing here?"

Thorne broke our stare to glance at his friends, which instantly allowed me to breathe easier. "Riku and Oz have agreed to observe our training sessions. Every move you make at this academy is under scrutiny, so our sessions shouldn't be any different. Think of them as an audience waiting for you to mess up. That way, you'll try harder not to."

Great, just what I needed right now. An audience to witness Thorne handing my butt to me.

It was on the tip of my tongue to protest, but Thorne must have anticipated it, continuing before I could open my mouth, "The more you desensitize yourself to the constant pressures of performing, the faster you'll acclimate. Those who continue to cave under the pressure don't make it. There were nearly two hundred students my first year here. That number was cut in half by the end of the year, then again the next year, leaving only fifty of us left. Many quit, some died, and a few took their own lives. But the number one reason why they failed was their inability to cope with the pressure. It's why the school board voted to incorporate a mentorship program this year. Heartstone was losing too many students."

"And parents were beginning to complain," Riku added, jauntily crossing his arms over his chest as he joined our group. When I glanced over at him, he gave me a saucy smirk.

Ignoring it, I asked, "So the mentorship program was a political move, then? To appease the families so they wouldn't try to have the school shut down?"

"They would never do that," Oz replied, coming to stand on Thorne's other side. Being this close to all three of them again was overwhelming, but I was too focused on the unsettling conversation to care right now. Sliding his hands into his pockets, Oz went on, "The families might be upset about the fatality rate at Heartstone, but they would never have it shut down. They want the Conclave of Magic to be a success just as much as we do and wouldn't dream of sabotaging our chance at earning spots on the council."

Oh. So the students weren't the only cutthroat ones. Their families were too.

"This *is* political, then," I said, lifting my gaze to Thorne again. I shouldn't be surprised, but it still bothered me.

"Welcome to the top, Snowflake," he replied in a tone that was almost mocking. "Up here, everything's political."

What did you expect, singalongs around a campfire? his eyes seemed to say before he turned and strode several paces off into the grass in preparation of our training session.

Riku called after him, "*Snowflake?* Cute, man, considering her name. Not as cute as Bambi, though."

Done with all the insulting names, I snapped a little louder than planned, "Stop calling me Bambi. I'm not a male deer."

Riku glanced at me in surprise, and I braced myself, certain he was going to put me in my place for reprimanding him. Instead, his expression softened as if I'd said something adorable, and he cooed, "Aww, our Bambi has tiny claws, Ozzy. Too bad she doesn't like to be teased, because it makes me want to tease her even more."

At the scowl I gave him, Oz shook his head with a quiet laugh. "Careful, Ri. Those claws aren't as tiny as you think. I saw the damage they inflicted yesterday."

"Well, it's a good thing I like dangerous women," Riku all but purred, dropping his arms as he sauntered toward me. I stiffened at the mischievous glint in his dark eyes but valiantly stood my ground, even when he slid up beside me and breathed in my ear, "You can sink those claws into my back any time, *Bambi*."

The comment annoyed me, but it was what he did next that shoved me over the edge. I didn't *see* him do it, but I didn't need to. Only an Air Elemental could make a sudden gust of wind flip up my skirt high enough to expose my entire backside. I gasped and whirled on him, instant fury rushing through me when I saw that his gaze was fixed on my butt.

Staring. Teasing. *Mocking*. Humiliating me. *Shaming* me.

"No thong?" He tsked, amusement dancing in his eyes as they finally lifted to mine. "School-issued panties are so boring. I'll have to send you a pair of—"

"You *bastard!*" I roared, so angry, so *mortified* that I was no longer thinking. Something else took over, a swift and volatile need that demanded I defend myself, that ordered me to *fight*.

I wasn't going to take it again. I was done being made fun of. Done being ogled at like I was some *freak* show.

Dimly aware that I'd finally snapped under the pressure but was too enraged to care, I let the dark energy coiled inside me rise to the surface. Thrusting my hand out, I willed it to come forth, to attack the gloating warlock. Only, it wasn't really Riku I wanted to attack. It was Blaze, the warlock who'd pushed me closer and closer to the edge all week until I'd finally had enough.

But my moment of clarity came too late.

I'd already lost control. Already let the darkness burst from my skin like deadly obsidian knives.

Horrified, unable to do anything, I watched as the shadows streaked toward Riku. It all happened in an instant, so fast that he wouldn't be able to block the magic in time.

Murdererrr, my intuition hissed.

No! I inwardly screamed, cracking, *breaking* as I watched history repeat itself.

An inch away from striking Riku in the chest, my magic suddenly exploded, the shadows dispelling in thick plumes of harmless smoke. It looked like a wall had stopped my magic from hitting him, nearly transparent save for the streaks of light spidering over the surface. Streaks that looked a lot like a static charge, like *lightning*.

Before I could feel any relief that my attack had been thwarted, something from behind slammed into me. I fell forward and hit the ground *hard*, so hard that all the air left me in a violent *whoosh*. Stunned, I didn't do a thing as hands roughly flipped me over and pressed me into the grass, as a furious face filled my vision and bellowed, "Don't you *ever* do that again, you hear me?"

Shocked senseless, I stared into Thorne's wild eyes, certain I wasn't the only one who'd just snapped. He gripped my biceps hard enough to leave bruises, his hands violently shaking. But he wasn't just angry. The longer he held me down, the longer his eyes bored into mine, the more I realized that he was terrified.

Terrified of what, I wasn't sure. Of almost losing a friend? Of knowing history had nearly repeated itself? Of . . . of me?

I didn't know why, but the thought of him being afraid of me brought no satisfaction. It made me feel ashamed. Made me feel . . . made me feel bad. *Wrong*.

"I'm sorry," I choked out, struggling to breathe. Not from having the wind knocked out of me but from the massive amount of *guilt* sitting on my chest. "I didn't . . . I didn't mean to."

The exact words I'd said to him nearly two years ago.

He flinched as if I'd struck him. An emotion flickered in his eyes so fast that I almost missed it. Almost.

Pain.

My words, my actions, had caused him pain. *Again*.

I was a terrible, *terrible* person.

"Thorne, you're hurting her."

Oz's softly spoken words might as well have been a shout. Thorne let go of me in a flash, jumping to his feet and stumbling back a few steps. He stared down at me for another moment, emotion, so much *emotion* in that gaze. Thunder rumbled in the distance, and I knew, just *knew* it was because of him. Because of the emotions brewing inside him like a howling tempest.

Then, as if he'd slammed a wall down, the emotion vanished. Stone cold nothingness took its place, and I shivered at the terrible sight, unable to stop my chin from quivering. He took me in, something akin to hatred slowly bleeding into his eyes, and I died a little. Died as those eyes looked away, *dismissed* me.

Without a word, he turned on his heel and stalked away. Comet shot from the sky to follow after him, and as they disappeared from view, a deafening silence fell over the grassy glen.

My eyes started to burn, but as usual, no tears fell. Expecting Thorne's friends to leave as well, I blinked in shock when a hand laden with topaz rings lowered toward me. Riku's hand.

An offer of help. From the person I'd almost *killed*.

I hesitated, certain he intended to make me pay for what I'd done. Then again, I deserved whatever he threw at me, so I lifted my hand and placed it in his. He easily pulled me to my feet, then gave my hand a light squeeze before letting go. The faint pressure almost felt like reassurance, like *forgiveness*, and the burn in my eyes grew unbearable.

"I'm so sorry," I whispered, trying and failing to look him in the eye.

"Forget about it," he quietly said, the usual amusement in his voice gone. He almost sounded sad now, making me feel even worse. "I should have known something like that would trigger you after what Blaze did."

The depth of his understanding surprised me, especially since it was him. He might be an arrogant playboy, but maybe I'd been too quick to judge his character.

"I really . . . I really screwed up," I tentatively said, still not sure how much they knew about what had happened two years ago.

Erring on the side of caution, I lamely finished with, "He won't want anything to do with me after this."

"Oh, Bambi," Riku softly groaned, reaching out as if to draw me into a hug. When I flinched back, he raised both hands placatingly. "Too soon, I get it. You'll surrender to my charm eventually, though. They always do."

I met his eyes to glare at him, and his lips twisted into a satisfied smirk.

"He's upset, but he'll get over it," Oz finally spoke in a serious tone, drawing my gaze to him. "Thorne is unfailingly committed to whatever he takes on, and that includes his mentoring of you. He might be pissed right now, but that won't stop him from honoring his word."

He studied me for another beat, his brows deeply furrowing the longer he stared. He opened his mouth, then shut it. Opened and shut it again.

Unease trickled through me. What did he see? What did he *know?*

"We should head inside. It's about to storm," Riku said, interrupting the uncomfortable moment. I looked to the sky, glad for the distraction, but my heart immediately sank at how fast the weather had turned. Dark, angry clouds were swiftly rolling in, completely blotting out the sun. More thunder rumbled in the distance, reminding me of the look in Thorne's eyes before his expression had gone stone cold.

Anger, pain, and fear all fighting for dominance, all directed at *me*. He might still mentor me after this, but he'd been triggered today, too. So deeply that hatred had simmered in his eyes.

The storm about to unleash its fury on us was proof of just how badly I'd messed things up. He might train me, but he was going to make me pay for it.

And he did.

Over the next several days, I learned exactly how Thorne had earned his ruthless reputation. Training with him was pure hell, not because he shouted in my face and called me names like a drill sergeant, but because he was coldly relentless. I wasn't allowed to think, wasn't allowed to *breathe.* He wanted results, and he wouldn't stop pushing until he got them.

Problem was, I couldn't give him what he wanted.

On top of our sessions, I was still struggling to sleep, keep up with my classes, and avoid confrontations. Blaze hadn't directly come at me again, but rumors about my magic mishap in Amplifying class had spread to the entire campus, leaving me more ostracized than ever. I'd even overheard a first year say that Blaze was forming alliances with other students who felt personally victimized by me. And then there was the gossip about me and Thorne, about him offering me protection for sexual favors.

It was all too much. Despite how badly I wanted to prove myself worthy of being here, I was failing. I knew it. The other students knew it. The professors knew it. And Thorne *definitely* knew it.

What I'd almost done to Riku hovered like a stormcloud over our heads every time we met for training. Each interaction was fraught with frigid tension, and no matter what I said, Thorne's responses remained icy. His merciless tactics wore me to the bone, but it was the cold looks and curt words devoid of any warmth that were starting to unravel me.

He loathed me. *Hated* me. I'd already known this, but as the days dragged into weeks, it became harder and harder to bear. He took great care to keep space between us at all times, and if our skin accidentally touched, he zapped me *hard*, a clear warning to get the hell away.

I was toxic to him, and the more we interacted, the more dangerous it became for both of us.

We were going to snap again. It was only a matter of time. And with tensions this high, I worried about our pactum. Neither of us had been hurt during our training sessions yet, but if he kept pushing, pushing, *pushing*, I was bound to break.

After nearly a month of watching this deadly dance, Oz and Riku finally had enough. I waited for them to arrive at the glen for our daily session, growing more and more nervous by the second when they didn't show. They always showed. *Always.* Their presence was the only thing keeping me and Thorne from completely tearing into each other. Without them here, we were doomed.

A shriek lit up the gloomy sky as Thorne's familiar swooped overhead, seeking out prey as usual. When Thorne arrived with his usual curt nod of acknowledgement and got right down to removing his blazer and tie, the tension became too much, and I blurted, "Where are Riku and Oz?"

Without looking at me, he cryptically replied, "Not coming."

I pursed my lips, waiting for him to say more. When he didn't, I pressed, "Why?"

He ground his teeth together, a muscle furiously ticking in his jaw. Yanking the tie free of his neck, he said, "Watching this disaster has become too painful for them."

Disaster.

Did he mean me or *us?* Probably both.

Hurt and anger warred in my chest, but I didn't let it show. Any complaint, any show of emotion, immediately earned me a cold lecture from Thorne. Weakness of any kind wasn't tolerated, and arguing was met with stern resolve.

We were here for one reason only: to get my magic under control before it accidentally killed someone, before I *ruined* his perfect reputation.

But my resistance to his training techniques was making that impossible. It wasn't that I wanted to defy him. More than anything, I desperately needed the control over my magic that he possessed over his. But the thought of injuring someone again, of *killing* them, stopped me in my tracks every time.

It didn't matter that the only person who could get hurt was Thorne. It didn't matter that any injury would be deemed an accident. Despite his coldness to me this past month, the thought of harming him froze me with fear.

He might be punishing me for my sins, but I had no desire to punish him in return. Maybe that made me weak, but every time I thought about getting revenge, I remembered the look on his face when he'd found out what I'd done to his sister. The look of utter betrayal, the *devastation* would haunt me forever, and every decision I'd made since had been because of that tragic day.

Which was why I already knew how this training session today would end. In epic failure like the dozens before it.

But as Thorne squared off with me in the grassy field like he'd done every day for the past month, the determined glint in his gaze was extra hard. After a month of enduring his hard looks, the one he was giving me now sent goosebumps skittering over my flesh. He was done being patient with me. Done *waiting*. Today, I would either bend to his will . . .

Or break.

"Thorne," I warned, slowly backing up a step. If he didn't stop looking at me that way, this session was going to end with one or both of us killed.

Before I could say more, he widened his stance and said, "Attack me."

No hesitation. No room for argument. He meant business and demanded my full cooperation.

I tensed as the darkness within me responded to the order, more than happy to oblige. It didn't care if he or anyone else was injured, a fact that was becoming more and more clear to me by the day. Knowing that terrified me more than anything else. More than the threats I'd received since coming here, more than Thorne's cruel punishments, and even more than failing my family.

The darkness couldn't be controlled. It wouldn't *let* me control it.

Which was why my immediate response to Thorne's order was, "You know I won't."

He pressed his mouth into a thin bloodless line. "We've been over this dozens of times, Snowflake. I won't let your magic touch me. I'll block it before it can leave a single mark."

I stared at him for a beat, taking in that *stubborn* determination, before tossing my hands up in frustration. "You know I'm not going to attack you, so what's the *point* of all this?"

"The point?" he repeated, his voice so low that I realized just how close his patience was to breaking. "The point is *this*."

He threw his hand out, and it was the only warning I got before a white hot bolt of lightning streaked toward me. It happened so fast that I couldn't react. I wasn't even able to *blink* before the lightning tip was an inch away from penetrating my eyesocket. The searing heat pulsing from it triggered my instincts, and I finally stumbled back, nearly falling on my butt.

Shocked, *horrified* that I'd been an inch away from being struck by lightning, the tether on my emotions snapped, and I screamed at him, "Are you *insane?!*"

"No," he barked back, recalling the lightning as swiftly as it left.

With a *crack*, it returned to him, the tattoos on his arms absorbing the energy. His gaze was dark, dangerous as he pinned it on me and spoke in a deathly quiet tone, "My magic is an extension of me and does *exactly* what I tell it to. Not for an instant do I allow it free will. If you can't learn to control your magic like that, then you'll fail in the upcoming trials. Now stop wasting my time and *attack* me."

Still shaking from how close he'd come to skewering me, I stammered, "I-I can't."

"Why not?"

"I just *can't*."

His brows slammed down, darkening his eyes even more. He took a step, then another, prowling toward me in a way that had all the hair on my body standing on end. "Do you think I'm afraid of you?"

He kept coming, and it took all of my strength not to run, to *hide*.

"*Answer* me."

The sharp command loosened my tongue, and I burst out, "Yes."

His hands formed tight fists, his gaze unrelenting. "The other students are afraid of you, including the professors. It's why they act the way they do toward you. They fear what you could *do* to them."

I stopped breathing as he halted inches away, forcing my neck to crane back. He lowered his head until our faces were a hair's breadth apart, the closest he'd been to me in weeks. His heat wafted over me, along with his wild scent, making my heart thunder erratically.

"I'm going to let you in on a little secret, Snowflake," he rumbled in an octave so low that it vibrated his chest. "Fear is what keeps you alive in a place like this. Fear is what gives you control. But if you allow that fear to control *you*, you're dead. Yes, I'm afraid of you, but not in the way you think. I fear you like a mortal fears a venomous snake. I'd be stupid not to. But I don't let that fear control me, unlike you."

"I . . . I don't—"

"Don't *lie* to yourself, Snowflake," he snapped, cutting me off. "You're afraid of me and my magic, which is smart. It's called self-preservation. But you're also afraid of yourself and your own magic. You're afraid of that most of all, so much so that you've allowed fear to *paralyze* you."

I stared at him unblinking, shocked that he'd figured me out so completely. He might as well have just shined a spotlight on the deepest, darkest parts of me. I couldn't run anymore, couldn't hide. He knew me. *Knew* me. So well that there was no point in denying his words. He'd only see them for the lie they were.

When it was clear that he'd found the root of my hesitation, something in his expression shifted. For the first time in weeks, cold cruelty didn't stare back at me. It had softened into something new, an emotion I never expected him to direct toward me.

Empathy.

"Train with me, Snowflake," he quietly said without any of the usual bite. "Turn your fear into a weapon. Use it to aid you, not control you. I won't ask again."

More like demanded, but at least he was demanding politely.

Still, I couldn't give him what he wanted, no matter how much I wished to. Not with magic like mine.

"I'm sorry," I whispered, watching with a sinking heart as that coldness returned.

"Then we're done here," he said, each word like chips of ice. "I can't help someone who won't help themselves. This is your last warning, Snowflake. Leave, or you *will* die."

He straightened and brushed past, obviously done with me. But as he stormed away, the blood in my veins froze, horror gripping me when I replayed his last words.

"Leave, or you will die."

Leave or die.

Leave. Or. Die.

"It was you," I breathed, turning around. Thorne slowed, then stopped dead when I said more loudly, "It was *you*."

My accusation slapped through the air, and he pivoted to face me once more. One look at his expression, and I *knew* that I was right.

"How could you?" I said, my voice shaking as a slew of emotions rose up. I didn't bother hiding them, wanting, *needing* him to see just how betrayed I felt. "I was terrified by that bloody message on my mirror. It made me lose sleep for *weeks!*"

He stared at me, taking in my anger, my *hurt*. "Winter—"

"No!" I snapped, balling my trembling hands into fists. "You don't get to finally say my name just because you were caught. What you did was beyond spiteful. You have no idea how . . . how *scared* I've been."

As soon as I admitted the words, I wished I could take them back. It was just one more truth, one more *weakness* he could use against me.

"I admit, I left the message to scare you into leaving," he said, and somehow hearing the confession out loud was ten times worse. "I didn't want to mentor you or be near you. I still don't, and I still don't think you'll make it out of here alive. But I stopped Blaze's attack in your Conjuring class and again in the infirmary. I could have stood by and let him kill you, but I didn't."

Shock sliced through me once more. *He* had been the one to block that fireball from incinerating me? Him and not Professor Seacrest? The admission was clearly meant to appease me, to smooth my prickly feathers, but screw that.

Marching toward him, beyond done trying to keep things civil between us, I spat, "Do you want an award, *Head Prefect?* You only stopped those attacks to save face, to protect your precious reputation. You yourself admitted that winning is all you care about, that my failure will reflect poorly on your leadership skills. You're doing all of this for *you*, not for me. You're stuck with me, and you hate it. You hate *me*. Admit it!"

"I *do* hate you!" he roared, freezing me in my tracks.

"And I hate *you!*" I roared back, hating that my eyes had begun to burn.

Anger, so much *anger* sparked in his eyes, but it was far better than stone-cold nothingness. The heat pouring off him was palpable, mixing with mine. And for one sadistic, unhinged moment, I didn't feel completely alone anymore. We were equally mad, equally hurt, equally hateful. It didn't make any sense, but knowing that he felt the same as me made all of this a little more bearable.

We stared at each other for a long beat, the tension between us supercharged. Then, without a word, he whirled and stormed off again.

It was the last straw.

A furious cry erupted from me, and so did my magic. As I felt it start to leave me, I raised my hand. Not toward Thorne, but toward the treeline several yards off. Like a whip, the dark magic sliced through the air, striking its target with deadly accuracy.

I froze. So did Thorne.

We both looked to the trees at the same time, just as a stout pine groaned and cracked, toppling over to hit the ground with a resounding *boom*.

I stared. Stared and stared.

Silence descended over the clearing again, until Thorne slowly turned to me and said, "Feel better?"

I blinked. Blinked again. Then murmured, "Yes."

"Good," he said, the slightest hint of satisfaction in his voice as he turned to leave again. "Then we'll meet back here tomorrow."

CHAPTER 14

The feeling of being watched pricked at my skin.

I peeked through the shower curtain, but the bathroom was empty save for me. At this time of night, it should be. Ever since Blaze had publicly humiliated me my first week here, I'd been taking showers late at night, the later the better. It was nearing midnight now, which was the best time to take showers since no one wanted to be caught out of their dorms once the clock tower tolled twelve. I always made it back to my own room in time, but the closer to midnight it was, the less chance I'd run into Blaze, Alma, or any of the other students out for my blood.

Chalking up the eerie prickly feeling to paranoia, I finished my cold shower and quickly toweled off my body. Unlike a lot of the students, I didn't feel comfortable strutting up and down the halls in only a bath towel, so I always brought my pajamas with me. They were school-issued, of course, consisting of black yoga-style pants and a white fitted t-shirt. I put them on, not bothering with a bra. Collecting my things, I made for the sinks and quickly brushed my teeth.

With minutes to spare, I poked my head out of the bathroom. All clear. Tiptoeing down the hall, I made for the end and soundlessly opened the door to my tower. As it shut behind me, I breathed easier, relieved that I'd managed another hassle-free shower. Navigating the five flights of stairs without a light had become the norm for me, so I slid up them in the dark, confident I would sleep like the dead tonight for the first time in weeks.

My training session with Thorne earlier today had been eye-opening, to say the least. We'd both admitted to things, things that I couldn't stop replaying in my head. But despite how preoccupied my mind had been after that session, finally knowing who had left that bloody message on my mirror was a huge relief. The threat had been real, but Thorne had only meant for it to scare me into leaving. I'd thought for sure it had been a death threat from Blaze or Alma, so knowing it wasn't them would allow me to sleep a lot more soundly.

I'd just reached the top of the stairs when that feeling of being watched skittered over me again. I paused and listened. When there was no sound of anyone following me up the stairs, I moved to the door and raised my hand, swiftly uttering the spell that would open it.

"*Sesamum, te aperi.*"

Yes, making the password *open sesame* was kind of lame, but it was easy to remember and better than no protection at all. At least it kept unwanted visitors out, which was everyone here.

As the spell fell away, I opened the door just as the clock tower started to toll. *Bong*. Well, that was close. Maybe I shouldn't push my showers back *quite* so close to midnight.

Shutting the door behind me, I did my usual cursory sweep of the room, double-checking that all was as I'd left it. Even with the protections in place, remaining cautious had kept me alive this long. I didn't take any chances and would continue to be careful, even with the knowledge that the mirror message had only been a scare tactic.

I checked the room over. Once. Twice. Everything was in its place, down to the flickering candles on my desk. As I focused on those candles, something about my desk made me pause. Crossing to the bed, I set my towel and toiletries down before moving toward the desk. Only the candles and a solitary spellbook covered the scratched brown surface. My notebook was on the bed, along with my other school-issued supplies.

But there was something off about the spellbook. It *looked* the same, but the longer I stared at it, the more uneasy I felt.

"It's just a harmless book," I scolded myself. "You're sleep deprived and paranoid."

But the feeling wouldn't fade. It grew and grew, twisting my stomach into knots as the bell continued to toll. *Bong.*

Annoyed that I was starting to feel unsafe in my own room again, I swept over to the book and picked it up.

"See? There's nothing to—"

A sharp bite of pain stung my palm. Startled, I glanced down just as a thin red line stretched across my skin. When blood seeped out and pooled in my hand, I dropped the book and stumbled back. As it thumped to the stone floor, pain sliced through my other palm. I lifted that one too, shocked when another thin line ripped open my skin. Blood leaked out, quickly forming a little puddle, and I rushed to the bed to grab my towel. But when I wrapped my hands in the white fabric to staunch the bloodflow, another sting lit up my flesh, this time on my wrist.

"What the hell?"

I watched with growing alarm as more blood slid out of me. Before I could press the reddening towel to the cut, another flare of pain sliced through my other wrist. Blood seeped out and dripped to the floor from both wrists, and when another cut formed a few inches higher only seconds later, panic started to set in.

Bong.

Cut. Cut. Cut.

Bong.

Cut. Cut. Cut.

By the time the bell had finished tolling twelve, I had more than a dozen cuts up both arms. Blood dripped steadily onto the floor, leaving my body at an alarming rate. When pain sliced through my neck, followed by the warmth of trickling blood, I knew I was in trouble.

"Stop!" I yelled at the cuts, only for another to form moments later. "*Cessa!*"

Terror gripped me when nothing I did slowed the cuts from forming. One sliced across my sternum, and I watched in horror as my white shirt bloomed red.

"Amulet, protect me. Pentacle, save me," I chanted, reaching up to grasp the necklace with bloodied fingers.

Cut. Cut.

The darkness within me stirred, drawn awake by the threat and my fear. For once, I didn't try to shove it back down right away. I called to it, beseeched it for help, my desperation to stop these cuts overriding everything else. It immediately came to my aid, rising up and manifesting into angry billowing shadows. They curled and whipped around my body, seeking out the threat, prepared to eviscerate it. But the more they sought, the more confused they seemed to become.

Cut. Cut.

The shadows faltered, unable to find the threat's source. They started to recede, to fade, and my alarm grew tenfold.

"No, don't leave. I need help!" I shouted at them. They sank into my skin once more, abandoning me to my fate. "*Seriously?*"

A wave of weakness stole over me, making me sway on my feet. No, no, no, no. I was losing too much blood. I was going to pass out soon if this didn't stop. Or worse.

I stared at my reflection in the mirror across the room, mortified by my bloodied state. *Death by a thousand cuts* came to mind, and as another one painted my shirt red, fear sealed my throat shut.

Go! a voice whispered, little more than a distant echo. It sounded so much like *her* that I suddenly knew exactly what to do. Stumbling across the room, I ripped open the door. My bloodied fingers lost their grip, and the door loudly banged against the wall. I didn't bother shutting it behind me, tucking my bleeding arms close to my chest as I staggered down the five flights of stairs.

More than once, I almost slipped and fell in the dark. A fall down these stone stairs would definitely break a few bones, maybe even my neck. I definitely didn't need *that* on top of everything else. Every few steps, a new cut sliced through my skin, allowing blood to saturate my clothing and leave a trail in my wake. I winced each time, the cuts starting to burn the more I moved. By the time I made it to the bottom, I was sweating, my breaths ragged and my heart frantically pounding.

I needed help. *Help*.

But when I closed in on the nearest dorm room, I stumbled right on past. They couldn't help me. They *wouldn't* help me. At the next door, I did the same thing, knowing in my bones that not a single soul in Jade Wing would come to my aid.

Dimly aware that I was breaking the out-past-midnight rule, I moved down the hall as silently as I could. Every few steps, a new cut burned my flesh, making me grit my teeth in pain. I kept going, kept dragging my body forward one step at a time. Just one more step. One more.

I didn't encounter a single soul as I staggered through hallway after hallway. Not even the professors were out. It felt like I was the only one here, and a huge part of me feared that I'd pass out in these hallways, that no one would find my body until morning when it was too late. I'd be bled dry by then, dead by a thousand cuts. Such a death seemed tragically beautiful, but I could also be growing delusional from all the blood loss.

Seconds became minutes became hours. At least, it felt that way. It felt like I'd been stumbling down hallways and lumbering up stairs for days. They never ended, and I silently cursed how massive this campus was. Eventually, the pain and blood loss got the best of me. I hit the stone floor hard, too weak to stand any longer.

So close. I was *so close.* I could feel it. *See* it. Only one more step. *One more.*

But I was spent. Trembling, exhausted, and racked with pain, I tried calling out and failed, my mouth drier than a desert. Frustrated, scared out of my mind, I did the only thing I could. I crawled. Inch by inch, I pulled myself forward.

Cut. Cut. *Cut.*

I dragged myself through my own blood, leaving a garish red streak in my wake. The blood was getting darker now. Not a good sign.

One more. Just one more.

Darkness edged my vision, making the hallway narrow and narrow. My frantic pulse began to slow, skipping every few beats. I dug my nails into the stones and pulled, desperate not to die in this blasted hallway. Not after everything I'd been through to get here.

A scent came to me anyway, settling over my skin like bitter smoke. Terror shot through me. Dirt. *No.* Decaying leaves. *No.* Despair. *No!*

I'm here, death breathed on my neck, scraping its icy fingers up my back.

NO!

I wasn't ready!

Just one more . . . One more step.

I collapsed in a heap, the last of my strength leaving me. As my vision went black, I raised my hand—one last effort, one last *stubborn* attempt to survive—and let it fall against the door.

Seconds passed. Minutes. Hours. *Days.*

The door clicked open.

CHAPTER 15

"Get me the Sano!" a voice roared, jarring me awake.

Strong arms came around me. Lifted me. Held me. I was weightless. Boneless. Helpless as someone picked me off the floor and carried me to who-knew-where.

Deep down, though, I wasn't afraid. Wasn't even alarmed. Instead, I felt . . . I felt relieved. Because I knew that voice, knew the rumbling timbre that sounded so much like distant rolling thunder.

I'd made it. I'd made it to my destination, and I was still alive. For now.

"Spirits and saints, is she—?" another voice said that I recognized.

"She's still alive but barely," the first answered, then bellowed again, "Oz, where the hell is that Sano?"

Chaos ensued. I couldn't see anything, but I heard several loud bangs as objects crashed to the floor. The arms around me shifted, disturbing numerous cuts all over my body. A sound escaped me. A pitiful whimper.

The voice above me swore, then gentled considerably. "Open your eyes for me, Snowflake. I need to see those big beautiful eyes."

I tried. I tried so hard to open them, but they were so heavy.

"I need a towel and bowl of water, Riku."

"On it."

As footsteps hurried away, something solid settled against my back and legs, pulling at more of my cuts. Another whimper left me, the only thing I seemed capable of doing at the moment.

"It's okay, Snowflake," the rumbling voice soothed. "I've got you now. You're safe."

Safe. I was *safe?* Not a word I ever expected him to say to me. I wanted so badly to contradict him, but not even my mouth would function.

"*Oz*," the voice barked, that anger not directed at me for once. The strong arms around me carefully fell away, barely agitating my injuries, but I knew he remained close by. I could feel him. Smell him. His scent swirled around me, shoving back the stench of death.

"Here," another familiar voice said. "She should take it all, Thorne. But it might not be enough to—"

"Don't say it," Thorne cut Oz off. "She's going to live. She *has* to."

Hands fell on me again. Gentle. So very gentle. They lifted my head up, cradled it.

"Did you hear that, Snowflake?" Thorne asked, his head so close to mine. "I won't let you die on me, so you'd better be prepared to fight. Now take this Sano like a good girl."

He lifted my head a little higher, and something cold touched my lips. A glass. A vial. I struggled to open my mouth, knowing he was trying to help me, knowing the Sano would *save* me.

Nothing. I didn't even have the energy for that.

Liquid moistened the crease of my lips anyway, but none of it got inside. Thorne viciously swore. "Oz, I need help."

More hands fell on me, coaxing my mouth open with firm pressure. That small action sent fiery pain through my face, making me aware that the cuts must have formed there too. I could only imagine how terrifying I looked right now, probably like death itself. The pressure didn't let up, allowing Thorne to pour the Sano into my mouth. As it started to slide down my throat, my gag reflex kicked in, forcing me to cough.

Agony ripped through me, setting my body, my *world* on fire. I tried to cry out but only choked more as the Sano mercilessly speared down my throat. Fingers massaged my neck, urging it down, down, down. The liquid kept coming and coming, persistent, *drowning* me. I was helpless to resist, unable to do anything but fight to keep breathing.

Time became pain, my body racked with convulsions as the Sano sought out the hundreds of cuts. One after the other, it attacked them, knitting the wounds shut and leaving me cold. *So* cold. Colder than I ever remembered feeling before.

"She needs heat," I dimly heard a voice say over the chattering of my teeth.

The hands on me shifted once more, and I was lifted again. As if I weighed no more than a feather, the arms supporting my back and legs carried me to a new location. But when they set me down this time, the surface beneath me wasn't flat like a table. Although solid, it intimately hugged my body, cradling me securely. When another full-body shiver racked me, the surface beneath me shifted in a way that felt like limbs. Like *legs*.

A lap. I was on someone's *lap*.

Hands guided my head to another solid surface, and when I heard a strong *thump-thump-thump-thump* beneath my ear, I knew that it was resting on a chest. One quick inhale confirmed whose body I was pressed against.

Thorne. I was cradled on Thorne Hudson's *lap*.

The need to get away trembled through me, but at the same time, a soothing warmth stole over my body. My shivering lessened, and my limbs ever-so-slowly started to relax, to *melt*. Into him. Into his blessed heat.

A deep exhaustion swamped me next, one that I knew I couldn't escape this time. It tugged and pulled, and I gladly let it to suck me under. Before it could completely devour me, something brushed my cheek, and I flinched.

"Go back to sleep, Snowflake," a soothing voice rumbled above me. "We won't let anything harm you."

I felt the brush along my cheek again moments later, but I knew what it was this time. A cloth. A warm one. Gently washing my blood away.

A relieved sigh shuddered from me, and I sank deeper into Thorne's warmth, finally allowing unconsciousness to claim me.

Regaining consciousness felt like clawing my way to the surface from deep underwater.

Everything was a struggle. Thinking. Breathing. Swallowing. Blinking. I tried moving, and my limbs felt like lead. When I finally managed to peel my dry eyes open, the first thing I saw was a blurry brown shape. Blinking to clear my vision, I focused on the shape again and froze when it materialized into a bird. And not just any bird. Thorne's *hawk* familiar.

He met my stare with an unblinking one, watching me in that hawky way of his. The animal was sitting on a wooden perch near the head of the bed, a bed that was *far* too comfortable to be mine. I stretched my hand out, feeling how silky the dark sheets were. The bed was large, probably a king size. Where the hell *was* I?

My gaze left the hawk and began to explore the rest of the room. Not far away was a stained-glass window. Barely enough light leaked through the panes to see, but I could clearly pick out shapes like a desk and chest of drawers. The door to the room was shut, but when I twisted my head around to see the other half of the bedroom, I spotted a figure sitting in a chair.

My heart leapt into my throat, nearly choking me. I jerked upright on the mattress, prepared to defend myself, but when the figure didn't move, I squinted harder through the gloom until I could make out their features.

What the hell?

It was *Thorne.*

Was I in his . . . his *room?*

His head was slightly tilted forward, allowing his tousled brown hair to fall across his cheeks and shadow his eyes. Judging by how still he was, I assumed he was fast asleep. Not in uniform for once, he wore a black t-shirt that hugged his chest and gray sweatpants. Seeing him so relaxed, so *vulnerable* was disconcerting.

As I watched him sleep, the events that brought me here suddenly came rushing back. The feeling of being watched, picking up the spellbook, the *cuts*. I didn't know how I'd managed to get to Thorne before completely bleeding out, but here I was. In his freaking bed.

The clock tower bell started to toll the hour, and at the first *bong*, I flinched, expecting a cut to form. Nothing happened. I glanced down at my arms, relieved to find that the cuts were gone.

That's right. They'd given me Sano. And I'd been so cold that Thorne had placed me in his lap to share his body heat.

I glanced at his lap now, at the way his legs were widely spread apart, and pictured my body securely between them.

Heat rushed into my cheeks, and I tore my gaze away, mortified that I'd fallen asleep on top of him. Spotting a glass of water on his nightstand, I reached for it and greedily gulped it down. As I did, the bell finished tolling the hour.

Six o'clock?

Panicking, I scrambled out of bed, nearly tangling in the sheets and falling flat on my face. A rustling of wings startled me, and I glanced behind me to see an agitated Comet.

"Shhh," I breathed, knowing the familiar could understand me. "I just need to use the bathroom. Can you tell me where it is?"

He stared at me as if annoyed that I'd left the bed, then gestured with his sharp little beak at a door slightly ajar across from us.

I gave him a small smile but avoided patting him on the head. Some familiars enjoyed being treated like pets but not all of them, and I didn't feel like adding a painful beak bite to my list of injuries. Certain Thorne would wake up, I breathed a quiet sigh of relief when I tiptoed past him and he didn't stir. The second I closed the bathroom door behind me, a lightheaded feeling swept over me, and I slumped against the door.

Okay, I wasn't completely healed then. The Sano had sealed my cuts, but I was still weak from blood loss. I wouldn't allow that to stop me, though.

Pushing off the door, I flicked on the light and paused, shocked that Thorne had this bathroom all to himself. Being Head Prefect definitely had its perks. Everything was black and slate gray, modern and decidedly masculine. I wouldn't be surprised at this point if he'd designed it himself. My drafty tower and co-ed bathroom felt like the stone ages compared to this luxury. He probably even had hot water.

A tremble started in my legs, but I pushed forward anyway, determined to keep going. The toilet flushed all on its own when I finished peeing, and the sink was automated too. I made the mistake of looking up then, taking in the waif of a girl in the mirror. Dark bruises ringed her big haunted eyes, her black hair matted in several places. Her full lips were bloodless, her skin whiter than it had ever been. But it was her shirt that grabbed my attention, filling me with horror.

It was red. Red when it should be *white*.

I lifted the hem, my gut twisting when more red greeted me underneath. The blood had long since dried, but it was caked to my skin, *clinging* to it, reminding me too much of death. Of how close I'd come to bleeding out.

The sight froze my insides, and I swayed again, nearly toppling over. I grabbed onto the counter at the last second, just as a voice from the doorway said, "You shouldn't be up."

I almost jumped out of my skin, whipping my head toward the door to see Thorne's big body framed there. Taking him in, noticing the *blood* smeared on his pants, nervous energy made me shake even harder. Still, I rushed to say, "I can't be late."

His brows rose. "Late? Maybe you forgot, but you almost *died* last night. Look at you. You're shaking so hard, you can barely stand."

I straightened as best I could, hating that he was seeing me like this. Hating that I'd gone to him in the first place. Knowing that I'd be dead right now if I hadn't didn't make me feel any better.

"Who hurt you, Snowflake? I need to know."

I blinked, caught off guard by his question, by the fierce gleam darkening his gaze. Swallowing, I replied, "I don't know. I placed protections around my room to keep intruders out, but someone must have gotten inside and put a hex on my spellbook. One touch, and the cuts started forming."

His gaze darkened even more. "Judging by how many cuts you received, it was more likely a curse. Such a malevolent act is prohibited at this school and punishable by expulsion. I won't let them get away with it."

Overwhelmed by not only the violence simmering in his eyes but in his voice now as well, I scrambled to think of some way to make him leave. The first thing that popped out of my mouth was, "I need to take a shower."

He studied me for a beat, then moved. Not away but *into* the bathroom. Shutting the door behind him, he made for the glass shower and switched it on.

"What are you doing?" I demanded, feeling my body tense all over. The bathroom had seemed huge before, but with him now in it, I was starting to feel claustrophobic.

"Helping you. There's no way you'll be able to take a shower on your own."

I gaped at him, certain I'd heard wrong. He couldn't have meant—

He whipped his t-shirt off and tossed it onto the counter, then tugged down his sweatpants. Before I could look away, I got an eyeful of his tight black boxer briefs and the giant mound of flesh they were barely containing.

My face burst into flames, and I tore my gaze away, saying with force, "No way. I'm not getting naked with you."

"Relax, Snowflake. We'll keep our underwear on. Now come here."

"Not a chance in hell. I can do it myself, see?"

Ignoring the fact that I was about to expose my panties to him, I let go of the counter and shimmied out of my yoga pants. But when I straightened, dizziness slammed into me again. I reached for the counter and missed. As I plummeted toward the floor, arms appeared and smoothly scooped me up. Finding myself pressed to Thorne's bare chest and heading for the shower, panic tightened my throat.

"Thorne, put me down."

He stepped into the shower and nudged the door shut. "Sure," he said and set me down. I immediately tried to leave, but he blocked the door with his huge body and grabbed the hem of my ruined shirt.

"Thorne!" I squeaked, unable to hide the panic in my voice. "I don't . . . I don't have a bra on."

Could I be any more *weak?* Pathetic didn't even begin to describe me right now. This was almost worse than my walk of shame. It *was* worse. At least then I'd been able to mask my humiliation and fear.

But instead of ridiculing my weakness, Thorne's expression softened, and he said, "I won't look."

Won't look. Did I believe him? No. But at least he wasn't making fun of or leering at me. I still had my bottoms on and so did he. Would it be the end of the world if he saw my breasts?

Yes.

When I didn't pull away, he took that as consent and resumed lifting my shirt. His knuckles grazed my ribcage, and I sucked in a quiet gasp. Not because he'd zapped me—because he hadn't—but because that swift yet intimate brush of skin on skin had just sent a thrill through me.

"Raise your arms," he quietly instructed, and I found myself obeying. The shirt slid up and over my head, then landed with a plop on the floor. When my eyes flicked up to Thorne's face, I found his gaze locked on my breasts.

"You looked," I blurted, surprised by how breathless my voice sounded. Where was the annoyance? The *anger?*

"Yes," he rumbled, continuing to study them. To *caress* them. "I'm a hot-blooded male. What did you expect?"

When he continued to openly take me in, goosebumps erupted over the sensitive flesh. My nipples hardened to rocks, and his eyes darkened. Not with anger. No, this was something new. Something that made my stomach clench with a thousand fluttering nerves.

"You have absolutely nothing to be ashamed of, Snowflake," he said, finally raising his eyes to mine. The emotion brewing in them hit me hard, stealing my breath. I tried to deny what I was seeing, tried to convince myself that my inexperience was playing tricks on me.

Because there was no way in hell that Thorne Hudson would look at me with desire.

CHAPTER 16

I let him guide me under the warm spray. Let him rinse my hair and start to wash it.

The water ran red with my blood, so much blood. Even my scalp had received multiple cuts. Thorne worked in silence, keeping his eyes above my neck as he washed my hair clean. His movements were gentle, achingly so, making our situation feel that much more intimate. We didn't speak, and that only served to heighten the experience.

Each sweep of his hands, each stolen look, felt deliciously new. Forbidden. It *was* forbidden in so very many ways. But he was only helping me wash my hair . . .

Right?

My skin tingled pleasantly wherever he touched, the soothing motions and warm water lulling me into a relaxed state. Struggling to keep my eyes open, I took the opportunity to examine the wing tattoos spanning his chest. At least, that's what I told myself. The inkwork was beautifully detailed, but it was the shifting muscles underneath that I couldn't stop staring at. His pecs flexed with each movement, and I remembered how it felt to have my head pressed against them.

My eyes wandered lower to the defined muscles on his stomach, tracing their uniform dips and swells. Would they jump beneath my fingertips if I touched them?

Shocked by the wayward thought, I grabbed the bar of soap in the cutout beside me and feverishly began to scrub the remaining blood from my skin. By the time my body was fully clean, I felt weaker than a newborn foal, trembling so hard that I could barely stand.

I hated to admit it, but he'd been right. I never would have been able to do this by myself.

Needing a break, I leaned against the tiles behind me. Thorne watched me, and I hesitated for a long moment before saying, "Thank you for not letting me die."

That look in his eyes intensified, and I knew for *sure* I was reading it all wrong this time. He looked protective, and *that* was impossible. He didn't want to be near me; he *hated* me. Even admitted so himself. He couldn't be feeling protective toward me—more like regretful that he hadn't let me die.

"Whether I want this responsibility or not," he said, his voice even lower than usual, "you're mine to keep alive."

Whoa. *Mine?* He couldn't mean it that way. He sure knew how to give a girl mixed signals, though, throwing around words like that and staring in a way that would make even the most hardened soul melt.

My legs chose that moment to finally give out on me. I started to slide down the tiles, and Thorne moved, wedging a leg between mine to halt my descent. As his muscular thigh pressed against my core, my body went haywire. Heat shot to the area, creating an ache I'd never felt before. Unable to control my reaction, a small gasp left me.

"Did that hurt?" Thorne questioned, a note of concern in his voice as he leaned a hand on the tiles beside my head.

He didn't remove his leg, though, using it to hold me up, keeping it pressed against me in a way that made it hard to breathe.

"No," I breathlessly replied, that one word saying far more than I'd meant to. At my confession, his eyes became dark pools of bottomless ocean. Confused, flustered, and feeling way too vulnerable, I reached out to push him back.

He caught both my wrists in one hand and lifted them above my head, securing them to the wall in one swift move.

"What are you doing?" I said, my eyes flying wide when his other hand left the wall and lowered to boldly grip my waist. Unused to being touched that way, my body quivered beneath his long fingers, a heady warmth that had nothing to do with the shower spray racing through me.

Instead of answering, he said in a quiet rumble, "Tell me, Snowflake . . . Have you ever been pleasured before?"

My jaw slowly dropped. When it was clear the question had rendered me speechless, he took the liberty of sliding that bold hand up my side. The sensation was electric, and I gasped again, unable to stop my spine from arching off the tiles in response. When I felt his thumb graze the underside of my breast and stop there, I stared wildly into his eyes, whether to plead that he stop or urge him onward, I didn't know.

"Answer me," he softly ordered.

I swallowed roughly, struggling to speak. "No," I said, the sound more whimper than a word.

Something filled his eyes then, and there was no mistaking it this time. He was excited. *Wickedly* excited. I started to tremble all over, on the verge of what felt like a panic attack. Air. I needed *air*.

"Relax, Snowflake," Thorne rumbled, adjusting his grip on my wrists before sliding that bold hand south once more. "I just want you to feel something good after the hell you endured. This won't change anything between us, and we can go on hating each other the same as before."

Before I could think to respond, to *stop* him, he slid his hand between my legs. The slightest pressure to my aching flesh had me jerking off the tiles with a breathy moan. His leg still wedged between mine held me in place, the gap he'd created allowing his fingers to explore the shape of me through my damp underwear.

"Since this is your first time, I'll make it slow and gentle," he said, the desire that I could no longer deny thick in his voice. I opened my mouth, but nothing came out, the feelings he was awakening in me erasing my mind.

Each sweep of his fingers over my center was achingly slow, just like he promised, stoking a fire in me that began to grow and grow and grow. He didn't breach that thin barrier of fabric between us the entire time, a choice that seemed decidedly intentional. It was like he knew just how wrong this was and keeping my panties in place would somehow absolve him of this sin. I didn't care either way at the moment, too busy drowning in forbidden pleasure.

The more he touched me, the more I wanted him to, and the longer he did, the stronger the sensation coiling low in my belly grew. I started to shake, to pant, the sensation building and building and building. His strokes quickened, shortened, targeting the most sensitive of all spots until my legs were stiffening, preparing for something huge.

Something *life* changing.

"Thorne," I whimpered, so much pleasure spiking through me that I couldn't stand it.

"Just a little longer, Snowflake," he rumbled near my ear, tightening his grip on my wrists and adding even more delicious pressure to my clit. "You're responding so beautifully, and I'm not done watching."

Ancestors, save me. His words alone almost unraveled me.

My breaths came in frantic pants, those deft fingers swirling and swirling, tighter and tighter. My core tightened right along with his movements, making me shake uncontrollably. I could no longer breathe. My whole world had narrowed to his fingers on my clit. It felt so good. *Too* good. I could no longer contain the feeling. I had to let it out. Had to . . .

"Come for me, Winter. *Now*."

I released the wall of tension, and it snapped. A strangled cry left me as pure adrenaline, pure *ecstasy* flooded me, filling every corner of my body. My world became bliss. I *was* bliss. Even my fingers and toes blissfully pulsed to the orgasm's beat, a beat I hadn't known existed until this moment. Thorne's fingers continued to work my clit, drawing out the pleasurable aftershocks. I felt like a specter in that moment, floating above my body in a state so peaceful that I didn't want to come down.

So *this* was an orgasm. Why the hell did I wait so long to have one?

Every inch of me hummed contentedly as I finally came down, so euphoric that I felt made out of jello. I tried gathering my legs beneath me, and Thorne let go of my wrists to help me stand. I swayed but eventually found my balance, fluttering my eyes open to glance up at him. Desire still simmered in his gaze, and before I knew what was happening, his head was lowering. Lowering toward mine.

Our noses brushed, and I froze, knowing what he was about to do. But we couldn't. *Couldn't*. It was too far. Too *much*. I'd already given him something I shouldn't have. Already let myself *feel* things.

"Thorne," I said in a trembling breath, stiffening even more when he slid a hand to the nape of my neck. Drawing us closer. Guiding my face to the perfect angle.

One slip. One little slip was all it would take. After the pleasure I'd just felt at his hands, I could only imagine how good it would feel to have his mouth on mine. Oh, the things he could teach me. He was my mentor, after all. Maybe I *should* let him kiss me.

What the hell was I saying? Thorne shouldn't kiss me. Kissing meant more than fleeting sexual desire. Kissing meant feelings. Kissing meant *caring*. I couldn't do this. *We* couldn't do this.

People who hated each other shouldn't be kissing.

Hudsons and Mayweathers were rivals. Sworn enemies. We didn't mix. There was too much bad blood between us, too much pain and betrayal. I was supposed to stay *away* from Thorne at all costs. It was bad enough that he had to mentor me. I couldn't stab my family in the back by selfishly indulging in a moment of sinful pleasure with him. I'd already let things go too far. What we were doing had to stop. *Now.*

His uneven breaths mingled with mine, the scant centimeter between us humming, *sparking* with want. Maybe just one kiss. Only one. Just to find out what he tasted like . . .

No. We *couldn't.*

Our lips touched anyway. Once. Twice. The contact was featherlight. An exploratory brush. A searching sweep. Barely a graze at all.

But I suddenly knew in my bones, in my *soul* that if I let this continue, I'd surrender, fully and completely. I'd get lost in him, in the pleasure he awakened in me, and I couldn't allow that—no matter how much I craved to know what he tasted like.

There was too much at stake. Too much to *lose.*

So when his lips descended on mine again, I forced out, "We can't."

The words were barely a wisp of air. Not convincing in the least. But at least I'd said them before I was too doped up on pleasure again to care what happened.

Thorne didn't let go of me, his half-naked body still dangerously close to mine. But he'd paused at my words, paused and rumbled back, "Why not?"

"Because it's . . . it's wrong." More convincing this time.

His fingers slid into the hair at my nape, eliciting a full-body shiver from me. "Doesn't feel wrong."

Dear ancestors, save me.

"It should," I persisted. "We hate each other."

"I hear that hate sex is extremely gratifying."

My eyes flew up to find him already watching me. Searching. *Challenging.*

"That's twisted," I hissed, but it came out weak.

His fingers continued to explore my scalp, making me want to melt into his touch. "You weren't complaining a minute ago."

He got me there.

"Well, I should have. It was a mistake and won't happen again."

His fingers stopped. Good. Ending this before he could change my mind, I firmly pulled away. He immediately let me go, and I convinced myself that was a good thing.

But when I exited the shower and reached for the nearest towel, I heard him clearly say, "We're not finished here, Snowflake."

I stiffened again, then wrapped the towel around me and tossed back, "Yes, we are. I'm not going to become your sex buddy just because you saved me. I don't owe that to you."

"Winter . . ."

I ignored him, snagging another towel on my way out to dry my hair.

"Winter, *stop.*"

Something about the command made me pause. The tone of his voice sounded alarmed. *Desperate.* Before I could turn around, he left the shower and erased the distance between us. He grabbed my hair, and I went poker straight, certain he was about to punish me for rejecting him, maybe even force himself on me.

The darkness within me immediately rose up, prepared to cut him in half if he dared cross that line.

But instead of using my hair to subdue me, he swept it over my shoulder and exposed my upper back. I froze, realizing too late why he'd come after me.

"Why do you have this?"

I didn't need to see his eyes to know what they were looking at. I tried to swallow and failed, my throat sealing shut.

"*Answer* me," he said, with enough bite that I flinched.

Struggling to breathe, to speak, I whispered, "You know why."

"I want to hear you say it." I hesitated too long. "*Say* it!"

"For *her*," the words tore out of me. "I wanted the butterfly . . . to remember her by."

He didn't speak for a long moment, and I started to tremble again, my stomach twisting into knots.

Then, he said in a deathly quiet whisper, "You had no right."

Hurt lanced through me, his words like a slap to the face. Ignoring his anger, I whirled around and cried, "I had no *right?*"

"No. Not after what you did to her."

My lip quivered, but that cold anger didn't leave his eyes. Knowing it was pointless but needing to get the words out anyway, I haltingly said, "I-I tried to explain what happened that day. You knew we both wanted to attend Heartstone and had started to prepare. We were just practicing, I swear. It was an *accident*, Thorne. I don't even remember how it happened."

"Do you think that makes it better?"

"No! But I never would have hurt her intentionally. Jewel was my best friend. My *only* friend."

He ground his teeth together, then gritted out, "She was my baby sister."

"She was my sister, too."

His eyes flashed in warning, and I swore I heard thunder rumble in the distance. "No, she wasn't."

"She *was*," I pressed despite the precarious line I was crossing. "Juliana and I were soul sisters. We had a connection, an empathic bond I can't fully explain. She meant more to me than you could possibly know."

"She was *my* responsibility," Thorne snapped. "It was my job to *protect* her, but I foolishly allowed you to continue seeing each other after the fallout. I *trusted* you."

"I know, and I'm sorry! I have to forever live with the guilt of what I did, so even though our pactum won't allow you to kill me right now, at least you know I'm already in *hell!*"

The door whipped open, and Thorne reacted at the speed of lightning. One second, I was in front of him, and the next behind, his body crowding me against the counter as he faced the intruder.

"Whoa! Chill out, bro," a familiar voice that was forever mocking said. "We heard the yelling match and just wanted to make sure everything was okay."

"Everything's fine, Tanaka," Thorne bit out. "Now leave."

Riku scoffed, not the least bit intimidated. "You need to jerk off or take a cold one, Hudson. Bambi's in no condition to deal with your hostility right now."

As Riku stepped inside, Thorne bristled, reaching back to grab my arm. "You're not taking her."

"*We* are going to dress and feed her while you cool off. Come out when you no longer look like a homicidal maniac."

Thorne's fingers tightened on my arm, a rumble that sounded way too much like a growl vibrating his chest.

"Trust us, Thorne," another voice said, this time Oz's. "We've got her."

His calm, reassuring tone had the desired effect. Thorne's grip on me slowly loosened, then fell away. As he stepped aside, allowing me to see his two friends, I made sure the towel around me was extra secure. Riku slid his gaze over me with an amused smirk, then barked a laugh when Thorne headed for the shower again.

"Jerking off, it is."

Confused by Riku's words, I made the worst mistake of my life and glanced over my shoulder, right in time to see Thorne toss aside his boxer briefs. With all of my might, I tried to look away, but my eyes betrayed me and zeroed in on his naked body. On the *appendage* between his legs. My mouth went bone dry as I took in how erect it was, how *hard*. The tip was engorged, and I couldn't help but wonder how something that big could fit inside a vagina.

Mortified by my train of thought, I made another huge mistake. Instead of turning around, I looked up at his *face*. When I found his gaze already on me, I could have died from humiliation. I *wanted* to die as he stared at me with that stone-cold anger and deliberately reached down to fist his thick shaft.

I gaped at him a moment longer, unable to look away. His eyes hooded, a spiteful gleam entering them right before he slowly stroked the length. The head swelled even more, pulling the slit open and allowing a little precum to leak out.

All the blood drained from my face.

"Okay, time to leave before you pass out," Riku said, amusement heavy in his tone as he slid a hand to the small of my back and nudged me toward the door.

Thorne's lusty groan followed us out, and I hurried from the bathroom like the hounds of hell were at my heels.

CHAPTER 17

I might not have much experience with men, but I did know that Thorne was masterbating in the bathroom right now to punish me.

He was upset at me for stopping the kiss, mad at me for the butterfly tattoo, and furious at me for killing his sister. All of that built-up angst would surely make for one explosive orgasm.

I tried not to picture what he was doing, but it was kind of hard not to when I was still within hearing range and about to pull on a pair of his boxer briefs. It had been Riku's sadistic idea to dress me in Thorne's clothing, and since I didn't have a better option at the moment, I hadn't protested much.

Thankfully, Comet had left the room with the guys to afford me a little privacy, but knowing that Thorne could enter the bedroom at any moment had me on edge. I hurriedly tugged the boxers into place, trying with all my might not to dwell on the fact that his dick had been inside them recently. A dick that was currently hard as a rock and seconds away from ejaculating.

I couldn't get that lusty *groan* out of my head. Would he groan like that again when he orgasmed? Would he groan like that if *my* hand was on his cock instead of his?

Stop it! I silently hissed at myself, hating that I was so fixated on him right now, that I was *surrounded* by him.

Only a single door separated us while he pleasured himself and I finished pulling on his clothes. Clothes that smelled like him, like the bedroom I was in. I shimmied into a pair of his gray sweatpants next and instantly knew they wouldn't work. His long legs were nearly twice the length of mine, and I would just end up tripping over the material the second I moved. Letting them drop to the floor, I grabbed the clean black t-shirt on his bed and yanked it on, desperate to leave before he finished jerking off.

The shirt was so huge on me that it fell to mid-thigh, and I decided that it was decent enough until I got back to my dorm. As I raced to leave the room, I heard a sound come from the bathroom, but I was already whipping open the door and hurrying outside. The second the door clicked shut behind me, I breathed a little easier, until I walked down the short hall and entered the common space of the dorm.

Correction—*apartment.*

There was a whole living room to my left with a huge suede sectional, three intricately-arched windows that overlooked the mountains, and a stone fireplace with a giant flatscreen on top. Comet was perched on the back of the couch, and his yellow gaze swiveled from looking outside to me, watching intently as I took in the space. To the right was a mahogany dining table with several chairs and a full kitchen with stainless steel appliances and granite countertops.

Surprised by how homey it was, I felt a swift stab of homesickness. I'd never been away from home this long before, and being here made me acutely aware of how much I missed the comforts of familiar surroundings and family. Doing my best to shake off the feeling, I was about to head for the exit when I spotted a leather book on the dining room floor. It was open and upside down, like someone had dropped it.

Or hastily swept it from the table.

I glanced at the tabletop again, my heart slowly beginning to pound when I realized that Thorne had placed me on it last night. My eyes traced the smooth surface but couldn't find even a hint of blood. I searched the floor next. The couch. Nothing. Nothing except that overturned book, a book that looked way too much like the cursed spellbook in my room.

"Whoops. I wondered where that wandered off to," a familiar voice said, right before the book suddenly lifted and flew through the air. In a flash, it went from the dining room floor to Riku's hand where he stood at the kitchen island. He and Oz were both there in their school uniforms, and I finally noticed the smorgasbord of food on the counter before them.

Catching me eyeing it a little too longingly, Oz said, "We don't usually order in, but this is a special occasion."

Not fully processing his words, I quickly swallowed before any drool could escape and looked away, even as my stomach loudly rumbled. "I'll be late. I have to go."

At a loss for more words, I beelined for the exit.

"Whoa, whoa, *whoa*."

I suddenly slammed into an invisible wall and stumbled back. Before I could fall, I felt another wall at my back, one that nudged me forward, *pushed* me toward the kitchen. Eyes wide, I looked to the guys again and saw that one of Riku's hands was encased in a translucent white glow. My confusion morphed into a scowl when I realized that he'd used the air in the room to stop me from leaving.

"Riku," I protested, trying to dig my heels in to no avail. "I'm going to be *late*."

"Late shmatte," he drawled unapologetically, continuing to reel me toward him with his air magic. "When you're with the Arcane Three, you're never late."

"But I need to get to the dining hall before all the food is gone."

"What do you think all of *this* is for?" he asked, pointing the book still in his grip at the buffet on the counter.

I stopped protesting, stopped fighting the pull of his magic as I came even with the island laden with food, their words finally sinking in. "This is . . . for me?"

"We've seen the way you eat, Bambi. A stiff breeze could knock you over."

I gave Riku a flat look. "It already did."

"Exactly, which is why you aren't going anywhere until you're stuffed to the gills. You lost a lot of blood last night and need to refuel."

His lips twisted into a devilish smirk then, his fingers curling in a "come hither" gesture as he pushed me closer and closer, leaving me no choice but to stumble right into his personal space. With a final nudge from behind, his magic pressed my front flush against his. The second I felt the magic recede, I tried to step away, only for him to snake an arm around my waist and firmly lock me in place.

"Riku," I started to warn, placing my hands on his chest to push him away.

Before I could, he leaned down and whispered in my ear, "You look good in a man's clothing. I'd love to see you in mine next."

At the insinuation, the *invitation*, heat flushed up my neck and into my cheeks. This wasn't the first time he'd flirted with and teased me, but after what I'd just done with Thorne, it felt *real* this time. Suddenly, I couldn't help but wonder if they shared females like they shared a dorm. Thorne had seemed awfully comfortable with his two roommates seeing him naked earlier. Maybe they even indulged in orgies on occasion.

Or a lot.

Flustered at the thought, my entire face on fire, I tossed back, "In your dreams."

"Oh, most definitely," Riku purred, a sound that sent a little shiver through me. "I've already had several dreams of you. Naked ones. Gives me plenty of fuel for when I jerk off in the shower, but Thorne got to see the real thing, the lucky bastard. No wonder he was so desperate for release."

At that, I went from hot to cold in an instant. Shoving him hard, I broke Riku's hold on me and snapped, "It's not like that between us, okay? I won't have sex with you, Thorne, or anyone else at this school. Just because there are rumors going around that I'm putting out doesn't mean I am."

Except that I almost had. Except that I'd let Thorne rub me to completion like the hussy the school thought I was. Maybe I wasn't so innocent after all. Maybe I *deserved* that red letter they so vehemently wanted to brand me with.

Feeling like a sellout, I prepared to leave with my dignity in tatters once more, this time of my own doing. How could I have been so stupid? How could I have let him *touch* me like that?

Angry at myself for giving in so easily, I turned for the door. It would be hard to go without breakfast, but at least I'd make it to the morning assembly on time.

Before I could take more than a step, Oz said, "Winter, wait." I pursed my lips and paused without turning around. "Who you do or don't have sex with is none of our business, and Riku swears to keep his hands and all sexual innuendos to himself while you eat your breakfast. Isn't that right, Ri?"

"That's right. Sorry, Bambi. I was out of line. Again." Then he ruined it by adding, "No more sex talk until after breakfast."

Rolling my eyes, I reversed course and muttered, "Good enough. A girl's gotta eat."

The pair went suspiciously silent as I picked up a plate from the counter and dug into the catered buffet. One glance at Riku's pinched expression confirmed that they'd taken my statement sexually.

I pointed the pair of tongs in my hand at him. "Not a word."

He lifted fingers to his lips and twisted the invisible lock before throwing away the key. Shaking my head, I focused on all the glorious food again. There were platters heaped high with fresh bacon, sausages, scrambled eggs, french toast, bagels, and various fruits. One platter stood out from the rest because it wasn't a platter at all but a pink box. A box that contained . . .

"Doughnuts!"

Unable to contain my glee, I grabbed one with white frosting and rainbow sprinkles and shoved it into my mouth. As the sugary carb goodness ignited my tastebuds, a happy moan slipped out.

"Oh, Bambi, you're not making this easy," Riku quietly groaned.

Ignoring him, I took another huge bite.

"Careful, or you'll get sick," Oz warned, picking up his own plate. "Your body's not used to rich food anymore."

Unable to stop now that I'd started, I demolished the whole thing in seconds without an ounce of regret and reached for another. As I bit into a cherry jelly doughnut this time, a noise came from Riku, and I flicked a distracted glance at his face.

"You look constipated," I remarked, darting my tongue out to catch the jelly smeared on my bottom lip. He tracked the movement, then lifted his eyes to the ceiling with another quiet groan.

Still feeling weak, I took my full plate and half-eaten doughnut with me to the island's other side, instantly relieved when I slipped onto a stool and gave my legs a rest.

As the guys started to dish up, I finished my second doughnut before saying, "I'm surprised you two are even speaking to me."

Maybe it was the sugar high talking, but after almost dying last night, I felt like clearing the air some more.

Oz looked up from his plate to ask, "Why is that?"

"Well, besides the obvious, which is me being a disgraced Mayweather, it doesn't take a genius to figure out that Thorne hates me. As close as you three are, I'm sure you've heard some pretty awful stories."

Okay, I was fishing, but I doubted I'd get another opportunity to learn what they knew about me without Thorne around.

"Oh, we've heard *all* the stories, Bambi," Riku said almost flippantly, too busy dishing up to notice the blood draining from my face.

Oz noticed, though. From behind his black-rimmed glasses, his hazel eyes watched me struggle and fail to swallow before I managed to whisper, "So you know . . . *everything?*"

Hearing the strain in my voice, Riku finally glanced my way. As he took in my expression, his voice gentled considerably. "Yes, we do. What happened was a terrible tragedy, but how Thorne feels about it doesn't mean we automatically feel the same. Plus, the whole 'fall on your sword for the mistakes of your ancestors' thing doesn't sit well with me. Our community can be pretty old school sometimes and could use a little twenty-first century reformation. I personally don't like to burn someone at the stake before getting to know them first, and after getting to know you better this past month, I'm pretty sure we should be friends."

I blinked, blinked again, certain I'd heard him wrong. "You want to . . . you want to be my friend?"

Please, don't laugh at me. Please, don't say it was a joke. Please, please—

"Pretty positive," Riku answered with a curl of his lips. A *genuine* curl, not a mocking one. "Maybe with a little friendly nookie on the side, but I'm not allowed to talk about that right now."

A small laugh burst from me. It was barely a laugh at all, but it was still a sound I hadn't made in a long, long time. Feeling a burn behind my eyes that wasn't brought on by pain for once, I replied, "I thought you said I was dangerous."

"Those were Ozzy's words, actually. I said that I *liked* dangerous women." He followed up the words with a teasing wink.

When I peeked at Oz again, he was staring at me in that disconcerting Oracle way of his. Feeling like he was looking right through me, *inside* me, I started to glance away when he said, "We all have the potential to be dangerous. Our magical affinity doesn't define if we're good or bad, nor does the celestial being that gifted us a part of its spirit. It's just that, your aura is . . ."

When he paused, I dryly supplied, "Shrouded in malevolent shadows?"

"Yes, but those shadows also feel deeply protective, which confuses me."

My spine slowly straightened, unease filling me. I should change the subject, but I found myself asking, "Why does that confuse you?"

"Because it's a contradiction. I saw the way you viciously attacked Riku a few weeks ago, but right afterward, you were extremely remorseful. And then for weeks after that, you refused to attack Thorne with your magic. He told us yesterday that you were afraid of yourself, and that makes me believe you only defend yourself out of fear, not maliciousness. But that contradicts your attack on Riku, so I don't understand. It almost feels like you're protecting something, maybe even hiding something. Something that would cause you to react out of character in violent ways."

My throat tightened and tightened, cutting off my air. He could see it. He could see my *darkness*. Fear rushed through me, not just from the thought of being exposed, but from what the darkness would *do* at being exposed. If it was both malevolent and deeply protective, it wouldn't react too kindly to the threat Oz's Oracle abilities posed.

Worried for myself, but even more worried for him, I was just about to jump off my stool and race for the door when a voice behind me rumbled, "I felt but couldn't see a chain around her neck in the shower earlier. She's probably hiding a spelled amulet."

Riku quietly snickered at the comment, his mind clearly in the gutter again, but I was too distracted by Thorne's looming presence to chastise him. As he joined us in the kitchen, stopping beside Riku across the island from me, I couldn't help but notice that the white shirt under his blazer was wide open. Beads of water still clung to his deeply tanned skin, and I hopelessly watched one slip down his six pack and disappear into his navel.

My mouth dried, images of our time in the shower bombarding my brain. My gaze sank lower and followed the trail of dark hair beneath his navel, my mind trying to conjure up a visual of him masterbating.

That groan, that lusty *groan.* Why couldn't I stop hearing it?

As usual, I made the mistake of looking up at his face next. But, for once, he didn't catch me ogling him. Not when he was too busy eyeing me in his shirt. Gone was the anger from earlier, the intense look he was giving me now more like the ones in the shower. Remembering how he'd stared at my bare breasts, I felt my nipples harden. No, no, no. Too late. I saw the moment he noticed, the desire flaring in his eyes unmistakable this time. Certain he was picturing me naked right now, a sudden ache pulsed between my legs.

Horrified, I shot up from my stool and scurried around the island toward the fridge. The guys silently watched me yank it open, clearly confused by my sudden agitation. I scrambled to think of an excuse. *Anything*. Recalling what Thorne had just said, I hesitated for a moment before grabbing a carton of orange juice and blurting, "I do have a spelled amulet, but it's harmless. My grandmother gave it to me for my protection and nothing more."

Gran would be so disappointed in me right now, but she'd told me to do whatever it took to survive. Exposing my amulet to keep my darkness hidden felt like the right move. It was far better they think the malevolence was coming from my necklace than from inside of me.

But then Oz asked, "Can I hold it?"

I stiffened, his words evoking a sudden rush of protectiveness. My hand itched to grab the pendant, to *defend* it if need be. Instead, I slowly shut the fridge and moved toward the cabinets in search of a glass. When I found one, I carefully poured the juice into it before replying, "Sorry, but I swore not to take it off."

An uncomfortable silence fell over the kitchen, one so quiet that I heard Comet's wings rustle. With my back turned to them, I had no doubt that the guys were looking at each other in silent communication. I tensed even more, worried that they'd try to take it from me by force. With three-against-one odds, there was no way I'd win.

Just when I was about to race for the door—*again*—Thorne said, "The spell on the amulet is probably what stopped the curse."

I turned from the counter with my glass of juice to gape at him. "*Stopped* it? The curse cut me to bloody ribbons!"

Without looking at me, he reached into the doughnut box and pulled out a glazed one before saying, "Yes, but I doubt whoever created that curse planned for it to stop cutting you. Without a curse reversal, the cuts should have kept forming until you were dead."

It made sense. Curses didn't just *stop*. But knowing that I'd be dead right now if not for my protective amulet was more than a little upsetting. Thank the ancestors for Gran's wise forethought.

"Do you know who cursed you?" Riku asked me, biting into an apple.

"No, but when I was taking a shower last night, it felt like someone was watching me. Then again when I climbed the tower stairs. I thought I was just being paranoid, but maybe whoever placed that curse used an invisibility spell to follow me."

"And bypass your dorm's protective spells," Thorne said as I sipped my orange juice, a slight growl vibrating his chest. "I bet it was Blaze, the sick bastard. I'm going to kill him."

I almost spit out my juice. Even Oz and Riku looked surprised as they stopped eating to stare at him.

Swallowing hard, I quipped, "If you do that, you'll all lose your bets."

I'd meant for the comment to be light, but when they all turned as one to stare at me, I instantly wished I'd kept my mouth shut.

Squirming under the weight of all three sets of eyes, I blurted a little defensively, "What? It's not the end of the world if you *lose* on occasion. It's just a stupid bet."

Riku snorted and shook his head like I was a naive little girl. "We never lose, Bambi."

I frowned, looking at each of them in turn before demanding, "Am I missing something here? If Blaze dies, you all lose." When no one said anything, I pressed, "Right?"

"Wrong, Snowflake," Thorne replied, raising the glazed doughnut to his mouth. "If Blaze dies, we win."

He devoured the doughnut whole.

CHAPTER 18

As the clock tower bell tolled the hour, I couldn't help but cringe.

"Relax," Thorne said from beside me as we walked down the hall. "You won't be punished for missing morning assembly."

I didn't respond, mostly because I didn't quite believe him. That and because my reaction wasn't purely about being late. Every time the bell tolled, I couldn't help but remember those awful cuts. I could feel them right now, stinging, burning, bleeding. Spilling my life force all over the stairwells and halls.

"My blood," I suddenly burst out.

Thorne glanced at me. He'd left Comet in his dorm while Riku and Oz had gone ahead to the morning assembly. But Thorne had other plans—plans that he had yet to share with me, the controlling brute. When he saw the panic stamped on my face, he replied, "We took care of it."

My eyes widened. "*All* of it?"

"All of it." His mouth formed a grim line. "It looked like a bloody massacre."

I could only imagine. A shiver raced up my spine when I tried to picture how gruesome I must have appeared when he'd found me. Grateful once more that he hadn't left me there in the hallway to die, I opened my mouth to thank him again, then promptly closed it, recalling his shocking confession about the bet.

This whole time, he'd let me believe that he had bet against me.

As annoyed as I was, I couldn't get over the fact that he'd actually bet in my favor. They all had. Did they really think that Blaze would die before I did? And was that the true reason why Thorne had saved my life? Not just last night but the times before that as well?

Realizing that he'd probably saved me because of a stupid bet definitely made me feel a little less grateful. I mean, I'd *known* he was competitive and didn't like to lose, but a *bet?*

What if touching me in the shower had been a bet, too?

I quickly shut the possibility down, certain I would yell at him if I thought about it too long. The last thing we needed was another heated shouting match filled with painful confessions.

Now that it was just him and me, I could feel that buzzing tension between us return. It felt stronger than ever, maybe even more so, the air surrounding us rife with old hurts and new. At least that spiteful anger in his eyes hadn't reemerged, probably because he'd temporarily released it with his explosive orgasm.

My mind started drifting down the gutter again, thinking of dirty forbidden things. Frustrated with myself, I said more forcefully than planned, "Wherever you're taking me, I need to get changed first. I don't want anyone seeing me like this."

And getting the wrong idea.

Thorne's gaze swung my way again, dropping down my front. When his attention lingered, taking in my form while I walked, I got flustered and slowed. He slowed too, matching his long strides to my short ones.

Huh. Well, that was new. So was walking beside me. Usually, he left me scrambling to catch up.

"That's our first stop," he evenly replied and faced forward again. Wait. No *I don't care if you're embarrassed* speech? Maybe I needed to almost-die more often.

More uneasy silence followed, but at least I could breathe easier knowing I'd be free of his clothes soon. The entire way to Jade Wing, we didn't cross a single soul. Everyone was in the morning assembly, and I could only imagine the whispered rumors about to fly with my absence. Blaze would be at the helm, of course, gloating that I'd finally gotten what I deserved. If it really had been him behind that curse, I wondered if he'd be stupid enough to claim credit and risk expulsion.

Probably.

When we reached the base of Jade Wing Tower, the itch for vengeance finally hit me. It carried me up the dark winding stairs, giving me the fuel necessary to drag one trembling leg forward after another. I'd let the abuse go on long enough. Whoever cursed me needed to pay. Thorne didn't comment about the lack of light, following closely on my heels, but when we hit the top, he maneuvered his big body in front of mine and pushed open the door.

That's right. I hadn't locked it in my hurry to leave last night. Terrific. Someone could have planted another curse in there for all I knew. Way to go, me.

I didn't protest as Thorne barged into my room without asking, too busy trying to calm my thundering heart. At first, I thought it was because of my weakened state, but when my limbs started to freeze up the closer I got to the door, I knew that it also thundered out of fear.

"Clear," Thorne called from inside, and some of my fear faded.

At least I didn't feel entirely alone anymore. A feeling like that should bring me relief, but I wasn't sure if I could trust it. So I pushed it aside, inhaling deeply before stepping through the door. Right away, my gaze shot to the floor near my desk. Finding it empty, panic gripped me.

"Where is it?"

"Where's what?"

"It has to be here. It's *evidence*."

"Winter . . ."

I hurried to the desk and started to search, my panic growing the longer I came up empty. "It has to be here."

Someone had been in my room. *Again*.

"Winter."

It had to have been Blaze, checking to see if I was dead. When he hadn't found me, he'd absconded with the spellbook to cover his tracks. He was going to get away with murder—*almost* murder—if I didn't find that blasted book.

I continued to frantically search, growing more desperate by the second. Where was my bloodied towel? Where was the dark pool of blood on the floor? Nothing made sense. It was like last night had never happened, like it had been nothing more than a *nightmare*.

I spun in place, feeling like the walls were closing in. This was a mistake. A cruel *mistake*.

"*Winter!*"

Large hands grabbed my biceps and shook me, forcing me back to reality. To the realization that Thorne was here. I wasn't alone. I wasn't *alone*. Which meant that it wasn't all in my head. Last night had happened. It had been *real*.

"I-I don't understand," I said, my voice sounding small, lost. "It's all gone."

"Look at me, Snowflake," he commanded, yet his tone was soothing. Gentle. When I continued to glance around the room, he let go of one of my arms to grasp my chin. Only when my eyes finally met his did he say, "We took care of the blood, remember? Even up here. As for the cursed book, I called Chancellor Grimshaw before we left and told him what happened. He came by personally to collect it and is expecting us in his office as soon as you're dressed."

I blinked, slowly digesting his words as I came fully back to reality. Oh. That made sense. Feeling foolish, I tugged my chin from his grip and started to ease back, only to find that I couldn't. Not because of his hand on my arm, but because my fists were clenched in his *shirt*. Mortified, I let go and quickly stepped back. He dropped his hand, watching me closely as if I was going to break.

Not gonna happen.

"I should get dressed then," I said, then paused, waiting for him to leave. When he continued to stare at me, I gave him a pointed look. "A little privacy, please?"

Slowly, ever so slowly, he crossed his arms over his chest. "It's nothing I haven't seen before."

My jaw dropped. Did he just—? Hell, no, he did *not* just say that.

"Thorne, leave," I demanded, not so kindly.

"Why? Do I make you nervous?"

Hell, yes.

"No, I just don't want to be ogled right now."

"Tough. I have to keep you alive, and that means my eyes stay on you at all times."

My eyes practically bugged out of their sockets. "Seriously? You can't follow me around *everywhere*."

"Watch me."

"I don't want to watch you. I want you to *leave* so I can get *dressed*."

He didn't move a muscle.

Gah! Fine. Two could play that game.

In a flash, I called the shadows to me and morphed into darkness. Exhaustion pulled at me almost immediately, but I stubbornly ignored it, silently slipping away from him.

"Snowflake," Thorne rumbled, the warning in his voice loud and clear despite my muted senses. I ignored that too, only staying in one spot long enough to grab the clothing I needed. "You're still recovering. You shouldn't be shadewalking right now."

I glanced his way, annoyed to find that his gaze was locked on my little pocket of shadows. With the only light to see by coming from the gloomy sky outside my broken window, he shouldn't be able to track me so easily. Maybe I was more fatigued than I thought, and my shadows were slipping. Gritting my teeth, I willed even more darkness to cloak me before gliding to another spot of the room.

I'd just started to undress with shaking fingers when I heard him expel a clipped sigh and say, "Fine, I won't look."

I paused, then tugged his t-shirt over my head. "Not falling for that again."

"I promise."

I paused again, considering. Maybe I was naive when it came to guys, but his words sounded genuine. Plus, I was starting to sweat from the effort of concealing myself, and I wasn't petty or stubborn enough to ignore his offer.

"Then turn around," I instructed him.

He did, and I immediately dropped the shadows, nearly swaying with relief. Checking to make sure he wasn't using the mirror's reflection to peek at me, I stripped off his boxer briefs and put on my own underwear.

Halfway through dressing, the silence became too much, and I said without thinking, "What happened to the student who lived up here last year?"

Right away, I knew that bringing up the topic was a bad idea. For all I knew, Thorne was the one behind the warlock's murder. Maybe he'd tried to scare him into leaving too but hadn't accounted for him falling out the window.

No, I couldn't picture Thorne being that sloppy. Every move he made was calculated and controlled. If he was behind the warlock's fall, he'd *meant* for it to happen.

Regretting my question even more now, I was about to change the subject when Thorne replied, "His death is still a mystery. Some say he committed suicide, but I believe he was murdered."

He *was* murdered, but I wasn't going to let Thorne know how I knew that.

"So, you don't know who killed him?"

Wow, I was really pushing my luck here.

"No, but you don't need to worry about that. I won't let that happen to you."

Why? Because it would make you look like an incompetent mentor?

I stuffed down the words, zipping up my skirt and saying instead, "Someone already broke in here and almost murdered me. There's a good chance they'll try to again."

"Which is why you're not staying here any longer."

My fingers froze halfway through buttoning my shirt. "Excuse me?"

"You're relocating to Sapphire Wing. To my dorm."

What. The. Hell? He said it so *definitively*, like I had absolutely no say in the matter.

"Like hell I am," I said, my tone laced with warning, with *bite*. He had no right to make decisions for me like that. *No right.*

Slowly, he turned around, his jaw set like granite. I set mine as well, preparing for a fight. He took in my defensive stance, lingering too long on the cleavage my half-buttoned shirt couldn't hide before replying, "Don't fight me on this, Snowflake. You'll lose."

"Why, because you always *win?* Well, I hate to ruin your big plans, but unless you're going to keep me *prisoner* in your dorm, I won't stay there."

His entire body went rigid. Anger flashed in his eyes, but something else did too. Confusion. "I'm offering you protection. Why won't you accept it?"

Wow, I'd really rattled him. I doubted he'd ever been turned down like this before. Two rejections in one day by the school's pariah must definitely sting. I wasn't rejecting his offer of protection out of spite, though. That would be stupid. Without a doubt, I'd be a lot safer in his dorm than mine, but . . .

"Because if I leave, it'll make me look weak," I told him. "You're the one who told me not to run and hide every time I'm afraid, and that I won't survive this place unless I'm willing to defend myself."

"This is different."

"Why?"

"Because you almost *died*."

I threw my hands in the air. "So? Then you wouldn't have to deal with me anymore. I know you have a reputation to protect, but so do I. This is my *one* chance to change things for my family, and I can't do that if you stuff me in a box and throw away the key. I'm sorry, but I can't hide behind you just because I almost died. I need to prove that I belong here, and staying in this drafty haunted tower is how I do it."

Thorne was silent for a long time, studying me in a way that made me worry I'd told him too much. But it wasn't like he didn't already know why I was here. Why I wanted so badly to *stay*. Why else would I risk dying?

Ever so slowly, I watched his anger and confusion melt away. Something else filled his eyes, then. Not resignation, but something that I most definitely didn't expect. Understanding.

Uncrossing his arms, he reached into his pocket and pulled

something out. "Here. My number is already in there, along with Oz and Riku's. If you won't stay with us, then you'll at least let us keep tabs on you."

Realizing he was holding a phone, I started to shake my head. "First years aren't allowed to have any devices."

"They are if I say they are," he said in that matter-of-fact way of his. "This is non-negotiable, Winter. Either take the phone, or I'll drag you to my dorm and throw away the key."

Cute. He thought I'd be cowed by that, but I would gladly accept the phone if it meant being able to call home. I desperately missed Wyatt and Gran's voices, and the thought of hearing them again gave me a fresh burst of energy. Striding forward, I took the phone from him, not surprised that it was the latest model.

"How will I charge it? I don't have a cord—or electricity, for that matter."

"I'll see to it that you have a charging cord and electricity restored to the tower. And a new window installed."

I almost protested that last part since it felt like cheating, then thought better of it. Almost dying should earn me at least *one* perk. I returned to the bed to put on my blazer and tie, then quickly ran a brush through my hair, wishing I had time to put on some concealer.

Oh, well. The dark circles further accentuated my ghostly vibe, which should unsettle a few of my peers, at least. When I finished and announced my readiness to leave, Thorne's expression darkened once more.

"Forgetting something, Snowflake?"

I glanced down at myself, then back up at him. "No."

Lips thinning, he stalked around me and grabbed something off my bed, then headed back, saying, "You need to carry this phone on you at all times. No exceptions."

Without warning, he strode right into my personal space and plunged his hand into my skirt pocket. My eyes flew wide, a small gasp escaping me when I felt his fingers graze my hip through the material. Pleasurable tingles erupted over my skin, making my body hyperaware of his.

He didn't pull back right away, keeping his hand where it was as he bent his head down toward mine and rumbled, "Do you understand?"

I swallowed hard, suddenly finding it hard to breathe. "I understand."

The words came out breathless, submissive. Where the hell did my backbone just disappear to?

"Good," he said, satisfaction heavy in his tone. He held his position for another beat, probably taking sadistic pleasure from the power move he'd just played, then slowly slid his hand free and turned for the door. "Then let's go."

CHAPTER 19

Chancellor Grimshaw stood behind his stately mahogany desk, absentmindedly stroking his short beard, his expression dead serious for once.

Phantom, his greyhound familiar, was curled up on a couch nearby, his coat blending into the leather so thoroughly that I hadn't seen him when we'd first arrived. Right away, I'd observed that the chancellor's office was more than just an office. The first floor had an impressive display of bookshelves on one side and a sitting area on the other, leaving the back wall free to showcase five intricately-arched windows and a majestic mountain view.

But in the middle of the room was a curved wrought-iron staircase that led up to what I assumed was a loft apartment. Talk about not being able to get away from your work.

With his gaze fixed on the spellbook that floated inches above his desk, Chancellor Grimshaw said, "I've analyzed the book as best I can without touching it but can't detect any residual magic. Whoever cast that curse was experienced and knew how to mask their signature, which makes me think that an upperclassman must be responsible. First years haven't been taught black magic yet."

"The other academies might not teach black magic, but they could have learned it at home," Thorne countered. "Many covens know black magic in some form and even possess grimoires."

True. The Mayweathers still had a family grimoire several

generations old. Gran had hid our Book of Shadows so they couldn't confiscate it after our excommunication.

Instead of focusing on the spellbook used to almost destroy me, I carefully watched Chancellor Grimshaw's expression. He appeared somber but not angry that one of the students under his authority had tried to curse another. Did situations like this happen often at Heartstone, or did he just not care that I'd almost died?

Remembering how quickly he'd dismissed the warlock's death during my Initiation Trial, suspicion churned in my belly. What if he'd been involved somehow? What if he *orchestrated* the occasional student death to cull out the weak and keep the student body as a whole on their toes?

Bile climbed up my throat, but I forced it back down, unwilling to show any more *weakness* by puking in the chancellor's office.

Still, my unease remained as he replied to Thorne, "I've considered this, but a curse that intricate would have taken years of practice to learn. My guess is that a third year chose to target Winter hoping that her death would weaken your position here. You've gone unchallenged for a while now, and some of your peers could be making their move. Like it or not, the mentorship program ties Winter's fate to yours. Many would see that connection as a golden opportunity to bring the Head Prefect down."

"I'm aware," Thorne said through clenched teeth, instantly making me feel guilty, "but outside of a trial, this level of attack is forbidden. I want a full investigation made right away and the perpetrator expelled the second they're caught."

Frowning, the chancellor glanced up at Thorne across the desk from him. "I doubt it will ever come to that, unfortunately. As I've said, whoever did this covered their tracks impeccably, and without any proof or witnesses—"

"I already have a pretty good idea who did it," Thorne interrupted him. "We can start there."

The chancellor looked surprised, studying Thorne's resolute expression before focusing on me. I wiped my face clean of all emotion, not wanting to give away that I now had *two* suspects.

As he opened his mouth to respond, the door to his office burst open. Thorne moved behind me in an instant, an intimidating wall between me and whoever had just barged in.

"Where is she?"

Recognizing the voice, I tried to peer around Thorne, only for him to block me with an arm. Annoyed, I shoved at the arm, but it didn't budge.

"*Thorne*," I hissed, and he finally lowered his arm, albeit reluctantly.

The second Professor Holt spotted me, the worry on her face melted into relief. "Oh, you poor thing. What a scare you gave us."

Us? More like just her. It felt good to have someone genuinely care about me, though. Not *everyone* here hated me, and that was definitely a consolation.

"I came as quickly as I could. You must have been so terrified," she continued, her heels clicking against the stones as she approached. Seeing my spellbook hovering just above the chancellor's desk, a scowl pulled at her full lips. "What a vile thing to do. How were you able to counteract the curse?"

I could practically *feel* Thorne stiffen, like he didn't want me to tell her. No worries there. My amulet would definitely be confiscated if I told a professor about it.

"I don't know," I began, doing my best to feign ignorance. "When I got to Thorne, I was pretty much dead. Maybe the cuts stopped because I didn't have any more blood to spill."

She exchanged a look with Chancellor Grimshaw before replying, "It's a possibility, I suppose. My, what a mess this is. I knew it would be hard for you here, but to curse you in such a manner is a disgrace. I've already informed the student body of the situation at morning assembly, reminding them that such behavior is forbidden and that the culprit will be punished accordingly." Heaving a sigh, she asked me, "Do you have any idea who did it?"

When Thorne didn't stiffen this time, I tentatively said, "Maybe. Blaze McGrath has threatened me multiple times. Cursing me is definitely something he seems capable of doing."

She crossed her arms beneath her full chest. "I've personally seen him try to attack you, so I understand why you think it might be him. That said, we can't officially convict anyone without proof. I'll start looking into his background and learn what I can about his family and coven. The more evidence we can find that he's capable of such a thing, the stronger our case becomes."

"We could also interrogate him," the chancellor said, finally suggesting something helpful.

"With Truth Potion." At Thorne's words, both professors turned to him wide-eyed.

"You know that Truth Potion can't be administered without consent, Thorne," Professor Holt reminded him. "Free will is sacred to our community, even more so these past one hundred years, ever since that fateful day when one witch's actions ignited a war between two powerful races. We've struggled ever since, which is why that rule cannot be tampered with. The consequences are too great."

"I understand," Thorne said, "but there are exceptions to that rule."

The chancellor frowned again. "Such as?"

"Such as wiping human memories to protect the supernatural

world. We never ask for their consent. We just do it."

"That's different," Professor Holt began, but Thorne didn't let her finish.

"I agree. Allowing humans to know of our existence would cause widespread panic and death, which is why I was all for excommunicating the elders after they tried to stop the vampires from breaking their curse. They *wanted* vampires to be exposed, all so they could end up on top again. So I'm all for taking away free will to protect our community, even if that means protecting the community from itself."

No one spoke for a while, his speech brutally cutting through to the heart of the matter. I wanted to be mad at his words. Although he'd been too young to vote on the disbanding of the elders a decade ago, it was clear he would have cast me and my family out if given the opportunity. But even knowing that, I couldn't really blame him. My ancestors had risked the safety of the community for ambitious gain, and in our world, that was unforgivable.

Eventually, Chancellor Grimshaw cleared his throat and replied, "I get what you're saying, Thorne. The safety of our community should always come first, and I commend you for standing firm on that. Without a doubt, you are exactly the type of leader this community needs during these troubling times, but to break one of our most sacred rules for one person's misfortune is rather rash."

Wait. One person's *misfortune?* Okay, I was definitely angry now.

Curling my hands into fists, I prepared to spout off at him when Thorne said in a scarily quiet tone, "Rash? If history has taught us anything, it's that one person's misfortune can befall us all. We need to band together when one of our own is in trouble, even if that means taking severe action to solve the problem. Freddy Goddard died in Jade Wing Tower last year, and we never solved who murdered him. Despite the need for this school to cull out the weak, I find that unacceptable, and I won't allow Winter to be the next casualty due to managerial incompetence."

Holy. Crap.

That last part had my jaw dropping, and not surprisingly, I wasn't the only shocked one. Both professors looked gobsmacked, but before they could respond to Thorne's harsh words, he pivoted on his heel and grabbed my hand. "Let's go."

In too much shock to protest, I let him pull me across the room and out the door, nearly choking on my spit when he slammed it behind him. Dear ancestors, did he really just *roast* the chief executive officer and vice-chancellor of Heartstone Academy? To their *faces?*

It wasn't until we reached the end of the hall that I realized he still held my hand. I tried to pull away, but his grip only tightened, anger practically pulsing from his skin and into mine.

"Thorne," I finally protested, pulling again as I struggled to keep up with his long strides. Noticing my struggle, he slowed and let go of me, then raised the hand to yank it through his brown tresses. Not wanting to agitate him more but needing to say something, I spoke barely above a whisper, "You shouldn't have done that. They could punish you."

"No, they won't," he replied, tailoring his speed to mine as we descended some stairs. "And it needed to be said."

I hesitated another beat, then said, "I didn't need you to defend me."

He slowed some more so I could pull even with him, glancing my way before responding, "Maybe not, but my words carry a lot more weight around here than yours. If we want justice for what happened, this is the fastest way."

I opened my mouth, then closed it, at a loss for words.

I was just about to thank him when he faced forward again and said, "And before you think I did this for you, I didn't. I just really hate that cocky, foul-mouthed bastard who did this to you and would like nothing more than to send him packing."

Aaand there he was, killing my gratitude once more.

"Even more than me?" I sardonically replied.

He was silent for a long moment, so long that I didn't think he would reply. Then, "Yes, Snowflake. Even more than you."

CHAPTER 20

I practically face-planted into my soup at dinner.

After refusing to miss any of my classes, I was beyond exhausted. At least Thorne hadn't made me train with him during my free period. In fact, he'd told me to lie down instead—which I hadn't done. If I had, I wouldn't have been able to get up again. Thankfully, he hadn't followed me around the entire day, but he was serious about the phone thing. He'd literally texted every hour to check if I was still alive.

He was watching me now, his gaze blatantly locked on my little corner of the dining hall as he conversed with Oz and Riku. I couldn't hear him, of course, the dozens of voices around me louder than usual. Everyone was talking about my curse, including Blaze. Alma seemed quieter than usual, at one point telling Blaze to shut up when he got too boisterous. I tried to listen in, to catch him confessing to the crime, but I kept dozing off.

In a few more minutes, everyone was going to know just how hard that curse had wiped me out. I'd be a sitting duck if anyone tried to pick me off at this point.

Valiantly trying to keep my head up and eyes open, I glanced over at Thorne's table again—and saw that Riku and Oz were missing. Before I could wonder where they'd disappeared to, two big bodies sat in the seats beside and across from me.

"So, here's the thing," Riku quietly said, his shoulder brushing mine as he leaned in close. "Thorne is pretty certain you're going to resist switching tables, so he sent *us* over to change your mind."

I frowned, my brain taking longer than usual to understand his words. Switch tables? As in, me sitting at *their* table? I didn't know what to think let alone feel about that, not when I was this tired, so I just mumbled, "And how will you do that?"

"By whipping out our dicks and wagging them in your face until you give in."

What the—?

"No, we won't," Oz said, shooting his friend a death glare.

Riku shrugged. "Suit yourself. But I will." Making good on his threat, he stood and reached for his belt to unbuckle it. When he popped the button on his pants and started to tug down the zipper, I knew he was serious.

"Okay, I give in," I groaned, waving at him to zip back up.

Something like disappointment flashed in his eyes. "Really? I was hoping you'd resist a little."

"Nope. I'm too tired and have already seen enough dick for one day."

Riku barked a laugh, and even Oz cracked a smile.

"Beautiful, dangerous, *and* witty? I'm smitten," Riku hummed while fixing his pants.

Despite my exhaustion, I melted a little at his words. I definitely understood why girls clambered to sleep with him. Charm practically oozed from his pores.

Pushing my chair back, I stood, only for a wave of dizziness to hit me. I gripped the table's edge, doing my best not to hunch over as the spell passed.

"Want me to carry you?" Riku crooned in my ear.

"Back off," I grumbled, reaching for my tray.

Riku plucked it up before I could. "Cranky, too. I like it."

As he led the way around the table, I finally realized that we had an audience. One quick peek confirmed that every eyeball in the dining hall was on us, on my walk of shame—or maybe walk of victory? I didn't really know yet. Thorne had publicly rejected me my first day here by booting me off the third year table. Now he was *inviting* me to it.

What would that say to the rest of the student body? That he'd accepted me? *Allied* with me? Not out of choice, anyway. He was simply saving face again before I made a fool of myself—and therefore him—by passing out in my food.

With each step, the room grew more and more quiet, the heavy attention making my skin feel too tight. Everyone knew that Thorne was my mentor and that the Arcane Three were a package deal, but none of the other first years had been invited to their mentors' tables or included in their alliances. Not that they were *actually* allying with me, but to everyone watching, it sure looked like it.

As we came even with Alma and Blaze, I prepared to receive twin glares. Riku was Alma's mentor, after all, and he wasn't carrying *her* tray over to his table. But I didn't expect Blaze to speak, to tell Alma loud enough for everyone to hear, "Whoever cursed her was an effing genius. If only I could have seen her bleeding all over the place like a stuck pig."

The words hit me a lot harder than I thought they would, and every inch of me went cold. When I faltered a step, a hand steadied me, fitting to the small of my back.

Oz.

In front of me, Riku's shoulders tensed. The only warning I got before my tray in his hands suddenly went airborne. As it flipped, my almost full bowl of soup and glass of water slid off the slick surface and struck Blaze. Liquid, along with chunks of meat and vegetables, sluiced down his head and clothing, plopping onto his lap.

As metal and ceramic crashed to the floor in a chaotic symphony, Blaze jumped up with a furious cry. "What the *hell?*"

"Whoops. How clumsy of me. It just flew right out of my hands," Riku innocently said.

Too innocently. Absolutely no one would buy that. The guy had the athletic grace of a ballerina and ninja warrior combined. He didn't know *how* to be clumsy.

Blaze whirled toward him, my soup still dripping off his dirty blond curls and onto his reddening face. Clearly not buying Riku's lame excuse, he balled his beefy hands into fists, wisps of smoke emanating from them.

Not intimidated in the least, Riku slowly took in his handiwork, looking Blaze up and down before saying, "Wanna start something, tough guy? I'd like to see you do something other than run your big mouth for a change."

Even more smoke came from Blaze's shaking fists, his lips pulling back in a silent snarl. Riku lifted his hands between them and made a show of cracking his knuckles. *Crack. Crack.* Each crack was punctuated by a flash of topaz, his rings, his *relics* catching the light. *Crack. Crack.*

Yeah, Blaze didn't stand a chance.

When Blaze hesitated, caught between ego and self-preservation, Oz spoke up from behind me, "I'd sit down if you value all that hot air. Fire is useless without it, and I'm guessing you are too."

"Good one," Riku said, sticking a fist out in our direction.

Oz reached around me to bump it.

Just like that, it was over. Blaze continued to stand, but it was clear he'd been put in his place. He silently fumed, his fists still shaking as he watched Riku turn away and approach Alma next. Leaning over the back of her chair, he spoke into her ear loud enough for those around us to hear, "You really should pick better allies, *mami*. This one's only gonna blow up in your face."

His free hand mimed a bomb exploding, then reached back and gently tugged her golden brown braid. She didn't respond, yet her eyes followed him as he resumed his stroll around the table. Oz pressed in close, his hand still on my back encouraging me forward. I hesitated for another moment, the need for revenge rearing up again. After what Blaze had just said, I was convinced more than ever that he'd been the one to curse me. He'd practically *admitted* to it.

I desperately wanted him to pay. Desperately wanted him cast out of this school like a discarded stray. He would know exactly how I felt then, and oh, how wickedly satisfying that would be.

Now wasn't the time to confront him, though. Besides being bone tired, I still didn't have any evidence to convict him with. Noticing my pause, Blaze swung his attention my way. Our eyes locked, and I felt the full weight of his wrath. Not letting my gaze waver, I looked deeply into those twin green pools of boiling hatred and told him without words that I knew. I *knew* he was guilty.

As a quivering sneer pulled at his mouth, I looked away and skirted around him, following after Riku. By the time we made it to the third year table, my body would have happily sat anywhere. Without an ounce of resistance, I gratefully sank into the chair beside Riku, stifling a relieved groan.

The second Oz and Riku took their seats, a deep voice across from me rumbled, "You two done making a scene?"

"No promises," Riku replied with an unapologetic smirk.

Thorne grunted, and I finally glanced up at him to say, "I thought we had an understanding about the whole hiding behind you thing."

He steadily met my faintly accusing gaze. "You're not hiding behind me. You're simply sitting across from me and socializing for once."

"And eating better food." Riku grabbed a plate from the table and motioned a server over, who hurried to fill the plate without comment.

When he placed it before me, my tired eyes widened a fraction. Salmon, mashed potatoes, and asparagus? This was like Michelin star level food. Despite how good it looked, I found myself saying, "I'm way too tired to eat all that."

"Do it anyway," Thorne quietly ordered. "You didn't eat enough at lunch."

He was watching my *calorie intake* now? Too exhausted to be annoyed, I picked up my fork without further argument and dug into the mashed potatoes. One small bite, and my appetite came roaring back. I was nearly done with the salmon when I finally realized how quiet it was around me. Glancing up, I caught all three guys staring at me.

Awkward.

Reaching for the glass of water Oz had poured for me, I took a sip before saying, "Did you all want me over here just to watch me eat, or what?"

With his elbow planted on the table, Riku propped his chin in his hand to better stare at me. "She's like a pocket-sized ball of sarcasm. Absolutely adorable. We should have brought her over here weeks ago."

I blinked.

"Conversation will definitely be more interesting, that's for sure," Oz remarked, making me blink again.

Carefully setting my water glass down, I looked across at Thorne and said, "Am I just here to *amuse* you?"

The slight edge to my voice didn't seem to faze him, making the food I'd just eaten sink to the bottom of my stomach like lead. Was I seriously just entertainment to them?

Before I could get up and storm off—let's see how they liked *that*—Thorne replied, "You were brought over here to make a statement. Anyone who messes with you now messes with us. Simple yet effective communication."

I stared. Stared and stared. Did he say what I think he just said? That by sitting at their table, I'd just announced to the entire student body that Arcane Three had my back? Not sure how to process this news, I didn't say a word.

"You're going to quickly find out how fickle politics are, Bambi," Riku drawled, leaning back in his chair. "I can singlehandedly change your social status at this school in a second flat."

Breaking my staredown with Thorne, I glanced at Riku with a frown. "How?"

"Like this." Reaching over, he deftly plucked me off my seat and onto his lap so that I was facing him. *Straddling* him. My hands automatically shot to his shoulders, my lower half sinking into his. Something hard twitched against me, against my *core*, and my eyes flew wide.

An explosive movement behind me announced that someone had just jumped to their feet, followed by a loud *bang* of a chair crashing over.

Before I could look to see who it was, before I could so much as blink, Riku slid both hands beneath my skirt. "See?" he purred, sliding them up, up, up, smirking when his thumbs grazed my underwear, and I gasped. "Everyone now knows that two of the most powerful warlocks at Heartstone are dying to get inside your panties.

One second flat, and you've been upgraded from social pariah to most desirable female on campus. You're welcome."

The bulge beneath me moved again, and I knew without a doubt that it was his dick. He was clearly aroused by this unexpected power play, uncaring that every eye in the dining hall was gaping at us. I felt his thumbs shift again, dangerously close to touching me through my underwear, and I finally moved.

The moment I scrambled to get off his lap, an arm snagged my waist and hauled me off him. Before my feet could fully connect with the ground, I was whisked away from the table at a fast clip. An *angry* clip. Without even looking, I knew it was Thorne. He practically carried me out of the dining hall, my legs unable to match his furious strides.

Realizing I couldn't pull away from him, I kept up as best I could, trying and failing to think of something that would calm him. Riku had definitely crossed a line, but he shouldn't be *this* mad. It was *my* reputation in question right now, not his. It wasn't like I'd sat on *his* lap in front of the whole school.

As we stormed down the hall just short of jogging, I finally settled on, "I had no idea Riku was going to do that."

Silence.

Wait. Did he think this was *my* fault? I hadn't asked for this. *Any* of this. When Riku had said he could change my social status, no way in hell had I thought he meant the school's most desirable female. I didn't even *want* that.

"Thorne, this isn't my fault," I tried again. Silence. "*Thorne*."

He didn't respond. Didn't even look at me. His arm stayed locked around my waist, dragging me to who-knew-where. So distracted by his furious state, I lost track of where we were. The halls and stairwells were empty, the only sound Thorne's angry footfalls. Suddenly worried that he was taking me somewhere quiet to punish me, my heart picked up speed. I had to do something. *Anything.*

I was just about to say his name again when he whipped us around a corner and shoved open a door. Dragging me inside, he shut the door behind us, and we plunged into darkness. My heart lurched into my throat, and when he finally let go of me, I blindly backpedaled to get away.

"Thorne—" My backside hit something solid, cutting off my escape. Before I could move around it, I felt Thorne enter my personal space again. Lightning quick, he grabbed my hips and hoisted me up onto the solid surface. A desk, by the feel of it. I tried to squirm away, but his grip was ironclad. "Thorne—"

"Where did he touch you?" he finally spoke, his voice like rolling thunder. Before I could fully grasp his words, he released my hips and slid both hands under my skirt. "Here?"

I jerked at the feel of his fingers on my inner thighs, at the thrill that shot through me. When I tried to close my legs, he wedged his body between them, prying my thighs further apart.

"*Where,* Snowflake? Here?" His hands went higher, dragging a path toward my suddenly aching center. "*Answer* me."

"Yes," I said, the word little more than air.

A growl vibrated his chest, vibrated his *hands.* The sensation wrung a startled gasp from me.

"How about here?" he demanded, sweeping his thumbs along the edges of my underwear.

I nodded this time, too breathless to speak.

He couldn't see the action, but he must have felt it. A savage curse left his mouth, right before he slid both thumbs over my underwear, over my *center* and pressed down. My hips bucked off the desk, and I grabbed onto both his hands with a sharp cry, pleasure spiking through my core. "Here?" he asked me. "Did he touch you here?"

I opened my mouth to respond, but nothing came out.

"I need an *answer*, Winter," he growled, that same vibration from earlier now going through my clit.

A moan of pleasure rolled up my throat, and with it a barely intelligible, "No."

He immediately responded by pressing harder on the sensitive flesh and rotating his thumbs in a circular motion. I moaned again, dimly aware that he wasn't punishing me after all. I'd passed some kind of test, and this was my reward. And, oh, what a wonderful reward it was.

As every inch of me began to burst awake with pleasure, everything else disappeared. Thought. Reason. Sanity. I didn't care about any of that, only what he was awakening in me. Certain he was going to keep the barrier of my underwear between us like last time, I wasn't prepared when he said, "I'm going to push aside your panties now, Snowflake."

He was going to . . . what?

His hands shifted beneath mine, tugging my underwear aside just like he said. Just like he—

One of his fingers touched my bare clit, and I almost lost it. Shaking, trembling, gasping, the foreign sensation crashed into me, robbing me of air.

"Relax, or you'll pass out," he murmured above me, tracing the tip of his finger over the sensitive flesh. When he suddenly flicked it, I jerked against the desk with a cry. Something that sounded way too much like satisfaction rumbled from him, then he flicked me again. And again. And again.

Overwhelmed by the new sensations spiking through my body, pretty sure I was going to pass out if he kept doing it, I let go of his hands and grabbed onto his shoulders instead. Something grazed my forehead, something warm, soft. His mouth.

"I'm going to check if you're ready now, Snowflake," his lips moved against my skin, but the words were lost to me. What he was doing between my legs was all I could focus on, the need, the desperate ache completely taking over.

His finger suddenly left my clit and slid further back. When it touched my pool of arousal, I jerked again. His mouth still on my skin shifted, stretching into a pleased grin.

"Oh, you're more than ready for me."

Ready. Ready for what?

Instead of pulling back, the finger slid further into my wetness, slipping into, slipping *inside* my entrance. Every inch of me tensed, and I gasped out, "Thorne!"

He paused, the tip of his finger still inside me. "You don't want this?"

I struggled to breathe. To think. Two things that were extremely difficult knowing that a part of him was inside my body. "I . . . I . . ."

"Tell me to stop, Winter, and I will." The words were strained, almost a plea. Making it sound like he *wanted* me to stop him.

"I . . . I can't."

I hadn't expected that confession to fall from my lips, but the second it did, he sucked in a hiss and pressed closer, forcing my legs even farther apart. The fingertip continued to inch inside me, penetrating a part of myself that had never been touched before.

"Relax, Snowflake," Thorne breathed against my forehead. "I can't enter you when you're so tense."

Drawing comfort from the calm reassurance of his voice, I relaxed my thighs as best I could, relaxed my walls, and his finger slid all the way in.

"That's my good girl."

The praise, combined with the feeling of his finger starting to curl against my tight walls, had another moan bursting from me. "Dear ancestors, save me."

"They can't save you from this," Thorne rumbled, slowly sliding his finger back out. "If you seek salvation, pray to me."

He pulled the finger all the way out, only to drive it back in again, firmly pressing on my sensitive walls as he did. He pumped in and out a few times, slowly, as if to prep me, to acquaint himself with my body. His finger explored, slipping farther and farther inside as if to reach something, pressing and curling, trying to—

He suddenly hit a spot deep inside me, and an immediate shockwave rocked my body. I gripped his shoulders for dear life, a ragged cry leaving me as my pussy fluttered and pulsed over his finger. It didn't feel like an orgasm, but hell if it didn't feel amazing.

"There's your sweet spot," he hummed, approval thick in his voice as I continued to spasm around his digit. "You're most definitely a virgin, Snowflake. Receptive to the slightest touch. Deliciously tight. Pure as snow and entirely untouched. But you won't be the same when I'm done with you."

No. I wouldn't. I already knew that. But as he slid his finger out again, only to add a *second* finger this time, stretching my entrance in a way I'd never felt before, something akin to fear fluttered in my chest.

Won't be the same, won't be the same.

His fingers pushed and pushed, stretching me more and more. My wetness helped, but it still burned, still hurt. It was a hurt I *wanted* to feel, though, and that terrified me most of all. By the time both fingers were all the way inside me, I was a trembling mess. Sweat had begun to bead my brow and trickle down my spine, and I was leaning more and more heavily on Thorne. He'd placed his free hand flat on the desk, which brought our bodies even closer together. My breaths were rapid, but so were his, the intimate moment affecting him as well.

He only waited a moment for me to adjust, then slowly began to thrust those two fingers in and out of me. Almost immediately, a pleasurable tension started building where his fingers rubbed against my walls, filling me with an ache greater than the one he'd given me this morning. This ache was fuller, *deeper*, reaching into parts of me I hadn't known existed.

Unable to help myself, I arched into him with a low moan, sliding my hands up to twine around his neck. I ached to be closer, *closer*. "What are you doing to me?"

"Ruining you," he breathed, curling both fingers until a pitiful whimper left me. "Ruining you like you have ruined me."

The confession should have alarmed me, but all I felt was more arousal, *excitement*.

If being ruined felt this good, then I *wanted* to be ruined.

He added his thumb to the mix, pressing on my clit again while his two middle fingers pumped in and out of me at an ever-increasing pace. I sank my fingers into the hair at his nape and pulled on the strands. A guttural sound left him, and he pumped his fingers even faster, *feverishly*. At the sound, at the realization that *I* had caused it, a thrill shot through me. My aching core tightened. *Squeezed*. Making me more and more sensitive to his fingers.

It was almost too much. It *was* too much.

I jerked my legs up and around him, using the leverage to frantically thrust into his fingers. My entire body was instinct, *need*, knowing exactly how to find the release it so desperately wanted. Thorne groaned again, burying his head in the crook of my neck as he drove his fingers in and out of me like a madman. Swimming, *drowning* in sensation, I tensed and tensed, so close to reaching my destination.

I didn't know what finally pushed me over the edge. His pumping fingers, his thumb working my clit, or his mouth hot on my neck. But when I felt him press his groin against the desk edge. Felt it rock, keeping time with my own thrusts. I exploded.

Throwing my head back, I belted out my release, unable to contain the powerful wave of ecstasy blasting through me. Thorne savagely thrust himself against the desk a few more times, then stiffened all over. One more thrust, and he groaned into my neck, the sound so raw, so *feral*, that pure excitement jolted through me, prolonging my orgasm.

Pretty certain that he'd just come in his pants, I felt a wicked sense of satisfaction. Even though I hadn't touched him, he'd found completion because of me. There was power in that, and it was a heady feeling. *Addictive.*

When we both finally came down, I was so spent that I could have fallen asleep right then and there. Thorne slid his fingers out, and I immediately felt less full. Less *whole.* I nearly told him to put them back in, but that would have made me sound crazy. The moment was fading, dying, allowing reality to crowd back in.

Crap. I'd let him pleasure me again. Twice. *In one day.*

If I wasn't so utterly exhausted that I could have curled up on this desk and slept forever, I'd be flogging myself.

He helped me down off the desk, allowing me a moment to resituate my clothes before heading to the door. As we left the room, neither of us said a word. What was there to say? *Thanks for the mindblowing orgasm, but we can't do that again?*

Already said that. It didn't stick.

Thorne obviously felt like he had some sort of dibs on my body. His reaction to Riku's move on me in the dining hall had said that much. How I felt about that, I didn't really know at the moment. All I knew was that this day needed to come to an end. Too much had happened for me to wrap my brain around it all. I needed sleep. *Sleep.*

We reached Jade Wing five minutes later, and I waited for him to turn and leave. He didn't. He walked with me all the way down the hall. Down the *crowded* hall. Oh, I was definitely feeling heavy walk-of-shame vibes right now. Everyone stopped and stared, making me think that they could see evidence of what we'd just done written all over my flushed face.

Thorne didn't even look at them. He walked right on by, his expression unreadable. Like nothing had happened. Like he took girls into dark rooms and pleasured them senseless all the time.

Maybe he did.

Something about that bothered me, *really* bothered me, and I shut the thought down.

As we reached the end of the hallway, it finally dawned on me that he was making another statement. Him coming here with me was a warning, a *threat* to anyone who tried to mess with me again. I was pretty sure the message was received loud and clear.

Opening the door that led up to my tower, he let me go through first before following close behind. Okay, then. He was making sure I safely reached my dorm. But as I struggled to make it up the stairs, I started to worry that he didn't plan on leaving at all. Our conversation earlier today had been about me not staying in his dorm. We'd said *nothing* about him staying in mine.

Crap, crap, crap.

I could barely stand when we finally made it to the top. Which was probably why I didn't think to resist when Thorne asked, "What's your password?"

"*Sesamum, te aperi.*"

He quietly scoffed, muttering, "No wonder someone got in. It's the same as making your password 'password.' Make sure to change it."

"I will."

As he uttered the spell to unlock my door, he conjured magic to his fingertips before pushing inside. I held my breath, waiting for something terrible to happen.

"Clear," Thorne said seconds later, coming back out with the blue orb still dancing around his fingers—the fingers that had pleasured me into oblivion twice in one day. I looked away, making the same mistake I always did by glancing up at his face. He was watching me, studying, *searching*. He opened his mouth to say something, then seemed to change his mind and only said, "Get some sleep. You'll sit with us at meals from now on, so I expect to see you at our table first thing in the morning."

He moved past me to leave, clearly not meaning to stay, and I felt panic beat at my chest.

Stay. Take me with you. Don't leave me here all alone!

The words tumbled through my mind, but I refused, *refused* to voice them. Instead, I murmured after him, "They'll call me a whore."

He paused. Without turning around, he replied back, "Then they'll regret it." I let the words sink in, let them soothe away some of my worry. He started to move again, and so did I, already half asleep on my feet. But only a few stairs down, Thorne paused again and said, "Oh, and, Winter? If Tanaka touches you like that again, I'll break his fingers."

With that, he was gone, leaving me reeling over his sudden possessiveness. Was that what this was? Or was it something even darker?

What are you doing to me?

Ruining you . . .

. . . Ruining you like you have ruined me.

CHAPTER 21

Someone was going to die today.

There was no mistaking the foreboding stench of death heavy in the air. The cold chills scraping up my spine and the disembodied whispers beckoning to me confirmed that death wasn't just on its way.

It was already here.

I'd been following the pungent smell for the past several minutes, my senses growing dimmer and dimmer the closer I got to death's target. I was close. *Very* close. My intuition urged me onward, yet my survival instincts shouted at me to run the opposite direction. Not because death was coming for me this time, but because I couldn't save whoever was about to die.

I never could. Which was why this gift, this *curse* had never made sense to me. Why allow me to sense death's approach if I couldn't save the victim?

Despite the despair trying to suck the life out of my very marrow, I pushed myself onward, needing to know who was about to be claimed. At least I knew it wasn't Thorne. He'd been texting and calling me for the past several minutes, obviously wanting to know why I hadn't shown up on time to our daily training session. Another buzz vibrated my hip, and I distractedly pulled the phone from my skirt pocket.

Call me. NOW, the new text from him said.

I was about to shove the phone back into my pocket when another text popped up: *Bambi, text us back. We're worried.*

A relieved sigh left me. Riku sounded okay, too. The Air Elemental might be oversexed and way too handsy, but he was starting to grow under my skin like obnoxious yet endearing fungus. After the dining hall lap-dance incident a month ago, things had cooled down between us, and I'd actually begun to enjoy our ridiculously flirtatious interactions.

Thorne didn't seem to like them all that much, but he didn't have a say in who I flirted with. After our sizzling rendezvous in that dark room, I'd woken up the next morning feeling like scum. Pleasure me once, shame on me; pleasure me twice, shame on me as well. I wanted to blame it on momentary insanity after almost dying, but I blamed him too for what had happened that day. Blamed him for touching me again when I'd told him we couldn't go there.

I'd spent hours, *days* after that reminding myself why we couldn't. We were enemies. Rivals. Competition at the very least. Our mentor and student partnership needed to stay professional. There was still so much unresolved hurt between us, so much pain and anger. Throwing sex into the mix was a recipe for disaster. I couldn't allow the lines between us to blur any more than they already had—even when I lay awake at night unable to sleep, my body aching for something that only he could satiate.

He'd ruined me, all right.

My body had never pined to be touched that way before. But ever since that one day of bad judgment, I couldn't stop thinking, couldn't stop *dreaming* about him touching me. It terrified me how easily I'd given in to him, how badly I didn't want him to stop once he'd started. It terrified me even more knowing that all it would take was one single touch for me to give in again.

So I'd kept my distance—as much as he would allow me to, anyway. I still had to train with him on a daily basis, still had to eat with him and text him, but not once in the past month had I let his body touch mine.

He hadn't pressed me, hadn't *pushed* me like that day I'd woken up in his bed, but every day since, I knew that he wanted to. Wanted to touch me again and hated that he did. Despised and craved that ache the same way I did. I saw that want in the way he looked at me. Needy looks. Haunted looks. Looks that lasted too long. Looks that cut too short.

This newfound desire was miserable, but I took comfort in knowing that he was suffering too. Petty? Probably. But he was the one who started it.

Another text came in from Thorne, even more insistent this time: *I swear, Snowflake. Call me back right now, or I'm going to tear apart this entire campus in search of you.*

Aaand there was the new Thorne Hudson I'd come to know this past month. He'd swapped the icy cold stares and angry insults for constant frustration and an obsessive need to know where I was at all times. His behavior was becoming borderline psychotic, and both Oz and Riku had expressed their growing concern.

Riku, of course, thought it was because Thorne wasn't getting any nookie—then majorly hinted that I could help him with said frustration. Oz thought it stemmed from the ongoing investigation into who had cursed me—which hadn't unearthed any evidence so far. The professors had voted against interrogating the students with Truth Potion, so whoever had almost killed me was still lurking around campus, undoubtedly waiting for another opportune moment to strike.

I, however, thought it boiled down to the stress of being partnered with me. Thorne couldn't properly focus on his own studies and upcoming trials when he was constantly checking if I was still alive. That, and my own trial was coming up in just a few weeks, marking the end of my first semester. I'd come in last place for my Initiation Trial, and we were both painfully aware that I'd almost failed to complete it at all. The need to win, to protect his pristine reputation, was everything to Thorne, and knowing that he wouldn't be able to help me with my trial once it started was taxing that ironclad control of his.

Whatever the reasons for his emotional shift, he'd become quite the cranky bossy pants lately.

Which was why I had no intention of answering him right away. The dude needed to take a chill pill before he had an aneurysm. Maybe turning my phone off for a while would help. Blaze had kept his distance from me all month, the Arcane Three's threats proving to be an effective deterrent. He'd also stopped verbally attacking me, and the rumors about my sexual exploits had all but died.

I'd overheard some gossip that he was putting his mentor Sydney through the wringer, though. His relationship with Alma even seemed a bit strained, making me wonder if their alliance would hold up much longer. The Fire Elemental was far from popular these days, and I mostly had Thorne, Riku, and Oz to thank for that.

Because of their protection, I didn't really need the phone anymore. I was holding my own, even in my classes. Besides, Thorne had rigged the phone so I could only dial his, Riku's, and Oz's numbers, the sadist.

Winter, please let us know you're okay.

The new text immediately allowed me to release another ball of anxiety, this one Oz-sized. Death was still leading me toward its victim, but at least it wasn't after one of the three guys who'd been there for me this past month. After all was said and done, I might just be a means to an end for them, but I knew without a doubt that I wouldn't have survived this long without their help.

Suddenly feeling guilty for ignoring them after everything they'd done for me, I was about to send a reassuring text to the group chat when my surroundings abruptly dimmed. The hallway plunged into shadow, as if the lights had just flickered out.

In here, both my intuition and death breathed in my ear, letting me know that I'd arrived. I slowed and peered through the darkness, a shiver working its way through me when I saw a closed bathroom door to my left. So distracted with following death, I wasn't sure which bathroom it was or even what building I was in. All I knew was that the hallway was devoid of life—which meant that whoever was on death's door had to be in that bathroom.

A cold sweat pricked my flesh, the heavy despair in the air nearly suffocating me. The last thing I wanted to do was see a dead body, but I couldn't help thinking, couldn't help *hoping* that I wasn't too late. They could still be clinging to life, still be *breathing*. I couldn't run away now, couldn't abandon them. They were alone, all alone, and no matter who was on the other side of that door, I empathized with how they must be feeling.

Hopeless. Forsaken. Scared.

I could help them. I could *save* them.

Shoving aside my fear, I rushed to the bathroom and pushed open the door. The second I was inside, I saw the body splayed on the floor. Saw and recognized the cute blonde pixie-cut hairdo.

It was Sydney Wright, Blaze's second year mentor.

"Sydney!" I hurried forward and dropped down beside her, immediately placing my fingers beneath her chin to search for a pulse. Nothing. "No. *No*."

I rolled her onto her back and pressed my ear to her sternum. Still nothing.

Death's presence started to fade, the despair and foreboding chill creeping away.

"No, don't take her!" I cried, my voice extra loud as my senses fully returned. "*Please!*"

Death ignored me, whisking Sydney's spirit away to a place I couldn't reach, fulfilling its mission without remorse.

Her body lay perfectly still beneath my hands, no longer breathing, no longer anything. It was empty. Devoid of life. Devoid of a soul.

Images of another time, of another body, flashed in my mind. Images of *her*, my best friend. My *soul* sister. Her body had looked and felt just like this. So very still. Too still. Lifeless. Soulless. All because of me.

Because of *me*.

A sound escaped me. Pitiful. Hopeless. Despairing. The sound of brokenness. The sound my shattered heart made the day I'd taken my best friend's life.

Suddenly, Sydney became *her*. Blonde pixie-cut hair lengthened to rich wavy brown tresses, her pale skin tanning.

I fell back with a horrified cry, frantically scooting backward until my spine smacked into the bathroom wall. Struggling to breathe, to discern reality from memory, I pulled my knees to my chest and stared wide-eyed at the body. One second, it was Sydney, and the next, my precious childhood friend. Back and forth, back and forth, present and past blurred together.

Bombarded by memory after memory, I couldn't move, couldn't *think*. My eyes stayed glued to the body, burning so fiercely that I thought for sure it would happen this time. I waited, waited for it to happen. Wanting it to happen, *needing* it to happen. The pressure, the *guilt* was too much. I had to release it somehow.

Cry already. CRY!

Something vibrated in my hand, and it took me way too long to realize what it was. Shaking, trembling so hard that I almost dropped it, I raised the phone to my ear and accepted the call.

"Winter?"

My lips were numb. I couldn't feel them.

"Winter, *answer* me."

I opened my mouth and uttered a sound. "Help." The word was so threadbare that even I couldn't hear it. Yet, somehow, he did.

"Where are you?" Thorne said, his annoyance and frustration suddenly gone. In their place was a quiet calm, a reassurance that I desperately latched onto.

"In . . . in the bathroom."

"Which one?"

Sydney's body became Juliana's again, and a panicked whimper left me.

"Winter, I can't get to you if you don't talk to me. Now, focus. Which bathroom are you in?"

I forced myself to swallow, to peel my eyes off Jewel's—*Sydney's*—body so I could better focus. Thorne patiently waited, his breaths steady over the speaker, so full and *alive* that I used them to ground me, to guide me back to reality, to the here and now.

He was alive, and so was I, and I needed to tell him where I was.

The words were garbled and all mixed up at first, but I finally managed to straighten them out, enough for him to roughly guess where to find me.

"I'm coming, Snowflake. Don't hang up."

I wouldn't. I wouldn't dare. His voice was the only thing keeping me in the present, keeping me *sane.*

"Keep . . . keep talking," I whispered, and he did. He talked about anything and nothing, mentioning the weather and how big the full moon was the other night. He talked about food, confessing that he needed to eat more fruits and vegetables. Talked about Oz constantly leaving his books everywhere and Riku sneaking girls into their dorm.

By the time I heard a noise at the bathroom door, I was able to breathe again, the tremors in my body no longer violent. The door opened, and I lifted my eyes, expecting to see Thorne come through. When he didn't, panic tightened my throat once more.

"It's just Comet," Thorne spoke through the phone. "I sent him ahead to make sure you were okay."

I dropped my gaze and finally saw the large bird, who'd somehow managed to push open the heavy door all by himself. His clawed feet faintly tapped the stone floor as he quickly scanned the bathroom's interior, taking in Sydney's body before zeroing in on me.

As our eyes locked, I heard Thorne murmur over the phone, "Good job, buddy."

The relief in his tone was clear, and I knew that the hawk familiar was using their telepathic connection to tell Thorne what he was seeing.

"He's going to approach you now," Thorne said to me. "Just hold still. He won't hurt you."

I watched the bird hop-walk across the bathroom, uncertain what he planned to do. When he stopped beside me, I just stared at him, too frozen to do anything else. He was suddenly on my forearm, then my bent knees, climbing up so swiftly that I barely felt the pricks of his claws.

His head was now even with mine, so close that he could easily dart forward and peck my eyes out. But that wasn't what he did. Instead, he leaned forward and nuzzled his forehead against my cheek. The feel of his soft feathers, combined with the weight of his presence, had an instant effect on me. Some of the panic holding me captive started to fade, along with the icy chill in my veins.

When the hawk rubbed against me again, I lifted my free arm and pulled him closer, surprised when he tucked his body beneath my chin and snuggled down like a pet. The second I felt the swift rise and fall of his chest, I squeezed my burning eyes shut and released a quiet sob. I gathered him tightly to me, burying my face in his feathered body. So warm. So full of *life*.

I heard a chuckle over the phone. "He doesn't mind the hug, but your grip is a little too tight."

"Oh." I relaxed my hold on the bird, and he chirped as if to thank me.

Less than a minute later, the door burst open. Comet didn't react, and his calming presence kept me from spiraling into a panic again. Thorne was the first to enter, and not surprisingly, Oz and Riku weren't far behind. They'd been preparing their own students for the upcoming end-of-semester trial, but they still watched me and Thorne train during my free period.

Seeing me huddled in the corner and clutching Comet for dear life while a dead body lay on the floor had them all filing in with somber expressions. As they took in the scene, it suddenly dawned on me how terrible it looked. How *damning*.

"I didn't . . . I didn't do it," I stammered. All three of them focused on me, no doubt hearing the hesitation in my voice. The *uncertainty*.

I didn't kill Sydney Wright. I *didn't*.

Didn't you? a voice breathed in my ear, sending another foreboding chill up my spine.

Comet squirmed in my grip, and I quickly dropped my arms, certain he'd picked up on the uncertainty as well, the *guilt.* With a flutter and hop, he left my lap, and I immediately felt lost again.

They didn't believe me. Of course they wouldn't. I'd killed before, after all. The body splayed in the grass had looked just like Sydney's. Untouched. Not a mark on it. No sign of how the murder had happened, only that it had.

And I was the only one who could have done it.

Panic shortened my breaths once more, the suffocating guilt making the walls around me cave in.

Murderer. Murderer!

Just when I felt myself start to break, to shatter, the sound of a glass rolling across the floor reached my ears.

"Look," Oz said. He bent down to pick up whatever Comet had nudged out from beneath the sinks, lifting what appeared to be a potion vial. One experimental whiff, and he jerked the bottle away from his face. "Yeah, that'll do it. A student last year took Nox Serum to stop their own heart. Looks like Sydney drank the whole bottle."

I heard his words, heard Riku sadly mutter, "Another suicide," but I was still lost. Still drowning in guilt, so much guilt. My gaze dropped to the body again, but before I could see if it was Sydney or Juliana this time, a big muscular wall blocked her from view. Long legs crouched before me, and a hand reached out, hesitating a moment before gently grasping my chin.

"Winter."

My eyes flew up to Thorne's. Expecting his face to be twisted in anger, hatred, or that terrible devastation I'd hoped to never see again, confusion swamped me when I found tenderness instead, his expression soft in a way I didn't know it could.

"I didn't do it," I repeated, waiting for that soft look to vanish, for condemnation to take its place.

Murderer.

Unable to keep the guilt inside any longer, I cried, "I'm sorry! I didn't mean to!"

I braced for the look to drastically change, to fill with hatred. No matter what I said, no matter how many times I apologized, he would always hate me for what I did.

And I couldn't blame him. I *didn't* blame him. Not even a little.

But the look only softened more, filling with *worry* instead of hate. How? How could he even stand to look at me, to *touch* me, after what I'd just done?

"Winter, you didn't do this. She killed herself," I heard Oz say.

I frantically shook my head, almost dislodging Thorne's grip on my chin. "No, she didn't. She would never do that. She was a ray of sunshine, overflowing with joy and always making me laugh. She would . . . she would *never* do this. Never *leave* me."

Another sound left me. Broken. Shattered. Dredged from the very center of my being. A violent tremor ripped through me, clacking my teeth together.

"I did this. I did this. I—"

"She's in shock," another voice said over my repeated confession.

Riku.

"I know," another voice replied, this time Thorne. Why did he sound so sad? Knowing that I had caused his sadness, more guilt pressed down on me. A choked cry left me, and I tried to lower my head in shame. Thorne cupped my face in both hands and lifted it back up, forcing me to meet his eyes again. "Come back to me, Snowflake. You didn't kill her. This isn't Juliana."

Looking into his eyes was too much. The pain. The *pain* in them. I couldn't *breathe.*

"Just kill me," I whimpered, *begged* him. "I know you want to, and it's what I deserve after what I've done. She was your sister. *Sister.* I can't live with myself anymore. Can't live with the guilt. So just kill me, Thorne. *Please.* Just—"

"Winter, stop."

Horror had flooded his gaze, but I couldn't stop now that I'd started. A dam that I'd tried to hold back for far too long had just cracked, just *burst*, and everything I'd been suppressing was gushing out.

"I'm a monster. I'm dark and evil, and witches like me shouldn't exist. I'm dangerous, and I need to be stopped, so just do it already. Just *kill* me."

"Winter, stop talking this way!" Thorne roared, shaking me hard enough that I felt my brain rattle. "It's not her. It's not Juliana! So just *stop*. Please, *stop!*"

His pain, his horror, his *panic.* It hit me all at once like a sledgehammer, and I stopped, just stopped, staring at him with wide burning eyes still dry as a bone, feeling lost, so very lost.

"Thorne."

One little whimpered word, and his expression crumbled.

"I know, Snowflake, I know," he whispered, the softness returning. "It's okay. Come here."

I didn't understand, too frozen in confusion to resist when he reached forward and pulled me to him. Still in a crouched position, he fitted my body between his legs and banded both arms behind me, locking me against him. My head fit perfectly beneath his chin, pressed to him in such a way that I quickly picked up the strong *thump-thump* of his heart.

Everywhere. He was *everywhere.*

In the back corners of my mind, alarm bells went off. But as his scent, his warmth, his *life force* wrapped around me, the warnings faded away. Relief, soul deep *relief* hit me like an avalanche, and I buried my face and fists in his shirt, melting into his comforting embrace. When a shuddering sob left me, he tightened his arms even more, his powerful thighs bracketing my lower half.

"It's okay, Snowflake," he breathed against my hair, warming my scalp. "I'm here now. You're safe."

Safe. There was that word again. A word that didn't belong in my world.

But in his arms like this, being held, being surrounded like I was something worth protecting . . .

I could no longer deny that I felt absolutely, assuredly safe.

CHAPTER 22

"Stop looking at me like that."

The dark eyes fixed on me didn't even blink.

"I'm fine. *Really.*"

"You cracked wide open, Bambi. Besides, if a woman says she's fine, she's really not. Female Psychology 101."

Sighing my frustration, I settled back on the couch pillows and closed my eyes so I could no longer see Riku's penetrating stare. "You're not the authority on women, you know. You don't know everything."

"Oh, I know everything," he said with a small laugh. "Every little nook and cranny."

I wrinkled my nose but kept my eyes shut. "Is everything *sex* with you?"

"Pretty much."

I sighed again. "Girls are good for more than just sex, you know."

"I know. I have use for you, and we haven't had sex yet."

"*Yet?*" I jerked my head up to throw a scowl toward the other end of the sectional where he was sprawled. "We're never having sex, Riku. You've been friendzoned, remember?"

His smirk was unapologetic as he interlaced his hands and lifted them behind his head. The move rode up his tight white t-shirt and exposed a sliver of tanned abdomen, which was *definitely* intentional. "Oh, I remember, but never say never, my little doe-eyed fawn. I have a way of charming off even the most tight-laced panties, friends included."

"Pervert." I grabbed one of the pillows behind me to throw it at him.

He caught the pillow midair with his magic, barely raising a finger as he smoothly guided it down to his lap. "Maybe, but you're looking less haunted, so I'll call that a win."

I paused at that, realizing what he'd been trying to do. On the couch back near my head, Comet let out a soft chirp, his close proximity yet another sign that they'd been worried. Ever since my little episode in the bathroom, one of the guys had been with me at all times, even during my classes. I'd tried to protest, tried to assure them I was okay, but none of them were buying it.

I hadn't just been in shock. I'd had a bonafide mental breakdown.

Seeing Sydney's body that way, *touching* her, had triggered something deep inside me, something that was still painfully raw and vulnerable like an exposed nerve. It took me hours afterward to finally realize the gravity of what I'd revealed in that bathroom. I'd basically admitted to them that *I* should be the one dead on that floor. That I deserved to die for what I'd done to Thorne's sister.

No wonder they'd refused to leave me alone for even a second. They probably all thought I was going to commit suicide next.

After a brief talk with Chancellor Grimshaw about finding Sydney in the bathroom, I'd been allowed to go about my day as normal. No guidance counselor, no "are you okay?", no nothing. The casual reaction to her death had nearly put me into a spiral again. Hours later, word of the suicide hadn't even reached the rest of the student body yet. It felt too much like she'd been erased from existence, like she no longer *mattered*, and that hit hard.

No one questioned my explanation for how I'd found her, but I could tell the guys weren't satisfied with it. My daily routine never took me by that bathroom, so it didn't make sense that I'd suddenly decided to go there. They didn't say anything, though, at least not yet. Not while I was this unstable.

Thorne had been called into the chancellor's office during dinner, so he'd left me in Oz and Riku's care, explicitly instructing them to watch me at all times. Which meant that I couldn't go back to my dorm. They'd brought me to theirs, saying that they were just following orders when I demanded they let me go.

That had been hours ago. It was nearing midnight now, and Thorne still hadn't returned. Which was why Oz had finally headed out to collect some of my things—and coerced me into telling him my new password. It was just me and Riku now—and Comet, who was probably giving Thorne a play-by-play of everything I was doing. At this point, it was too late for me to even make it back to my dorm in time.

It seemed like I was having another sleepover whether I wanted to or not.

Annoyed but also more than a little relieved that I wouldn't have to be alone all night with my haunted thoughts, I focused on Riku again and said, "So how is mentoring with Alma going?"

He blinked at me as if surprised that I'd asked. *See? I'm perfectly fine*, my eyes silently told him.

"She's an avid learner and aims to please," he slowly replied, watching me closely. "It's really hard to keep it in my pants around her, and most days, I don't know why I even try. Maybe it's our pactum holding me in check, but this mentor-student thing we have going on is super hot. I should just screw her and get it out of my system, you know? But I don't think that's what you asked."

"It's *not*." I threw another pillow at him, and he deftly caught that one midair too, lowering it back to the couch with an insufferable smirk.

"You really want to know about Alma? I thought you two were frenemies."

My expression flattened. "Frenemies? She tried to drown me during our Initiation Trial and nearly filled my lungs with my own fluids in Conjuring class."

"Exactly. You've got this fierce competitive thing going on but also a begrudging respect for each other's talents. Which is also super hot, by the way."

"Uh, yeah, no. I'm pretty sure she doesn't respect anything about me."

"You'd be surprised, Bambi," he said, picking at a loose thread on the first pillow I'd tossed at him. "You've come a long way in just a few short months. Everyone has noticed."

"And yet I'm still just a disgraced Mayweather to them. No one will talk to me except you, Oz, and Thorne."

Riku barked a laugh. "That's because Thorne has spent the past month glaring at anyone who dares to even look at you."

"Great," I muttered, yet something fluttered in my belly at the realization. The word "possessive" came to mind again, making me think of all sorts of forbidden, confusing things. Before my brain could jump down that rabbit hole, I blurted, "Alma and I could never be friends, at least not while she's allied with Blaze. I still think he placed that curse on my spellbook, and I think he's responsible for Sydney's death too."

At that, Riku straightened from his relaxed position, his expression sobering. "Whoa, why do you think that? We saw him at dinner earlier, and he was completely unscathed. Which means that he didn't break his pactum with Sydney by intentionally harming her."

"I don't think he *forced* Sydney to drink that Nox Serum. I just think he drove her to it." When Riku continued to stare at me expectantly, I went on, "I personally know how it feels to be bullied by Blaze. He made me walk naked down Jade Wing hall for everyone to see. He's made countless degrading comments to me both in public and in private, has tried to physically attack me, has spread false rumors, and turned people even more against me, all for the purpose of breaking my spirit."

The crestfallen look on Riku's face made a painful lump form in my throat, but I pushed on, needing to share my theory.

"He might not have done all of those things to Sydney, but I heard he was extra hard on her lately, publicly complaining about her skills as a mentor and saying he wished he'd been paired with someone better. Those kinds of comments stick with you, even if they aren't true. So I can't help but think that the pressure he put on her—combined with the pressures she already put on herself and the stress of the upcoming trials—tipped her over the edge."

With a soft curse, Riku shoved both hands through his hair, making the black strands stick up every which way. "I think you're right, Bambi. He probably needed an outlet for all his frustrations, and she was the closest target. Based on the fact that he walked away unharmed, I bet the bastard didn't even realize how miserable his accusations were making Sydney."

Knowing that Blaze had probably gone after her because he could no longer go after *me*, guilt closed in once more. Before I knew it, my knees were locked against my chest and my arms tightly wrapped around them.

Something on my face must have clued Riku into the reason for my abrupt posture change, because he gently said, "Wanna talk about it? And before you say no, you should really talk about it."

I huffed a wry laugh, unused to seeing Riku so serious, so attentive. I must have really freaked them out earlier. A slight rustle above my head reminded me that Comet was listening to every word we said, but the need to unburden myself was too great, too *tempting*. So, before I could stop myself, I was voicing words I'd never shared before, allowing the Air Elemental a peek into the dark center of my being.

"I'm upset about what happened to Sydney, but I didn't know her like . . . like Juliana. I still see and feel her everywhere. When I look at myself in the mirror, when I feel the sun warming my face, when I dream at night, I think of her. I swear I can hear her whispering to me sometimes. She *haunts* me, Riku, and when I saw Sydney's body lying on the bathroom floor, I just . . . That awful day came rushing back to me. Sydney became Juliana, and I couldn't stand losing her all over again. Couldn't bear the *guilt*."

When a shuddering sigh left me, Riku silently rose to his feet and approached my end of the couch. Before I knew what was happening, he'd slid his long body between mine and the couch back. With one smooth movement, he had my head pressed to his chest and one of my legs draped over his.

Feeling the hand behind me tug my collared shirt free of my skirt, I started to stiffen. "Riku . . ."

"It's just a friendly cuddle, Bambi," he said, slipping the hand beneath my shirt to rest on my lower back. "I won't try to cop a feel. Promise."

Except that I'd never *cuddled* with a male that wasn't a family member before. This position might seem innocent to Riku, but I was more than aware of his body intimately pressed to mine. His hand on my back started to move, tracing circles that felt oddly comforting instead of sensual. I let him do it, surprised when the skin contact along with his steady warmth relaxed my tense muscles. In no time, my eyes drooped, and I began to drift off.

What only felt like seconds later, I heard the main door to the dorm click open. I jerked upright in a flash, scrambling to disentangle myself from Riku as if we'd been caught doing something naughty. A chuckle rumbled from him, and I smacked his chest in irritation before managing to lurch off the couch and face the door.

When I found Thorne frozen in the doorway, staring at us like he'd seen a ghost, heat crept up my neck and into my face.

"Don't worry, man," Riku drawled, dropping his legs to the floor so he could sit up. "I wasn't making a move on your precious Snowflake. Her virginity is still intact."

What the—? How did he know? Had Thorne *told* him?

I whirled on Riku, utter mortification making me snap, "Why do you assume I'm a virgin?"

"Oh, Bambi," he replied, a teasing grin lifting his mouth as he looked up at me. "It's as plain as the cute little button nose on your face. You might as well have a blinking neon sign on your face that says 'I'm a virgin.'"

My jaw dropped. Could he really tell just by looking at me? Feeling way too exposed, I scowled and snapped again, "Did you just compare me to *Rudolph* this time?"

His grin widened.

"Who's Rudolph?" a new voice said, and my humiliation deepened even more.

"Bambi is," Riku replied to Oz, who was now in the doorway as well.

"Wait, Bambi is Rudolph? I don't get it."

"It's simple. Both deer are innocent little virgins, and so is she."

I threw up my hands with a groan, then turned for the door. Refusing to look at Thorne's face again, I focused on Oz as I walked across the room and said, "Thanks for getting me my stuff, Oz, but I really can't stay here. I know it's past midnight, but I'd rather be punished than—"

"Why do you think I want to kill you?"

At Thorne's softly spoken words, I stopped dead. Still looking at Oz, I saw his eyes widen, then flick behind me to Riku. Wow. Okay. So he wanted to do this right here and now, in front of Riku and Oz, no less.

Except that his two friends suddenly moved as if in response to some unspoken cue. When they quietly left the main room and headed for their own, Comet lifted off the couch and followed after them. As their doors clicked shut, Thorne silently closed the door behind him and leaned against it, crossing his arms over his chest. A wall. A *barrier*. Keeping me trapped inside so I couldn't run or hide from his question.

Seconds dragged by. Minutes.

"Answer me, Snowflake."

His quiet tone, completely devoid of anger, cracked apart the last of my resistance.

"Because you told me you wanted to," I said, unable to hide the tremor in my voice.

Still not looking at him, it was the shift in his tone that gave away his shock. "When?"

I savagely bit my lip before forcing myself to say, "That day. The day my world fell apart. I tried to tell you what happened, but . . . but you were so angry and filled with . . . with hatred and rage. The sky darkened, and a storm blew in. Rain started pounding on our heads, and lightning forked through the sky. You *were* the storm in that moment, just like you were during your demonstration in my Conjuring class. You were covered in blue sparking electricity, the air heavy with so much deadly current that I knew you were about to strike me dead."

Struggling to breathe, I pressed a shaking hand to my chest before continuing, "'I'll kill you,' you told me. *Screamed* at me. I could see in your glowing eyes how much you meant it. And I was terrified, so terrified that I . . . I ran. I ran and hid like a coward. Instead of facing your righteous wrath, the punishment that I deserved, I used a portal to escape. And I'm sorry. I'm sorry I didn't let you kill me then, and I'm sorry you can't kill me now. I didn't plan on this. I didn't plan on *any* of this. Being admitted to Heartstone, getting partnered with you. I know you hate being stuck with me, and I don't blame you. I don't even blame you for wanting to kill me. We both know I deserve it."

He didn't say anything for a long time. The only sounds in the room were my frantically beating heart and unsteady breaths. Now that I'd reminded him of his promise, that old fear crowded in once more. Fear that he was about to exact his revenge on me for taking his sister's life. He deserved to. I'd always known that right belonged to him. But as the seconds ticked by, I suddenly didn't want him to. The feeling grew and grew, until every molecule of my being wanted to fall down at his feet and beg him not to end me.

Before I could, before I could utter a single word, he finally replied, "I never said that I would kill you."

My eyes snapped to his. "What?"

"I never said that I would kill you," he repeated, carefully enunciating each word. "It seems to me like there are many things about that day you can't remember. I was angry, yes. I called down a storm, yes. But I never said those words to you."

Feeling like my world was turning upside down, I shook my head, certain *he* was the one who didn't remember things correctly. "But our pactum. You didn't want to bind yourself to me because then you wouldn't be able to kill me."

"I didn't want to bind myself to you because every time I'm near you, I'm reminded of *her*," he shot back. Not in anger, but . . . but in pain. *Raw* pain. "I was finally in control of my life again until you came back into it, forcing me to reopen scars and relive old memories. But I never *once* said that I would kill you, Snowflake, and I don't want you to *ever* talk about deserving to die again. I need you alive. *Alive.* Do you understand me?"

Eyes wide, my heart in my throat, I weakly whispered, "I understand."

"Good," he said, lifting a hand to jerk it through his hair, revealing just how upset he was. After another long moment, he said in a much quieter tone, "You're sleeping here tonight in my bedroom. No arguments."

Panic rushed through me.

Before I could protest, he added, "I'll be on the couch. Text if you need anything."

With that, he pushed off the door and headed for the kitchen, our conversation officially over. Still reeling from what I'd confessed to him and what he'd confessed to me, I continued to watch him. Did he really not want to kill me? Had I made up those words in my mind that day, so certain that he wanted to? That I deserved it?

Overwhelmed with uncertainty, too confused and drained to sort it all out, I silently turned away. Not toward the exit but toward the hall that would lead me to his bedroom, to the place I swore to myself I would never return.

CHAPTER 23

It was the smell of death, the promise of another nightmare, that had me jerking awake.

Heart thundering, breathing heavily like I'd just run a mile, I glanced around the strange room with wide eyes, trying to remember where I was. The faint glow of the moon through the window allowed me to pick out objects in the dark room, and after a few seconds, I expelled a shuddering sigh of relief.

I was in Thorne's room. Thorne's *bed.* Alone but not alone, aware that three powerful warlocks were sleeping only a wall or two away. I was safe here. Safe.

"I'll kill you!"

No. No, that wasn't true. At least, Thorne had told me it wasn't. But I could still remember it so *clearly*, see the pure rage on his face as he stormed toward me, deadly lightning crackling at his fingertips.

Confused, frustrated, still struggling to push the recurring nightmare from my mind, I whipped the sheets aside and scooted off the bed. My only intent was to splash some water on my flushed face, but instead of heading for the bathroom, my feet carried me to the bedroom door.

Just one peek, I told myself, reaching for the handle. *One peek at his sleeping face, and I'll be able to rest easier.*

I didn't know why, but seeing for myself that Thorne was only a stone's throw away would help me fall back asleep—hopefully without nightmares this time.

"I never said that I would kill you."

Never said. Never said.

"I need you alive."

Alive. Alive.

For his own reputation? So he could win? Or for another reason entirely?

Needing to put my mind at ease, to silence the doubts and fears, I turned the handle and soundlessly opened the door. Just one peek. Just to see that he was actually asleep on the couch, that he wasn't concocting some plan to murder me in my sleep. Just one—

The door swung open, and I bit back a scream, nearly jumping out of my skin as a huge shadow darkened the hallway. It moved toward me, and I raised my hands, prepared to defend myself. At the last second, I recognized the gait, the confident and controlled movements that could only be Thorne. I dropped my hands and stepped back instead, retreating as he came inside the bedroom after me and quietly shut the door.

Halfway between the door and bed, he erased the distance between us and stepped into my personal space. With no warning whatsoever, his hand came around me and slid under my night shirt, pressing to my lower back. The move drove us closer together, and I sucked in a gasp as his front brushed against mine.

In an instant, I realized two things: he was shirtless, and I'd made the terrible mistake of sleeping without my pajama bottoms.

Only a scant inch of air and a few scraps of clothing separated our bodies, and we were alone together in a darkened room. *Again.*

My body immediately warmed at the realization, filling me with that terrible ache I'd tried so hard to ignore this past month. I couldn't see Thorne's expression in the dark, but I could feel the heat coming off him in waves, the want pulsing from his body as it leaned toward mine.

It took my breath away, leaving me stunned and unable to move. He didn't say a word, but it was his hand still hot on my lower spine, splayed out in an almost possessive way that clued me in to his thoughts.

"We didn't do anything," I spoke in a hushed whisper, my voice little more than air.

"I know," he said in a low rumble, the sound vibrating through his palm and into my spine, making me want to arch against him. "I talked to him."

"You didn't break his fingers, did you?"

"No."

I swallowed, not sure what to say next, worried that if I didn't keep talking, something was going to happen. Something I wouldn't be able to—wouldn't *want* to—stop. "Can't sleep?"

Okay, that much was obvious. Based on how alert he seemed, I doubted he'd even tried.

"No," he replied, using the hand on my back to reel me closer. "Not when you're in my bed, twisted in my sheets, and smelling like me."

I blanked at the confession, wholly in denial that this was happening. Maybe I was still dreaming. That had to be it. My very first wet dream.

My nipples grazed his hard body, and I shivered at the electric sensation, feeling the buds grow stiff at the friction. Okay, this felt too good, too *real* to be a dream. My imagination wasn't this powerful.

Time to stop this reality from going any further. *Now.*

"Thorne."

He pressed into me, making me feel parts of him I'd never felt before. Something between his legs, something *huge* brushed my lower belly, and I quickly stepped back. He followed, not giving me an inch.

"Thorne, we can't," I warned, continuing to retreat.

"Then stop me," he said, his body moving in sync with mine. "Tell me to stop, and I will."

I opened my mouth, but nothing came out. What the hell was *wrong* with me?

Doing the only thing I could, I stepped back again. My legs abruptly hit something solid, and I lost my balance. I started to fall backward and instinctively shot my hands up to grab hold of Thorne's shoulders. Instead of halting my descent, he came down with me, his hand on my back slowing my fall to his bed.

His bed. I was on his *bed*, and he was hovering above me, his legs planted between mine so I couldn't roll away. Placing his free hand on the mattress beside my head, he leaned down so our faces were inches apart and quietly rumbled, "You can't tell me to stop, and you know why?"

"Why?" I whispered, the sound pathetically weak.

"Because you need this as much as I do."

My lips parted, and his eyelids shifted, his gaze lowering to them. He softly hissed through his teeth, and my toes curled at the sound. His hand still pressed to my spine shifted lower, sliding over my underwear to cup my backside. When he squeezed, a breathy moan escaped me. Encouraged by the sound, he curved his fingers inward, seeking out the spot that so badly ached for his touch.

"Please," I whimpered, digging my nails into his shoulders. "Please, I . . . Please, don't touch me."

Please don't, please don't. Please do, please do.

He froze, his fingers inches away from my throbbing center. After a painfully long beat, he said, "You don't want me to touch you?"

I do. I do *want you to touch me.*

I bit my lip, so hard that I tasted blood. Forcing myself to speak, I uttered a faint, "No."

The hand immediately slid away, and I inwardly cried my disappointment.

"Fine, I won't touch you," he said, his voice not sounding mad, per se—more like determined. "But I know you want me to. If I were to touch your panties right now, I'd find them damp with arousal."

Wow, the *ego* on this guy. Then again, he was probably right.

"I know what my touch does to you," he went on, sliding that hand out from beneath me. I didn't see where it went, but I suddenly heard the metallic clink of a belt buckle shift. Just like that, my pulse skyrocketed through the roof. "Do you want to know what your touch does to me?"

My mind blanked again. Utterly blanked.

Before I could respond, before I could even realize what he was asking, he slid the buckle free and tugged down his zipper. In one swift move, he pulled one of my hands off his shoulder and plunged it into his pants, into his *boxer briefs.* As my fingers connected with something thick and hard, I froze, in too much shock to pull away.

His dick. I was touching his *dick.*

Taking advantage of my moment of stupor, he wrapped my fingers around the stiff appendage before placing his hand over mine in a tight grip.

"*This* is what you do to me, Snowflake," he said in a quiet growl, gripping my hand so hard that I had no choice but to squeeze his dick. I immediately felt it swell in my hand, becoming so thick that my fingers could barely connect around it. A sound left him, pure need, pure *bliss.*

I stared wide-eyed at his shadowed face, still not fully computing that I held his dick in my hand. I should have tried to pull away then, but that sound he'd made, that needy little *groan*.

He'd made that sound because of me. Because of my *touch*.

Tugging his manhood free of his pants, he kept his fingers firmly clasped over mine. When his hand started to move, so did mine, sliding up his cock in a slow pump. His skin was taut and surprisingly soft, but the thickness underneath was what shocked me the most. I didn't know what I expected a penis to feel like, but not like this. Silky smooth yet powerfully unbending, pulsing with virile energy and life.

It felt incredible.

He moved our hands in another slow pump, then another and another. My eyes widened further, my brain finally registering what he planned to do.

Masterbate with my hand. *Mine*, not his. Even though his hand was the one making the motions, it was my hand that was touching him, stroking him, *squeezing* him.

Remembering the last time he'd masterbated in my presence, I couldn't help but wonder if this was another punishment. I'd kept my distance from him for a solid month, not letting him touch me once. But now that he had me in his control, in his *bed*, maybe he'd finally snapped. Maybe Riku had been right about him being sexually frustrated, and he'd decided he was done waiting.

My breakdown from earlier today had been the catalyst, my own haunted past triggering his once more. He'd said that being near me made me think of her, that I'd torn open old wounds. That hurt, that *pain* was in his movements now, in the coiled way he held himself above me and the unrelenting grip on my hand.

The line between desire and hatred was razor thin, and he was teetering on the edge of both.

"Ruining you . . . like you have ruined me."

So this was it, then. This was his revenge. Taking my innocence piece by piece, destroying it until there was nothing left. No wonder he didn't want to kill me.

Why would he when slowly breaking me was so much more satisfying?

Knowing his endgame should have filled me with anger, with *fury*, but it didn't spark a reaction in me at all. If anyone deserved to destroy me, I'd always known it would be him. I didn't owe him my body for saving or protecting me, that much was true. But if this was how he wanted me to pay off my life debt to him, then who was I to deny him that right?

Besides, he hadn't been wrong. I did need this. I just hadn't known how much until now. Until he'd taken my hand and started to jerk off with it.

He was pumping faster now, his movements more choppy, more frantic. His breathing had become labored, hitching every time he squeezed my hand which in turn squeezed his cock. Knowing that he was enjoying this, that his body was humming with pleasure by my hand, did something to me. Something entirely unexpected. The ache—not the one currently between my legs, but the one I'd carried with me for the past two years—had begun to throb less. Watching him seek out his pleasure somehow calmed me, *soothed* me, acting as a balm that spread through my veins like Sano.

When the jerking motions of his hand grew rough, *desperate*, I finally moved. Finally gripped his manhood all on my own and started to mimic his actions. The second he felt me take over, a loud groan vibrated from him. My pussy spasmed at the guttural sound, and it was all I could do to keep my free hand from reaching down and rubbing the ache.

"You're such a good girl for giving me what I want," he gruffly said, letting go of my hand to let me pleasure him on my own. The mattress dipped as he splayed the hand on my other side, shifting more of his weight above me.

I continued the frantic pace he'd set, marveling at how hard he was. The term "boner" suddenly made a lot more sense to me now. It *felt* like a bone. Despite how much a part of me wanted to preen at his praise, I found myself replying, "I'm not your possession, Thorne."

"And yet here you are, in my bed with my dick in your hand," he said, the words little more than a growl. "I own you now, Snowflake. You will bend for me. You will break. You'll do whatever I want you to because you're *mine*."

Ancestors, save me.

His possessive words and tone only served to excite me, and a little whimper burst from my lips. The sound had an instant effect on him, and he gripped the sheets on either side of my head, tensing all over.

Oh. *Oh*.

This was it. The shift, the energy poised on the edge, the quivering of his thighs that announced he was ready. I pumped even faster, my movements shortening as he became so hard, so swollen, that the skin felt ready to split.

He was about to come. His body was stiff as a board above mine, his breaths coming in pants.

I squeezed him harder, as hard as I could, and he violently jerked. Something shot up his shaft like a discharging weapon, and he darted a hand down to yank up my top. A long guttural groan left him at the same time, almost distracting me from the sudden warmth squirting onto my belly.

His sperm. He'd *ejaculated* on me.

His remaining arm propping him up gave out then, and he dropped to his elbow, nearly falling on top of me. Not knowing what else to do, I continued to hold onto his dick as he rode out the orgasm, his heaving chest brushing against mine as he lowered his forehead to the mattress.

After a long moment, his breathing evened, and he slowly lifted off me. I let go of him, watching the dark shape of his silhouette as he tucked his dick back inside his pants and turned to leave.

Well, then. Guess I wasn't going to get a thank you for a job well done. Then again, punishments didn't usually end in praise.

But instead of leaving, he went around the bed and entered the bathroom. A light flicked on, but I didn't move or even cover myself, his cum still sitting on my belly. He'd only lifted my shirt high enough to expose my midsection, his intent on clearing a landing pad for his sperm, not sneaking a peek at my breasts again.

Seconds later, he came back out with what looked like a washcloth. Approaching me, he slowly took in my body, sweeping his gaze over my bare legs that were still parted, then higher to my black underwear. As his eyes lingered there for a moment, staring so intently that I was certain they were imagining me without the panties on, I squeezed my aching thighs together and immediately felt how wet I was.

Yup. He was right, the arrogant bastard.

Something that looked a lot like satisfaction curled one corner of his mouth as he stopped beside the bed and reached toward me with the washcloth. When the damp, slightly rough fabric grazed the sensitive skin just below my belly button, I jerked, sucking in a quiet gasp. He did it again, taking his time cleaning up the mess he'd made. Able to see his face now, I took in how relaxed he looked compared to earlier. He almost looked . . . content.

When he was finished, he took the washcloth back into the bathroom and returned less than a minute later, switching off the light. The room plunged into darkness once more, so I wasn't prepared when I suddenly felt arms slide beneath me and scoop me up. A startled sound left me, but I didn't protest as he carried me to the head of the bed and laid me back down. With a few deft moves, he had a pillow situated beneath my head and the comforter securely tucked under my chin.

Before I could panic that he was about to join me, he leaned down and rumbled in my ear, "You asked me not to touch you, Snowflake, so I won't. But you might want to touch yourself and relieve that ache between your pretty thighs, or you won't be able to sleep tonight."

I blinked. Blinked again when he shifted just enough to brush his lips over my forehead, then straightened and quietly exited the room, leaving me to deal with the terrible ache he'd left behind.

CHAPTER 24

I hated to admit it, but being able to take a hot shower in the morning made staying overnight at the Arcane Three's dorm almost worth it.

It was heavenly not having to rush or worry about people like Blaze barging in. And after last night's little disruption, I'd actually slept peacefully for the first time in weeks. I'd had to take Thorne's advice and pleasure myself first, but after *that*, I'd slept like a baby.

Oz had managed to scrounge up all my essentials, including some makeup, so I took my time in the bathroom doing my face and hair, ignoring the fact that Thorne probably needed to use it. After the stunt he'd pulled last night, he could wait.

Own me? *Bend* me? *Break* me?

Had I seriously let him get away with saying those things to me?

"*You're mine.*"

Mine. Mine.

I couldn't deny that a big part of me still thought he deserved to ruin me, but this thing between us was growing more and more toxic. Anger and hatred were turning into lust and obsession, and I wasn't sure which was more dangerous.

If I wasn't careful, he was going to end up breaking more than just my body. I could feel it, feel how much I was drawn to him. Not just physically but emotionally, too. During my breakdown in the bathroom yesterday, I'd sought out his voice for comfort, not just his body. He'd calmed me, made me feel safe, even after yelling at and shaking me.

I didn't know how he managed to have that effect on me, but I was terrified of what that meant. Once our mentor-student partnership was over, we'd go our separate ways. We'd become rivals, *enemies* again. He'd have no need to protect me, and this thing between us would end.

I'd go back to being the school's pariah, alone and unwanted. But I wouldn't be the same person anymore. Once Thorne was done with me, I knew I'd never be the same again, just like he'd said. My innocence would be gone, and so would a piece of me that didn't belong to him. Problem was, I was pretty sure he already owned that piece, and there was no way I could get it back.

So much for thinking last night hadn't been that big of a deal. He hadn't even touched me the way my body craved for him to, but the intimate moment had left a mark on me anyway. I might have needed it at the time, but if I didn't get my suddenly active libido under control, I was going to keep giving in, keep handing him pieces of me that couldn't be returned.

Own me? Maybe parts of me. But I couldn't let him take everything, even if the guilt still gnawing at my insides insisted that my life was his to claim.

He didn't want to kill me. He wanted me *alive*. And the only way I could stay alive in a cutthroat place like this was by protecting myself, which meant protecting myself from him, too.

Staring at my reflection in the mirror, resolved to not keep repeating the mistakes of last night, I whispered to her, "Sorry I keep getting naked with your brother."

No response, but I didn't need one. I knew my best friend, and without a doubt, she wouldn't approve of what Thorne and I were doing. She might have been the sweetest person on earth and loved me like a sister, but even she understood that Hudsons and Mayweathers were like oil and water. The two couldn't mix, and her death was proof of that. If only I'd listened to my parents and Gran all those years ago instead of sneaking off to see Juliana behind their backs.

If only I'd listened, just like I should be listening to Gran now.

"Stay away from Thorne Hudson at all costs."

I could only imagine how horrified she'd be if she found out what I'd done to his dick last night.

Cringing at my reflection, I collected my things and left the steamy bathroom behind. Suddenly starving, I dropped my stuff on Thorne's bed, deciding to ask them if I could come back for it later. Not because I planned to *stay* here another night, but because I wanted more time at the dining hall to stuff my face.

But the moment I left the bedroom, the smell of food wafted toward me, along with the sound of male voices. When I emerged from the hallway and they saw me, the chatter stopped.

Great. What were the odds that they were talking about last night?

Right away, I noticed that Thorne still didn't have a shirt on and that all three of them were in the kitchen cooking breakfast. So distracted by the unexpected sight, I forgot to blush at the thought of them discussing the hand job I gave Thorne.

"Didn't think we were the domestic types, eh, Bambi?" Riku said, his tie and shirt askew as usual. I didn't respond, too surprised that they were *cooking* and nothing smelled burnt. He waved a spatula at the island and added, "Pull up a stool. Eggs are almost done."

Um, yeah, not a good idea. Not after what Thorne and I had done last night. If he hadn't told them what happened yet, there was a very good chance that they'd *heard* it. Thorne had groaned awfully loud when he'd . . .

I accidentally looked at him just as I recalled that euphoric groan. Our eyes locked, and I was suddenly back in that moment again, squeezing his dick as he came all over my belly. Something on my face must have given away my thoughts, because his eyes abruptly hooded. With Oz and Riku busy at the stove, he took the opportunity to reach down and adjust himself through his pants. The move was definitely deliberate, a reminder of what we'd shared last night.

I own you, his heated gaze seemed to say, slowly sliding down my front. When it lingered on the apex of my thighs, that stupid ache returned, forcing me to squeeze my legs together. Satisfaction curled his mouth, and I wanted nothing more than to throw something at his head for torturing me.

The bastard knew; he *knew* that my body still yearned to be touched by him. Did he have to get me all hot and horny this early in the morning?

A sharp shriek and rustle of wings broke the cruel staredown, and I glanced toward the living room just as Comet launched off a perch near the windows and shot across the room. Thorne held out his arm, and the hawk landed on it, digging his claws in none too gently.

"Watch it," he grunted at the bird, shooing him up to his shoulder so he could inspect the damage. Little puncture holes dotted his skin, a few of them starting to ooze blood.

Comet let out another ear-piercing shriek and flapped his wings, hitting Thorne in the head. When Thorne ignored him, he darted his sharp beak out and caught the warlock's cheek.

"*Okay*," he growled at the bird, dislodging him from his shoulder so he could press his hand to the bleeding cheek.

Comet smoothly dove back to his perch in the living room,

turning his back to the room as if annoyed.

"What has his feathers in a bunch?" Riku asked as Thorne moved toward the kitchen sink.

"Nothing," Thorne replied, turning on the water and grabbing a towel.

As one, Riku and Oz glanced at me, their gazes more than a little discerning.

Great. They thought *I* had something to do with that little squabble? Then again, maybe I had. Comet could hear Thorne's thoughts, and maybe the familiar hadn't liked what he'd been thinking. Thinking about *me.*

Huh. Maybe that cuddle session we'd shared in the bathroom yesterday had made the hawk warm up to me a bit. The thought of a bird defending my honor was kind of adorable, actually.

Even so, I felt more awkward than ever standing in a place that I clearly didn't belong. I was an intruder in their peaceful sanctuary, and my presence was ruining that. Knowing that staying here any longer would further stir the hornet's nest, I started to move toward the exit, murmuring, "I should go."

I wouldn't be able to sit at the third year table without them, but if I headed toward the dining hall now, I should still have enough time to—

"Oh, no, you don't," Riku said, suddenly beelining toward me. Before I could stop him, he grabbed me around the waist and picked me clean off the floor. Ignoring my sound of protest, he marched back to the kitchen and plopped me onto a stool.

"Riku—"

"Stay," he said, pointing a finger at me. "I mean it, Bambi. We don't cook meals often, and when we do, it's never for a girl. This food was made specially for you, and you're gonna eat it."

I stared at him wide-eyed, too surprised by his passionate little speech to speak.

"I think you broke her," Oz remarked when the silence stretched.

"No, that's Thorne's job," Riku replied, so definitively that I nearly swallowed my tongue. "Although . . ." He crouched down a bit so we were eye-level, cocking his head to the side as he studied me thoughtfully. After a moment, he straightened and said, "Nope, still a virgin. Thorne's got the restraint of a Zen Buddhist. I don't know how he does it."

My cheeks burst into flames, and I swiped at Riku with my foot. He easily dodged the kick with a light chuckle, rounding the island to finish making breakfast. Thorne failed to comment on Riku's observation, and that somehow only made it worse. I'd already assumed his friends knew about what Thorne and I had done, but it was clear they thought we'd gone all the way. Even *expected* it. Riku had, at least.

If they were making bets on how long it took for me to give up my virginity, I was seriously going to break some balls.

Reluctantly deciding to stay after Riku's guilt-trip speech about the food being special, I swiveled on the stool to watch them finish cooking. Riku was manning the eggs, Oz the bacon and sausage, and Thorne the french toast—while also cleaning the blood from his face and arm.

Suddenly feeling like an entitled princess while they slaved away, I slipped off the stool and rounded the island in search of the plates. It wasn't easy with three big bodies in the way, but when I found them, I stood on tiptoe, straining to reach them. A hand came up over mine and plucked four plates off the shelf, then lowered them to my level.

I immediately recognized the hand as Thorne's, the jagged strands of lightning tattooed on his skin a dead giveaway. Hyperaware of his body directly behind mine, so close that I could feel his heat, I accepted the plates without comment and quickly scooted away.

"As cute as it is to see our little Bambi on tiptoe, we should move the plates to the bottom shelf," Riku casually remarked, turning off the burner.

"That's okay," I rushed to say, alarmed by his suggestion. "It's not like I'm moving in." I set the plates on the island, noticing how quiet it had suddenly become. One glance confirmed that all three of them were acting suspicious. I narrowed my eyes and firmly added, "I'm *not* moving in."

"Whatever you say, Bambi," Riku said with a shrug, coming up beside me with a steaming pan. I held up a plate for him, and he scooped some scrambled eggs onto it. "But I know you like it here. We have nice beds, hot water, and all the food you can eat. Plus, there will always be a pair of arms waiting to cuddle with you after an exhausting day. And a dick to help you sleep at night."

"*Riku*," Thorne snapped before I could, surprising me.

"Chill, bro. I wasn't talking about *my* dick." Riku winked at me, and I almost shoved the plate of scrambled eggs into his face.

It got quiet after that, each of us dishing food onto our plates in tense silence. More than aware that they wanted me to give in, to *move* in, I stubbornly set my jaw and refused to comment. One mental breakdown didn't give them permission to make me stay here.

This little alliance between us was temporary. *Temporary.*

Plus, I still had to prove myself to the other students, and letting the Arcane Three coddle me more than they already did wouldn't look good. The other first years weren't living in Sapphire Wing, so neither could I.

Realizing the topic wasn't up for discussion, Oz slid onto a stool with a heaping plate before him and said, "I'm curious how you knew where to find Sydney yesterday."

Everyone froze.

About to take a bite of my eggs, I heard them plop back onto my plate as I stared at the Oracle across the island from me. Out of the three, I knew Oz the least. We barely spoke to each other, not because he was naturally quiet or had his nose in a book half the time, but because his abilities were hazardous to a witch like me.

His keen observation skills had already made me expose my protection amulet in order to keep him from looking deeper. Now, he was poking at my walls again, trying to expose even more of my dark secrets.

Still standing beside me, Riku took one look at my pensive expression and said, "Maybe we should discuss that later. She's probably still shaken up by what—"

"I'm curious, too," Thorne interjected, sliding onto the stool next to Oz. One glance at the determined glint in his eye, and I knew I wasn't getting off the hook this time.

Slowly setting down my fork, I tried to wipe all emotion from my face before saying, "Intuition. It's kind of my thing. Something didn't feel right, so I followed that feeling until it led me to the bathroom."

The truth. With one huge omission.

Thorne watched me for a beat, then glanced at Oz. When I saw what looked like suspicion darken the Oracle's hazel eyes, my appetite promptly vanished. Reaching up to adjust his glasses, he replied, "Intuition is kind of my thing, too. As an Oracle, I can sense things other magic wielders can't, namely the spirit plane."

I tensed all over. Those keen eyes of his narrowed, picking up on my growing unease.

"When my third eye opened a few years ago," he continued, "I was able to access abilities like astral projection. Being able to see and sense things beyond the limits of the earthly plane is something only an Oracle can do, so I'm more than a little curious to know how you managed to feel something not of this world."

Dear ancestors, he was referring to death. To my ability to *sense* it. How? How did he figure me out so *completely?*

I opened my mouth but nothing came out. What could I even say? Not the truth, that was for sure. Darkens shouldn't be able to sense death, to *smell* it. Admitting what I could do would only further convince everyone here that something was wrong with me, that I didn't *belong.*

"She also said my sister's spirit haunts her," Thorne broke the silence to say.

I swung my gaze back to him, my mouth still askew, then shot an accusatory glare up at Riku.

He raised both hands placatingly. "Hey, it wasn't me. Our couch confessions never left my lips."

I directed the glare toward the living room, but Comet kept his gaze glued to the windows, pretending like he couldn't hear. So much for our bonding moment.

Needing to nip this in the bud before they completely unraveled me, I focused on each of them and sternly said, "Look, I feel things intensely and have a vivid, sometimes morbid imagination, okay? Even humans can occasionally sense things, so let's drop it and finish eating. I don't want to be late for the morning assembly."

Not waiting for them to reply, I shoveled a huge bite of eggs into my mouth, ending the discussion. After a moment, they dug into their own food, everyone but Thorne.

"About that," he said, and I felt my hackles rise again. "I need to prepare you all for something Chancellor Grimshaw told me last night." My hackles lowered, but the sudden tension in his voice kept me on edge. "After what happened yesterday with Sydney, he decided to call an emergency board meeting. None of you are going to like the decision they made."

As he began to share what awaited us in our near future, my heart sank and sank. Nope, I didn't like this decision one bit. In fact, I *hated* it.

Things were already complicated here, but they were about to get a whole lot worse.

CHAPTER 25

"It saddens me to say that a second year Air Elemental, Sydney Wright, took her own life yesterday afternoon. Not everyone is suited for the pressures of Heartstone, and some would rather end their own lives than face the disgrace of their failure and the disappointment of their coven."

Even knowing what Chancellor Grimshaw was about to say couldn't curb the dread I felt when he started to tell the student body about the board's decision.

"Which is why the school board has decided that a gala is needed to lift heavy spirits and remind students why they're here in the first place."

An excited murmur surged through the crowd, the promise of a party piquing everyone's interest.

My phone vibrated my hip, and I used the pleats of my skirt to peek at the screen.

Poor unsuspecting souls, the text said, from someone called Sex God.

What the—?

Another text came in through the same chat, this time from Lightning Daddy. *Riku, you sick bastard.*

What? Sex God replied back. *The names fit.*

Uh, someone called The Brain responded. Probably Oz.

I sent an eye-rolling emoji, then immediately wished I hadn't.

Lil' Virgin? Lightning Daddy—aka Thorne—texted. *We're going to have words, Riku.*

The group chat name suddenly changed to Lil' Virgin and the Three Dicks.

Feeling heat creep up my neck, I texted back, *You suck.*

No, that's your job, Lil' Virgin, Sex God replied back, then added a tongue and eggplant emoji.

A full-blown blush blasted my cheeks, and I shoved the phone back into my pocket just as Chancellor Grimshaw began talking again.

"The Legacy Gala, as we've decided to call this event, will be extra special. Not only because it will be held the evening before the first years' end-of-semester trial, but because every student's family will be invited to attend."

At that, the room went dead silent.

Yup. There was the reaction I'd expected. I wasn't the only one shocked that they were inviting *family* members to visit Heartstone Academy. And right before a *trial*. The chancellor was making it sound like a good thing, like a visit from family would cheer the students up and give them courage to face the upcoming trials.

In reality, it was just another test, a trial in itself. The gala was a political move, pure and simple. The expectations of such an event were meant to put even more pressure on the students who were beginning to flounder, to weaken. After the gala, I wouldn't be surprised if some students failed to show up for their trial the next day, too overwhelmed to go through with it.

Legacy Gala, indeed. Even the name put undue pressure on the next generation of potential leaders. This was another culling opportunity, a way of cleaning house, and the very families that were supporting their scholars could end up being their downfall.

The pressure, the pressure to be *perfect*, could break even the strongest mind. The purpose of this gala was sadistically brilliant, actually, and I applauded whoever had come up with the idea. But I already knew it was going to test my limits, to push me *beyond* them if I didn't prepare myself.

A deadly magical trial I could handle, but navigating a roomful of protective parents who hated that I attended the same school as their children? Even worse, facing a roomful of Mayweathers and Hudsons who'd been feuding for the past decade?

Yeah, I didn't know if I could survive that.

CHAPTER 26

The day of the Legacy Gala arrived all too soon, bringing with it a plethora of nervous energy that could be felt in every dark corner of the campus.

But that wasn't the only event today that was heavy on my mind. It was also the second anniversary of Juliana's death.

For the past few weeks, I'd dreaded this day so deeply that I'd begun to eat and sleep less. Preparing for my end-of-semester trial had felt easy compared to the mental and emotional strain of this day. I desperately wanted to see my family again, but not like this. Not here. Not today of all days. Only adults were allowed to attend, so Wyatt wouldn't be coming at least. But Gran knew what this day meant to me. My emotions were already high, and having her here would only sharpen those painful memories more. On top of that, seeing my grandmother surrounded by hostile faces, by judgmental people she'd once called friends after everything she'd endured this past decade, was going to be hell.

It would be a miracle if tonight ended on a positive note. In my gut, I already knew that it wouldn't. Old grudges, old *hurts* were about to be inflamed once more, and I would be smack dab in the middle of it all.

Which was why I'd wisely erected the barrier between me and Thorne again, only interacting with him when absolutely necessary. He'd helped me prepare for my trial and ate across from me at meals, but that was it. No more sleepovers. No more touching. As if aware of what I was doing, aware that I *needed* that boundary, he hadn't tried to invade my space again.

The looks didn't stop, though. The glances that whispered of dark nights filled with passionate heat.

He wasn't done with me yet, not by a long shot. He'd simply chosen to pause his sex revenge so I could stay focused on my upcoming trial. How nice of him, except that his consideration wasn't truly for me. He just didn't want me to fail, which in turn would make him fail.

Still, I appreciated the distance, even if I was starting to suspect it only worsened the restless nights and decreased appetite. He might not be touching me, but my body continued to crave what he could do to it, encouraging my imagination to go places it shouldn't. I'd had to pleasure myself nearly every night the past few weeks just so I could get some sleep, but nothing I did compared to what *he* could do.

Curse him for awakening my libido. I'd been perfectly fine without orgasms in my life, but now, they felt like a necessity. An *essential* one.

Those heated little glances we'd been sharing couldn't happen tonight, though. Not that I thought they would. Not today when feelings would be raw, when hurt and hatred were bound to resurface. The more we ignored each other, the better off we'd both be. Gran couldn't suspect that there was anything between us besides mutual loathing. One little *hint* of something more, and she'd unravel me faster than a spool of yarn.

"Two years ago today, I lost my soul sister. Yet I can't stop thinking about doing naughty things with her brother," I muttered at my reflection in the floor-length mirror, sweeping one last critical look over my appearance.

Families had been allowed to send the students formal attire for the event, and Gran had surely outdone herself with the dress she'd chosen for me. The chiffon fabric appeared black at first, but with the addition of light, it transformed into a gorgeous midnight purple. The neckline plunged nearly to my navel, exposing more cleavage than I ever had before. A risque choice, but one that clearly sent a message.

I'm all grown up, it said. *Ready to be taken seriously and seen as a potential leader.*

The sleeves were almost sheer, cinched at the wrists similar to the waistline. The skirt flowed all around me like the robes of a ghostly specter, allowing a scandalous peek of my upper thigh through the high slit. A pair of black heels completed the outfit, giving me a much-needed vertical boost.

As usual, I kept my hair down but had added a little extra curl to the long wavy mass. It spilled down my back, the color nearly identical to my dress. My school makeup kit wasn't nearly as good as the one back home, but tucked into the folds of the dress Gran had sent over was a tube of my favorite lip color. I wore the dark red shade now, along with heavier eyeliner that made my pale blue eyes pop even more.

The only jewelry I wore was the protective amulet around my neck, still invisible to the naked eye. I couldn't wait to tell Gran that it had kept me alive more than once this semester—but probably omit the part about getting cursed and almost bleeding to death.

"I wish you were here, Jewel," I spoke to the mirror, praying that on today of all days, I would get a response. "This gala would be so much more bearable if you were facing it with me."

I waited. Waited some more. Nothing.

"I'm sorry. This day should be all about you, not me," I whispered, feeling guilty that I was thinking of other things besides her today. Last year at this time, I was sitting in the snow-encrusted field where she'd died, my heart so heavy with thoughts of her that I'd stayed there until I was blue with cold. I'd considered lying down in that snow and dying there, too. It would have been fitting. Gran had found me and brought me back home before the hypothermia could take hold.

Unable to look at myself in the mirror any longer, I turned away, waiting for the cue to leave my dorm. Our guests would be arriving by portal just outside Heartstone's main entrance. To avoid any disruptions in the process, the students were to wait in their rooms until the clock struck eight.

Hearing the buzz of a text come in, I moved to my desk to check it.

Can't wait to see you in something besides your school uniform tonight. I hope there's lots of skin.

Shaking my head, I quickly replied back to Riku, *No ogling or sexual innuendos allowed around my grandmother. I'm Switzerland tonight, remember?*

He sent back a sad face, along with, *Fine, then at least send me a selfie so I can ogle you in private.*

With a sigh, I snapped a quick pic for him, knowing that he wouldn't behave tonight otherwise. I'd already asked that he, Oz, and Thorne keep their distance from me and Gran during the gala, but the Air Elemental had a tendency to go rogue in public settings. He couldn't seem to help it.

It was almost a full minute after I sent the selfie that he finally texted back, *Wow, Bambi. I get why Thorne is always staring at your chest now. You've got a gorgeous rack.*

Instantly regretting sending Riku the photo, I hurriedly texted back, *He does not.*

Does so. He won't be able to keep his eyes off you tonight.

I heavily doubted that. Not when today was the anniversary of his sister's death. He probably wouldn't even be able to *look* at me.

Yup, it was official. Getting through tonight was going to be so much harder than I thought.

The first *bong* finally sounded, the cue I'd been waiting for. As the clock tower announced the eight o'clock hour, I set my phone on the desk, unable to take it with me this time. As beautiful as this dress was, it hadn't come with pockets.

Nervous energy fluttered in my stomach as I left the room, not because of the bonging noise that still reminded me of that godawful curse, but because I was about to be reunited with my grandmother. She would be happy to see me, of course, but I worried about what she would witness tonight, what she would *hear*. Most of the students still openly rejected me by pretending I didn't exist, but there were a few like Blaze who might try to make a scene tonight.

If he wanted to psych me out for our trial tomorrow, then this gala would be the perfect opportunity to do it. All he had to do was badmouth me in front of Gran. She'd expect me to defend myself, of course, to *remind* him of who he was speaking to. I didn't even want to think of what her reaction would be if I failed to do so.

When I reached the bottom of the tower stairwell and opened the door, I prayed that the other first years had already left ahead of me. No such luck. The hallway was teeming with students, many of them lingering in groups as they admired each other's formal wear. As I moved past them, every single one stopped talking to stare.

Fantastic.

Even after my time spent in the Arcane Three's company, my infamous reputation remained. I received more jealous and covetous looks now than hatred, but none of my fellow first years intended to include me in their alliances any time soon—or ever.

Yet one more reason why I needed to get through tonight in one piece.

Thorne had warned me that one of the main focuses of tomorrow's trial would be alliances. Those who'd already forged strong relationships with other first years would have a major leg up in this trial, and because I would be all alone, having my wits about me was even more imperative.

Up ahead, Alma emerged from her dorm, followed by Blaze. The Water Elemental looked stunning in a deep blue mermaid dress that accentuated her shapely figure and made her glowing skin look golden. Her signature braid was coiled high on her head, giving her a regal appearance. Spotting me walking toward her, she paused to give my outfit a once over, then arched a brow as though mildly impressed with what she saw.

Blaze wore a white tuxedo that somehow managed to make him look even broader, his dirty blond curls carefully gelled into place. He noticed me as well, fixing his gaze on my cleavage for far too long. A typical leer pulled at his mouth, but I didn't miss the unmistakable spark of lust in his green eyes. I immediately felt sick to my stomach as he raked those eyes down my front, no doubt trying to picture me naked.

If it wasn't for Alma, I would have walked on past without a word. Blaze and I hadn't spoken directly to each other in almost two months, and it needed to stay that way. Although he hadn't officially been accused of placing that curse on me, I still believed he'd done it. Combined with the part he'd played in Sydney's death, the need for revenge, for *justice* still simmered in my blood. There was no knowing what the darkness inside me would do if he tried to talk to me right now.

He hadn't seemed remorseful at all over his mentor's death, immediately inquiring about getting a new one. Since none were available right now, he'd been leeching off of Alma more and more, even intruding on her training sessions with Riku. As a repercussion, the alliance between the Water and Fire Elemental had begun to fray, and I'd seen them quietly bickering with each other almost every day this past week.

Despite how Alma had treated me in the past, I couldn't help but feel a bit sorry for her. She should have heeded Riku's warning about picking better allies, because Blaze was clearly dragging her down at this point.

Which reminded me of something else Riku had said a few weeks ago, that a part of Alma might respect me, albeit begrudgingly. Friends? Not a chance. Frenemies? I was curious. Curious enough that I slowed, that I allowed myself to suffer Blaze's close proximity long enough to say, "That dress looks pretty on you, Alma."

Surprise flickered in her sepia brown eyes. "Thanks, *sombra*," she replied in her melodic accent, then slid a covert glance toward Blaze before adding, "This should be an interesting night for you. Might be a good time to practice your shadewalking."

With that, she turned to sashay down the hall. Blaze followed after her, but not before giving me one last look. Something about it instantly put me on edge, and I replayed Alma's words in my head. I'd thought them a light insult at first, a reminder that I was about to receive a lot of negative attention from angry parents. But with the addition of Blaze's creepy glare, I wondered if she was actually warning me.

Interesting night. Shadewalking.

Was Blaze planning something?

My stomach was practically in knots by the time I made it to the great hall. The sound of an orchestra playing reached my ears, along with the steady hum of hundreds of voices. Not just students, but their parents. Their families. Their *covens*.

Pretty sure I was about to hurl, I slowed, reaching up to touch the invisible pendant resting on my sternum. Whatever awaited me in there, I was protected. And once I was reunited with my grandmother, with my *own* coven, no one would dare touch me. For the first time in months, I'd finally have someone watching my back. Someone without an agenda, someone who cared, who I could implicitly *trust*.

I was just about to step forward and reveal myself to the room when a voice whispered in my ear, "I see you still have it on."

I whirled, but no one was there. My eyes instinctively darted to the nearest patch of shadows, and when I saw them shift, a smile, a *real* smile, pulled at my mouth for the first time in months.

"Gran!"

My small, albeit feisty grandmother dramatically emerged from the shadows, a huge smile plastered on her own pale face. "Oh, Winter Snow, how I've missed you!"

She opened her arms as I hurried toward her, enveloping me in one of her comforting hugs. I clung to her fiercely, squeezing my eyes shut to stave off the burn.

"I've missed you, too. So much," I whispered, breathing in her juniper scent. My tense body immediately melted into her familiar shape, and for one blissful moment, I was home again.

All too soon, she pulled back to hold me at arm's length. "Now, let me get a good look at my granddaughter. Oh, ancestors preserve my old bones, you are breathtaking!" she gasped, her pale blue eyes so like mine brimming with pride. "A little thinner than I remember but still healthy. I'm so relieved. You're handling this challenge so beautifully, Winter. If only your parents could be here to see how well you're doing. Your aunt Clarice too, rest her soul."

At the mention of our absent coven members, the burn behind my eyes increased. "I wish they were here, too. How is Wyatt?"

"Oh, the same. Playing video games far too much and studying way too little. I'd let you talk to him, but it's ten o'clock back home, and he's already asleep."

"Did Pearl stay with him?"

Gran laughed at that. "Hell, no. She would never miss an opportunity like this. The old girl is already inside spying on past acquaintances. You know how familiars like to keep tabs on each other, enemies or not."

I shook my head, not the least bit surprised that the familiar hadn't bothered to greet me first. Typical cat behavior, only interested in their own agenda.

"Speaking of enemies," I started, then bit my lip, not sure how to tell Gran that Thorne was my mentor. She was bound to find out eventually, and I'd rather her hear it from me than through the gossip chain.

"What was that, darling?" Gran asked, staring at me quizzically.

I continued to hesitate, not wanting to destroy our happy reunion. As soon as I told her, she'd bombard me with questions, and I was in no state to fudge the truth right now. She'd see right through my lies, and I couldn't face her disappointment, not when she was the only one in my corner tonight.

"Nothing. I'll tell you later," I replied, relieved when the music changed at that moment and distracted Gran.

She let go of my arms to pat her white hair, which was swept into an elaborately braided updo. Her black dress was far more modest than mine with graceful bell sleeves and a neckline elegantly wrapped around her throat. Dark stones glittered in her earlobes, and

I recognized them as her signature relic, obsidian. Even fresh from traveling via portal, she looked flawless and poised. Not much rattled my grandmother, and if she was nervous right now, I couldn't tell.

"Well, that's our cue, darling," she said, slipping her arm through mine. "Ready?"

No. I wanted to stay out here where it was safe, where I could pretend that I was back home among friendly faces.

"Yes, Gran," I replied, nervous energy fluttering in my stomach once more as we turned to face the great hall's open doors.

Just a few steps, and we would be exposed to a world that had shunned us, *hated* us. It felt like my first day here all over again, but somehow, it was even worse now. Most of the students at Heartstone had been too young to be fully impacted by the vampire war and the elders' downfall, but the generation before them had been in the thick of it. They'd felt the disgrace firsthand, so I expected their reactions to our presence here tonight to be more severe than anything I'd endured thus far.

Amulet, protect us, I inwardly prayed and took a step forward. Then another.

Just one more step.

"Hold your head high, darling," Gran murmured for my ears alone as we took that final step together. "Mayweathers don't bow to anyone."

CHAPTER 27

The great hall was unrecognizable.

It looked like a winter wonderland, complete with rolling hills of snow and ice sculptures that jutted up like columns. All of the chairs were gone, leaving the center clear. Enchanted snowflakes gently fell from above, but it was the *ceiling* that had my mouth opening in awe. It was as if there was no ceiling at all, as if the roof had been removed to allow the outside in. The dark sky littered with stars was nearly obscured by an undulating wave of greens, blues, and pinkish reds. The spelled *aurora borealis* danced to and fro, encouraging the viewers below to do the same.

Except that they were too busy mingling in little groups, most of them sipping from flutes of champagne or nibbling on hors d'oeuvres served by the school staff.

But the second Gran and I entered the great hall, a ripple effect occurred. The groups closest to us stopped talking to stare, which then prompted neighboring groups to do the same. Within moments, the entire great hall had fallen quiet except for the music playing, everyone turning to witness our entrance.

A few more seconds, and even the music died, plunging the room into deafening silence.

All the hair on my body rose as hundreds of eyes focused on me and my grandmother. The weight of them was unbearable, but I forced my chin up anyway, unwilling to let Gran down when she so desperately needed me. How I handled this moment didn't just affect me. It affected her, too, maybe even more so.

This was her first time seeing these faces in a decade, faces that had once looked upon her with reverence and awe. She'd been a legend back in her day, and there wasn't a soul in the witch community that didn't know who Katherine Mayweather was.

As those faces focused on her now, not a single one was filled with reverence or awe. Gran stood tall anyway, the air about her like that of a queen entering a roomful of subjects. Something brushed past my skirt, and I didn't have to look to know that it was Pearl, no doubt answering Gran's call to stand united against the hostile masses.

Gran was a pillar of strength beside me, refusing to wither under the hundreds of cold stares. Out of habit, I searched for Professor Holt, knowing that I could count on her sympathy, at least. I couldn't find her, my gaze hitting glare after glare from faces that despised me and my grandmother for no other reason than our Mayweather bloodline.

It didn't matter that Gran had once been considered royalty, that she'd been lavishly respected and praised for decades of service to her community. It didn't matter that she'd lost her husband in a skirmish with the vampires, that she'd spent almost forty years trying to keep Syphons safe. It didn't matter that she'd retired with honor, that her actions had never directly disgraced the community.

I might be paying for the sins of my family, but she was equally paying for them. Her daughter was dead, her son and daughter-in-law currently locked up in prison, but that made no difference. Someone still needed to pay for their unforgivable mistakes.

Ten years. Ten years of isolation, and it was like that time meant nothing to the unfriendly faces before us. Distrust was heavy in the air, their harsh opinion of the Mayweather name as unrelenting as ever.

Gran suddenly reached over her shoulders and flipped up a hood I hadn't known was attached to her dress. A *black* hood. The reactions around us were instantaneous, shocked gasps and whispers rippling through the crowd. Even I struggled to keep my composure, beyond surprised that she'd chosen to make such a bold statement tonight of all nights and here of all places.

Mysteriously cloaked in black, she looked like an elder prepared to do battle. The image was a slap in the face of everything the Legacy Gala stood for, and it was obvious that Gran's intent came across loud and clear to the community who'd shunned everything *she* stood for.

"Elder Mayweather," I heard someone whisper.

"*Ex*-elder," someone hissed back.

"How obscene."

"Who does she think she is?"

If Gran heard the comments, she didn't let on, her queenly air and cloak an impenetrable shield around her.

Until she spotted *them.*

As the Hudson family came into view, our outward reactions were identical. Stiff necks, even stiffer spines. Gran's fingernails dug into my arm, a low hiss leaving her as she locked eyes with Thorne's grandmother, her greatest nemesis.

They hadn't seen each other in ten years, but it was clear that the animosity Gran felt toward her ex-best-friend hadn't faded with time. A deep, rumbling growl from Pearl further confirmed Gran's feelings.

Beatrice Hudson's expression was unreadable as she took Gran in. The air thickened even more with tension, the bad blood between the pair more than obvious. A calico cat emerged from beneath

Beatrice's sparkly maroon skirt, and Pearl hissed at the familiar who used to be her friend.

My eyes cut to Thorne without permission, only to find his gaze already fixed on me. His expression matched his grandmother's, and my heart sank, then sank even lower when I saw that the entire Hudson family was looking at me the same way—save for Comet, whose expression never changed no matter what he was feeling. Thorne's parents had come to the gala, of course, but so had a member that I hadn't expected to see.

His younger brother, Sterling.

Juliana's twin.

At the sight of him, my throat painfully closed, cutting off my air. I slowed, forcing Gran to slow with me. Seeing him standing there was like looking at a ghost. He'd always favored his sister in appearance more than Thorne, his features softer than his older brother's. Even though he'd significantly filled out since the last time Juliana had shown me a picture of him, he was nowhere near as broad as Thorne. Both looked devastatingly handsome in black tuxes perfectly tailored to their tall frames.

Why hadn't Thorne warned me that Sterling would be coming?

My mind immediately went to the worst case scenario, painting an ugly picture of deceit and revenge. Gran had warned me that the Hudsons might have been behind my admission to Heartstone, that they sought to destroy me like I had destroyed Juliana. It was the anniversary of her death. This was the *perfect* opportunity to expose my shameful secret—in front of the most prestigious witches and warlocks in the community, no less. Gran would be forced to watch the last of her legacy die, helpless to stop it.

If they wanted to crush the Mayweather name once and for all, this was the time to do it.

We were surrounded by hostiles, unable to escape even if we tried. The wards wouldn't allow us to portal. We were *trapped*.

I focused on Thorne again, desperately trying to see past the aloof mask he wore. Had he only kept me alive so I wouldn't die before this moment? So his family wouldn't miss out on getting their own revenge?

It made sense. It *all* made sense.

The obsessive need to keep an eye on me, the growing frustration. He'd been impatient for this moment, *anticipating* it. He'd known that suicides often happened before trials, that the board was trying to reduce the casualty count. He'd been in a meeting with Chancellor Grimshaw and the school board for *hours*, no doubt suggesting the idea of a gala himself. Our sexual encounters had been his own personal revenge, but exposing me as a dangerous witch killer was a family matter.

He'd *wanted* them to come here, to witness for themselves the Mayweather's final downfall.

And like a *fool*, I hadn't figured it out until this very moment. Until it was too *late*.

His betrayal hit me hard, harder than I wanted to admit. It felt like he'd just brutally plunged a blade into my heart and was now watching me bleed out—like he'd undoubtedly wanted to do months ago.

The pain intensified when I realized that it could have been him. Thorne could have placed that curse on me and then played the hero so as not to break our pactum. Maybe my amulet hadn't stopped the curse after all. Maybe *he* had, reversing it for the sole purpose of breaking me down piece by piece, lulling me into a false sense of safety.

Making me *trust* him.

How could I have been so naive? So *stupid?* He'd been my enemy all this time, and I'd let him in anyway, so desperate not to be alone anymore that I'd ignored every warning sign.

Gran had told me to stay away from the Hudsons, but I'd failed to listen. Juliana had paid the price the first time, and now, it was my turn.

Dying on her death anniversary would be tragically poetic, though, I had to admit.

Despite the turmoil eating me up inside, self-preservation demanded I think of a way out of this. Shadewalking was at the top of the list, but I heavily doubted that Thorne would let me sneak away. He'd find me and drag me back like he was always threatening to do, forcing me to face my greatest fear, to *pay* for the sins I'd committed against his family.

I could practically hear him ordering me not to run. He couldn't win if I did, and I knew how badly he wanted to win. Winning was everything to him, and he'd played me perfectly until the bitter end. I'd known he was ruthless, but this was downright diabolical.

He'd ruined me, all right. He'd bent and broken me, because I was his. I owed my life to him, and he'd taken it, *claimed* it. There was no undoing that now.

Running was pointless, because I'd already given him everything he needed to control me. He'd spent months training me, learning my weaknesses. I'd practically served myself up to him on a silver platter, *begging* him to destroy me.

Poor Gran. Still so proud of her legacy, and she had no idea how epically I'd failed our family.

Just when I felt myself start to crack under the weight of it all, a pretty Asian girl in a tight white dress that left little to the imagination cut between the two groups and grabbed Thorne's arm. "Guess what?"

she exclaimed, bouncing up and down on her ridiculously high heels. "I sent in my application to Heartstone for next year!"

Thorne blinked as if coming out of a trance, breaking our stare to glance down at the excited girl. Obviously recognizing her, his impenetrable mask melted away, and he gave her a soft smile. "Yumi."

Smiled. He *smiled* at her. He'd never smiled at me that way before. Something about that realization made the knife in my heart twist a little. I completely stopped in my tracks, torn between watching their interaction and making a break for it.

"Riku suggested that we dance while I chat your ear off," the girl said, reaching up to stroke Comet's chest. The bird bent his head to affectionately nip at her fingers, and she giggled. "Unless you have a special someone here I don't know about?"

So fast that I might have imagined it, Thorne's eyes flicked back to me before dropping to the girl again. "No one special."

The blade gave an extra sharp twist.

"Oh, good," Yumi said with a relieved smile. "I don't want to make anyone jealous. Let's go. I've got *so* much to tell you."

As they turned and headed for the empty center reserved for dancing, something in me cracked. Broke. Yup, it was official. Thorne had stolen a part of me, something essential. Whatever he'd taken was following him onto that dance floor, leaving the rest of me to cope with the loss.

Dumb. I'd been *so* dumb to let my guard down around him.

Watching him walk away with another girl was almost worse than the knife of betrayal he'd just stuck into my heart.

Now that he was gone, everything felt off. The tension between the two families remained, but without Thorne here, it grew unbearably awkward. Instinct screamed at me to run while I had the chance. But another part of me, the part laden with guilt, urged me to break the silence, to *apologize* for what I had done to the Hudson family.

I'd wanted to for so long, but I'd been too afraid. And even though I was still afraid, I *needed* them to know how deeply sorry I was. Words wouldn't change what happened, and I didn't expect them to forgive me, but I had to tell them how much I loved Juliana. They deserved to know, even if they condemned me to death right afterward.

I was just about to risk everything when someone else decided to come between the Mayweather and Hudson standoff.

"Katherine Mayweather, as I live and breathe. I'm honored you decided to come."

Gran finally broke her stare with Beatrice as Chancellor Grimshaw stopped before her with his hand extended. I blinked, surprised by his friendly greeting. Did he really mean the words, or was he just trying to keep the peace?

Either way, Gran looked him over with a critical eye before replying rather saucily, "Cyrus Grimshaw. I must say, you've aged like fine wine. Being chief executive officer of the community's most prestigious academy must suit you."

That creepy smile of his stretched a mile wide. "Oh, indeed. It suits me quite well."

With a light laugh, she placed her hand in his, and he bent down to brush a featherlight kiss over her knuckles.

I clamped my mouth shut before it could fall open. Were they . . . *flirting* with each other? Or was this a simple play of politics? Probably the latter. I understood politics enough to know that smiles and kind words could cut just as deeply as outright disdain. Gran clearly had history with the chancellor, although I had no clue who or what they were to each other. Ex-lovers? Doubtful. There was at least a twenty-year age gap between them, and Gran had never shown an interest in men after Grandad died.

Not that I was aware of anyway.

It suddenly dawned on me how little I actually knew about my grandmother's personal life before I was born. I'd always seen her as a surrogate mother, the woman who'd practically raised me and my brother while my parents were off doing important elder business. She'd relocated from London to the states shortly after our grandfather had been killed, wanting to be closer to her best friend. My dad and aunt moved with her, and shortly after, my parents met and married. We'd lived as one big happy family for years, setting down roots in New Hampshire alongside the Hudson family, who officially joined our coven.

My world had been perfect before the exile. Since then, everything kept falling apart. The Hudsons left our coven and moved away, my parents' attempt to restore the Mayweather name ended in failure and landed them in prison, and my continued secret friendship with Juliana resulted in her death.

And now, here I was, fighting to restore the Mayweather name, praying I didn't fail like my parents had. But watching the ease with which my grandmother spoke to Chancellor Grimshaw, looking for all the world like she *belonged* here, I'd never felt more inadequate. She made it look so *easy*.

It was one thing to hear about her past exploits during her years as an elder but quite another to see her in action. Gran was a formidable force, commanding the room's attention with her presence alone. She oozed confidence and charm in a way that baffled me, especially considering how she'd been treated the past ten years.

The chancellor was clearly basking in her attention, enamored enough with their conversation to ignore the glares many around us were giving them.

In that moment, one thing became painfully clear to me. Gran was born for this cutthroat lifestyle. So had my aunt Clarice who'd been Head Elder *and* the headmistress of an academy before she died. My dad had thrived in this atmosphere too, along with my mom, despite not having a drop of Mayweather blood in her veins.

But me?

I didn't fit. Making polite conversation didn't come natural to me, neither did smiling in the face of my enemies. I'd rather cut the pretense and tell people *exactly* how I felt about them, consequences be damned. Smiling while I was dying inside felt like an impossible task, and forcing myself to do so wasn't an option.

I might be standing tall in the middle of Heartstone Academy despite the great odds against me, but in that moment, I'd never felt more like a failure, like a *fraud*.

This wasn't me. *None* of this was.

I was like a flopping fish on dry land, unequipped to survive in this world. Everyone around me easily breathed in the air while I gasped, my body unable to cope where it didn't belong. Feeling like a useless lump, I stood silent as a tomb while the world ebbed and flowed around me. Someone else approached the Hudsons, and I lost my chance to apologize. Gran and the chancellor continued to talk like old friends, and more and more people started to dance.

One head stood taller than the rest, and before I could stop myself, I was watching Thorne and Yumi gracefully cut across the dancefloor. Not much taller than me, the dark-haired girl had to crane her neck back while she talked to Thorne. He responded to something she said, and she laughed loud enough for me to hear. When he smiled, that pain in my heart twisted again.

I hated to admit it, but they looked good together. Easy. Natural. Unlike when Thorne and I were together. There was nothing *easy* about our relationship. We didn't even have one, and after tonight, I doubted we'd ever speak to each other again.

Despite the fact that he was about to betray me, the thought of this thing between us ending tonight filled me with even more pain. Yup, I was broken. Broken and pathetic.

As I continued to stand like a statue, not knowing what to do with myself, voices filtered toward me, close enough to overhear but just out of sight. I tried to tune them out, but the mention of two names sank into me like vicious claws.

". . . Benedict and Miranda . . ."

My parents.

"I heard the SCA is refusing to shorten their sentences. Too much of a liability, they say. Personally, I hope they rot in that prison for what they did. Sacrificing the community's safety once for personal gain was bad enough, but twice? I'm still in shock that Heartstone's school board voted to admit a Mayweather, especially after Clarice's failure to protect the students at Thornecrest. I, for one, loathe the thought of a Mayweather rising to power again. The apple never falls far from the tree, and I say the whole family is rotten to the core and should have been disposed of years ago."

The condemning words gouged deep, hitting bone. I struggled to breathe through the pain ripping my insides to shreds, to stand tall when all I wanted to do was curl up into the insignificant ball the speaker of those words made me feel like. They'd wanted me to overhear them, to know just how much the community didn't think I belonged here. I'd survived countless verbal attacks this semester without breaking, but this one cut deeper. This one was targeting my *family*, painting them as *villains*, and I couldn't . . . I couldn't do it any longer. Couldn't *be* here.

Knowing I was about to let Gran down but unable to listen to these people badmouth my family a second longer, I moved toward my grandmother, interrupting her conversation with Chancellor Grimshaw to quietly say, "I'm not feeling well, Gran. I'm so sorry, but I need to leave."

She turned to me, concern and confusion warring on her face. One look at my own expression, and she saw far more than I wanted her to. Her pale eyes narrowed as she swept them over the crowd, no doubt in search of whatever had upset me.

Worried that she would find and confront whoever had said those awful words, I hurriedly added, "I'm fine, Gran, really. I just need to—"

She lifted a hand, and I reluctantly stopped talking, my gut clenching when her gaze locked on something behind me. Certain she was about to make a scene in front of everyone, to fight a battle that *I* should have fought, I tried to brace myself. But she didn't say a word. She simply stood there with her hand up. *Listening.*

Oh no.

If she heard anyone badmouthing the members of her family, this political little charade would be over. Gran wasn't the turn-the-other-cheek type, and after ten years of living in forced purgatory, I knew without a doubt that an explosion was imminent.

"Let's just go," I said, needing to stop this from escalating, from turning into a bloodbath that ended with *both* of us dead. I tried to slip my arm through hers, but her hand came down and grabbed mine. *Hard.*

"Is it true?"

At the change in her tone, dread sank like a rock in my stomach. Pearl must have overheard someone talking about the mentorship program and relayed the message back to Gran that Thorne and I were partners. Curse those furry little eavesdropping ears.

"Is what true?" I asked, choosing to take the coward's way out by playing dumb.

"Are you *sleeping* with Thorne Hudson to get ahead?"

At the bite, at the *anger* in her voice, my insides turned to ice. But it was the sudden stillness around us that had me swaying on my feet, on the verge of passing out. They'd overheard. Worse, they already *knew*. Just like with our arrival, silence rippled over the crowd. It spanned outward as the gossip spread and spread, reaching every single ear in the great hall.

The dancing stopped. The *music* stopped.

Everyone turned our way, turned to *me*, waiting for an answer to Gran's question. I swept a glance over the room and immediately regretted it when I saw that Thorne had stopped as well, his gaze locked on my face.

Had *he* started this rumor?

Just the thought of him doing something so cruel cracked the final pieces of my composure. Feeling my hands start to tremble, I curled them into tight fists before looking Gran straight in the eye and replying, "No, I am not sleeping with Thorne Hudson to get ahead. The mere thought of doing such a thing sickens me."

Seeing the truth written in my eyes, Gran's expression fell. "Winter . . ."

Too humiliated to stand here for even one more moment, I quickly cut her off, something I *never* did. "I have to go, Gran. Thank you for coming tonight, and please tell Wyatt I miss him."

Leaning forward, I swiftly kissed her cheek and turned away. She let me go, as silent as the rest of the crowd while I swept toward the exit. I kept my head held high even when my chin quivered, even when tears threatened to pour from my eyes.

They didn't. Even today, they were as dry as bone.

I thought for sure I wouldn't make it, thought I would trip and fall, making an even bigger fool of myself.

Just one more step. One more.

The stares were unbearable, the silence even more so. Did they believe me? Or had they already labeled me as nothing more than an opportunistic slut?

Oh, how the Mayweather name had fallen.

Barely able to force one foot in front of the other, I was nearly to the doors when Riku appeared beside me. "Bambi . . ."

"Don't," I curtly said, refusing to look at him. "Don't ever call me that again."

He stopped in his tracks, and I hurried past, the burn behind my eyes making my whole face hurt. Realizing that Riku must have betrayed me too, pretending to be my *friend* so I'd open up to him, I almost lost it.

By sheer force of will, I managed to exit through the doors and leave the Legacy Gala behind, all while my heart shattered into a million pieces.

CHAPTER 28

I didn't know why or how, but instead of returning to my lonely tower, I ended up outside.

Worse, in the glen. *Our* glen. The place where Thorne and I had trained nearly every day for months. Where I'd learned to face my fears, to face *myself.* To finally let others in and trust again. I'd started to think of this place as a haven, the one spot on this campus that didn't constantly remind me I didn't belong.

I was just another student here, not a Mayweather. My time at the glen had been about learning and growing, not protecting my back from threats.

But that was all gone now. That sense of belonging had been fake. A *lie.* Just like everything else.

The air was bitter cold, matching how frozen I felt inside. Unlike in the great hall, there were no stars or Northern Lights decorating the night sky, no snow gently falling and dusting the ground. Clouds obscured the moon, the threat of a storm heavy in the air as always.

I could barely see, but I didn't need to. The shadows surrounding me felt like friends tonight, cloaking me in the darkness I so desperately sought. The glen might not feel like a safe haven anymore, but it was the only place that could shield me from prying eyes while I fell apart.

The pain inside me swelled, along with the darkness I carefully kept contained. Both needed release, and I wasn't strong enough to keep it all inside anymore. So I let go. Let go and threw my head back, belting out a scream of pure agony. As I did, I whipped my hands out and released the darkness, allowing it to explode from me in angry bursts of deadly shrapnel.

I heard the furious magic rip into tree after tree, eviscerating the trunks until they collapsed under the attack and crashed to the forest floor. I kept screaming, frantic to expel the pain I was drowning in, desperate to find relief.

The well of hurt and anger felt endless, and I took it out on the helpless trees, watching the dark outline of one after another succumb to my relentless assault.

I didn't know how long I expelled the darkness and screamed myself hoarse, but a sudden shriek had me whipping around, my hands glowing dark violet as I prepared to defend myself.

"Easy," a voice said, the deep timbre scraping across my raw nerves. When I squinted past the glow of my magic and saw a familiar tall shape only yards away, I bared my teeth in a low hiss.

Comet shrieked again and launched into the sky, and I let him go, my sights solely trained on the warlock who'd caused all my pain. Thorne took another step, and I hissed again, crouching into the defensive stance he'd taught me.

He paused, no doubt taking in my unhinged state. I let him, wanting him to know just how *furious* I was. One false move, and I would attack. Pactum or no pactum, my need for revenge was too strong to control at the moment. He could try to subdue me, of course, but he wouldn't succeed. Not this time.

I was too enraged, every inch of me burning with a desire that used to terrify me. Not anymore. I wanted to kill. *Kill.*

"I didn't do it, Snowflake."

"*Don't* call me that," I snapped, pointing a glowing finger at him.

I needed him to be afraid. *Terrified.* So he'd leave and never speak to me, never *look* at me again.

He didn't even flinch, his face calm and his hands loose at his sides. The nonthreatening posture made me see red. I felt wild. Reckless. Invincible, like no one could touch me. Even him.

It felt good, *so* good, and I wouldn't let him take that away from me.

"Admit it," I said, my voice little more than a growl. "This was all a ruse, a *set up*. Right from the start, you wanted to see me fail. It was your family who advocated for my acceptance to Heartstone, who wanted me here so they could get revenge for what I did to Juliana." When he didn't respond, I shouted, "*Answer me!*"

He watched me, watched as I slowly came undone and didn't even blink. Finally, he replied, "My family voted in favor of your admittance to Heartstone, yes. But—"

"I *knew* it," I interrupted, trembling so hard that my teeth clacked together. "Gran warned me that your family was behind this, but I stupidly let you near me anyway. I let myself feel *safe* around you. I never should have agreed to the pactum, never should have even *come* here. This was all a sick elaborate hoax to lure me out of hiding so you could destroy me for good."

"That's not true," he carefully said, as if speaking to a cornered animal.

"You wanted to ruin me, to *break* me. You said so yourself."

"Not in the way you're imagining, Winter."

"What other way *is* there?" I exploded. "You pursued me, touched me, stirred awake these needs, these . . . these *feelings*. I didn't ask for this. Didn't *want* this. But you took pieces of me anyway. You broke me apart, and I *let* you, perversely believing that I owed that to you. And I would have continued to let you until my life debt was repaid, but then tonight happened, and I finally understood that you didn't want to destroy just me. You wanted to see the last of my family's reputation obliterated in the most humiliating way possible by painting me as nothing but your little whore. In front of my *grandmother*. Do you have any idea what that did to me? To *her?*"

"I didn't spread that rumor."

"Enough!" I roared, flinging my hands out, my *magic* out. It streaked through the darkness and plunged into its targets without mercy. "No more lies, Thorne. Admit that you came out here to drag me back inside so your family can tell everyone what I did to Juliana."

"What? I would *never* do that," Thorne vehemently said, sounding so appalled that I almost believed him. "I came out here to see if you were all right, to *comfort* you."

"*Comfort* me?" I practically shrieked, furious that he wouldn't drop the ruse. "You hate me, Thorne. *Hate* me. Everything you've ever done to me was to further your revenge plot, so just stop already. Stop pretending to care, because I know you don't. You only care about winning and seeing me burnt at the *stake*."

"No, I *don't*," he snapped, the words punctuated by a low rumble of thunder. "I don't hate you, and I don't want you hurt."

That knife in my heart twisted again, and I lashed back with far too much emotion, "Stop lying to me. Stop *punishing* me!"

"I'm not. I'm being completely honest with you, Winter. And if I'm punishing anyone, I'm punishing myself. Every second that I'm near you, I'm in pain, but I can't stay away. I keep coming back for more like a drug addict desperate for another fix. You're my sweet venom, my deadly obsession. I crave you more than I crave anything, more than I crave *winning*. I didn't want this either, but you're all I can think about now, and it's killing me. *Ruining* me. When I saw how much that rumor hurt you tonight, I wanted to destroy the entire room until I found who started it and then destroy *them*. I still do. The need to protect you is all-consuming."

I shook my head, unwilling, *unable* to believe him. "You're lying."

Lightning lit up the sky. "I'm not."

"Doesn't matter. I killed your sister, and you'll never forgive me."

Another rolling rumble shook the air, this time closer. "It was an accident."

My breath caught.

When I failed to respond, he took a slow step toward me. "I believed you were the villain for so long, that you killed my sister for your own revenge against my family, but I don't believe that anymore. I can't. You've proved yourself truly remorseful for what happened, and I can see how much her death tears you up inside."

He took another step.

"Thorne," I warned, raising my hands higher to ward him off. "Don't."

"Then stop me."

Lightning forked across the sky again, illuminating his determined expression. Oh, no. He took another step as thunder boomed, vibrating the ground.

"I've been hiding my anger behind a steely wall of control for so long. But then you arrived at Heartstone, and that wall started to crack, allowing my anger to finally come out. I hated and blamed you for my sister's death, but I can't anymore." Oh no, oh no. "Juliana loved you, and you loved her." No, no, no, no, no. "You don't deserve to die for something you don't remember doing, and you don't deserve my anger any longer. Juliana would want me to forgive you, so—"

"Don't," I weakly whispered.

"I forgive you." The first raindrop struck my cheek as he closed the gap between us. Unable to move, unable to stop him, I let him grasp my arms and gently lower them to my sides. "I forgive you, because we both need to heal and move on. Because I *care*. Because I want you to be free of your guilt."

It was the slight break in his voice, the raw *emotion* that made the chaos wreaking havoc inside my body start to recede, along with the angry magic at my fingertips.

He forgave me. Forgave me. He cared. *Cared*. Despite the pain still sharp in my chest, I so desperately wanted to believe him.

Seeing my hesitation, sensing the shift, he slid his hands up my arms to cup my face. Another raindrop fell, then another and another. "Let me show you what you mean to me, Snowflake. Let me kiss you."

I stopped breathing.

How was this happening? A minute ago, I wanted to kill him, and now *this?* It was all too much, and I didn't know what to do.

"You'll hurt me," I managed to get out, trembling for a different reason this time, afraid, *so* afraid that he was going to destroy what was left of me.

"I won't," he murmured, sweeping his thumbs over my skin. "You don't owe me a single thing, but I want this. Let me kiss you, Snowflake. Please. If you want me to beg, I'll beg."

I trembled harder, so hard that I gripped his forearms to steady myself. More lightning brightened the sky, revealing his pleading look. I could practically *feel* how desperately he wanted to kiss me. My lips parted, and his gaze dropped to them, filled with yearning.

"Let it happen," he breathed, lowering his head toward mine, blocking out the stormy sky until all I could see, all I could smell was him. I dug my nails into his jacket, struggling to breathe, to *think*. I shouldn't do this. I *couldn't* do this.

"Thorne," I whispered, *begged*. "Our families . . ."

"Don't need to know. No one needs to know but us. Comet is in the trees standing watch. He won't let anyone see us."

Why, oh, why did he always know just what to say? My anger was gone, my guard lowering to let him back in, and that terrified the hell out of me. I felt helpless, drawn to him by a force stronger than myself, unable to pull away even if I wanted to. Which I didn't.

"I promise you're safe with me," he whispered reassuringly, stretching his thumb out to catch my bottom lip. I gasped as the slightly rough pad ran over my sensitive skin, immediately awakening a want, a *need* for more. "Let it happen. That's all you need to do."

Let it happen. He made it sound so easy. So uncomplicated. All I had to do was surrender to the kiss. And, oh, how I ached to be kissed by him.

He must have sensed how badly I wanted this, too. I didn't say a word, but he suddenly knew, *knew* that I wouldn't stop him. That I didn't *want* to. Because he erased the final inches between us and . . .

Kissed me.

CHAPTER 29

Rain started to soak through my hair and dress, but I barely noticed.

I was too consumed by the fact that Thorne Hudson was kissing me.

The second his mouth touched mine, lightning forked down and struck the ground. As the powerful energy dispersed, I could have sworn, *sworn* that it traveled up through my body and into my lips. The shock of it wrung a gasp from me, and Thorne pulled back.

Our eyes met and held. The rain dripped from his wet hair and onto me, onto my mouth. He focused on the drops, inhaling sharply when I parted my lips again and . . . let them slide in. An invitation. One that he eagerly accepted.

He swooped back down and captured my mouth, the contact firmer, more insistent this time. A command. He wanted me to reciprocate. His warmth seeped into my chilled skin, stealing all the way down to my toes. All too soon, he broke the kiss again to check on me, our breaths slightly uneven as we stared at each other.

Hungry for more of that delicious warmth, I pushed up and initiated the kiss this time, firmly pressing my mouth to his. He made a sound like rolling thunder in the back of his throat, then dropped one of his arms and crushed me to him. My body lit up like a firework at the intimate contact, and when I gasped again, he took full advantage and deepened the kiss.

His bottom lip slid between mine, and I got my first taste of him.

My tongue happily lapped up the salty flavor, seeking out more by tracing his skin. He went wild at the feel of my tongue on him, kissing me harder, *deeper*. My bottom lip slid into his mouth, and he greedily sucked it inside to taste me.

As a euphoric groan left him, butterflies detonated in my stomach and my toes curled.

Rain saturated our frantic kisses, wetting our lips so they pleasurably slid over each other, *inside* each other. Needing more, I raised my hands to grip his strong neck and parted my lips wider. His tongue immediately plunged into my mouth and tangled with mine. And just like that, I was lost. *Drowning*. Bliss unfurled low in my belly, forcing a moan from me. Thorne swallowed the sound, holding me to him so tightly that I could no longer tell where he ended and I began.

My body was pressed to his in a way I'd never experienced before, but instinctively, I knew it could get closer. All on its own, my lower half sought out his, gratified when it found something rock hard. I pushed up even more and fit the length between my aching thighs, driven by a need I barely understood but desperately wanted to experience.

"Snowflake," Thorne groaned into my mouth, sliding his hand down to cup my butt and grind me against him. The blast of sensation wrung a cry from me, and I felt my pussy flutter with a mini orgasm. He ground his erection into me a few more times, then uttered a curse and broke our kiss. His breathing was as ragged as mine, his pulse thundering beneath my fingertips, but he pulled back enough to look me in the eye and say, "I won't take you like this. Not when you're still unsure about me, about us. But I desperately want to taste more of you. Please, let me do it. Let me taste you."

Taste me . . .

Oh, dear ancestors, was he saying what I thought he was saying?

My pussy fluttered again, suddenly aching for what he was suggesting. A helpless whimper burst from me, and that was enough for him. He kissed my lips again, then kissed lower, tipping my head back to expose my throat. He pressed his warm mouth to my thundering pulse, and I sucked in a sharp breath as his tongue darted out to taste my skin. The storm raged around us as he kissed lower and lower, sending goosebumps over my flesh everywhere his mouth touched.

When he found my cleavage, he slowed, and I pried my eyes open to watch him. He pressed his mouth to one swell, sliding his eyes shut as if in rapture. My toes curled again as he repeated the kiss to the other swell, then slid his hand over my shoulder to slip my dress down. I let him, struggling to breathe while he slowly exposed one breast, then the other, both nipples hard enough to cut glass.

"I've wanted to do this for so long," he roughly said, his gaze heatedly caressing my flesh before he leaned down and captured a nipple in his mouth. When I felt him suck on the sensitive nub, all the air punched from my lungs, and I gripped his shoulders for dear life.

Oh, but that wasn't all he did. After working the nipple into a frenzy of sensation with his tongue, he gripped it between his teeth and gently bit down. I jerked and cried out as pleasure shot through me, traveling through my veins like lightning until it hit my aching clit.

"Anscestors, save me," I gasped, and Thorne chuckled, the vibrations further stimulating my flesh.

When he finally released my nipple, it was only to kiss his way to the other one. We were thoroughly drenched by the time he was finished, but I was too blissed out to mind the cold.

He suddenly dropped to his knees in the grass before me, and the sight instantly rendered me speechless. I didn't know why, but it was the sexiest thing I'd ever seen. Knowing what he was about to do, I quivered with nerves and anticipation. Was I seriously going to let him do this right here out in the open?

Yes. Yes, I was.

"We can do this standing up or on the ground," he said, pausing to look up at me.

Oh, wow. Both. Both, please.

But I was really enjoying this power reversal where I was looking down at *him* for a change. "Like this," I found myself saying, to my utmost surprise. One corner of his mouth curved upward, and I knew he'd figured out my train of thought.

Without taking his eyes off me, he slid both hands inside the slit of my dress and spread the dark fabric wide, revealing my panties. Hooking his thumbs into the material, he started to tug them down, down, down. As my pussy was exposed to the night air, all of my attention went to that area, to the realization that he was about to see me naked down there for the first time.

He didn't give me time to feel self-conscious, though. Lifting one leg, then the other, he slid my underwear free before spreading my skirt again. His head was suddenly between my legs, kissing a slow path up my inner thigh. I tensed all over, overwhelmed by how intimate it felt to have his head down there, how *vulnerable*. My heart began to pound, harder and harder the higher up he went. My nerves were on fire, along with the ache he was so close to reaching.

He darted his tongue out to lick the rain from my skin, and I almost died.

"Open your legs for me, Snowflake," he rumbled against my sensitive flesh, and I obeyed without question, without thought. All I could think about was the throbbing ache between my thighs and how close he was to—

The moment I gave him clearance, he focused on that aching spot and placed his tongue on it, licking all the way up the center.

My mind stopped. My heart stopped. Everything stopped as that one lick filled me with pure ecstasy.

Unable to process, to *contain* the feeling, I opened my mouth to scream, but nothing came out. He licked me again, and my whole body bowed forward, forcing me to drop my hands to his shoulders so I wouldn't fall over. On the third lick, a strangled noise finally made its way out of me. I sounded like a drowning cat, but I didn't care. As long as he didn't stop, I didn't care about anything.

"Perfection," he hummed against my clit, his hot breath sending a thrill through me. "You taste like mine."

Mine. There was that word again. Only this time, it felt like I was.

He found a rhythm after that, thrusting his tongue against me like he'd done with his erection earlier. I gripped his shoulders tightly, my body buzzing with so much pleasure that I felt faint. I locked my trembling knees, but they threatened to buckle beneath me with every new thrust. He held my thighs to steady me, spreading them a little wider so he could delve deeper.

It was when that powerful, talented tongue of his began to swirl over my clit in tight little circles that I started to lose it. Pitiful whimpers left me, my body struggling to keep up with the overload of sensations shooting through it.

It felt too good. It was too *much*. I wasn't going to survive.

I dug my fingers into his hair, my breaths coming in frantic pants as I barrelled toward my destination at breakneck speed. Too much, too much, too *much*.

"Thorne!"

He didn't slow, didn't let up. He wanted me to come, and he

wasn't stopping until I did. My whimpers grew louder, turning into cries. His tongue swirled faster and faster, harder and harder.

Terrified that I was about to explode, unable to stand the assault a second longer, I tried to pull back. Thorne tightened his grip on my thighs and bore down even more, lashing his tongue over my clit so savagely that I broke. *Shattered.* My entire body detonated like a bomb, the pleasure so intense that I threw my head back and screamed.

At the same time, lightning struck the glen, closely followed by a clap of thunder so loud that my screams were lost to the storm.

Him. It was him. He'd orchestrated this storm, *conducted* it. Using it to drown out my screams of rapture so no one would hear.

So completely blissed out, I had my first full out-of-body experience. From an orgasm, anyway. I was lighter than air, floating in the tumultuous sky without a care in the world. My earthly body gave out on me halfway through the experience, forcing Thorne to catch it. He gathered me against him, tucking my head beneath his chin while I came down. When my breaths and pulse evened out again, he slid my dress back into place and collected my underwear before standing with me in his arms.

I snuggled against him, still a mile high as he carried me down the steep pathway. A sudden rustle of wings announced Comet's presence as he swooped down and gracefully landed on Thorne's shoulder. Only when we were nearly to the dorm building did my common sense start to return.

"Someone will see," I whispered, squirming in his arms to be put down.

He tightened his grip and rumbled back, "Then cloak us."

Okay, so he was feeling a bit possessive, apparently. Not that I minded at the moment. After what he'd just done, he deserved to carry me for as long as he wanted.

Doing as he suggested, I gathered the shadows around us, which wasn't hard this time of night. They easily rose to do my bidding, shielding our forms from prying eyes. It was still early enough that we could have returned to the gala, but it was clear I was done, and Thorne didn't even bother to ask. I let him carry me inside, listening closely for anyone roaming the halls. All clear. If Thorne was bothered by the feel of my cold shadows surrounding him, he didn't let on.

"Is she still here?" I quietly asked, and he immediately knew who I meant.

"No. Your grandmother left right after you did. So did my family."

Relieved, I sank into him a little more. "I didn't expect to see Sterling."

"Neither did I. He made a last minute decision to come."

Well, that would explain why Thorne hadn't warned me. I'd really assumed the worst about him. Feeling bad, I couldn't help but say, "I'm sorry I accused you of lying and stabbing me in the back. And starting that rumor."

I'd really been a jerk to him.

"It's okay," Thorne replied. "I understand why you did. You were stressed, humiliated, and there's a lot of unresolved history between our families."

To put it lightly.

Biting my lip, I dared to ask, "Are they mad?"

"About the rumor?" He paused before admitting, "I don't know. I told them it wasn't true, but they seemed troubled by the thought of us together."

Oh. I shouldn't be surprised, of course. Hearing that the heir to the Hudson legacy might be screwing his sister's killer would concern me, too. I'd downright forbid such a heinous thing if I were in their shoes.

Still, I found myself not wanting to dwell on the consequences of what we were doing. Not right now, not when being in Thorne's arms felt so good, so comforting. After the stressful day I'd just had, I really, *really* needed this. Which was why I changed the subject, saying as nonchalantly as I could, "The girl you were dancing with seems nice."

"She is," Thorne replied without missing a beat. "Yumi is Riku's cousin but is more of a sister to him. You'd like her."

I raised an eyebrow at that. "Did you two ever date?"

The moment the words came out, I knew they were a mistake. I sounded jealous. *Was* I jealous?

"We briefly had a thing last year, but we're just friends. She's a lot like Riku in that way."

Oh, that was reassuring. *Not.*

When I didn't respond, he asked, "Does that bother you?"

Yep.

"Nope."

Yeah, he wasn't convinced. I was acting weird, and it was annoyingly obvious. Turning another corner, he made sure the coast was clear before saying, "What I said at the gala about not having someone special in my life wasn't true. I only said that to protect you. Even though this thing between us is complicated, I think it's more special than either of us realizes."

I blinked. Blinked again.

Did he just . . . confess that I was special to him?

At a loss for words, I didn't respond, but I felt the jealousy fade away. He'd probably had sex with several girls over the years, but that didn't mean he was going to jump into bed with them now. I was the one currently in his arms with my lady bits still blissfully tingling from his thorough attention.

A comfortable silence lapsed between us, but when he rounded the corner that led toward Jade Wing, I blurted without thinking, "I don't want to be alone tonight."

Oh, wow. I'd gone and said it just like that. No taking it back now.

Thorne slowed, and I stopped breathing, worried that I'd allowed myself to be too vulnerable. I'd stayed strong all these months, insisting on remaining in Jade Wing Tower no matter how miserable I was. But now that my trial was looming before me, only hours away, I didn't . . . I didn't want to spend this time alone.

Would Thorne consider that weak?

Nervous that he was about to lecture me, I opened my mouth to retract the words when he suddenly turned and headed the opposite direction.

Toward Sapphire Wing.

A heavy dose of gratitude spread through me, and I reached up to twine my hands behind his neck. Without a word, he ducked his head and ghosted his lips over my forehead, making my toes curl again. By the time we reached his dorm, I was relaxed enough that I could have fallen asleep in his arms. But when he uttered the spell to open the door, we were greeted by two familiar faces. Two *worried* faces.

Comet launched off Thorne's shoulder, and I released the shadows just as Riku and Oz stood from the dining room table to approach us.

"Is she okay?" Oz asked, and the genuine concern in his voice melted me.

"She will be," Thorne responded for me, and I was okay with that. Now that the blissful high had worn off, all I wanted to do was curl up on his heavenly mattress and sleep like the dead.

"Bamb—" Riku started, then paused, something akin to pain tightening his features.

"You can call me Bambi," I said. The pain on his face melted away, and his mouth curved into a soft grin.

Thorne didn't stick around for further talk, somehow knowing that I needed to be alone. Alone with *him*. He carried me into his room and nudged the door shut, plunging us into darkness once more. I didn't mind, and neither did he, familiar enough with the room that he maneuvered around it with ease.

When he finally set me down, he immediately got to work undressing me. The sodden dress was pooled on the floor in no time, leaving me in nothing but my heels. With my nakedness concealed by darkness, I didn't feel awkward. He left me standing there for a moment but came back seconds later, slipping one of his shirts over my head. Kneeling down, he unstrapped my heels, then slid a pair of his boxer briefs up my legs.

The act was so intimate, so *caring* that I felt a telltale burn behind my eyes. I blinked, blinked again, trying to ease the burn, but as he began to undress himself, it wouldn't go away.

By the time he was in a fresh t-shirt and sweatpants, I was more than ready to crawl into bed and shut my gritty eyes. I doubted even the unfamiliar sensation of sleeping beside someone would keep me awake, regardless of how sexy my bed companion was. When Thorne pulled the sheets back, I gladly climbed in, then felt the mattress dip as he climbed in after me.

For a second, I wondered if he planned on doing more than sleep tonight. But as I settled down and the room fell into silence, he simply curled an arm around my middle and pulled me back against him. His body lined up with mine, cocooning me inside its larger shape, and my senses sprang awake once more.

No doubt feeling how alert I'd suddenly become, he placed his mouth near my ear and breathed, "Sleep, Snowflake. You're safe here."

The soft reassuring rumble sank into my bones, and faster than I thought possible, I started to drift away.

I didn't know how long I slept, but I suddenly woke up with a gasp. Thorne violently reacted to the sound, springing up to brace his body above mine in a second flat. "What's wrong?" he said, his frame taut as if prepared to shield me from an attack.

I didn't respond right away, uncertain at first what had startled me awake. Something tickled my cheek, and I reached up to swipe at it. And that's when I knew. A sound left me, half laugh, half sob. "Nothing's wrong," I whispered as another tear slid onto my cheek. "I'm crying."

"And that's a good thing?" Thorne asked, sounding confused as he lifted a hand to wipe the tear away.

"A very good thing," I sniffled, feeling another tear, then another slide down my face. "It means I'm finally starting to heal."

CHAPTER 30

I stared at my foggy reflection, certain I was going to be sick.

This was it. The day of my trial. Ride or die time.

Out of habit, I almost started talking to the image in the mirror, something I did when my emotions were high. She'd always known just how to comfort me in times like these, reminding me that I was stronger than I thought.

But even though it was her older brother in the steamy shower behind me, I stopped myself from speaking out loud. He wouldn't understand. *I* didn't even fully understand why I felt closest to my dead best friend while talking to a reflective surface.

This thing between me and Thorne was still so new and uncertain, and I didn't want to ruin that by admitting that I talked to Juliana like she was still alive.

I'm scared, I spoke in my head instead, which wasn't as good but better than nothing. *I almost failed my last trial, and I'm so afraid that I'll fail this one or wind up dead.*

No response, as usual.

Feeling tears well in my eyes, I hurriedly blinked them away and finished securing the braid in my hair. Ever since the dam had broken last night, I couldn't seem to stop the tears from leaking out. I guessed that was to be expected after two years of blockage, but the timing kind of sucked.

Today of all days, I needed to be tough, no weakness allowed.

Tears weren't weak, but tell that to the students who'd been waiting months for this moment, a moment where they were finally allowed to attack me without punishment. I couldn't see the attack coming if my vision was obscured by unending tears.

The shower switched off, and I studiously focused on my outfit, which Oz had picked up for me after my arrival last night. Used to wearing a skirt and blazer during the day, it felt weird to be dressed so casual. My yoga pants were black and so was my long-sleeved tee, the only color a silver-stitched H and A crest on the upper left side. I'd been told enough about my upcoming trial to know that it was physically strenuous, so I was glad for the change in wardrobe.

The shower door opened, and I looked everywhere but in that direction, unused to this level of intimacy. Sure, I'd seen Thorne naked before, but it felt different between us now. We'd confessed things, *feelings*. And we'd kissed, *more* than kissed. After what had happened between us last night, taking in all that delicious wet skin fresh out of the shower made our changing dynamic that much more real. And I wasn't ready for that yet, not when I had a trial to focus on.

He didn't seem to have the same sentiment, though. After I'd slipped out of bed and taken my own shower, he'd joined me in the bathroom, stripping down to nothing before I'd even finished dressing. At least he hadn't masterbated in the shower while I was getting ready. I wouldn't have been able to focus at *all* if he'd done that.

As I dropped my braid to let it swing down my back, Thorne came up behind me and picked it up. I tensed, all too aware that his naked *dick* was inches away from my backside. Didn't he know what a *towel* was?

"I like your hair like this," he commented, his voice still slightly gruff from sleep. Before I could prepare myself, he wrapped the length around his hand and tugged my head back. As I naturally fell against his chest with my face tipped up, he leaned down and covered my mouth with his. Still wet and warm from the shower, his skin melted into mine, instantly making me weak-kneed and pliant against him.

Holy crap, this was dangerous. One kiss, and I was putty in his hands. Literally.

"Did I tell you how beautiful you looked in that dress last night?" he murmured against my lips, the compliment making me warm all over. "You looked even more beautiful when I started to take it off."

Shock zipped through me, along with a flash of heat that settled between my legs. Was Thorne Hudson *flirting* with me? Well, this was new. And more than a little distracting.

Thankfully, he had better control over his faculties at the moment, straightening and going about his business like he hadn't just blown my mind—and made my panties embarrassingly wet.

Struggling to regather my wits, I left the bathroom post-haste, in desperate need of air that didn't smell like his wet body. As I entered the dorm's main living space, Oz and Riku were in the kitchen just like the last two times I'd stayed over. Comet turned from looking out the living room windows to give me what sounded like a "good morning" chirp.

I gave him a small smile, suddenly wondering how much he'd seen—and heard—last night. He might *look* like a bird, but there was a highly intelligent celestial spirit inside that feathered body. I wanted to be embarrassed by the thought of him overhearing my orgasmic screams, but I was too busy trying to keep my stomach down when I caught a whiff of the catered breakfast spread out on the island.

"Morning, Bambi," Riku called, holding what looked like a Starbucks drink. Since when did we have Starbucks? "You're looking all doe-eyed and rested. Here, this is for you."

I approached the kitchen slowly, taking in Riku and Oz's relaxed postures and smiles. Something about it creeped me out, and I commented while accepting the drink, "Why are both acting like this?"

"Like what?" Oz asked, still smiling at me pleasantly.

"Like the sun is shining and everything is right with the world." When they both kept smiling at me like weirdos, my expression flattened, and I reminded them, "I have a trial today."

"We know," Riku replied, nudging me to try the drink. "We didn't want to freak you out."

Uhh . . .

"Well, now I'm *more* freaked out," I muttered, raising the cup to take a tentative sip. Caramel Frappe, my favorite. Except my throat was so tight that I almost choked on it. Pointing my drink at them, I added, "Those smiles are especially freaky, by the way."

With a sigh, Riku wiped the smile from his face. "Fine, would it help if I confessed that I didn't sleep a wink last night?"

"Me neither," Oz admitted.

My stomach soured even more, and I set down the drink. "Um, no, that doesn't help."

"Well, it looks like Thorne slept well for the first time in weeks," Riku commented with a wicked little smirk.

I glanced behind me just as Thorne entered the space, his black slacks riding dangerously low on his hips and his white collared shirt still wide open. Forgetting how to breathe, I took in his sun-kissed, slightly damp skin and marveled at how his muscles moved and flexed with each step.

"Hope you weren't mad that I sent Yumi to run interference last night. It looked like a fight was about to break out."

I blinked, realizing that Riku was talking to me. Tearing my gaze from Thorne's body, I replied, "No, I wasn't mad. The distraction was needed, so, thank you."

"But, like, Yumi wasn't trying to steal your man, just so you know. They've known each other for a long time and had a little fling last year, but that's way over now. It would be like you and me hooking up. Super enjoyable but temporary, you know? Like spring break at a nude beach, or—"

"Riku," I loudly said. "Shut up."

Riku closed his mouth with an audible click.

Oz made a choking noise that sounded a lot like laughter. Thorne brushed past me on his way into the kitchen, firmly enough that I knew he'd done it on purpose. It felt like a great big cat had just rubbed up against me, the move purely affectionate—and maybe a bit possessive.

If he considered me his, did that mean he was mine? And if so, for how long?

"You should eat," he said and dropped a box of doughnuts before me. "You need all the fuel you can get."

At the reminder of what awaited me in less than an hour, that sick feeling came roaring back. One look at the gooey doughnuts, and my stomach violently lurched. I was across the room in a flash, barrelling toward the bathroom. Dry heaves left me the second I was hunched over the toilet, my whole body trembling like a leaf.

Moments later, I felt the presence of someone behind me. Unable to stop them, unable to do anything but gasp and choke as tears streamed from my eyes, I felt a large warm hand splay on my back. Two more bodies entered the bathroom, but I didn't bother trying to shoo them away. Not when their presence was the only thing keeping me from spiraling into a panic attack.

"I'm fine," I said when I could speak again, carefully straightening so I wouldn't further upset my sensitive stomach. "I'm just a little nervous."

"It's okay to admit you're afraid," Oz said from the doorway, surprising me. "I was terrified of my first year trials."

"So was I," Riku admitted from beside him.

Thorne didn't say anything, but when I reached up to wipe my face, he gently caught my wrist and turned me around. As our eyes met, he brushed his thumbs over my cheeks, catching every last tear before saying, "The waiting period before each trial is almost harder than the trial itself. It drains you mentally and emotionally, but once the trial starts, instinct takes over. It's why I've been training you every day, so your reactions under pressure aren't fear-based. You're still learning, but your stamina and control over your magic have increased significantly. I know you can do this, Winter. You've proven that you deserve to be here."

He couldn't have said the more perfect thing. The words were sweet music to my ears and a balm to my battered heart. I'd nearly given up hope of ever hearing those words, and I certainly never thought that Thorne of all people would be the one to say them.

What's more, I could feel how genuine they were. He hadn't spoken the words simply to placate me. He *meant* them.

"Thank you," I whispered, my gratitude reaching into my core, into the deepest depths of my soul.

He responded by pressing a kiss to my forehead. Not a quick brush, but a lingering one, a kiss that warmed my insides and filled me with reassurance.

"Let's get some food in you," he murmured against my skin, and I nodded, fairly certain I could keep it down now.

Now that he'd given me the words, the *confidence* to face my trial.

CHAPTER 31

"This year, the end-of-semester challenge our first years will face is called the Labyrinth Trial," Chancellor Grimshaw said. He stood at the top of the stairs just outside Heartstone's main entrance, along with Professor Holt and the other teachers. "Your mentors should have prepared you for this day with the knowledge and experience they gleaned from their own trials. Although no two trials are exactly alike, they faced a similar trial during their first year."

His commanding voice echoed over the gloomy clearing and down the stairs to where the student body congregated in pairs. Thorne stood beside me, tall and imposing. The warlock's arms were crossed, yet his posture was relaxed, calm. He didn't touch or even look at me, and I was grateful for his businesslike demeanor. I could tell that last night's rumor was still on everyone's minds, and I didn't want to fuel their imaginations by acting too chummy with my mentor.

At least the trial was keeping them properly distracted. Well, except for Blaze, who kept giving me dirty little looks every few seconds. I wasn't the only one who noticed his attention, and after a dozen or so looks, Thorne shifted his body to block Blaze's view.

"It was him," he muttered under his breath, just loud enough for me to catch the words. When I saw one of his hands form a tight fist, I knew exactly what he was referring to.

"Probably," I murmured back, feeling dumb that I hadn't

suspected Blaze in the first place. He'd been acting extra sketchy last night before the gala, and I couldn't forget Alma's cryptic warning.

He'd probably hoped that publicly humiliating me in front of our community's most prestigious members would finally break me, and it almost had. If not for Thorne, it would have.

"Wait until I get my hands on him," Thorne quietly seethed, and the promise of violence in his tone sent a shiver up my spine. Not of dread. Of *excitement.*

"Not if I get to him first," I grumbled back. My reaction should have troubled me, but I was too busy feeling vengeful. Maybe this bloodthirsty school was finally starting to rub off on me.

Or I was just really, *really* tired of that douchebag picking on me.

I wasn't the sad, meek little stray anymore. I'd started to accept myself, to *prove* that I belonged here. I might not have allies to watch my back during this trial, but I had the Arcane Three. Their belief in me alone would get me through this trial, of that I was certain. And a vindictive bully like Blaze wasn't going to stand in my way.

"The goal of this trial is to use your intellect, instincts, and abilities to find your way out of a dangerous underground maze," the chancellor went on. "If you're going to lead our community someday, you'll need those tools to face *real* challenges. But a council is not made up of just one individual, which is why teamwork is heavily encouraged for this trial. There are traps and all manner of unpleasant surprises along the way, so having someone to watch your back is essential."

He paused, and I could have sworn he looked directly at me before continuing, "I hope you have all chosen your allies wisely. If not, they could hinder more than help you, even cause you to fail. Unlike your class demonstrations, failure to complete this trial will result in expulsion from Heartstone Academy. Exploitation during trials is allowed, yet another reason why forming trustworthy alliances is so important. You can complete the maze together or individually, but the first student to reach the end and portal back to school will reap the most rewards. *Audentia et Fortitudo* to you all, and may the most worthy among you succeed."

Cheers and clapping erupted all around us, the chance to earn better accommodations and social status whipping the first years into a frenzy of excitement.

Oz was close by with Damien, his first year partner. The Fire Elemental rarely spoke to me, but he acknowledged my existence in a respectful way, so that was something. Alma stood beside Riku and didn't look as excited as I thought she would. This was her chance to climb back to the top, but she was too busy flicking glances at Blaze, who was hooting and hollering beside his new mentor.

Two first years hadn't shown up for the trial this morning. Seeing their families again must have proven to be too much, and they'd left Heartstone sometime in the middle of the night. I hadn't really known either of them, but I still felt bad that the pressure had broken their spirits. At least they hadn't committed suicide. Then *I* would be the broken one. Blaze had immediately jumped on the opportunity and secured himself a third year mentor, which he seemed particularly pleased about.

"Mentors, prepare your portals," Chancellor Grimshaw shouted over the chaos. "Once you deliver your first year to the designated drop-off point, the Labyrinth Trial will begin!"

More cheers as portal after portal sprang into existence. Swirling vortexes of greens, blues, whites, oranges, and purples lit up the gloomy morning. Nerves tumbled in my stomach, but excitement did too, the energy around me contagious. I'd never seen so many portals at one time before, and certainly not this diverse.

Thorne lifted a hand, and a portal edged in crackling electric blue emerged out of thin air. I'd never traveled with anyone besides family members before, but the thought of stepping into the Ether with him didn't fill me with terror like I thought it would. The binding oath we'd made to each other aside, his confessions last night had affected me deeply. I wanted to trust him. I *did* trust him. Despite everything, I knew that he wouldn't let anything harm me inside that void of endless darkness.

Knowing that the second Chancellor Grimshaw gave the word, the time for speaking would be over, I looked up at Thorne and said, "Any last words for me?"

"Don't die. I'll be very upset if you do."

I cracked a weak smile. "We can't have that. You'll lose your bet."

He focused on me, his expression dead serious. "I don't care about that anymore. All I care about is you making it back to me alive."

My eyes widened a fraction, my heart skipping a beat.

"First years, get into positions," the chancellor shouted over the humming portals.

Before I could move an inch, Thorne snaked an arm around my waist and pulled me against him. It was far more intimate of a position than was needed, but I soaked up his nearness like a bone-dry sponge.

"On my command," Chancellor Grimshaw said, raising his hand. I glanced at Professor Holt to find her gaze already on me, reassured when she gave me a small, albeit encouraging smile. "Set!"

I fisted my trembling hands in Thorne's shirt. "Don't let me go."

"Never," he replied, tightening his hold.

The chancellor dropped his arm. "*GO!*"

Thorne lunged for his portal with me firmly locked against him, and the darkness swallowed us whole.

CHAPTER 32

I didn't have time to think. Didn't even have time to glance at Thorne one last time as the sucking, swirling portal spit us out.

The second my feet hit solid ground again, he released me and roared, "Go, go, go!"

I was off like a shot, my senses firing on all cylinders as I beelined toward the black, yawning mouth of a large cave carved into the mountainside. Normally, the sight would have freaked me out, but I didn't have time to be scared either. Any hesitation could cost me, and I wasn't going to start this trial like I did my last one. If I fell behind, I might never catch up again, and I was determined not to finish dead last this time.

More shouts bounced off the rocky mountainside as mentor after mentor dropped off their first years. Since I couldn't see anyone ahead of me, I assumed Thorne had gotten here first, which gave me a much-needed head start. I churned my legs as fast as they would go, knowing that I was most vulnerable to my peers out here in the open with my back exposed.

Sure enough, the telltale *whoosh* of magic alerted my senses to an incoming threat, and I threw up a shield just in the nick of time. The magical attack pounded into my invisible shield with lethal force, and when I spotted orange flames in my peripheral, I knew exactly who'd lobbed it at me.

Gritting my teeth, I ran faster, annoyed that Blaze had already forced me to expend some of my energy. At least I'd defended myself against the bastard this time. Two months ago, that fireball would have hit me. Muscle memory from blocking Thorne's attacks during our training sessions was saving my butt already, and I was beyond grateful for all he'd done to prepare me for this moment.

I could feel the darkness inside me roar awake at Blaze's attack, encouraging me to retaliate instead of flee. I ignored it, along with my need for revenge, knowing that engaging him right now would be foolish. He had allies, and I didn't. Plus, after spending almost the entire semester eating with the Arcane Three, there were probably dozens of other first years who'd love nothing more than to eliminate me.

Permanently.

If I was going to survive this trial, I had to be level-headed like Thorne had taught me. Every move needed to be calculated and controlled, and going on the offensive when I was at a clear disadvantage would be stupid. I had to be patient. *Smart.* The dark cave ahead would offer me protection and the perfect advantage, so I raced toward it without looking back even once, determined to lose myself in the shadows before anyone could reach me.

Just a few more steps. A couple more. *One more step.*

I heard the roar of another fireball heading my way, but my feet had already made contact with the darkness. With a single thought, I called the shadows to me, ordering them to surround me, to *protect* me. They immediately plunged me into pitch black nothingness, whisking me from sight just as the deadly magic streaked inside the cave. It harmlessly sailed past, its tail of light growing dimmer and dimmer as the deep darkness swallowed it whole.

Now that I was concealed, I breathed a bit easier but didn't allow myself to lower my guard even a little. Being the first one inside the cave was an advantage, but it also meant that I would be the first to blindly face the challenges ahead. How I handled them would pave the path for the other first years, giving *them* an advantage, but I didn't let that slow me down.

After the challenges I'd faced yesterday and managed to overcome, I was more than ready to prove myself. Add in Thorne's encouragement, a restful night's sleep, plus a whole lot of caffeine, and I was feeling pretty awesome.

Setting off into the cave at a fast walk, I immediately realized that it wasn't just dark. It was the *darkest* of darks. There wasn't a speck of light in here, and the cave walls felt oppressively close. Each step was heavy yet somehow weightless, the still air dead but also frightfully alive.

Despite being a Darken witch, even I was intimidated by the cave's inky interior, the darkness so absolute that I couldn't see my own hand in front of my face. If this had been my Initiation Trial, fear would have rendered me immobile, but I wasn't that afraid of the darkness in and around me anymore. Little by little, I'd begun to accept it again, thanks to Thorne's insistence that I face what scared me most. My magic still felt like an entity of its own most of the time, intent on destroying anything that posed a threat, but I could wield it again without worrying that it would hurt someone.

Problem was, completing this trial without hurting anyone might be impossible.

I could already hear some of the other first years entering the cave, their footfalls and voices echoing off the jagged walls. The sounds were muted due to my shadows, and I relinquished them a bit to hear better. Sudden shouts, followed by a flurry of commotion, announced that a fight had already broken out. Colorful flashes of magic lit up the darkness as the skirmish turned deadly, cries of pain ringing through the cave.

Seconds later, I felt a presence behind me, and all the hair on my body stood on end. I whirled around, my hands extended as I prepared to defend myself.

No one was there. It was just me and the darkness.

My senses suddenly muted again, making it hard to see and hear the fight yards away. But I didn't miss the shift in the damp air, the foreboding chill creeping up my spine closely followed by a scent, one that could only mean one thing.

Death had arrived.

I froze, torn between stopping it from claiming a victim and self-preservation. That split second of hesitation decided for me.

A wail penetrated my foggy senses, the mournful sound sinking deep into my bones.

"Nadine! No!"

Recognizing the name, my heart sank. It was one of the girls who'd sat closest to me at the first year dining hall table. She and her friend Sage were always gossiping about the Arcane Three and dreaming of being noticed by them. They'd ignored me but had never been outright mean either.

"*Nadine!*" Sage wailed again, and I knew, just *knew* that death had already claimed Nadine's spirit.

Sure enough, death's chill and scent started to evaporate, allowing my senses to come roaring back. Knowing that there was nothing I could do to save her, I set off into the darkness again, wanting to get as far away from the grieving girl and bloodthirsty pack as I could.

Hurry, hurry, hurry, my instincts screamed at me, knowing that Nadine wouldn't be the only casualty of this trial if the other students found me.

As the cave plunged me into black nothingness once more,

I veered to the right, searching for a wall to guide my path. When my fingers hit something hard and wet, I jerked back, my brain immediately convinced that the cave walls were covered in blood.

Shouts echoed behind me, closer this time. Ignoring the wetness, I placed my fingers on the wall again and took off at a light jog, determined to stay in the lead. Every time I considered conjuring a small orb of magic to light my way, I dismissed the thought, unsure how the cave would react. It hadn't reacted so far, even with my shadows cloaked around me, but I didn't want a repeat of the Initiation Trial.

The more discreet I was and the more I conserved my energy, the greater chance I had of making it to the end.

Minutes ticked by, and the shouts gradually faded. Not because they'd slowed or passed me, but because the cave must have chambers. The majority of the students had taken a different path from mine, making me wonder if I'd chosen the wrong one. Even so, I kept up my steady pace, trailing my fingers along the rough stone wall despite how raw they were becoming.

It felt like hours passed. Time started to lose meaning as I walked and walked, the darkness feeling more and more oppressive the deeper I went into the cave. All I could hear was my footsteps and slightly labored breathing, and something about that creeped the hell out of me.

Where *was* everyone?

I picked up speed, trying my best not to panic. This cave had to end eventually. It wasn't like I was going in circles or anything. As soon as I had the thought, my stomach dropped.

What if . . . What if I *was* walking in circles?

I hadn't seen anything, hadn't *heard* anything in what felt like hours. Something wasn't right.

My chest tightened, and I stopped dead, struggling to breathe. Allowing myself a moment to calm my racing heart, I took a risk and conjured an orb to my fingertips. When the glowing violet strands barely made a dent in the darkness, I released my shadows and willed the orb to brighten.

The light cast eerie shadows on the wall beside me, and I nearly jumped out of my skin before realizing the shadows belonged to me. Shaking my head, I held the orb higher and took in my surroundings. One glance, and my stomach dropped even more. I was in a narrow passage that resembled a crude hallway, the width barely six feet. When I noted that it was slightly curved, my stomach threatened to expel my breakfast.

I started to move again, my steps frantic, *panicked.* It couldn't be. I must be mistaken. Maybe the passage would twist left soon. It *had* to. I started to run, my breaths coming in panicked spurts as the corridor continued to twist right. The longer I ran, the more I knew in my gut that I'd been going in circles this entire time.

I swore sharply, too upset to even care that the sound echoed off the walls of my hellish wheel. No one would hear it anyway. I was alone. *Alone.* And the others were no doubt far ahead of me by now.

Swearing again, I searched for a way out of this endless cycle, switching my attention to the opposite wall. Precious minutes raced by, but eventually, I found the exit and barrelled through, not even pausing to make sure the coast was clear. The time for stealth was over. If someone was lying in wait to attack me, then I would attack them back.

But no one was.

The cave opened up again, yawning wide like a mocking laugh. It had bested me this time, but I wasn't going to let that happen again. I was hellbent on catching up with the others, and this stupid cave wasn't going to stop me.

Like a shot, I took off into the abyss, letting the magical orb guide my way.

CHAPTER 33

A bloodcurdling scream alerted me that I was on the right path.

Instead of slowing, I ran faster. Racing toward danger was definitely a first for me, but the adrenaline pumping hotly through my veins didn't let me dwell on it.

Hurry, hurry, hurry, it demanded, and I obeyed, using that scream to guide me forward.

Another scream bounced toward me, and I raised my orb higher, trying to find the source. The chamber I'd selected had been open and uneventful up until this point, but just ahead, I could see that it abruptly narrowed. The cave walls smoothed as if someone had sanded them down, the passage appearing manmade instead of natural.

As I neared the narrow entrance, a familiar chill crept up my spine. Death was near. Or had been. My intuition went haywire, and I forced myself to slow, heeding the warning. With the orb still lighting my way, I silently slid into the corridor. The air immediately felt different inside the tight quarters. Still. Aware. Like a predator about to pounce. I braced myself for an attack, uncertain if it would come from a student or some kind of magical trap.

Thorne had warned me that every trial I'd face would be rigged with dangerous spells meant to challenge me. He hadn't known what sort of spells would be awaiting me in the Labyrinth Trial, though. Each trial was handcrafted with care, and they were different every year.

Whatever challenges I was about to face, I had to rely on my own wits and intuition to get me through them. Thorne couldn't help me, and if I was in danger, he wouldn't be coming to save me.

With that sobering fact in mind, I crept down the eerie passage with caution. Only a few yards later, another tight passage opened up to my left. I paused for a moment, then continued straight, not wanting to get stuck in another dead-end loop. A few more yards, and a passage opened up to my right.

Nope. Not falling for it.

I kept straight as an arrow, even when death's presence grew stronger, an unseen breeze carrying its pungent scent to me.

This waaay, it urged me forward, making goosebumps skitter over my flesh. But my senses didn't dull like I expected them to, and I found out why a second later.

A scream pounded into my eardrums, so loud, so *close* that I jumped, my heart lodging in my throat.

"Help me!"

The cry came from directly ahead, and I broke into a run, *certain* I was going to beat death to its victim this time. But as I neared, a scent hit me. Sharp. Metallic. Not death's scent.

Blood.

I glimpsed the carnage before I could brace myself, and the sight was too much for my stomach. I bent over and lost my breakfast, splattering it all over the cave floor. My orb flickered, and I frantically willed more light into it, not wanting to be in the dark with what I'd just seen.

"Help!" the cry came again, weaker this time.

I straightened, my hand and orb shaking as I forced myself to face the carnage again. A crushed body lay on the floor, the limbs all angled wrong and the head missing.

Oh. There it was. Lodged in a corner.

Blood saturated the ground and soaked the walls, pooling beneath the neck where the head used to be. The face was pointed away from me, but I could tell that the body was male.

"Please," a male voice croaked, and I looked up past the headless body to see a warlock with dark auburn hair standing there at an odd angle.

His face was splattered with blood, but I recognized him as Levi Pierce, the Earth Elemental who'd pricked my leg with a thorny vine during Conjuring class.

Careful, my intuition hissed in warning. *It could be a trap.*

No, I didn't think so. It was Levi who was trapped, pinned to the passage wall somehow. My heart sank when I noticed the passage had come to an abrupt dead end.

"Please, help me," he said, sounding so desperate, so *vulnerable* that I couldn't help but respond. Doing my best to keep my eyes off the carnage below, I carefully stepped over the body and approached Levi.

The second he saw that it was *me*, his expression changed. He didn't look mad, per se, or even disgusted, but he wasn't particularly pleased either.

I paused, and his expression morphed into panic.

"No, please! Don't leave me here. You're all I have!"

Wow. No one had ever said *that* to me before. Taking in his pale sweaty face, I hesitated another moment before giving in with a sigh. At this rate, there was no way I'd finish the trial first, but I couldn't ignore someone in need.

So much for being cutthroat.

"What happened?" I asked, raising my orb higher so I could see where he was pinned.

"We weren't . . . fast enough," he panted, his breaths shallow and uneven. "The walls started to move, and everyone panicked, and Simon just . . . Oh God, he's dead. I can't believe he's dead."

Trying not to panic at the thought of the walls moving, *crushing* anyone who stood in their way, I reached around Levi and gingerly touched his shoulder. I expected him to cry out in pain, but he didn't even flinch. "Does that hurt?"

"What? No. I didn't even feel it."

He must be in shock then, and no wonder. His right shoulder was butted up against the wall, but his connected arm . . . It was trapped. *Crushed.* Wedged between two huge slabs of limestone. He must have been leading the way with an orb when the spelled walls had slammed shut on his extended arm, while another set had crushed Simon. Well, except for his head. It had been chopped off, but the skull was still wholly intact.

Focusing on the smooth walls, I finally noticed the seams separating the gigantic slabs that allowed them to move independently. Great. Just great. This was a deadly underground maze, all right, one that wanted to crush us into oblivion.

"We need to get you out of there," I needlessly told Levi, urgency filling my body once more. Those walls could start moving again at any time, and I didn't want to be standing here when they did.

I dug my fingers into the crack holding Levi's arm captive, but it only took me a second to realize that he wasn't getting out of there without magic. A *lot* of magic. Worry shivered through me, not because expending so much magic would weaken me, but because I could *hurt* him.

Then again, he was already hurt and could lose that arm if he didn't get medical attention soon. Not to mention the walls, which could start moving again at any moment.

Clenching my jaw, I set aside my worry and said, "I'm not an Earth Elemental, so I can't push stone this heavy. But you can."

He made a weak scoffing sound as if I was dense. "Don't you think I would have already done that if I could? I can't *feel* my hand, let alone conjure magic to it."

"But you still have your left hand. I need you to use it."

Pursing his bloodless lips, Levi raised his trembling free hand and rested it on the wall. "Fine. And what will you be doing?"

I let the orb fade out, then dug both sets of fingers into the crack on either side of Levi's shoulder before replying, "I'm going to destroy the stone."

I was a Darken, after all. Destroying was what I did best.

Not waiting for a reply, I shut my eyes against the darkness and focused on the darkness brewing inside of me. The second my attention locked onto it, it sprang awake, beyond eager to be used.

Easy, I warned the chaotic force as if it was a sentient being. Far too often, it felt like my magic *was* sentient instead of an extension of me. I knew that wasn't possible, but ever since Juliana had died, I couldn't get the notion out of my head. Something was definitely wrong with my magic, but I needed it right now. So, despite my misgivings, I called on it anyway, willing the dark destructive mass to my fingertips.

It snaked through my veins like an undulating serpent, beelining for the target I'd chosen for it. Without hesitation, the magic raced from my body and *struck* the stone. Cool light flared behind my closed eyelids as the stone cracked. Levi sucked in a startled breath, but I dug deeper and ordered the darkness to attack the stone again.

Strike. *Crack*.

Dust and pebbles pelted my face and head as the slabs started to break under the magical assault.

"Push!" I shouted at Levi, directing another attack at the stones.

Just as I released another wave into the stone and more splintering cracks echoed through the corridor, a green glow joined my dark violet. Levi grunted beside me as he pushed his own magic into the stone, so forcefully that I felt it shudder beneath my hands.

It was working.

"Keep going!" I yelled, pumping another round into the limestone. It cracked and groaned and shuddered. Dust choked the air, but I refused to cough, all of my attention on breaking apart the rock.

I'd never attempted to destroy anything this dense, this massive before, and it took an immediate toll on my body. Sweat slid down my spine, every inch of me beginning to shake from the strain. I sent another wave into the rock, and the crack that followed was almost deafening.

"Aahhh!" I belted, striking the weakening stone one final time.

It exploded.

The two smooth slabs buckled, transforming into huge deadly chunks. Before they could rain down on us, Levi released a guttural cry of his own and pushed them forward. The avalanche of stone tumbled and clattered down the dark passage, and his crushed arm dropped to his side.

As Levi stumbled, I grabbed his good arm to keep him upright and conjured another orb into existence. One glance confirmed that we'd broken through to the other side, where the passage stretched on into the darkness.

"We have to go," I said, firming my grip on his arm. I took a step forward, careful not to trip over loose rock, but he didn't budge. "Levi, come on."

"I can't," he weakly groaned, casting a look behind us. "Simon."

I faced him to sharply say, "He's *dead.* And we're next if we don't leave right now, so *move!*"

I would apologize to him later once we got out of here, *if* we did, but this wasn't the time for empathy. I pulled on his arm, and he stumbled forward with a pained grunt, no doubt getting sensation back into his crushed limb. He needed medical attention *fast*, but the only thing I cared about right now was exiting this passage before the walls started moving again.

Picking our way past the stone rubble, we'd only made it a handful of yards when a loud scraping noise filled the corridor. Levi stopped dead, and we glanced at each other at the same time. The pure terror on his face told me everything I needed to know.

The walls were about to move again.

"RUN!" I bellowed. Sinking my nails into his arm, I took off, relieved when I felt him lurch forward with me.

The scraping grew louder and louder, a deep rumble vibrating the ground beneath us. One swift glance behind me confirmed that the walls were indeed moving.

Wham!

A set of stone slabs slammed together, and I jerked my head around again, horror climbing up my throat. This was *not* the way I wanted to die.

Apparently, Levi felt the same way, because he jerked away from me and all-out sprinted down the passage, cradling his crushed arm to his chest. Even with his injury, he passed by me, his legs much longer than mine. I lit his path as best I could, my orb's light casting crazy beams through the darkness.

Wham!

The slabs were shutting faster, *closer*. They were only feet behind me now, and I had no idea how long this corridor was.

I ran for all I was worth, keeping my eyes straight ahead in case the walls ahead of us decided to move as well. If that happened, we were screwed.

Wham, wham!

Air violently whooshed directly behind me, letting me know just how close the walls had been to crushing me. My heart thundered wildly, every inch of me alive with terror.

Hurry, hurry, hurry!

Levi shouted something, but the words were lost to a deafening screech as another pair of stone slabs activated. Ones that I could *see*, because they were on either side of me. About to *squish* me like a pancake.

I wasn't going to make it.

Like hell I wasn't.

My survival instincts kicked into overdrive, and just as the slabs screamed toward me, I pushed off the ground with all my strength and dove forward.

CHAPTER 34

WHAM!

The boom shook my bones as I hit the ground and rolled free of the stones just in the nick of time. I scrambled to my feet, ready to take off again, when Levi panted, "It's okay. We made it."

Buzzing with adrenaline, my instincts still in hyper-survival mode, I reconjured my orb and whirled around, searching the walls for even the slightest movement. With surprise, I noted that we were no longer in the narrow passage. We'd entered a massive cavern, and I willed more light into my orb, trying to see how high it went. The ceiling was blanketed in shadows, but over Levi's labored breathing, I heard the screech of bats from somewhere above.

"Look," he grunted, jerking his chin toward the far side of the cavern. "Do you think it's a shortcut?"

I glanced that way and immediately stiffened when I spotted what looked like a free-standing portal. Its glow was colorless, dim, and entirely eerie.

Enter me if you dare, it seemed to taunt, the glow of its magic undulating, *beckoning*.

Um, nope. I didn't trust it. Not after almost getting squished.

"You can go that way if you want, but I'm not," I told Levi and started forward again.

"Where will you go?" he asked, lurching after me.

"I don't know, but I won't enter a portal without knowing where it's taking me."

"Maybe it's a test to see if we're brave enough to face whatever's inside," Levi suggested.

"Maybe." Probably. I still wasn't ready to hand my life over to it.

We fell silent as I began searching for another way out of the cavern. After a few minutes, I still hadn't found an exit. The portal continued to beckon, urging us to take a chance.

I clenched my teeth together until they ached. Nope. There *had* to be another way out.

"I'm gonna go," Levi suddenly said, and I turned to see him standing in front of the portal. Half his face was cast in shadow, but the other half was eerily illuminated by the portal's glow, making him appear even paler. Or maybe that was because he looked about ready to pass out. I hadn't dared look too closely at his crushed arm, but I could only imagine the agony he was in.

"You should," I replied, understanding that he was willing to take the risk on account of his injury. "For your arm's sake, I hope that it's a shortcut."

"Yeah, me too," he said with a weak laugh. Then, "Thanks for saving me. I owe you one."

I blinked, caught off guard by his sincerity. "No problem."

He hesitated a moment, as if feeling guilty for leaving me here, then turned toward the portal and stepped inside. It swallowed him up, and when nothing bad happened, I was almost tempted to follow after him.

Almost.

I wasn't desperate enough for that yet.

There *had* to be another way. The portal was too obvious, too easy. It felt like a trap, one that I hoped didn't injure Levi even more. He had enough strength to finish this trial, but not if it required more use of his magic.

Setting my worry for him aside so I could focus, I closed my eyes and tuned into my senses. If there was another way out, my intuition would let me know. It had led me to Heartstone during my Initiation Trial, so I had to trust that it would guide me through this one.

A full minute ticked by. Precious seconds that I didn't have time to spare.

My senses reached out to every corner of the cavern, listening to the fluttering and squeaks of the bats above, smelling the earthy, slightly musty scent of the cave, feeling the cool dampness of the air. I focused harder, digging *deeper.*

Drip. Drip.

Water.

My eyes snapped open. If there was water in this cavern, then it had to go somewhere. I focused all of my effort on those faint drips, a last-ditch attempt to find a way out. Water was my ticket. I just had to locate the source.

Another precious minute raced by, but the drips were louder now. I frantically cast my orb of light over the cave walls, trying to find those elusive water droplets. A tiny flash caught my eye, a *reflection.* I hurried toward it, nearly crying out in relief when another drop of water fell and hit the cave floor. I followed the thin, winding stream of water along the cavern's edge, praying I wasn't wasting my time.

The stream gradually widened inch by inch as more water from the cave walls dripped into it. I kept going and going, hope trickling through me the farther I went.

This way, my intuition finally whispered, and I couldn't help but break into a grin.

I'd been right. There was another way out.

I followed the stream until I couldn't follow it anymore, until it disappeared inside the cave wall itself. Before I could spiral into a panic that I'd reached yet another dead end, I dropped to all fours and felt along the wall. As my hand met the spot where the water disappeared, I watched my fingers vanish from view. I jerked back, only to reach out again and watch my entire *hand* vanish.

An invisibility spell. Clever.

The exit was cloaked, something I should have considered from the start. Quickly standing, I felt along the wall until my hand disappeared again, then let the rest of my body follow after it. A second later, I was on the other side, once again in a narrow corridor.

Great. My favorite place to be.

Pushing my fear down before it could suffocate me, I started down the passage, paying extra close attention to the walls. They weren't smooth like the last corridor, but that didn't necessarily mean they wouldn't try to crush me. The stream widened even more, making it hard to walk without stepping in it.

Minutes later, it stretched from wall to wall, and I had no choice but to get my shoes wet. The water was slowly becoming an underground river, and I could hear the current now. In no time, my shoes were completely waterlogged, the depth up to my ankles, then my calves.

Trying not to panic, to trust that my intuition hadn't steered me wrong, I kept plowing forward. Just when the water reached my knees, the current strong enough that I struggled to keep my balance, my foot slipped. I frantically pinwheeled, but the current took full advantage of my error and knocked me over. I fell backward, managing to gasp in air before fully submerging. My orb winked out, plunging me into darkness once more, and I flailed about, trying to grab hold of something, *anything*.

The current forced me along, sabotaging my attempts to slow my speed. I couldn't see a thing, but it suddenly felt like I was going faster. The passage beneath me abruptly dropped, and I fell over the edge. A feeling like hurtling down a rollercoaster sent my stomach into my throat, and I belted out a terrified scream. Water rushed all around me, forcing me down, down, down. I desperately tried to keep my head above it, gasping in air whenever I could.

The water rushed faster and *faster*. Just when I thought it would never end, the passage floor disappeared completely, and a wall of water swallowed me whole. Fear spiked through me when everywhere I felt, there was only water. I was surrounded, *sinking*, but there was no bottom.

Self-preservation kicked into overdrive again, and I started to flail my limbs, desperate for air. I didn't know which way was up or down, if I was swimming sideways or deeper into the inky gloom. But I kept flailing, kept fighting to claw my way out of the watery abyss. My lungs were on fire, screaming for oxygen. I fought and fought, grasping at the endless cavern of darkness.

This was what being lost to the Ether probably felt like, I randomly thought to myself, then fought harder, desperate not to die alone in the dark like this.

Just when my body began to convulse, the need for air too great, my head broke the water's surface. I immediately sucked in life-giving oxygen, dragging in mouthful after mouthful like it would be my last. Only when my lungs were satiated did it finally dawn on me that I could see the world around me.

I blinked in awe at the massive cavern, at the glowing blues and greens surrounding the huge underground lake and dotting the ceiling. Glowworms. They were *everywhere*. Despite my close brush with death, I took a moment to appreciate the rare natural wonder, one that was created solely for this earthly plane and had nothing to do with celestial beings or magic.

Growing tired from treading water, I started toward shore. My feet had just connected with the bottom when a sudden *whoosh* and blast of bright orange disrupted the quiet chamber. I looked up and spotted a fiery ball headed straight for me. Doing the only thing I could, I plunged my head under the water again. The ball hit a second later, exploding over the surface. A heatwave pulsed toward me, and I ducked even lower.

Another ball exploded over the surface, then another and another. I backpedaled, sinking deeper into the lake's abyss. Several more fireballs struck the water, each one fizzling out before they could reach me. Only when my lungs started to scream at me again did I dare approach the surface. I swam farther out first, hoping the darkness masked my movements, then slowly rose. Just one quick breath was all I needed. I wouldn't even have to fully breach the surface.

I lifted my face out of the water only enough to draw in air, then dove below the surface again.

More fiery explosions rained down on me, but I was already out of melting range. I didn't know how long this cat and mouse game went on, but my exhausted body couldn't keep up much longer. I needed air and solid ground. Something had to give before my strength gave out.

Desperation started to claw at my chest once more when the fiery attacks abruptly stopped. I waited. Waited some more.

A trap. It had to be.

My lungs didn't care, forcing me to the surface again to draw in air. But when I breached the water this time, shouting reached my waterlogged ears. Hesitating, I rose up a little more, just enough to hear better.

"We don't have *time* for this, Alma. Either help me out, or we're done."

Blaze. Why was I not surprised?

Alma said something back to him, but I couldn't quite make out the words.

"What the hell is *wrong* with you?" Blaze barked, clearly upset by whatever she'd said. "She's a disgrace. A *Mayweather*. Since when did you become a stray-lover?"

"I'm not," Alma replied loud enough for me to hear. "I just don't want to *drown* her."

Silence.

I was about to duck down again when Blaze said, "Fine. Then you give me no choice."

I flinched as an explosion lit up the cavern once more. I prepared to slip beneath the surface again, but before I could, a scream of pain bounced off the cavern walls. Unable to help myself, I jerked my head out of the water and looked toward shore . . .

Just as Blaze sent a fiery blast of magic toward Alma.

CHAPTER 35

I really did have a death wish.

Instead of watching my two enemies destroy each other, I raced toward shore, my only thought on stopping Blaze from killing Alma.

She was on the ground now, screaming in agony as fire engulfed her entire left side. Even as her body shook and writhed, she raised a hand, clearly trying to call water to her—water that was so close yet too far away. Before she could, Blaze prepared another attack, his mouth set in an unforgiving leer.

Pure instinct took over. The second my feet found solid ground, I stood up and called on my magic. It eagerly responded to my urgency, knowing *exactly* what I wanted it to do. With deadly force, it streaked from me like obsidian blades and embedded itself deep into Blaze's fiery outstretched hand.

The impact knocked him sideways, and he fell against a thick limestone column jutting up from the cave floor. Before he could recover, I lashed out again, willing the shadowy blades to harden, to solidify. To *become* actual knives. It wasn't actually possible for my magic to take on a permanent corporeal form, but it could temporarily.

And it did.

Almost faster than my eyes could track, the hardened magic streaked toward Blaze and sank into his flesh. He bellowed in pain as the blades went all the way through his beefy arms and dug into the pillar behind him, effectively pinning him to the stone. *Trapping* him. His eyes found me just as I prepared another attack. Seeing my intent, he jerked against his restraints with a furious roar, murder in his hateful expression.

I flung my magic toward him, gratified when it thunked into his thick thighs and skewered his lower half to the column. He continued to struggle, spittle flying from his mouth as he raged at me.

"You're *dead*, stray, do you hear me? *Dead!*"

I approached him quietly, my entire body singing with revenge. I felt powerful, *invincible* as I watched my tormentor helplessly writhe against the stone.

Kill him. Kill him! the darkness inside me urged, drunk on the sight of our victim so weak and pitiful before us.

After everything he'd put me through this semester, I wanted nothing more than to sink a shadowy blade into his neck and watch him slowly bleed out. I could envision it now, his hateful words turning into pleading gasps as he realized that the only one who could save him . . . was me.

A yard away from reaching him, I stopped, my need for revenge boiling so hotly that I shook from head to toe. A flick of my wrist. That's all it would take to end his life.

He must have seen something in my expression, something dark, something *malevolent*. Because the barest hint of fear flickered in his forest green eyes. The darkness inside me practically hummed with pleasure, basking in his terror.

Kill him now!

It would be so easy, and no one would bat an eye if I did. This was a trial. Killing was allowed, *expected* even. I could finally prove that I had the ability to be cutthroat, that I was bloodthirsty like the rest of my peers. They'd have no choice but to respect me after this.

Or fear me.

The thought came out of nowhere. It was faint, weak compared to the powerful darkness brewing in my blood. But it gave me pause. Made me *think*, until painful memories of my haunted past came crowding back in.

They were like a slap to the face, forcing me back to reality, to the realization that I was about to *kill* again. I'd already been down that road, and it had almost destroyed me. I could practically feel Juliana's disappointment that I'd let my darkness control me again, *consume* me.

A tear spilled down my cheek before I could stop it.

Noticing the sudden shift in my demeanor, Blaze's fear vanished, replaced by that signature leer of his. "I knew you couldn't do it. You're too weak, too—"

"*Dormeo*."

The spell I pushed toward him immediately shut Blaze up. His eyes rolled back, his head dropping forward as I forced him to sleep. At the same time, the blades holding him captive crumbled to dust, and he pitched toward the ground facefirst. I smoothly stepped aside as he fell, feeling a sick sense of pleasure when his big body smacked against the cavern floor with a meaty thump.

Checking that he was out cold, I turned to Alma. She was still alive, I knew that much, but I braced myself for whatever I would find. A burn like the one she'd just endured could be disfiguring, and even Sano couldn't mend something like that. I found her at the edge of the lake, the burnt half of her body fully submerged in the water. She was still awake, her breaths coming out in short wheezes, and I grimaced at the thought of how much pain she was in.

When I stopped beside her, she tried to lift her head and failed, laying it back down on the ground. "Is he . . . ?" she rasped, then coughed, unable to finish the rest.

"He's still alive," I answered, taking in the angry burns visible above the waterline. One side of her clothing barely covered her charred skin, which allowed me to clearly see the damage Blaze had inflicted. The fire hadn't touched her long golden braid, though, which floated limply on the water.

A painfully dry laugh left her. "I don't get you, *sombra*." Cough, cough. "At all."

"That makes two of us," I muttered, glancing around the cavern. "Is there a way out of here?"

Another cough. "No. We've been stuck here."

Terrific. I assumed they'd come down here the same way I did, so they'd probably already searched for a hidden exit. Which must mean . . .

"It has to be underwater."

Alma didn't respond.

"There must be another chamber attached to this one that's only accessible underwater," I told her, reaching down to pull off my shoes. They'd become a hindrance more than a help lately, and I gladly tossed aside the dead weight. Now that my body was no longer hyped up on revenge, I could feel how fatigued it actually was. I'd used a *lot* of magic today, and all the adrenaline spikes and crashes weren't helping. Stepping into the water again, I hesitated for a moment before saying, "We need to go, Alma."

At that, she peeled her eyes back open and barked another dry laugh. "We? I'm cooked, *sombra*. Literally. This is the end of the line for me. I've failed."

I pursed my lips, hating how defeated she sounded. This wasn't the confident Water Elemental who'd won first place in the Initiation Trial. "You didn't fail, Alma. You were *betrayed*."

"I should have . . . known better. It's my fault."

"Maybe, but you could have drowned me earlier, and you chose not to. I owe you a life debt, so I'm not going to just leave you here."

She slowly blinked. "You don't owe me . . . anything."

"Fine, maybe I don't. But I need your Water Elemental abilities, so you're coming with me anyway."

Without waiting for a response, I bent down and started to help her up. I targeted her good side, doing my best to avoid any burns. Still, she sucked in a pained gasp when I grabbed her arm and looped it around my neck.

"Stay strong, Alma," I said instead of apologizing. "Pain is temporary. Push through it."

Something Gran would have told me.

She groaned as I lifted her off the ground, leaning heavily against me with only one good leg to stand on. I practically dragged her into the lake, grateful when the water took over carrying her weight. She kept her arm around me as I kicked off the bottom and started to swim, heading for the sheer rockface on the other side. If there *was* an underwater entrance to another chamber, then it made sense for the location to be on the deeper side.

Problem was, it was a long swim, and I was already tired—not to mention the addition of Alma's weight.

"I need you to get us to the other side faster, Alma," I panted. She didn't respond. "*Alma.*"

A weak groan left her.

"You can't pass out right now," I told her forcefully. "We'll both drown if you do."

"No. Just me," she quietly rasped.

Sudden anger barrelled through me, and I snapped, "I'm *not* letting you die, so stop moping and *help* me."

Another dry laugh left her, but seconds later, I felt the water stir around us. The ripples were faint at first, then grew in volume, swirling faster and faster until I felt them *push* us forward. It felt like a cresting wave had lifted us onto its shoulders to give us a ride, making it so I no longer had to paddle.

Alma still hung limply from my neck, but she'd clearly found the strength to use her magic. In no time, we were across the lake and grabbing onto the jagged cave wall. My breathing was uneven, but Alma's sounded alarmingly weak.

"Stay with me, Alma," I urged her, knowing that the hard part was still ahead of us. "Catch your breath. I'm going to check if I can find anything."

Lifting her arm off my neck, I made sure she had a firm hold on the wall before filling my lungs with air and submerging beneath the water. Almost immediately, the world around me darkened, and my heart sank. Finding an exit was going to be next to impossible if I couldn't see. I tried conjuring an orb to my fingertips, but the water quickly drowned it out.

Remembering my Initiation Trial, I willed a shield to form around my right hand. As soon as the protective bubble was free of water, I conjured an orb again. Purple light bloomed into existence, illuminating the dark waters. The magic wasn't significant, but keeping it steady while I searched for an exit would be draining. I glanced below, using the light to see just how deep the lake went. My orb failed to reach the bottom, and I tried not to panic. Finding an exit could take hours, and I doubted I'd have the strength to last that long.

I started my search anyway, determined not to fail this trial. I probably wouldn't come in first place, but I could beat Blaze at least. Plus, I needed to get Alma out of this cave before she gave up. I could see now that she'd rather die than return home a failure, and that upset me more than I thought it would. She might have played a part in my misery this past semester, but she'd also tried to warn me about Blaze before the gala.

Blaze was pure evil, and I didn't care if he rotted in here, but I didn't want that fate for Alma. We weren't friends, but we weren't exactly enemies either.

Riku had been right. Alma and I were frenemies.

That didn't exactly make us allies, but I didn't want her to fail either.

With that thought in mind, I continued the search, needing to find that exit for *both* our sakes. But I wasn't able to hold my breath for long, and I was forced to the surface way too soon. As I popped up gasping for air, I found Alma right where I'd left her.

"It's so deep," I sputtered out, grabbing onto the wall beside her. "I don't even know where to begin."

She didn't respond, and I prepared to duck down again. Before I could, she quietly said, "Let me try."

I blinked at her. "But your injuries."

She shook her head. "Not like that. Like this." Closing her eyes, she inhaled a few raspy breaths, then released a low, lilting hum. It sounded dry and broken, but after a few moments, it grew in volume, strengthening. And then, she began to sing. "*Water mine, please aid my call. Thine power is great, and I'm but small. Your grace is unmatched, your path more than wise. Please guide the way for my failing eyes.*"

I stared in awe at her, at the peace that had transformed her pain-riddled face. The water immediately responded to her song, the spell urging it to seek out an exit. I felt it stir beneath my bare feet, forming a current whose sole purpose was to guide our way.

A small smile curved Alma's mouth. "Found it. Let's go."

CHAPTER 36

I struggled to keep the shield around my magical orb while the current carried us deep into the belly of the lake.

If Alma wanted to betray me, now was the perfect time to do it. I'd put her arm around my neck again before we'd submerged together, but this was *her* domain. One flick of her wrist, and she could draw the oxygen from my lungs and take off without me. I would be helpless to stop her and unable to reach the surface again before my lungs gave out.

I'd always known that trusting the wrong person could spell my doom, but I had to hope, *pray* that Alma wouldn't stab me in the back. I needed her, maybe even more than she needed me. The fact that she'd chosen not to drown me earlier had to mean something, and I clung to that as the current whisked us down, down, down into the watery bowels below.

Just when I started to worry that Alma had indeed sent me to my watery grave, the current veered left toward the cave wall. I held my orb higher and squinted through the inky gloom, relief filling me when I saw an opening in the wall. An *exit*.

The current pushed us through it and changed course again, lifting us up, up, up. I started to kick, desperate to reach the surface. Alma kicked as well, and we breached seconds later, sucking in twin gasps for air. Alma's strength suddenly failed, and she went limp against me. I let my orb fizzle out so I could keep us afloat, glad when

I discovered that this cavern had glowworms too. And that wasn't all.

"Look, Alma. Light!" I shouted, excitement zipping through me when I spotted a tiny bright dot on the far side of the chamber. It was an exit. *The* exit. "We're almost there!"

She didn't respond, and I glanced at her face to see that she was barely holding on to consciousness. Fresh determination rushed through me, and I began to swim toward the nearest shoreline. Seeing that little speck of light was all I needed to fuel me onward, to carry Alma's limp body through the water until my feet finally, *finally* connected with solid ground again.

"Alma. *Alma*," I panted, dragging her deadweight out of the water. She was a good five inches taller than me, and being barefoot sure didn't help. The jagged rocks cut into the soles of my feet, but I ignored the pain, unwilling to leave Alma behind when we were so close.

"I'm sorry," she abruptly moaned, trying and failing to make her legs work.

"It's okay. You got us through the water, so I'll get us the rest of the way."

"No," she rasped, her breaths shallow and faint. "I'm sorry for . . . for what Blaze did to you. At the gala."

Beyond surprised that she was apologizing to me, I easily responded, "That wasn't your fault. Neither were the other awful things he did to me, including the curse."

"Curse?" she said, sounding confused.

I slipped on a wet rock and caught myself. "Yeah, the curse that was placed on my spellbook a couple months back. The one that almost killed me."

She dragged in another weak breath before saying, "Blaze didn't curse you. Believe me, he would have . . . would have bragged about it if he had."

I stumbled and barely caught myself again, almost losing my grip on Alma. Blaze hadn't cursed me? If he hadn't, then who had?

My mind reeled with the possibilities, dread tightening my chest when I realized it could be anyone. I'd been so certain that Blaze was the culprit that I'd focused my suspicion on him this entire time. In reality, I should have been focused on everyone *else*.

Someone besides Blaze was out for my blood, and hearing that firsthand made me feel nauseous all over again.

Focusing on the task at hand so I wouldn't throw up, I lapsed into silence and continued the trek toward that glimmering speck of light. Alma did her best to help, hobbling on one leg as I propelled us forward one awkward step at a time.

Almost there. Only a few hundred feet. Only a dozen. A few more. One. More. Step.

After so much time spent in darkness, the light coming from outside was almost blinding. I kept my eyes wide open, hoping to never set foot in a cave ever again after this. A blast of cold air blew into the cave, racking my wet body with shivers, but nothing had ever felt so good.

"We made it, Alma," I panted, my trembling legs ready to give out. All we had to do now was portal back to Heartstone.

"You go first," she said and stopped just shy of exiting the cave. "It's only fair."

Wow. I definitely hadn't expected her to say that. Hesitating, I nodded before carefully leaning her up against the cave wall. But when I let go and stepped outside, raising my hands to form a portal, I heard a fleshy *thump* behind me.

I whipped my head around to see Alma splayed on the cave floor, passed out cold.

"Alma!"

I turned toward her just as a voice called out my name. I whirled again, blinking in surprise when none other than Professor Holt materialized before me. Certain it was an apparition spell, one last test of the Labyrinth Trial, I raised my hands to defend myself.

"It's me, Winter," the apparition said, sounding so lifelike that I paused. "There's nothing to fear, child. I'm here to assure students when they've reached the end of their trial. You *made* it."

She sounded so pleased, so *proud* that my suspicion started to fade. It was her. It was really her. The one person at Heartstone who'd shown me nothing but kindness from the very beginning.

I let my hands fall back to my sides. "Alma is badly injured. She needs help getting back to Heartstone."

"Oh, the poor dear," Professor Holt clucked, moving forward to check on her. After a quick examination, she added, "I'll have to portal her back. Those burns look serious."

"And she won't be penalized?"

The professor glanced at me as if surprised by my question. "She will be, but she made it through the trial, so she won't be expelled."

Not ideal, but at least the school wouldn't fail her.

"You, on the other hand, are the first to reach the end, so I believe congratulations are in order."

My heart stopped, then started up again with a jolt. "Really?"

She smiled at me warmly. "Really. You've come a long way in just one semester, Miss Mayweather. Everything's going to change for you after this."

I continued to gape, struck speechless. I was in first place?

The professor laughed, then raised her hands to conjure a portal. It sprang into existence, the edges glowing a vibrant green. "I'll take Miss Ramirez directly to the infirmary so we don't disrupt your moment of glory. Help me lift her up, dear."

I turned toward Alma again, and just as I did, arms snaked around me and yanked. Thrown off balance, I fell back, unable to catch myself in time. I saw the glowing portal closing in around me, but it was too late. I tumbled inside, helpless as the darkness swept me away.

CHAPTER 37

It all happened in an instant.

One second, I was turning to pick Alma up, and the next, snatched away to another dimension. The arms still wrapped around my middle kept me from freefalling through the Ether, and even though I wanted to break away, I knew how dangerous that would be. I could get stuck. *Lost.* Unable to find my way back to the earthly plane.

So I didn't struggle. Didn't do a thing but allow my captor to whisk me away to who-knew-where.

In the back of my mind, I knew that the person who'd portaled me from the cave was Professor Holt, but I couldn't understand why. It didn't make sense. *None* of this made sense.

Before I could come up with a single plausible excuse for her actions, the dark twisting world around me abruptly vanished, along with the professor's arms. I stumbled forward into a world of vivid green, one that was suddenly *alive* and rushing toward me.

Snakes—no, *vines*—shot around my body. They were everywhere, winding in and out through my limbs, whipping around them, pulling them apart. They stretched taut and slammed me back against what felt like a window, trussing up my arms and legs like ropes. Except that they were riddled with thorns, and when the vines forced my limbs apart spread-eagle, I felt thousands of sharp thorn-tips sink into my flesh.

A pained cry burst from me. I didn't have to look to know that blood was now leaking from the thousands of burning puncture wounds. I tried to pull away and instantly regretted it as the thorns dug deeper, wringing another cry from me. Two more vines snaked around my middle and dug into the sensitive flesh, further anchoring me in place.

When I opened my mouth to scream for help, another vine shot toward my neck and quickly coiled around it, squeezing so tight that I could barely breathe. Thorns punctured my throat, and more blood spilled from my body, trailing down my skin and soaking my clothes.

Trussed up so thoroughly that I could no longer move, my gaze at last fell to Professor Holt. She stood before me with her hands encased in green magic, her brown eyes burning with an emotion I'd never seen in them before, an emotion that didn't make *sense*.

Hatred. Pure unadulterated hatred.

I stared at her in shock, in disbelief. This had to be a test. Nothing else made sense. She'd always been so *kind* to me.

A lump formed in my throat, one that I couldn't swallow due to the vine cutting off my air. Still, I needed to make sense of this, to *understand*. So I forced out a strangled, "Why?"

She watched the blood trickle down my neck and drip from my arms and legs. As the drops hit the stones beside my bare feet, her full mouth curved into what could only be described as wicked satisfaction.

"Poor naive Winter," she crooned, not an ounce of warmth in her tone. "So ignorant about the world she's stumbled into. So tragically oblivious. Did you honestly think that you could survive in this world? That you would belong? You should have remained in exile where it was safe."

She curled a finger, and another vine animated, gracefully

twisting through the air to stop beside her head. As it did, something moved inside her poofy black afro. It was so small that I could barely see it, but when it finally emerged from her coiled curls and stepped onto the vine, unease filled my stomach.

A spider. A black widow, to be precise. This whole time, she'd been carrying around her familiar, and I hadn't even known.

"Zola has been spying on you for months," Professor Holt went on, curling her finger again. The vine bent to her will and trailed forward, carrying the deadly little spider toward me. "She's been dying to sink her fangs into you, so be a good girl and hold still while she injects you with venom, hmm?"

My heart started to pound, faster and faster as the spider approached me. I tested my bonds again and paid the price, the thorns mercilessly digging in deeper. As the vine stopped beside me, the spider jumped off and onto my shoulder. I lost sight of it a second later as it crawled toward my vulnerable neck.

Fear coursed through me, and I choked out, "Please, Professor Holt. I—"

"Silence!" she snapped, her gaze locked on her spider familiar.

I felt the moment it reached my neck, its skinny legs tickling my skin. I instinctively tried to jerk away, but the vines held me in place. Seconds later, a sharp pain lit up my insides as the spider bit me, sending venom into my bloodstream. A tear spilled down my cheek, then another and another. A second painful bite followed the first, and a pitiful whimper burst from me.

Professor Holt looked on with pride, but the look wasn't for me. It was for her familiar.

How could I have been so oblivious? So *trusting?* I'd so easily been fooled by a warm look and kind word, so desperate for acceptance that I'd ignored every instinct, every warning my body gave me.

Another sharp bite of pain raced through me. The bites hurt like hell, but I didn't think the venom would kill me. I'd be writhing in agony soon, though, a fact that Professor Holt seemed to be looking forward to.

"Do you know how my daughter died ten years ago?" she abruptly asked, smiling a little as her familiar bit me again. "She was bitten and drained of all her blood, attacked by a vampire just outside the protective wards of the academy responsible for her safety. And do you know who the headmistress of the academy was at the time? The one who was supposed to protect my Jordan at all costs?"

My heart dropped to my feet.

Seeing the sudden look of understanding on my face, the professor's mouth gave a sardonic twist. "That's right, Winter. Your aunt Clarice. The Head Elder whose sworn duty was to keep the children of Thornecrest Academy safe, who abused her power by allowing a Syphon inside the wards and risking the lives of all who depended on her. My Jordan never would have been outside that night if not for your aunt's selfish choices. She used my daughter, *exploited* her for her own personal gain and managed to fail even then. My only child died for nothing, and *that*, Miss Mayweather, is why you're here."

Another tear slid down my cheek as the pieces slowly came together. She was getting revenge by reversing her tragic story. My aunt had been responsible for her daughter's death, so killing me would finish that vengeful loop. An eye for an eye. Or, in this case, a niece for a daughter.

"You almost foiled my plans, though," the professor continued, curling her finger again. The spider on my neck skittered off and hopped onto the vine, retreating back to its hidden spot in Professor Holt's hair. "The moment your application letter to Heartstone arrived, I knew fate was telling me that justice for Jordan's death had finally come. Convincing the board to admit you was a challenge, but they were intrigued by the thought of a Mayweather struggling to rise against the odds. No one thought you would succeed, of course.

"When the cauldrons chose Thorne Hudson to be your mentor, I knew your days at Heartstone were numbered. The Head Prefect paired with the disgraced outcast? Fate couldn't have chosen more perfectly. I watched you struggle to survive, each day worse than the last, until finally, I knew it was time."

She paused then, staring at me so intently that it suddenly hit me. Realizing what she'd done, I sucked in a ragged gasp and whispered, "The curse."

"That's right, Winter. Death by a thousand cuts was destined to be your fate. Just as my daughter bled to death, so was that to be your end. But you survived, somehow, a phenomenon that shouldn't be possible. I had to retreat then and alter my plans, making sure to choose a time for your death that wouldn't cast suspicion on me.

"Your end-of-semester trial was perfect, as no one would be looking at the professors that day. I could come and go as I pleased, and none would be the wiser. All I had to do was wait for you to fall into my hands. You trusted me so easily, and no one witnessed our departure. Of course, I'll return you to the cave soon enough, as it's necessary for everyone to believe that a fellow student killed you during the trial. I only wanted to take you someplace private where no one would interrupt us. Isn't my greenhouse lovely? Jordan and I tended it together, even before she manifested her Earth Elemental abilities."

She sniffed and dabbed at her eyes, then slipped a hand inside her jacket pocket to pull out a green stone. An emerald. Her relic. "It's not that I hate you personally, Winter. I would have much rather your aunt Clarice be punished, but destroying her legacy is the next best thing. My daughter died under your aunt's care, and you will die under mine."

"Please," I whispered, silent tears tracking down both cheeks. "You don't have to do this."

"Yes, I do. My daughter deserves justice, and this is the only way I know how to give it to her."

Her expression changed then, flattening to one of deadly concentration, of *determination.* She raised both hands, along with the emerald, and clenched them into fists. The vines around me viciously squeezed, forcing the thorns in so deep that I cried out in agony, in *fear*.

This was seriously happening. My professor was going to *kill* me.

Amulet, protect me. Pendant, save me! I inwardly cried as the vine around my neck completely cut off my air.

Terror and desperation twined together, and I frantically fought against my restraints, cutting myself even deeper.

"It will all be over soon, Miss Mayweather," Professor Holt said over my struggles. "The more you resist, the faster you'll bleed out."

So it was death by blood loss, after all. She truly thought her daughter's fate was to be mine.

Feeling blood slide down my arms and legs, my life force slowly but surely slipping away, I did the only thing I could. The darkness within me immediately responded to my desperate call, rising up to challenge the threat. I didn't shrink from its eagerness this time, didn't balk as it boiled and hissed, intent on killing whoever was harming me.

It surged through my veins and into my hands, but before I could release the angry maelstrom, the vines around my arms swiftly shot to my hands and sealed them shut. The thwarted darkness went wild with rage, and I cried out again as it pushed and shoved, determined to get out. The vines tightened further, and blood ran in rivulets down my trapped fists.

A chill suddenly crawled up my spine, followed by a scent I knew all too well. Dirt, decaying leaves, despair.

No. *No!*

Death was coming. Coming for *me.*

Angry shadows leaked past the vines' stranglehold, billowing into the air, but they weren't enough to save me.

"You can't win," Professor Holt shouted over my cries. "I have the strength of a relic on my side. You might come from a powerful bloodline, but I've been watching you, Winter. You're afraid. You don't have what it takes to—"

She abruptly gasped, and the vine around my neck loosened, then slithered away. I dragged in air, violently coughing and wheezing as I gulped down too much.

"It can't be," I heard her say in disbelief. She was suddenly inches away, her expression one of shock as she gaped at something just below my neck.

As she lifted a hand toward me, I finally realized what had caught her attention. My amulet. The invisibility spell must have worn off. Everything in me went cold.

"No wonder the curse didn't kill you. A heartstone's power is unmatched. Oh, to touch it, to *hold* it. I can only imagine how it must feel to—"

The second her fingers made contact with my amulet, something shot through me. A need. A *demand*. It rose violently, consuming me completely. The stone pressed to my skin heated. And as Professor Holt closed her hand around it, the darkness within me expanded and expanded, stretching my insides until I could no longer contain it.

I threw my head back and screamed, releasing all of that boiling tension in one powerful explosion. It whipped from me like striking serpents made of shadow, shooting from my bleeding cuts, from my very *pores*. The raging magic attacked the vines, strangling them, obliterating them to dust.

The professor's grip tightened on my necklace as she prepared to yank it off, and I simply reacted. No thought. No instinct. Nothing. My body was no longer my own. I was a passenger, an observer as my gaze locked with hers, as my hand broke free of the vines and shot toward her. Just shy of touching her, it stopped. Stopped and savagely twisted.

One swift *pull*. That's all it took.

Her eyes flew wide. She released my necklace and stumbled back, looking at me like she'd seen a ghost. "Impossible," she whispered, clutching at her chest. She opened her mouth again, but her brown eyes suddenly dulled, the life in them fading.

As she started to fall, I fell too, darkness consuming me before I could hit the ground.

CHAPTER 38

By the time I came to, death was gone and so was Professor Holt.

Rather, her spirit was.

Her body still lay where she'd fallen, her sightless eyes wide open as though in shock. Pain racked me from head to toe, the cuts and venom making it hard to breathe, to think. At the same time, I felt oddly detached, like this was only a dream, a *nightmare.*

What had happened? How was the professor dead?

Lightheaded from pain and blood loss, I struggled to pick myself up. Something moved in my blurry peripheral, and I glanced over in time to see a black spider skitter behind a potted plant.

The professor's familiar.

I let her go, the spider no longer a threat to me. Instead, I tried to remember how I'd gotten free of the vines, but everything after the professor had grabbed my necklace felt murky. Dark.

I couldn't . . . I couldn't remember.

Just like I couldn't remember how Juliana had died.

Panic speared down my throat, and I scrambled to my feet, swaying so hard that I fell against the greenhouse windows. Did . . . did *I* do that? Had I *killed* her?

My heart started to race, faster and faster until darkness edged my vision again. I stumbled away and bent over to throw up, but only a choked sob came out.

What had I done? What had I *done?*

Straightening, I caught my reflection in the greenhouse window. I could practically *feel* my best friend's condemnation.

Murderer.

"No," I whimpered, shaking my head. "I didn't . . . I didn't mean to."

Something glinted in the window's reflection, and I reached up with trembling fingers to grasp my amulet. The stone was cool to the touch and wholly visible. For a split second, I thought about taking it off. Yes, it had protected me, but at what cost? My professor was dead. *Dead.*

Staring at my reflection a moment longer, I tightened my grip and whispered, "Shadows mine, aid my spell. Cloak this necklace, shield it well."

The necklace immediately disappeared from view, and I hesitated for another beat before releasing it. The amulet hadn't killed Professor Holt. *I* had. There was no one to blame but me. Pain continued to rip through my body, making my muscles spasm and twitch. I desperately needed Sano, but the only places I could get it were back at Heartstone or . . . home.

A sudden yearning filled me, a need to hide, to seek the safety of my family. But if I did that, my time at Heartstone would be over. I'd be expelled for not completing the trial, and . . . and I'd probably never see Thorne again. The thought of him no longer in my life, of never being touched by him again, of never being kissed and held in his arms . . .

No. I couldn't run from this.

I might be guilty of killing Professor Holt, but she'd tried to kill me first. It was self defense.

Right?

Trying not to let panic consume me, I turned from the window and raised my hands to form a portal. Maybe I was in shock and denial, but I couldn't let Professor Holt's death stop me from completing my trial. There would be questions, an interrogation to face, but I would get through it. I *had* to.

The professor had tried to destroy my family's legacy, but I wasn't going to let her. She'd been right about me being afraid, but I wouldn't allow that fear to control me anymore. I had what it took to survive in this world. Naive or not, I was more determined than ever to prove her wrong. To prove them *all* wrong.

So when the black portal edged in dark violet formed before me, I stepped inside without hesitation, setting my course for Heartstone.

When I stumbled out of the sucking maelstrom seconds later, my strength finally gave out, and I crashed to the ground. Pain seized my limbs, my muscles trembling as the venom wreaked its havoc on my nervous system. I tried to stand and failed, but before I could crash back to the ground, a pair of strong arms hauled me up.

"Thank the moon and stars, you're alive," a familiar deep voice said, right before I was crushed against a hard body.

The contact sent agony roaring through my injuries, and I couldn't hold in a whimper.

Thorne pulled back, sucking in sharply through his teeth when he saw the condition I was in. "How badly are you hurt?"

When I failed to answer, he swept me into his arms, striding for the steep stairs in front of Heartstone at a fast clip. The swift move was so abrupt that my senses reeled, making everything swirl around me.

"Move!" Thorne barked, each step urgent as he carried me up the stairs three at a time. I tried to speak again and failed, too dizzy and overwhelmed. Right before entering the front doors, he came to a sudden stop. "Please step aside, sir. Winter's been injured and needs

Sano."

"That will have to wait, Mr. Hudson," I heard Chancellor Grimshaw gravely reply. "Please set Miss Mayweather down."

Thorne's grip on me tightened, but when I let out another faint whimper, he carefully lowered me to my feet. The moment he did, the chancellor stepped forward and said in a formal tone, "I, Cyrus Grimshaw, Chancellor of Heartstone Academy, bind your magic."

Something latched onto my wrist, and I glanced down just as a round silver object encased in fiery magic shot from his hand and encircled my other wrist. They looked like twin silver bracelets, but I knew better. They were cuffs. *Shackles*. Spelled to bind the wearer's magic.

Almost immediately, an odd feeling swept through me, one I'd never felt before. It was cold. Hollow. Empty. So vast that it burned a hole straight through me, stealing my strength, robbing me of something essential.

My magic.

One second, it was coiled inside me, and the next . . . gone.

Deep suffocating despair wrenched a sob from my lungs, and my legs completely gave out.

"Winter!" Thorne lunged for me, but the chancellor beat him to it.

Grabbing one of my biceps to keep me upright, he solemnly intoned, "Winter Mayweather, you have been charged with the murder of Juliana Hudson, and it is my duty as chief executive officer to arrest you on behalf of the entire witch community."

Gasps filtered toward me, and one look down the stairs confirmed that most of the student body was present, along with the professors. I spotted Riku and Oz in the audience below, their expressions horrified.

Every inch of me went numb as the chancellor's words finally sank in. He hadn't said Professor Holt's name. He'd said Juliana's.

Before I could stop myself, I sought out Thorne. His handsome face was a blank mask, devoid of all emotion. As eyes of ocean blue stared back at me, I felt my heart start to break.

"Come with me, Miss Mayweather," Chancellor Grimshaw ordered and firmed his grip on my arm to lead me away. I had no choice but to follow, my body nothing more than an empty husk. I lost sight of Thorne, the chancellor guiding me through the front doors of Heartstone.

I waited. Waited some more.

Thorne didn't follow.

My heart shattered.

We walked in silence, each step more difficult than the last. There was too much to feel, too much to think, but I was too broken, too *lost* for any of it. I didn't know how long we walked, but it felt like ages. By the time Chancellor Grimshaw stopped before a door, I had no idea where we were. Nothing looked familiar. He produced an ornate iron key from his pocket and fitted it into the lock. Uttering something under his breath, the key flared brightly, and the lock scraped open.

As the chancellor pulled the door wide, darkness greeted us. A foreboding chill crept up my spine, and I finally managed to whisper, "Where are you taking me?"

"To the dungeons, Miss Mayweather," the chancellor grimly replied. "Where you will await your trial."

ALSO BY BECKY MOYNIHAN

HEARTSTONE ACADEMY

Dark Witch

Storm Prince

WOLVES OF MIDNIGHT

Midnight Vow

Midnight Claim

Midnight Queen

Midnight Hunt

Midnight Bond

A TOUCH OF VAMPIRE

Shadow Touched

Curse Touched

Fate Touched

Sun Touched

Forever Touched

THE ELITE TRIALS

Reactive

Adaptive

Immersive

GENESIS CRYSTAL SAGA

Dawn till Dusk

Fall of Night

Stars till Sun

ACKNOWLEDGMENTS

This story was such a challenge to write, and I loved every second! For those who don't know, Heartstone Academy shares the same world as my A Touch of Vampire series and Wolves of Midnight series. I wanted all three series to interconnect somehow, so the backstories and worldbuilding were super important for this series. If you've read my other series, I hope you picked up on all the connections! I loved digging deeper into the witch/warlock world and wasn't surprised at all to discover how truly complex it is. I'm so excited to see where the next couple of books take us!!

I have the best beta readers in the world, and I just want to thank Allie, Morgan, Kate, and Melissa for your unwavering support and invaluable feedback.

I also want to thank Amber for joining the team!! I can't believe you've been on this journey with me from the very beginning!

I am always indebted to my fabulous ARC team for loyally reading my books and leaving incredible reviews. I don't have enough words to tell you how grateful I am for your enthusiasm and support!!

To every single one of my readers, you have no idea how lucky I feel to be living this author dream, and I have YOU to thank for it. From the bottom of my heart, thank you for loving on my books and making my dreams a reality!!

BECKY MOYNIHAN is a bestselling, award-winning author of fantasy and paranormal romance. Her books include the A Touch of Vampire series, Wolves of Midnight series, Heartstone Academy series, The Elite Trials series, and the co-written Genesis Crystal Saga.

When she's not writing, you can find Becky curled up on the couch in her North Carolina home, binge-watching shows and sipping Mountain Dew.

To stay up to date on new releases, sign up for her monthly newsletter: www.beckymoynihan.com/newsletter

www.ingramcontent.com/pod-product-compliance
Lightning Source LLC
LaVergne TN
LVHW100506110826
845146LV00002B/531

* 9 7 9 8 9 8 8 3 7 3 7 6 6 *